ALL
VISIBLE
THINGS

Incorporating illustrated extracts from the
diaries of Paolo del Rosso,
assistant to
Maestro Leonardo da Vinci

BRIAN MCPHEE

Published by Entente Publishing

www.ententepublishing.com

hello@ententepublishing

Revised edition

For
Marianne
and Adam

'...*painting, which is the only imitator of all visible works of nature...for all visible things are produced by nature.*'

Leonardo da Vinci
Treatise on Painting

LIST OF ILLUSTRATIONS

PART

ONE

May 2nd 1503

I have never seen Maestro Leonardo so angry. He announced his return from the home of Signor del Giocondo by slamming the door. He then swept his eyes around our bottega before fixing on Salaì. In a loud and harsh voice, he scolded Salaì for the untidiness of his workspace, then cast him out with a command to stay away until he could swear an oath to mend his ways. Maestro then stormed across to Agostino and berated him for the slovenliness of his vestments, driving him out also, declaring he should return only when newly bathed and attired in fresh clothes. I confess, at this I became extremely anxious, worried that I too would incur Maestro's wrath for some fault.

Fortunately, his harsh words with Salaì and Agostino had sated my master's temper, although not his anger.

Still with a rough tongue, he addressed me. "That despicable creature, that pretentious cloth merchant, had the temerity, the insolence, to demand—I tell you, Paolo, the scoundrel actually demanded—that I paint his miserable mouse of a wife, Mona Lisa."

"No matter, Maestro, we will find another, a more worthy commission, I am certain of it."

At this, I witnessed a peculiar transformation of my master. His entire person seemed to shrink as he threw himself onto a chair where he lowered his head into his hands.

His voice was muffled when at last he responded in his normal, pleasant voice.

"I regret very much, Paolo, that I had to accept Giocondo's appalling commission. And you will weep at the miserable fee I was compelled to accept."

Present Day – Oxfordshire

Lauren Patterson slumped back in her green leather chair and stared, mesmerised, at the extraordinary document in her hand. After what seemed an age, but was in fact no more than two minutes, she lifted her eyes and gazed blankly around the room, her thoughts in a tumult as she contemplated the implications of what she held in her hand. Absently, she admired the way the louvred blinds beside her sculpted the late afternoon sun into a pleasing arrangement of stripes marching resolutely across the gleaming surface of her desk. She tracked the alternating procession of light and shade, finally arriving at the battered box crammed with musty papers. The old container was newly beguiling, its siren whispers promising new secrets.

Dust motes danced lazily in the warm glow, undisturbed by the ornate longcase clock tolling the quarter hour.

The first time Lauren had been shown into this room she had to suppress a giggle. This was, by some margin, the most elegant room she had ever visited, and then, to her delight, she was informed that it had been assigned for her exclusive use. The antique furniture glowed, the Chinese carpet luxuriously cushioned her steps, and the faces in the family portraits arrayed around the walls welcomed her into their private domain.

The clock's cheerful chimes startled the young woman from her trance. Carefully she put down the diary page, grasped the arms of her chair and pushed herself upright. She leaned across the desk to rifle through the stack of papers in the box. The remaining contents consisted of more of these distinctive sheets–hundreds of them, and all written in what appeared to be the same flowing hand.

She lifted the next document from the pile and examined the paper. It was heavier and had a smoother finish than the coarse sheets she had been working with up until now. At first glance, it appeared to be from the period, as did the hand of the writer. Even through her thin cotton gloves, she could feel the quality of the paper.

Lauren didn't have to be a Leonardo scholar to recognise that the manuscript on her desk was incredibly important.

She replaced the sheet in its box and eased off her gloves. Deliciously barefoot, she strode across the room to stand at the window beside the tall clock. From this vantage she could see all the way down the aisle of majestic oak trees, patiently cultivated by generations of gardeners to conduct visitors to the house's main entrance. As she surveyed the now familiar scene, Lauren was acutely aware that this was a pivotal moment, a once in a lifetime opportunity. She had to think, plan, concentrate. She drew strength from her surroundings; the unbroken line of Englishmen who had nurtured this environment had been raised to a quiet but certain confidence. Now, by some mysterious alchemy, the ancient house and its ghosts lent the young woman a measure of their store of serenity and resolution.

She would seize this opportunity with both hands.

She returned to her desk and scanned a few random pages in the pile. She glimpsed dates – 1508, 1519, 1502. The sheets were not in order–at some point they had been jumbled up. It was clearly an extensive chronicle, but when did the entries begin?

1501

March 25th

An auspicious day; the first of the new year and the first of my new life.[1]

My name is Paolo del Rosso. I am fourteen years of age. Because of the close friendship between my grandfather and Ser Piero da Vinci, father of Maestro Leonardo, I have today joined the household of that most illustrious artist to train as his assistant. Not as his apprentice, for I have but little skill with a brush. But my grandfather assured Messer da Vinci that I am reliable and have been well tutored in Latin, writing and the manipulation of numbers, and so I am to assist Maestro Leonardo with matters of his household and with the business of his clients and commissions. It is a great honour. Maestro has only recently returned from a stay of seventeen years in Milan. It seems his assistant in that city chose to remain close to his Lombard family. This is my good fortune.

---

[1] Prior to the adoption of the Gregorian calendar, many countries counted the new year from March 25th, the feast of the Annunciation. However, in this volume, years have been divided in accordance with modern usage.

And perhaps I may learn something of drawing and painting.

My eminent master has already instructed me to observe everything and note in this journal all that I see, every day. I must study people carefully in the streets, in the piazza, and in the fields.

March 28th

*I*t is now the afternoon. Maestro Leonardo read my chronicle of yesterday and was not pleased. He asked if there is a deficiency in my sight, that I see nothing; or in my lips and ears, that I ask and hear nothing.

It seems I must write more.

Maestro spoke to me most forcefully.

"Describe how the weather is, if this is important. Tell of unusual people and portents. Describe the events you witness or participate in. Particularly the latter. Write about the baker and the carpenter, but especially of great men you encounter."

You will have noted that I just quoted my master as if he had dictated these exact words to me.

"You must make your reader feel they are with you, in the room or on the street, wherever you are describing. Whenever possible do not describe what happened but re-enact it. See here, where I painted this gown, draped over the model's legs? My goal is not to make something that merely

looks like the fabric, but rather that *is* the fabric. I want the viewer to pause, shyly look around to confirm he is unobserved, then reach out to stroke the painting, to confirm that the folds are real."

We, that is to say the household of my master, we are comfortably accommodated in the monastery of Santissima Annunziata, which is, as you must know, in the city of Florence.

I have just asked my master, who are you? For whose eyes do I write?

He answered that I should write for the grandsons of my grandsons, who will, he assures me, be interested in all that happened to their forebear.

"But you will be writing also for yourself. It is a sound discipline to record your thoughts, ideas, impressions, each day. This encourages clear thinking and will assist in developing your opinions and philosophy. And, young Paolo, you are now part of the household of a great man—posterity will be interested in your reports."

Maestro has a healthy regard for his own reputation.

I am writing in a corner of the bottega, now my own space. My corner is that closest to Maestro's bedchamber, where he sometimes works when he requires quiet. The workshop is large. In addition to the long table where we take our meals, there are a number of distinct areas for painting, carving and displaying our work to clients.

There are four students working today, plus Maestro Leonardo, who has three areas for himself. In one he is making a large study of a dramatic image of the Holy Mother with her child and blessed mother St Anne, and the infant Baptist. It is a most remarkable work. The composition is unlike any other I have seen. My master explained that when he is finally satisfied with the design, it will become an altarpiece, painted in vibrant colours to capture the very likeness of the scene.

Beside this is another area, where stands a large easel covered in a confusion of drawings and sketches of people and animals and flowers and everything else that you cannot imagine.

Finally, my master has an ingenious sloping table of his own design, on which he plans effects for masques and parades and also perplexing machines and structures that do not exist, save in his immense imagination. In the days to come, he promises to explain the purpose and workings of these bizarre objects.

*Image 1: Cartoon of the Virgin and Child with
St Anne and John the Baptist.
(National Gallery, London)*

*I have studied the apprentices working around me. They are
all older than I, but still young, and all are pleasing of visage
and figure. Among them is Gian Giacomo Caprotti from
Oreno, who we call Salaì. He is the great favourite of my
master, although Maestro Leonardo had occasion this
morning to scold him, although to little effect. Indeed, I have*

11

been told our master gave him his nickname, Salaì, although I do not yet know why.[1] There are at present two more apprentices, but they are presently installing another altarpiece in a church in Santa Croce.

None of the students are as pleasing to the eye as my master himself. Although he is old, his eyes are clear, his face strong and he wears the most magnificent costumes, even when he works.[2] As for me, I am plain of face and so I seem to myself an oddity in this company. My master assures me this is of no matter—he employs me for my mind, not my features.

October 26th

A most frightening and inauspicious day.

This morning the sun disappeared completely. For many minutes there was darkness, although the sun had been well on her daily journey across the heavens. The air itself became absolutely motionless. All conversations halted. The birds ceased their singing. The cats stood rigid, spines arched and the fur on their tails erect. The dogs were seen slinking away under chairs and tables. Suddenly, the perfect silence was broken, and we stared at each other amazed, as from beyond the walls came the dreadful howling of the wolves. The soothsayers made fortunes

---

[1] Salaì means Little Devil
[2] At this date, Leonardo da Vinci was 49 years old.

selling protective amulets of all kinds. Maestro forbad me from buying any, but Salaì sold one to me.

We heard rumour that a young woman walking past Torre dei Barbadori suddenly fell dead for no reason. One moment she was talking with her sister, the next she simply collapsed, dead before her body reached the ground. A chicken was born with two heads. Six houses were closed up on account of the plague. It is all connected.

Maestro discovered the amulet later in the day.

"An eclipse is in the natural order of things, Paolo, nothing more. It is predicted to the hour. There is nothing to fear. Get back to your tasks. Now, where is that wretch, Salaì?"

Still, like most of the city, I attended vespers in the Cathedral.

Maestro was there also.

Lauren

Lauren Patterson was a first year PhD student from the University of Chicago. At thirty-one, she was a few years older than the majority of students starting out as postgrads. She was tall and slim and could have stepped out of a recruitment brochure for a mid-west university–she had the classic 'preppie' college look peculiar to those whose fortunate genetic heritage was a blend of Scandinavian, Irish and, in her case, Italian forbears. Her striking looks– vivid blue eyes, faintly olive skin, long black hair and the end product of excellent orthodontics–were animated by a sharp and occasionally combative intelligence.

Lauren's doctoral thesis, provisionally titled, *'Connections: The wool trade between England and Florence 1490-1600'*, was to be based on the family papers of William Chance, 18th Earl of Blythswood. These manuscripts had been languishing in a basement in the family home, Blythswood House, in Oxfordshire. They documented the family's participation in the Tuscan wool trade, dating from when a distant ancestor, Sir Robert Chance, married Margaret Pennant, a wealthy wool trader.

The father of Robert Chance had permitted the union to go ahead only because he assumed that, at thirty-nine, Margaret was past child-bearing age, meaning her considerable fortune would find its way to the children of Robert's younger brother, their father's favourite.

In the event, twenty-six years after their wedding, Margaret and Robert's only son, Walter, took over the management of an admired and successful international trading business. And before Margaret died, she was in attendance when Queen Elizabeth I invested Walter as the first Earl of Blythswood.

Lauren remembered thinking, *'You go, girl!'* when she read this. And now, thanks to a modest research grant and some money saved since graduation, for the past few weeks she had been living and researching in the home of the current Earl of Blythswood, Margaret's direct descendant.

Her plan had been to use the collection of papers to create a detailed picture of the family's dealings with Renaissance Florence. The archive had lain undisturbed, most probably since it was crated up around 1740 when the family wool business had been wound up. Indexing the trading records had accelerated the rate at which Lauren could read and simultaneously translate the 500-year-old script, written in archaic Tuscan—not too dissimilar from modern Italian.

Until she turned up the diary pages, the documents Lauren had been examining had been routine commercial communications: orders, receipts, requests for payment, enquiries about future orders and the like. She had picked up a straightforward order for a shipment of wool dating from 1522, when underneath, she spotted the 1503 diary page, looking unlike anything she had come across previously.

When the initial shock wore off, Lauren composed herself. The first task was to sort the sheets into chronological order, all the while fighting the temptation to read each random entry as she worked. The writer's habit of meticulously dating his entries meant this stage shouldn't take too long. Although the sequence had been disturbed, there were long stretches of entries that had survived in order. Lauren guessed that at some point the entire stack of pages had been dropped, hurriedly gathered up, and unceremoniously dropped into the box.

Around eight p.m. Lauren suddenly realised she was ravenous. She badly wanted a least a sandwich and a cup of strong coffee, but that would mean going down to the kitchen, two floors below. The lure of the documents proved stronger than her hunger. She rubbed her eyes, gathered up her hair and, with practised ease, wound a pencil into it to hold it in position. She figured she'd be working a while longer.

By one in the morning she was confident that the entire chronicle was in its proper sequence. Despite her resolution, she hadn't been able to avoid reading snippets from the material. Leonardo's name turned up time and again. She was desperate to dive into the text, but reluctantly accepted she had to get some sleep. She was now too tired to eat, never mind concentrate on translating. She locked the study door and wearily dragged herself to bed.

Early the following morning, after a hurried breakfast–she was too hungry to skip eating entirely–Lauren was back at her desk, engrossed in the intriguing chronicle of the young clerk, Paolo.

The early pages were a continuation of his opening entries: descriptions of the activities and projects in Leonardo's studio and a recital of the tasks to which the young assistant had been gradually introduced– negotiating for materials and carrying messages and instructions from his master to various suppliers, clients and prospective clients around the city. Paolo was excited about everything he saw—it was all new to him. Lauren thought he may have been raised in the countryside or perhaps a small village. Now he delighted in the sights, sounds and smells of the vibrant and wealthy city, one of the largest in Europe. As instructed by his master, Paolo dutifully committed his observations to his diary, which was now a spellbinding time-traveller's guide to Renaissance Florence.

When Lauren was eight, she had joined her town library, and over the years she discovered Judy Blume, *The Lion, the Witch and the Wardrobe* and, thanks to an elderly librarian, *Nancy Drew*. She cried when Harry Potter saw his son off at Platform 9¾, devastated to have finally reached the end of the saga. When she returned the final volume, the same old librarian surreptitiously reached into a drawer where she kept her own copy of *The Golden Compass*, which had been vehemently rejected by the library committee. Once again Lauren immersed herself in a totally different world.

Reading Paolo's diary gave her that same sense of vicariously inhabiting another world, one full of adventure and discovery.

The young academic's mind was now working on several problems at once. Uppermost was how to protect her personal access to The Paolo Chronicles, now capitalised in her mind, so she could retain intellectual ownership of their publication. These documents would create a tremendous furore among art historians, indeed all historians and scholars of the Renaissance and of the many branches of knowledge to which Leonardo had contributed. Lauren feared that, as soon as word of the diary's existence got out, senior academics would attempt to take over. Her doctoral adviser, Professor Hildebrand, was a prominent figure on campus and although Lauren didn't know him particularly well, intuition warned her he would not be someone to rely on for support–indeed he would more likely be one of those she would have to fend off, if she was to achieve her ambitions. Economic History was not a glamour department, and the never-ending struggle to secure funding engendered fierce competition for publication in prominent academic journals, and even more especially for breakout projects that garnered attention in the wider media. Lauren suspected that, despite loud protestations to the contrary, most academics would trade half-a-dozen scholarly articles in even the most prestigious journal for an extended profile in the *New York Times* or *The Economist.* Some would trade a kidney.

Lauren had secured her doctoral grant by wearing down the assessors until they finally succumbed to the determined young woman who had pestered them remorselessly for advice, guidance and finally, acceptance. Now she knew she would need allies as well as all of her tenacity, to fend off the academic competition for first publication of the diary.

At the same time, she had to consider her responsibility to the Earl, owner of the papers, who would no doubt have his own priorities for the diary. He too was essentially an unknown quantity. Since her arrival, William Chance had visited Lauren twice, each time taking a genuine and informed interest in her work. But she knew from the staff that he had his own challenges to contend with. He depended on an informal network of academics and heritage organisations to provide the expertise, research and additional funding vital to safeguarding and restoring the estate's myriad fabrics, materials and structures representing five hundred years of English history. How would these relationships be impacted by the emergence of the diaries?

While all of this was tumbling through her head, yet another part of her brain was processing the highlights of each handwritten page. Suddenly, her entire focus zoomed onto this task, as once again she spotted a familiar name.

1503

April 12th

T oday I was alone in the new studio when a man appeared, unannounced, at our door. He was dressed in the customary attire of a wealthy merchant. The quality of his silks announced the nature of his business.

Although his vestments spoke of wealth, his manners were uncouth and his accent uncultured.

With no preliminary polite words, he commanded me. "Tell your master, Messer Francesco di Bartolomeo di Zanobi del Giocondo wishes to speak with him on a matter that could be greatly to his benefit."

"Signore, I regret to advise you that my master remains in attendance on His Excellency, the Duke of Valentinois. I expect his arrival within the week." [1]

"Your master would be better advised spending his time with the leaders of his own city, and not with those of rivals bent on our destruction. In any event, his friend, Dottor

---

[1] The Duke of Valentinois is better known to history as Cesare Borgia, son of Pope Alexander VI.

Machiavelli, is calling upon the members of our council, seeking a great commission for your master, and I am in a position to be of considerable assistance in this matter. Or not," he added pointedly. "Have him call on me the moment he returns."

Although I had never spoken with this man before, the name del Giocondo is familiar to me. He is a rich merchant, trading mostly in silk, but also occasionally in wool. He is said to be ruthless, a common enough trait among the fiercely competitive merchants of our city. I have been told that some years ago he took a third wife, a young woman of fifteen years and no more than average beauty, but with an old and honourable name, Madonna Lisa Gherardini.[1]

As to the great commission of which he spoke, I know a great deal about the matter, having carried messages to various acquaintances of my master seeking their support.

We had recently been on an extended sojourn to the court of that fierce and shrewd man, Cesare Borgia. But the cruel intrigues constantly swirling around his Excellency and his father, the Pope, disgusted Maestro and so I have been sent on ahead, to prepare our new home and studio for the return of our household.

---

[1] 'Mona' or 'Monna' is a contraction of 'Madonna', more or less equivalent to Mrs. in modern English usage.

Sadly, despite the many wonderful and valuable services provided by my master, the past months have not seen an increase in our fortunes and we now find ourselves in great need of a grand commission. Fortunately, such an opportunity has arisen—indeed, this is another reason for our return.

The Gonfaloniere of Florence, Messer Piero Soderini, has decided that the council chamber, the Salone dei Cinquecento, in the Palazzo della Signoria, should be graced with two enormous frescoes.[1] This is the great prize del Giocondo was referring to. The work will be even larger than the renowned depiction of the last meal of our Saviour and his apostles created by my master in Milan.

Although I have not seen the monumental work executed in Milan, I have seen many of the preparatory full-size drawings created by Maestro and his assistants. As the drawings are covered in little scratches used to transfer the image to the wall, the sheets cannot be used again, so we use them as packing material to protect delicate work.

The proposed frescoes for the Palazzo della Signoria would provide work for our bottega for some years. It is essential, for both silver and honour, that Maestro wins the commission. By the grace of God, we have the wise and wily

---

[1] The Gonfaloniere or 'Standard Bearer' of the city was leader of the Signoria, the Council of the Florentine Republic. The Signoria met in The Room of the Five Hundred in the Palazzo della Signoria, today known as the Palazzo Vecchio.

Dottor Machiavelli assisting us in this cause. Now Colonnello of the Militia, he too was present in the court of the Duke and there became a trusted friend of my master. It is one of my delights to listen to these two wonderfully clever men discuss matters from the redirection of rivers, to the true responsibilities of rulers and commanders and a thousand other questions.

April 11th

*M*aestro read my chronicle today, the first time in some weeks.

"It is good, Paolo," he pronounced. "I will not ask for it again. I trust you will maintain your discipline and I understand the need for privacy if you are to record your true thoughts in all matters."

I am pleased.

April 21st

*I*n the night, the Arno flooded and we awoke to exceedingly strange sights. Every building stood silent— solitary islands surrounded by swirling water. Uprooted trees and bushes floated amidst benches from the churches, dead animals and some poor family's furniture. Small animals, cats and rats mostly, but here and there a few dogs, clung fiercely to floating tree limbs until the local boys cast stones to make them fall into the water, where many of them *drowned. Maestro raged at the miscreants, but the dangerous currents rendered him impotent to stop them. He was greatly angered and frustrated at this.*

Fortunately, being on an elevated site, our new studio is undamaged.

May 23rd

*E*ven now, I am amazed at the huge number of artworks we produce here in the bottega. I have just finished the accounting for this week:

- ❧ *4 small Madonnas*
- ❧ *3 small St John the Baptists*
- ❧ *2 St Reparatas for her feast day next month*
- ❧ *1 medium Annunciation for the sisters in Carmignano, completed by Jacopo, with a little help from Agostino.*
- ❧ *A portrait of the daughter of Ser Antonio Coldiroli done by Cecco, which Maestro pronounced to be very good indeed and which he himself did not touch, save to enhance the young lady's hair.*

Also today, we presented Maestro's design for a new processional altar of St Zenobius for the guild of bankers.[1]

This is a most important commission and Salaì has been charged with completing the painted element of the work from our master's design. There is a large altar table, six braccia deep and nine braccia wide, with long poles for carrying.[2] On this table there is a raised platform covered in silver and above that another, slightly smaller, decorated in gold leaf. Here stands the ancient statue of our saint, containing the relics of his bones. Behind and above the statue, our master will cause to be made an elm tree, in silver. By means of an ingenious mechanism of Maestro's design, the tree will suddenly be clad in leaves of green silk, four times in every hour.

This representation of the true miracle God produced to attest the holiness of the saint will be a wonder to all who see it. Behind the tree will be Salaì's painting of the holy saint presenting the resurrected child to his mother.[3]

---

[1] *St Zenobius is one of Florence's patron saints, along with St Reparata and St John the Baptist. There are two particular miracles associated with the saint. When a child was run over by a cart, the body was brought to Zenobius, who brought him back to life and gave him to his mother. And at Zenobius's funeral, his body touched a dead elm, which immediately burst into leaf.*
[2] *One braccio fiorentino (an arm's length) was approximately 58 cm or 23 inches.*
[3] *This painting is lost.*

The officers of the guild pronounced themselves pleased with the design and agreed to advance the first half of the payment, admonishing us to preserve the secret of the tree so to ensure the astonishment of the city next May.

How much more we could achieve if only we were in more commodious surroundings! This studio is most unsatisfactory, being too cramped and losing the light much too early in the afternoon to permit delicate work.

June 3rd

L ast night I looked back at my earlier entries. Most, in truth almost all, are exceedingly tedious. To my heirs who are reading them—I apologise. However, I realise I have failed to give a portrait of Maestro Leonardo. If there is anything of interest in this journal, it will surely be in regard to my most excellent master.

First, as to his appearance.

My master is an extraordinarily well-favoured man. He is very tall, with an imposing head and an excellent profile. He wears his hair long, and he uses a cream of his own devising to keep it looking well. As you may guess from my last observation, Maestro is more than a little vain concerning his appearance. He wears only the most fashionable clothes, so long as they allow him to show off his figure. For this reason, he favours short tunics with hose, the better to display his legs. He never leaves his bedchamber save he is fully dressed and perfumed. He is also unusual in disdaining the general belief that washing is harmful to the skin and the essential essences. He bathes weekly, even in cold weather, and insists we follow his example. Maestro also demands that our clothes are clean at all times, even in the bottega. At first, I confess, I found this obsession with constant bathing and cleaning most unwelcome, especially in winter when I was accustomed to restricting my toilet to washing my hands daily and, once or twice a week, my face. My body was cleaned when the river became comfortable for swimming in the spring. Now however, I am an enthusiastic convert to Maestro's beliefs, except now I suffer the appalling stench of enclosed spaces other than our own.

Every time we receive funds from an important client, Maestro indulges himself in a new vestment, passing on to one of us something that is old to him, but often seldom worn.

Maestro Leonardo is generally of a very pleasant disposition. He enjoys conversation with friends and strangers. I can say that when we walk in the city, many men come up to greet him and to seek his views on matters of the day. However, he is not active in the affairs of the Guild nor of our gonfalone[1]; he says he does not have the time for petty politics

––––––––––––––––

[1] *Medieval Florence was divided into 4 quartieri (quarters), each of 4 gonfaloni. Each gonfalone had its own symbol and flag. In time the word gonfalon came to be applied to the flag, and not the district. Each family was associated with and loyal to its particular gonfalone.*

and has not the patience for unnecessary socialising with dullards.

It is true that occasionally he loses his temper with the stupidity of clients or the corruption of politicians, but in truth, the person who irks him the most is Salaì. Which is surpassing strange, as Salaì is also the one he most indulges.

This brings me to the final, most delicate subject. My master is the subject of rumour that he is one who prefers the carnal pleasures of men to women. Indeed, those of us who work for him are the butt of many slurs in regard to these rumours.

I can only give evidence of matters of which I am aware.

It is true he selects unusually handsome boys to be his apprentices. He is not married, nor has he taken a mistress. He gives clothes and money to Salaì and accepts him back every time he is thrown out for stealing, or impertinence, or causing disruption. As I acknowledged, Maestro is extremely attentive to his clothes and his hair. He is left-handed, a sure sign of the devil's influence in many eyes.

To give the counter.

Maestro loves beauty and would always choose to surround himself with beautiful things and people, a ready explanation for the boys he selects. I am the exception.

He paints women above all things and with a love and appreciation greater than any man before.

I am with him the large part of every day, and in all that time he has never shown any odd behaviour, neither to me *nor to anyone else. He has never asked me to absent myself so he might be alone with another. I am permitted to enter his bedchamber at any time if I must bring him news or announce a visitor.*

The mystery is Salaì.

But compared with the mystery of Maestro's genius, this is a small matter indeed.

And Giorgio, the older brother of my friend Filippo, terrorises the young women of the city. Afterwards, he re-arranges his clothes with his left hand.

June 15th

Our gonfalone won the palio yesterday morning. The procession of San Giovanni was particularly good this year. Our own Jacopo was one of the spiritegli and we watched and cheered as he marched by the studio.[1] In the evening I rode in a girandole and we set off many fireworks to entertain the populace. There was no curfew last night and the air was warm and pleasant. Not everything I did was something of which I am proud.

There was wine. There was a young woman, a serving girl from the tavern. I have noted her before and for her part, I have twice caught her watching me.

---

[1] Spiritegli were men on stilts, representing giants.

She led me to a dark corner of the cellar. Everything was rushed, fumbled, confused. I was a fool. And this morning I awoke with a dry mouth and remembered, and I am ashamed. Tomorrow, or the next day, I will see her and will feign friendship, but I will not engage in conversation. She is some years older than me—perhaps she will not care. But what if she looks at me expectantly, and I disappoint her? It is cruel. It is shameful. I must hurry to my confessor in the morning.

There can never be another first time. My imaginings of how special this important occasion would be are now so many shattered dreams. Instead of a romantic moment to be recalled with tenderness and affection, it was a sordid affair best not recalled at all. I <u>am</u> a fool.

But I must learn from this. I will try to be guided by what is important worthwhile and not what is merely convenient or pleasurable for the instant.

I dread meeting her again.

August 23rd

Madonna del Giocondo visited us today for her first sitting. Maestro Leonardo is reluctant to admit this, but while Mona Lisa can be said to be less than beautiful, she is kind, gentle and obliging.

Bartolomeo is the newest addition to our number. He is eighteen and fair of feature. His father is a Ferrara nobleman, and so we call Bartolomeo, 'Count'. He will be with us for a few years, to study and learn from Maestro. In the few days he has been with us, he has already demonstrated great skill with the brush. He is also kind and generous to me. He laughs easily and is not offended by our name for him. Today he has given our master a nickname, which we will now use, but only when Maestro cannot hear us.

This morning, Bartolomeo came from talking with our master and turned to me, saying,

"Paolo, Dimmi has an errand for you."

"Dimmi?" I asked, puzzled.

"Our master. A dozen times each day, he commands me: 'Dimmi!' If I say I have seen an unusual flower—'Dimmi!' If I report a new shop in the piazza—'Dimmi!' A new colour of blue from Mantua?—'Dimmi!' This is my name for him now—'Dimmi'. There is nothing new he does not want to hear and understand."[1]

October 16th

We are saved!

Dottor Machiavelli arrived, breathless, to announce that we will have the contract to create the vast frescoes on the walls of the

---

[1] 'Dimmi!' means 'Tell me!'

Salone dei Cinquecento. And, thanks be to God, we will be housed in a new studio in Santa Maria Novella. Our relief was palpable, our joy unbounded. My main task in the coming days will be to make the new space suitable and ready for my master to create a magnificent work for the Signoria and the city.

Meanwhile, the portrait of Mona Lisa del Giocondo has taken a strange path. The lady came twice to sit for Dimmi so he could sketch her face and experiment with her pose. He explained she would not be permitted to see the painting until it was delivered to her husband. The lady accepted this without complaint. In truth, her ignorance is required so Dimmi can execute his plan of revenge on her husband.

My master had been forced to accept the commission of Francesco del Giocondo because of his political influence with the Signoria. It came to us that he controls several positions in the city government and his brothers and cousins are also active in politics. Together, the Giocondo clan is a formidable political force.

But Dimmi has been vexed by this situation from the first. Months ago, soon after he accepted the commission, he exclaimed to us all. "Every week, I give offence to gracious ladies of the highest rank and to their husbands, explaining that I am too busy to paint them. Yet here I am, forced to exercise my talents for this cloth merchant. But now we have the signed contract from the Signoria, and I will make him regret his blackmail." [1]

Dimmi had been silent as to how he would revenge himself on his unwanted patron. But although he could prevent the lady from seeing her portrait in progress, it was impossible to prevent his assistants from being witness.

"We shall see what the great merchant thinks when we unveil our image of his modest wife."

Not for the first time with a commission, Dimmi had set aside his sketches of Mona Lisa del Giocondo and did not commence upon the actual oil painting. However, the requests and threats from Messer del Giocondo had become ever more urgent and so he finally turned to the task.

Today we saw at last the design from which Maestro will work. He will render Mona Lisa naked. I am reluctant to write of this. It seems most unseemly to me.

The face, sketched in a most unflattering manner, is clearly hers, and Dimmi is skilful and knowledgeable enough to imagine the lady's body beneath her modest dress. True, she is seated and visible only to the waist. While some artists

---

[1] *This is almost certainly a reference to Isabella d'Este, a powerful noblewoman, who had been pestering Leonardo incessantly to paint her portrait. He had already painted Cecilia Gallerani (The Lady with Ermine), mistress of her sister's husband, and had produced another portrait, either (experts disagree) of yet another of his mistresses or, more aggravating still, the sister herself, Beatrice (La Belle Ferronnière).*

have recently taken to depicting female nudes in antique fables or representations of Adam and Eve, it is a shocking pose for a recognisable wife and mother.

Image 2: Study for The Nude Mona Lisa.
Previously attributed to the studio of Leonardo da Vinci. Now possibly attributed to Leonardo himself as a rough preparatory sketch for a painting never executed by him. (Musée Condé, Chantilly)

Jacopo and I were shocked into silence. It was Bartolomeo who spoke and gave voice to our thoughts. In pleasing words and cultured manner, he bravely expressed all of our thoughts.

"Maestro, the arrow of your revenge will surely divide and more grievously wound an innocent bystander. You will shame a lady who has been gentle, kind and modest. I believe you will have cause to regret this action, perhaps not immediately, but one day for certain. And it is not worthy of you."

We waited for our master's response. Since we have been crammed into our temporary studio, tempers have been ever shorter. Fortunately, today emotions were at their happiest, following Dottor Machiavelli's excellent news from the Signoria.

There was silence for several moments before Dimmi nodded to Count, smiled and turned to me.

"Paolo, tomorrow morning, go to the del Giocondo home and ask Mona Lisa to loan us her dress. Explain that, to spare her more hours in this draughty studio, a model will take her place for the final sittings. Then go to the home of my goddaughter, Chiara, and tell her she is required once again to model for me."

He continued, "Count, prepare a board for the new painting. No, I believe I will use a canvas. Prepare a canvas according to these instructions."

With that, Dimmi found some pages of instructions he had already written, on the preparation of canvases, and handed them to Bartolomeo, who, under my instruction, was learning to read our master's difficult writing. The preparatory nude design was set aside.

I am curious to meet Chiara, having heard much about her from Salaì and Agostino. Her father was a childhood friend of Dimmi's. Her mother had been a pretty maid in the household. As a favour to his old friend, Dimmi had agreed to stand as godfather to the baby, perhaps because of his own illegitimate parentage. I knew that for some years the family had resided in Urbino, but on the recent death of their father, Chiara, her young sister and their mother had returned to Florence, where they occupy a small house, paid for by my master.

"As you manage my money and my accounts," Maestro instructed me one day, "you will see that each quarter we will be paying the rent on a small house in San Giovanni. This provides a home for my goddaughter and her family, following the death of my friend, Tomasso. I know you keep private all of our business affairs, but this matter in particular is to be kept strictly between you and me. It is of concern to no one else, and I want no gossip attaching to this family."

Chiara had been the model in several paintings by Dimmi, copies of which I have seen. In the paintings, she is beautiful, but Maestro could have created this effect. I shall see for myself tomorrow.

The Professor

The mahogany desk was bathed in a comforting glow from the old-fashioned brass lamp in the otherwise dark room. Lauren had spent almost every waking moment since her discovery in this sanctuary. Yet again, she had passed an entire day and evening immersed in Paolo's world, leaving only to run downstairs for rushed meals. When the clock struck ten, she forced herself to put down the latest manuscript. She rubbed the back of her neck where a crick had formed, her eyes closed to ease the dry sting that developed when she spent too many hours engrossed in the Chronicles. For a moment, she gave herself up to the sensual pleasure of scrunching her toes even deeper into the rich pile of the carpet.

Paolo's diary was an incredible document, full of astonishing insights into one of the most dramatic and critical periods of Western civilisation. Lauren was hoarding the secret of these pages, and she knew it. It was well past the time when she should have revealed her find. She didn't want to share yet, but she couldn't put it off any longer.

She turned to her laptop and spent thirty minutes writing and re-writing an email to David Hildebrand, chair of the Department of Economic History at the University of Chicago.

Professor Hildebrand,

My early examination of the Chance documents began well. I uncovered a great deal of new material touching on many aspects of the trading relationship between England and Florence.

However, something unexpected and exciting has arisen, and I feel I should bring it to your attention.

In one of the larger storage boxes, under yet more of the commercial documents, I came upon what appears to be an extensive personal diary opening in Florence in 1501. Remarkably, the diarist is a young assistant to none other than Leonardo da Vinci.

I have indexed the diary entries up to and including 1503. Among much fascinating minutiae of daily life in Renaissance Florence, and in particular in Leonardo's workshop, I have noted detailed material relating to the commissioning of the Mona Lisa, information which I am certain will have a major impact on the interpretation and provenance of the painting in the Louvre.

It appears that the diary contains entries at least thru 1522, although I don't yet know if it is complete. Nor have I yet uncovered the provenance of this remarkable document.

Assuming for the moment that it is genuine, it is clear this diary is of primary significance. I have therefore suspended my research on the wool trade papers and devoted myself full-time to summarising and indexing what I am provisionally entitling, 'The Paolo Chronicles', after Paolo del Rosso, author of the diaries. I should mention that a Google search confirms there was indeed a Paolo del Rosso active in Leonardo's household from some date prior to 1504 until Leonardo's death. While this fact of itself is not, of course, evidence of the document's authenticity, it is nonetheless reassuring.

I estimate it will take me around one month to produce an overview of the entire corpus, 1501-1522. After this, I will produce a detailed transcript, in Italian and English, of each diary entry. No doubt as the transcript emerges, experts from a wide range of disciplines will have to be involved.

While the university will presumably wish to seek primacy for itself regarding these initiatives, we will have to consider the views of the Earl. I will brief him later today.

I hope these decisions meet with your approval.

Lauren Patterson

When she was finally satisfied with her effort, Lauren saved her draft, closed her laptop and picked out a few key pages of the diary for tomorrow, before finally heading to bed–tired, but still exhilarated by her discovery.

She deliberately sent her email at eight the following morning, two a.m. Chicago time, confident she would have at least five hours or so before a response reached her. As soon as she hit 'Send', she went down to the kitchen for a light breakfast–the butterflies in her stomach dissuaded her from choosing any of the cooked options.

Lauren didn't feel guilty about having delayed disclosing her discovery to her professor, but she did feel bad about not confiding earlier to the Earl, whose property the papers were and whose hospitality had enabled her to uncover this treasure. It was time to make good on that omission.

From her lunchtime visit the previous day, Lauren knew the Earl was at home. She ran back to her study to collect the pages she had selected the previous evening and made her way down to the library. When she had arranged things there to her satisfaction, she set off to find the owner of the house and the Chronicles. This was not necessarily a straightforward undertaking. The main house was a rabbit-warren of corridors and stairways, many of which Lauren had yet to explore. Then there were the many outbuildings–ranging from a large chapel and several barns, to stables, cottages and garden sheds. But the sun was shining, so it wasn't too long before she tracked down her host in the rear vegetable garden. The Earl and Joe, one of the younger gardeners, were having an animated discussion. As Lauren came close, she overheard the end of their conversation, which transpired to be about the best strategy to get rid of leaf spot on the tomato plants.

When Joe turned away to attend to his next vegetable patient, Lauren spoke up.

"Lord Blythswood, may I have a word?"

"By all means, although if we are to talk like normal humans, why don't you call me William?"

"Thank you. Can we talk in the library? I have something exciting to show you."

Blythswood House would never be a contender for the title of England's most beautiful stately home–over the centuries too many opinionated owners had made too many eccentric contributions. But it was one of the quirkiest. Traces of Medieval, Renaissance, Tudor and Jacobean architecture competed for attention with the most recent High Victorian embellishments, rarely in perfect harmony. Blythswood's fame rested, not on the house, but on its magnificent gardens; the spectacular thirteenth century tithe barn, popular with brides and event organisers; and the historic art collection, now displayed in the former chapel.

From the garden, Lauren and the Earl entered the house by a rear door and passed along a corridor lined with oak wainscoting darkened by the centuries to a gloomy brown-that-was-almost-black. Lauren opened a heavy door, and the atmosphere lightened dramatically as they stepped into the elegant library, designed in the eighteenth century by William Kent for an earlier Earl. Translucent, full-length blinds were permanently lowered over the room's tall windows, protecting the leather volumes shelved in serried rows around the walls. On a sunny day like this, the entire room was bathed in a diffuse, pearlescent glow, reflecting off the spines of thousands of books with their patinas of warm browns and shades of rich burgundy. Lauren led the Earl to a long mahogany table on which she had arranged the carefully selected pages of Paolo's diary.

First, she explained how she had found the papers. Then, drawing his attention to key passages, she gave her host an overview of what she had learned so far.

"Basically, you appear to own an insider's view of the workings of the studio and household of Leonardo da Vinci. And there are hundreds of pages, covering almost twenty years, so there's much, much more to learn. It's unbelievably exciting."

Lauren paused to allow William time to absorb the impact of what she had set out before him. She forced herself to still her nerves as she studied him intently, looking for even the tiniest hint that would signal his reaction.

"I am just stunned, Lauren. I had no idea this was here. Well, of course I didn't–what a silly thing to say."

He grinned at her, shedding ten years in the process.

"You've made the most important discovery at Blythswood since 1533, when a maid found the ring Anne Boleyn had given Henry VIII. He lost it in the gardens while he was having his way with said maid and threatened to have the entire household, my ancestors included, all sent to the Tower if it wasn't recovered. There might never have been an Earl of Blythswood.

"Seriously," he continued, "this is a wonderful surprise. Have you given any thought as to what we might do next? Although I don't suppose you've had too much time to think about it."

"I'm sorry to have to confess that I've had these papers longer than you might suppose–I found the diary pages nearly a week ago." Lauren's words now tumbled out in a rush. "At first, I was just thrilled, and eager to read the documents. Then I became a bit obsessed, and couldn't drag myself away from the amazing world I was immersed in."

She paused. "And, I must be honest, I enjoyed having the secret to myself–I was learning things about Leonardo no-one has ever known or even suspected. I'm sorry. I should have told you earlier."

He dismissed her concerns with a wave of his hand. "I'd have felt exactly the same in your shoes. Don't worry about it. You've told me now and that's what's important. I don't suppose a few days after five hundred years will make the slightest difference. The main thing is you found the papers. Now we need to determine the proper course of action to protect them."

Feeling a large weight lift from her shoulders, Lauren handed William a printed copy of the email she had sent to Chicago.

The Earl was an intelligent and shrewd man.

"I imagine this will create a stir in academic circles?"

"I'm certain it will create absolute uproar in all manner of places. It's Leonardo da Vinci and it's the *Mona Lisa* after all."

Then Lauren took her gamble, the one she had been wrestling with since reading Paolo's first entry.

"Lord Blythswood, William, whoever translates and publishes this material will be, for a while at least, the most famous academic historian in the world. I'd like to be that person. You own this diary. Whatever you wish to do with it, is your absolute right. I'm asking you to trust me to treat its contents in a manner that respects the diary while allowing me to kick-start my career. If you permit me to finish my work on the Chronicles in the manner I outlined to Professor Hildebrand, I promise to do right by them."

Lauren waited for his decision, once again attuned to the significance of the moment. Her breathing became shallow, her chest tight. The next words she heard could make or break her career.

William Chance's question about the likely reaction to Lauren's discovery had been more about giving himself thinking time than eliciting information. He was already the custodian of a moderately important art collection, and he understood very well the seismic impact the papers would have on the art establishment.

Lauren's straightforward petition had struck just the right note. The Earl admired the young researcher's honesty and he was sure his late wife, Katherine, would have lobbied on Lauren's behalf–she had always sought to advance the careers of young women to whom she had taken a shine, and he was certain she would have liked Lauren and admired her spirit.

An exchange overheard years ago, between his wife and their friend, Jeremy, a prominent barrister, had had a considerable impact on him, challenging his own comfortable assumptions.

With some vigour, Katherine had declared, "If men in positions of influence don't make a special effort to help them, young women will never be given the opportunities to achieve their potential."

"That sounds like unfair positive discrimination," their friend replied.

Before he could develop his case further, Katherine retorted, "What it sounds like, Jeremy, is precisely what your sons, and the sons of your friends and classmates, have relied on and benefited from for generations."

The fact remained, however, the academic politics that would arise around a discovery of this magnitude had to be carefully managed, or the reputation of the papers and their owner would be jeopardised.

The Earl carefully lifted one of the diary pages and examined it, before setting it back down. Gently, he nudged the paper until it was precisely aligned with its fellows. Lauren stiffened even more, her body an overtightened guitar string.

When he spoke, William looked directly at Lauren. "I've always admired the American way of avoiding false modesty and being open about one's ambitions. I'll support you in your research, Lauren. You may continue as you outlined to your Professor, although I trust you'll keep me regularly advised on what you're discovering. And once translated, there will be no restrictions on other scholars with a legitimate need to examine the originals. We will have to find a home for the manuscript to facilitate that—we certainly can't accommodate an unending stream of academics here."

Lauren forced herself not to yell out her joy at his answer. She also resisted the urge to hug her host. As wave after wave of relief swept over her, from far away she heard the Earl continue. "It's a bit early in the day for champagne, but we should celebrate. I'll ask cook to prepare a special lunch and we'll indulge then."

* * *

At the start of lunch, the Earl stood up and called for attention from everyone gathered around the long kitchen table.

"In the course of her research, Lauren has uncovered some very important historic papers. She'll tell you much more about them herself soon, but for now I'm asking that you don't pester her for information. I'm sorry to be mysterious, but certain arrangements have to be made before we can tell you anything more. In the meantime, cook has prepared lunch with the pheasants from the weekend's shoot. Then there are some delicious looking fresh strawberries. And, if Tom would please do the honours, we'll start with a glass of champagne."

After a leisurely meal, everyone remained at the table enjoying the last of the sparkling wine. A loud ping interrupted Lauren's conversation with Emma, Blythswood's wedding planner. Reluctantly, she slipped her phone from her pocket and glanced at it before passing it across the table to the Earl, an email open on the screen.

Lauren,

I'll be on the first available flight. Do nothing. Speak to no one until we talk. That includes your host. I'll send my flight details. Meet me at Heathrow Airport.

Professor Hildebrand

Two hours later, in the serenity of her study, shoes off and toes luxuriating in the carpet, Lauren was once more absorbed in the lives of Leonardo and his household. Until she received a text message:

Arriving London Heathrow 11.35
a.m. tomorrow on Flight AA46.
Meet us there.

'Us', Lauren thought. So already there were two of them.
Or more.

* * *

Lauren watched from her study window as the black
minicab crunched its way up the gravel driveway. Even
though the Earl's reaction to her proposal had been so
positive, she couldn't help remaining a bit apprehensive.
In addition to having the Earl onside, she needed the
support of an academic organisation to properly research
and analyse the contents of diary, and she needed funding
to keep herself in England. She found her shoes and made
her way to the front entrance to greet the visitors.

She opened the heavy door before anyone knocked,
but before she could utter a word of welcome, Professor
Hildebrand complained, "I expected you to meet us,
Lauren."

"I'm sorry, Professor, but we were really busy this
morning. Things have moved on since my email. I had
already talked with the Earl before I received your reply.
We've made space in a basement strongroom to house the
Chronicles. It isn't the perfect environment—the light isn't
great—but it's secure, dry and fireproof and it'll do until the
Earl makes more permanent arrangements. We can see
them whenever you wish."

Any observer could see that David Hildebrand was not
at all happy. Things were not playing out the way he had

rehearsed. He had intended to have a conversation with Lauren while she should have been driving him from Heathrow: Only he could deploy the resources required to execute this major project, Lauren needed to focus on her PhD, perhaps later there could be a role for her to assist in the project.

"Lauren, I wonder if you understand just how important this matter is. It's essential I take control immediately. I need to meet with the Earl, as soon as possible. Can you make an appointment with him in, say, two hours or so, and meanwhile, where are our rooms? We need to change and freshen up."

"I'm sure the Earl will be available whenever you're ready, Professor, he knows you're arriving today. As for your rooms, I'm afraid I have the only remaining guestroom in the house. But I've reserved two rooms in the village. Blythswood is a popular destination for tourists and visitors, so the only nearby hotel is full. But I'm told the local pub rooms are comfortable, although you will be sharing a bathroom, I'm afraid. I'll drive you there now if you want."

* * *

Three hours later, in Lauren's splendid study, the two jet-lagged professors sat across the desk from their student. As they took in the paintings, antique furniture and ornamental plasterwork of the room, both men were mentally contrasting these stunning surroundings with their own utilitarian accommodations back in the department's austere 1960s building in Chicago.

David Hildebrand opened the discussion. "You've clearly given this a considerable amount of thought, Lauren. What do you wish to propose?"

"I think we should do what I outlined in my email, Professor."

"When you say, *'we'*, you mean *'I'*, I think. You want to do it all yourself, don't you?"

"Only the initial phase. I can index, summarise and translate the material as well as anyone. And yes, I do want the recognition, let's be frank."

"Very well, if we're being frank, there's no way I can allow an inexperienced post-grad to retain custody over what might turn out to be the most important document for Renaissance studies discovered in decades, perhaps the most important ever. That just can't happen."

"Why not? Because I'm a post-grad, not a professor? Because I'm a woman? Because I'm not you?"

"I don't appreciate your tone, Lauren, or your implication."

"Men rarely do when challenged by women, Professor. The fact is, I am absolutely competent to carry out the initial work—I'm familiar with the period and I'm fluent in the language. Surely that's all that should be at issue—not my seniority or status, and certainly not my gender. I'm well aware that specialists will ultimately do most of the interpretation and analysis, but that's not what we're talking about. And, may I point out, control of the Chronicles is not in your gift—that decision is in the hands of the owner of the papers."

As if on cue, William Chance knocked and entered the room.

"Professor Hildebrand? Pleased to meet you. Sorry to have kept you."

David Hildebrand regained his composure and held out his hand.

"Lord Blythswood, it's a pleasure. This is my colleague, Jackson Greensmith, Associate Professor in my department. Lauren's news is exciting."

"Very exciting indeed. You must be thrilled to have one of your students uncover such an important document."

Lauren interjected. "William, Professor Hildebrand is an expert on economic history, especially the fifteenth and sixteenth centuries. You should ask him about the trading connections between England and Italy during the Renaissance."

"Perhaps you might indulge me over dinner this evening, Professor?"

"I'd be happy to. The trade in wool was of paramount importance, both here and in Florence. Many hundreds, even thousands, of families were involved one way or another. I'm sure Lauren's thesis on your own ancestors will be a valuable addition to the literature."

"I suspect we may have to wait somewhat longer before we see that particular document, now Lauren has bigger fish to fry. Are you an art historian, Professor Greensmith?"

"Indeed not–"

Before Jackson Greensmith could say anything else, Hildebrand interrupted. "I was just explaining to Lauren that one of the challenges we face with the diary is the wide range of academic disciplines we will have to call upon to fully evaluate the material, such was the enormous range of Leonardo's activities. This is the primary reason why I must insist a more senior person take charge, one who can speedily deploy whatever specialists are required."

William Chance cut directly to the crux of the matter.

"Professor Hildebrand, I respect the fact that you are Lauren's supervisor, with every right to direct her academic work as you deem appropriate. That said, the diary is my responsibility. It seems to me, Lauren has set out a course of action both reasonable and appropriate. It is, of course, for you to determine her role vis-à-vis her doctorate and her relationship with the University of Chicago. However, as the diaries are translated, the contents, and indeed the original documents, must be made accessible in a responsible and controlled manner to all accredited academics with a demonstrable need to study them.

"For multiple practical reasons, that access cannot be granted here at Blythswood. But nor, I'm afraid, can it be done in Chicago. The papers will remain in England. It is my intention to transfer them to an appropriate facility, and I have already set that matter in train. Discussing those arrangements is what delayed me just now."

David Hildebrand couldn't summon up a persuasive argument to counter the Earl's pronouncement. This only added to his deep sense of frustration. Here he was, within touching distance of a project that would bring unimaginable exposure to whoever brought this material to the public, and he was being thwarted by a doctorate student and an English dilettante.

He addressed his student.

"Lauren, you can't simply drop your PhD research and pick up another project on a whim. You're here as a result of a grant awarded in respect of a specific proposal. You must continue that work. With the Earl's permission, Professor Greensmith will remain here to progress work on the diary pages until I return."

Lauren had hoped to avoid this eventuality. Still, she had prepared for it. With a glance at the Earl, she addressed her adviser directly. "In that case, Professor, I resign."

Everyone accepted the Earl's advice to sleep on things and allow tempers to cool. The two American academics were taken to see the diary pages and later endured a strained early dinner with the Earl. Lauren excused herself. However, when they all met up again the next morning, nothing had changed. Lauren handed a formal note to her professor, resigning her position at the university and committing to repaying the grant money she had received.

The following day, two distinctly unhappy academics boarded their plane for the long flight back to Chicago, still jet-lagged and with nothing to show for their travels. Jackson Greensmith could help tormenting himself by occasionally looking at a couple of pages of the chronicle that he had surreptitiously photographed with his phone. How he would have loved to have staked a claim to this discovery!

1503 – Chiara

October 17th

I now understand that Petrarca was truly a genius.[1] Many times someone, invariably someone with grey whiskers, has insisted that the poets have expressed all we would wish to say concerning our emotions. I have always been sceptical. Until now. That most worthy master captured exactly the feelings that overwhelmed me this morning:

> Blessed be the day, and the month, and the year,
> and the season, and the time, and the hour, and the
> moment,
> and the beautiful country, and the place where I was
> joined
> to the two beautiful eyes that have bound me.

Our eyes were joined; my heart is truly bound.

This most excellent morning started well.

Mona Lisa del Giocondo was gracious and kind, and she bid me take a cool drink while her maid fetched the dress and wrapped it in a cloth.

---

[1] The poet Petrarch (1304-1374)

I then went to the address I had been given for Chiara. She too was gracious, but oh! how her beauty instantly bewitched me. I shall try to describe her.

She is young. Well, she is twenty-four I learned this afternoon, and so eight years older than I—but surely that is of little matter. Her eyes are the palest blue, the morning sky after rain. Her skin is flawless; smooth and radiant. Her full lips are red, her teeth pearl white, the better to illuminate her beguiling smile. Her hair is long and full and glows with the deep, rich colour of the finest old Tuscan wine. I blush to try to describe her figure. It is enough to say—perfect.

But even greater than her physical beauty is the radiance of her true self. She smiles, she laughs, she walks with a light step, greeting everyone and leaving a trail of smiles behind her. The world is a better place for her presence.

Too soon, we arrived back at the bottega and to gloom.

Dimmi had just learned that Gonfaloniere Soderini has been beguiled by Michelangelo Buonarroti, a talented young artist, but no friend of my master. There are also some among the Signoria unhappy that my master has worked with the Pope and the Milanesi, neither well-disposed to our city and Republic. All of this means that the Gonfaloniere has divided the great commission. We will have one wall, on which Maestro will create a representation of the Battle of

Anghiari, while Maestro Michelangelo will have the opposite wall for the Battle of Cascina.[1]

I fear there will be tension all the while they work.

Despite his dark mood, Dimmi embraced his goddaughter, of whom, it is plain, he is exceedingly fond.

"Chiara, tesoro, I am sorry. My mind is troubled by this news of Michelangelo. I cannot paint today. Please be so kind as to return the day after tomorrow."

Before I could stop myself, I blurted out, "I will escort you back to your home, Chiara."

Salaì laughed at me.

"The child is smitten!" he called.

But Chiara gave me a lovely smile and replied in voice at once sweet and kindly, "That would be delightful, Paolo. Come, let us go."

I can tell you only little of the rest of my morning—it passed as if in a dream. As we made our way back to Chiara's home, I insisted on taking a longer way, avoiding the piazza. She was at first confused and then teased that I was simply making longer our journey together. However, when we arrived at her door, her mother was awaiting her.

---

[1] *Paolo actually refers to Maestro Buonarroti. However, as the sculptor and painter has come down to us simply as Michelangelo, this usage has been adopted in this translation.*

"Were you upset, cara?"

"Upset? Why would I be upset?"

"The hangings, of course! Six men are to be horribly tortured and then hanged today in the piazza, before their bodies are chopped up. Surely you knew? Everyone has been talking of it. The worst of the mob will be there."

"I did not know." Chiara turned to me. "Paolo, did you know about th… You did, didn't you? Is that why you would not let me enter the piazza?"

She waited for no answer, but instead took my hand and squeezed it.

"Thank you."

And now, before I must close my eyes to think of her more clearly, I will copy out more from that genius of love, Francesco Petrarca:

> Bitter tears pour down my face
> with an anguished storm of sighing,
> when my eyes chance to turn on you
> through whom alone I am lost from the world.
>
> Yet it is true that your soft gentle smile
> quietens my ardent desires,
> and saves me from the fire of suffering,
> while I am intent and fixed on gazing.

October 18th

Today, Maestro Leonardo da Vinci was inducted, once again, into the Confraternity of St Luke. In his honour, we spent much of the day scrubbing and tidying the bottega for his return, knowing how much he likes everything to be clean and well organised.

This evening, to mark the ceremony, a bull was let into the enclosure of the lions, but little happened. One lion did eventually leap on the back of the huge bull, but it was immediately thrown off, after which both lions ignored the bull, while it was equally dismissive of the great cats.

It is still amazing to me that the Republic keeps lions for no reason but the entertainment of its citizens! Can there be another city anywhere so well-favoured in the beauty of its architecture, the transcendent genius of its artists and the sagacity of its leaders?

October 19th

This has been the greatest day of my life.

I rose early and eased myself out of our bed. This is not so easy. As the youngest and the latest to join the studio, Bartolomeo and I sleep in the middle of the bed, while Jacopo and Salaì have the favoured places on the outside. Agostino and Francesco, who we call Cecco, are the oldest and Cecco by far the biggest of us, so *they have their own cot along the foot of our bed. There are complaints if anyone awakens the others before the appointed hour. I woke Jacopo, but today I did not care if later he would scold me—in fact he did, and I didn't.*

I took especial care with my toilet. Dimmi says we should dress well every day—with care and with colour. Today, I tried my best. I wore my new rose doublet and my fine coat with its velvet collar, and I was pleased as I could be with the results. My face is my face, and there is nothing to be done about it. I picked the last of the parsley to chew but could find no anise in our stores[1].

I left the bottega before anyone else stirred, excepting Tessa, our housemaid, who was building a fire.

I wandered around the market, searching for anise (successfully I must say—although the price was shockingly high) while trying all the while to still my racing heart. (In this I was signally unsuccessful.) When I could wait no longer, I knocked on the door of Chiara's house. I have written before that Chiara lives with her mother and much younger sister. I learned today that she is saving for her sister's dowry.

---

[1] *Fresh parsley and anise (aniseed) were thought to combat bad or stale breath.*

"Maestro Leonardo first painted me as a young girl, as the Angel, with the Madonna and the babies, Our Lord Jesus and St. John. Since then he has permitted me to model for his friend, Maestro Botticelli. My padrino insists no one else may employ me—to protect my reputation.[1] But I have been told that Maestro della Robbia will petition him to permit me to sit for him, for a Blessed Virgin."

Chiara told me this as we walked to our studio. My friends who saw us walking side-by-side will be overcome with jealousy. I hope there were many who did.

At the studio, Chiara retired to change into Mona Lisa's dress.

I then watched as my master tried various poses—guiding Chiara to hold her head like so, or to move her hand a tiny fraction left, now right. Finally, he pronounced himself happy.

It was clear he had determined on a slightly different approach to the portrait. Count's words have caused Maestro to change his heart and his head with regard to the lady.

---

[1] *Padrino = godfather*

Image 3: The Virgin of the Rocks.
With a young Chiara as the pointing angel
(Louvre, Paris)

"Now, Chiara, your face. You have just been delivered of
your third child. It is a boy, your second son. Your husband

is delighted—with two sons, his line is now secure. He will soon present you with a beautiful jewel, and next month you will move into your new home. At this moment everything in your life is blessed. These are the thoughts I wish you to live while I paint your eyes and your smile. Sadly, my dear, the eyes will be Mona Lisa's boring brown and not your own dramatic blue, but still I want to read her thoughts in your eyes."

As Dimmi spoke, I watched, amazed, as the emotions he described played across Chiara's face. I had assumed she was chosen as a model because of her radiant beauty and presumed ability to sit still for many hours, but now I saw there was another, more important reason. Chiara can invoke any emotion on demand. My master believes that a painting comes alive only if the artist paints the thoughts and emotions of the sitter as well as her skin and hair.

The morning passed delightfully as I gazed at the vision before me. Soon enough, Chiara realised my attention was completely fixed on her, but she did not betray me.

Finally, Dimmi laid down his brushes.

"A good morning! Thank you, mia cara. We will continue tomorrow. Paolo, after you escort Chiara home, take some lunch and then meet me at the house of Benvenuti Fonte. We need to extract some more money from that old miser."

Dimmi left the room, but before Chiara could rise from her chair, Salaì appeared behind her chair and wrapped his *arms around her, clutching her bosoms. In a flash, Chiara leapt up and spun around, easily breaking his grasp. A deadly stiletto had miraculously appeared in her right hand, its needle-sharp point a blur that came to rest a whisker from Salaì's terrified eye.*

"You had better decide how much you enjoy feeling my breasts, Caprotti, because the next time you touch them, it will cost you dear. You assume because I am a model, I must be a whore? Even though you see how Maestro, my padrino, treats me with honour and respect? You are a prick. You understand nothing of women. I pity those poor girls and boys you pay to lie with you. Now, get out of my sight."

It was delicious to watch.

And then, as if nothing had happened, Chiara turned to me and beamed her lovely smile. "Give me one moment to change, my protector, and you can walk me home."

I have no idea when or to where the knife disappeared.

As we passed along Via dell'Oriuolo, Chiara linked her arm through mine. I thought I might expire from happiness.

"I saw you looking at me this morning, caro. It is good for a young man to fall in love with an older woman—to feel the drama, the excitement. But do not let your heart be broken. In a few years, you will meet a girl your own age, or younger. Perhaps she will look like me, perhaps not. But you will meet her. So, for now, by all means be my protector, but have a care also to protect your heart."

Why would I seek to protect my heart from these joyous sensations? Who would not relish the soaring excitement and pride of walking beside her? Not savour the closeness between us as two joined conspirators? Who would seek an end to these glorious feelings? Not I.

After, I went to rendezvous with my master at the home of old Messer Fonte. Recall that I had delivered the portrait of his granddaughter last week, but he refused my request for an additional fifteen florins.

"Here is the fee as agreed, seventy florins. Tell the maestro I am pleased with the portrait."

When I arrived at the Fonte palazzo, Dimmi was already there, speaking with great animation.

"Messer Fonte. Yes, we agreed seventy florins for a painting of your granddaughter. But then you arrived at my studio with the puppy and asked that I add it into the scene. I have done as you requested. For the extra work, I ask only fifteen florins, as I am a reasonable man. Look at the fur, the eyes—I am sure your granddaughter cried with joy to see her beloved pet in her painting."

"She did indeed. It is most excellently done. But you said nothing about an extra fee. Therefore, I need pay nothing more."

"I assumed a man of culture would understand that an extra figure meant extra work and was thus deserving of an additional fee!"

"Then, on this occasion, you assumed wrong. Now, I must bid you good day, Maestro. I am old and in the custom of taking a nap at this hour."

I could see Dimmi was not in the mood to let this matter rest. I had an idea.

"Maestro, we should leave," I said, making the old miser smile, anticipating his victory. "Just let me retrieve our frame and we can leave Messer Fonte to his much-needed rest."

I went over and lifted the painting from its easel. The little dog was indeed charming. Carefully, I laid the painting face down on the table.

"What are you doing, boy?" the old man demanded.

"I'm recovering our frame, which we loaned you. The contract said nothing about a frame. We were obliged to provide you a painting of the agreed size and subject, and there it is."

I pointed to the painting, resting back on the easel, now naked and much less impressive when shorn of its golden frame.

"If you come to the bottega, Messer, we can show you many styles of frames which can be made for your painting."

"But everyone knows that a painting comes in a frame!"

"No, Messer, everyone may assume so. On this occasion, I fear, you assumed wrong."

The old man was not pleased, but he knew he had been bested.

"Very well, very well. How much is the frame?"

"Made to order, twenty-five florins. But we have a policy of charging only twenty when we sell a frame with a painting. Is that not correct, Maestro?"

My master was struggling to keep his joy from his face.

"Quite so, Paolo, quite so." [1]

As we crossed the piazza, Dimmi ruffled my hair.

"Here, take the half, ten florins. You deserve them. You did well today, Paolo. And I have had an idea. The sketch of the Virgin and her mother with the infants, the Saviour and St John the Baptist–I am going to change the composition. It has been in my mind for so long, but I was never completely certain how I wished to proceed. This morning, looking at my goddaughter, it came to me that I must focus the viewer more clearly on her face. Chiara will still be portrayed as the Virgin but now with her cousin, Elizabeth and her child, the Baptist. A lamb will represent our unborn Saviour, foretelling the Baptist's later meeting with him. In this manner the story will feature more strongly Mary in the form of Chiara. We will need my goddaughter in the studio constantly, until this painting too is finished."

What a day!

---

[1] *The Fonte commission painting is lost.*

Image 4: The Virgin and Child with St Anne.
Now believed to portray Mary, Elizabeth and St John the
Baptist, with Chiara as Mary, the rearmost figure
(Louvre, Paris)

November 20th

I do not understand why my master loves Salaì so. He causes nothing but trouble and his skill in painting is *merely proficient–far inferior to Count, Jacopo or even Agostino.*

I thought in May, when he banished Salaì for a week, I had never seen anyone so angry as Dimmi was that day. Today was a thousand times worse.

Cecco burst into the bottega after lunch and, once he had recovered his breath, he grasped Salaì by the shoulders and shook him.

"Did you make a painting from Maestro's first study of Mona Lisa del Giocondo, and then sell it?"

Now you must consider that Cecco is older and much bigger and stronger than Salaì, than any of us. As Cecco shook his shoulders, Salaì's head bounced first one way and then the other.

"What is it to you?" Salaì finally blurted.

"You fool, you idiot, you twice-pox'd arsehole!"

With that, Cecco lifted Salaì completely off his feet and threw him backwards, directly into his easel and everything came crashing down. Awakened by this uproar, our master came running from his chamber, his long hair dishevelled.

"What is going on here? Can a man get no rest after his lunch? Am I in the jungle, surrounded by wild animals? Cecco, what is happening? Why do you assault Salaì? Dimmi!"

"Maestro, I fear to tell you the calamity this piece of putrid dog shit has brought upon us. I was taking a cup of wine with some acquaintances when I overhead Messer

67

Baldovinetti boast to his friends that he had recently bought a painting of Madonna del Giocondo, naked.

" 'Her breasts are surprisingly firm for one who has had five babies, but then she will have suckled none of them, although I assume her husband has enjoyed them well enough. I will unveil them to everyone next week at the feast.' Those were his exact words, Maestro, I swear."

There was a frightening silence while Salaì tried, without success, to wriggle past Cecco, who again held him, arms pinned firmly by his side.

Finally, my master spoke, in a voice hard as slate and cold as ice.

"Count, Paolo, go to Salaì's box. Find every soldo, every denaro. Find everything that can be sold and bring it here."

We ran to do his bidding. When we returned, it appeared no one had moved or spoken. We laid money and some small items before Dimmi. There was a surprising amount of cash, over two hundred florins, I guessed.

Now he addressed the trembling Salaì.

"How much did you charge for the painting, parasite? Dimmi!"

"150 florins," he mumbled.

150 florins is a huge amount. Few of the Maestro's portraits bring so much. In this instance, the value is in the power the painting gives, not the worth of the artist. Baldovinetti is well

known to be a bitter rival of Francesco del Giocondo. With this painting, he will humiliate his enemy, and the torment will never end.

Dimmi shook his head in despair. "Paolo, we must retrieve the painting. Bring all of this money."

He turned and spoke again to Salaì.

"You ungrateful, spiteful, dishonest wretch. Leprous cur, vermin, cockroach. Leave here and do not let me put my eyes on you again. If you see me approach in the street, turn and run away. If I pass you on the bridge, throw yourself into the river."

With that, Maestro picked up a leg of the broken easel and began to beat Salaì about the head and shoulders until, after a few well-placed blows had landed, Cecco released him and allowed him to run into the street.

There were many problems associated with Salaì's insane action. Apart from theft from the bottega and the terrible discourtesy to our client, there is the huge problem concerning the fresco for the Signoria.

In short, it is not going well. My master had decided upon a novel method of working and, so far, it is proving to be a disaster. The Signoria, and in particular Gonfaloniere Soderini, are extremely unhappy at the slow pace of work. And they are giving us only a little money each month. They could stop paying at any time and we would be in dire trouble. The only small relief is that Maestro Michelangelo has yet to even begin his fresco. Nonetheless, this is absolutely the last *moment we need to make an enemy of a powerful political faction such as that around the Giocondo clan.*

In the end, my master had to hand over all of Salaì's 210 florins and promise to paint, for no fee, a portrait of Baldovinetti's wife, a surpassingly ill-favoured woman of fifty-seven years.

The money cost my master nothing. Painting the most infamous harpy in Florence will bring him a mountain of pain.[1]

---

[1] *It is not clear that this Baldovinetti painting was ever begun. It is not known today and there is no further mention of it in the Diaries, nor in the literature. Given Leonardo's record, it is highly probable that he succeeded in putting off this unwelcome task indefinitely.*

Image 5: Mona Vanna or the Nude Mona Lisa.
Salaì's painting that caused so much trouble.
(Hermitage Museum, St Petersburg)

Chance Encounter

Jonathan Granville's mood bounced between euphoria to high anxiety as he looked around the pristine gallery. He had sunk every penny he owned into Access Art. Most of it had gone on the drawings, etchings and watercolours arrayed dramatically on the freshly painted satin grey walls. Each had been tastefully framed by a friend from the Courtauld Institute. The overall visual impact was stunning.

In just over a week he would have his opening. He had invited an eclectic mixture of friends and family; lecturers and professors from the Courtauld; collectors he had met over the years, often with his grandfather; journalists and a few other dealers. The major auction houses would each send someone and Frederick Henderson of Cheltenham Auctions would be there. Jonathan had hung his very first purchase, bought with Mr Henderson's assistance many years ago. The tiny cherub's head was marked *'Sold'*, as were a few other private pieces he had no intention of selling. The always courteous auctioneer had sent an acceptance note in immaculate copperplate handwriting.

'I am delighted to accept your kind invitation to the opening of your new gallery. I well remember our first meeting on your birthday and your excitement over your first acquisition. Your late grandfather was a valued client, a fine connoisseur, and a man with a keen eye for a bargain. In all of our dealings over the years, buying and selling many works of art, I do not believe I ever witnessed him taking a loss on any trade—a most remarkable

track record. I am certain he would be extraordinarily proud of your initiative.

If there is anything I can do to assist in your new venture, please do not hesitate to call on me. I look forward to seeing you at the opening.

Cordially,

Frederick Henderson

P.S. You may wish to take a close look at Lot 312 in our upcoming sale; an interesting Flemish watercolour.

When he read the note, Jonathan had an intense flashback to one particular day, when he was only twelve years old and alone in the big house with his grandfather.

* * *

"You have to pick an area, and study it intensively," the elderly man instructed his grandson. "That's the only way you can compete with the dealers, auctioneers and other buyers. You need to know at least as much as they do, preferably more. Then you can trust your judgement. Take this drawing here for example."

Jonathan watched his grandfather lift a lovely drawing from the wall and place it on a display easel where it could be examined more easily. One of the things he loved most about being with his grandfather was that he talked to him exactly as he would an adult.

"I spotted this in an auction catalogue several months ago, attributed only to '*Venetian School, Early Seventeenth*

Century'. But I knew something else about it. There's a painting in a Paris museum by an artist called Pietro da Cortona. In the left-hand corner there's a girl with a basket. It is *this* girl. I realised this sketch was a study for that painting. So, I bought it, for £2,000. Now it's worth perhaps £50,000. I like this sketch, but I'm not in love with it. If I saw another I thought was a bargain at £50,000, I'd sell this to pay for it. Don't tell your father I said that, by the way," Grandfather finished with a conspiratorial wink.

This conversation lit a spark in the young boy and gradually he became at first interested, and then obsessed, by the drawings, sketches and watercolours in his grandparent's rambling house in Stow-on-the-Wold. Together, Jonathan and his grandfather studied each artwork in turn. The old man explained the techniques used, the story of the artist and the period, and the subject matter–generally portraits, landscapes or episodes from mythology or the Bible.

* * *

Jonathan snapped out of his reverie and realised he was exhausted. For the past three weeks he had been working non-stop: helping Andrew rig the lighting system, painting the walls and ceiling and, for the past few days, laying a new floor. Being friends with a professional lighting designer had been another huge bonus, saving him a great deal of money. All in all, his friends had been great, he mused. Without them, none of this could have happened.

And he'd have to depend on the kindness of friends for a while more. He had no money left to pay wages, but he was saved when his sister-in-law and two good friends agreed to work two or three days a week each, without pay, to help him staff the gallery when it opened for business.

Right this minute Jonathan was sorely in need of a few hours out of this space. He finished unpacking and shelving the reference books from his grandfather's bookcases, grabbed his North Face jacket and headed out.

Jonathan's favourite place to decompress on a damp, blustery day was the National Gallery. No matter how often he visited, there was always something new to enjoy–sometimes a new exhibit, but more often a picture he had overlooked in his previous visits. Today he decided he would visit an old friend. He made his way straight upstairs to Room 20 and Leonardo's magnificent cartoon, *The Virgin and Child with St Anne and St John the Baptist.*

He supposed it was only about the fortieth time he had stood before the masterpiece. But on this occasion his concentration was broken. Actually, it never got fixed properly in the first place. An attractive young woman stood before the drawing.

He waited discreetly for a minute, giving her time to appreciate at the magnificent work before moving on. When it became clear she wasn't in any hurry, he ventured, "It's wonderful, isn't it?"

She responded immediately, and straight away he picked up on her American accent.

"It is, although I can't help wishing I had seen it when it was new. I imagine it must have been much brighter."

"I'm sure you're right. It has suffered abuse over the years but then again, it's surprising that anything so fragile has survived at all. You know a man attacked her with a shotgun, from as close are we're standing now?"

"Really! A shotgun! In England, yet! When did this happen?"

"About twenty years ago. The man was mentally ill, and the damage was repaired. Poor old girl, getting shot when you're 500 years old."

"So, it's a girl is it?" she teased.

"Well, yes. The two main figures are women, even if St Anne is a bit unfinished, as if Leonardo hadn't made up his mind about something. She's a bit fuzzy, don't you think?"

"Leonardo had made up his mind, but then he changed it." She pointed to the adjacent oil painting, *The Virgin of the Rocks*. "Because of her."

Jonathan glanced over at the other Leonardo. "I'm sorry, I don't understand."

"Because of the young model for the angel in that painting over there. She grew up, and Leonardo changed his mind, because he wanted to feature her prominently in *this* composition. So, he did, as Mary."

Lauren was living on her nerves. The episode with Professor Hildebrand had been extremely stressful, although she thought she had done a pretty good job of hiding her anxiety. She was grateful to William for proposing a break for a couple of days, which had given her time to think. The Earl was busy today and so they had arranged to meet first thing tomorrow. She hoped he wasn't having second thoughts. Her future depended on it.

Years ago, Lauren had come across the deliberately twisted phrase, *'Ready, Fire, Aim!'* and recognised her own behaviour now. She had acted with no clear plan for what would she would do next. She was in a foreign country and, even if she had the support of the Earl, she was going to have to deal somehow with visa problems, money issues and finding a university to support her doctorate.

But right now, she needed a break. She had decided to travel up to London to finally see a couple of the artworks she had been reading so much about.

"There's a diary, by Leonardo's assistant. He explained exactly when and why Leonardo had a change of heart about this composition."

"I've never heard of such a document. Which is very odd–I must look it up."

"Actually, you can't. It hasn't been published yet. It will be soon though."

"Really? And you're working on it? That must be exciting."

"Well, yes, at least, I hope so. I'll know tomorrow, for better or worse. I'm a bit on edge about it, to be honest."

"I've got a big day coming up myself. That's why I'm here, to get away for an hour or so. Look, will you let me buy you a cup of coffee? Actually, I can do better than that. They do a proper cream tea here. I'm guessing from your accent you may not have had that experience. I'm Jonathan, by the way."

She immediately shook the hand he offered.

"Thank you, Jonathan–that would be great. I'm Lauren, pleased to meet you."

Jonathan guided them to the gallery's restaurant. When they were settled at a table and had placed their orders, Jonathan asked about the diary.

"I've just started translating it, it's fascinating. I'm only part way through, but already it's incredibly exciting."

"I'm sure it must be, but, well, to be honest, you don't look too excited."

When Jonathan returned to the subject of the diary, Lauren realised she had slipped up, badly. She hadn't been thinking of what she was saying. Whether it was the friendliness of the Englishman or the fact that she was distracted; for whatever reason, she had said more than she should have. She had to be more careful.

She took the opportunity to move the conversation away from the content of the Chronicles. She told him about the disastrous episode with Professor Hildebrand.

"So now I feel guilty, that I've been incredibly selfish. I'm worried William, the Earl, might have second thoughts, that he may be regretting offering his support."

"I don't know the Earl of Blythswood, although I have seen his art collection. I assure you, families like the Chances don't hold on to their titles, their land, their heads even, by being easily pressured into doing things they don't want to."

After a pause, during which he thought he saw some of the tension lift from Lauren's shoulders, Jonathan continued. "What will happen next?"

"I don't know, and I can't think about it anymore. Let's talk about something else."

"Before we do, Leonardo never did paint that Virgin and St Anne, the cartoon I mean. It should be pricked with lots of tiny holes used to transfer the outline onto a panel for the final painting. The cartoon we were looking at has no holes. The final painting was never done. You could go to Paris and see their version of the composition."

"Now, that *would* be lovely." Lauren sighed.

Jonathan told her about the upcoming opening of his gallery.

"Please come along, I need all the support I can get, and you'll meet lots of interesting people. I'm sure it wouldn't hurt to get away from your musty old papers now and then."

"You're right, it wouldn't hurt at all. Thank you. If I possibly can, I'll come to your opening, promise."

The rain had stopped by the time they were served their cream teas. Lauren was charmed by the rituals and laughed when Jonathan explained the great controversies.

"In Devon they slice the scone and spread each half with clotted cream. Then they dollop a spoonful of jam on top. In Cornwall it's jam first, then the cream."

"Which do you recommend?"

With mock indignation, Jonathan replied. "Are you serious? How can you even ask? Jam first, of course. The Devon approach is all wrong, just plain weird. I hope you agree—I could never be friends with a scone heretic."

When Lauren stopped laughing, she pointed out, "You said, controversies. What's the other one?"

"Well, moving right over the *con*troversy con*tro*versy," he said, exaggerating the alternative pronunciations, "there's the whole issue of whether it should be *'scone'* like *'bone'*, or *'scone'* like *'gone'*."

"Is this a Devon and Cornwall thing as well?"

"A little bit. But mostly that's a north–south thing."

Lauren shook her head. "I can see I've got lots to learn."

A weak sun elbowed its way through the clouds as they walked from Trafalgar Square to Paddington. All the while Jonathan told Lauren stories of London and its history. They talked about their favourite places to visit and about her impressions of England.

Lauren noticed the flag on the Italian Embassy as they strolled through Grosvenor Square. This prompted her to tell Jonathan about her Italian great-grandfather and how she learned Italian as a child.

"He paid for me to stay with him most summers when I was a kid. My mom's grandmother had died years earlier and he married again, a sweet lady who was almost perfectly spherical. Lucia had no kids of her own, so I guess she enjoyed having me under her feet for a few weeks each year. I developed a love for Italy and the Italian language. I still adore visiting Italy, it's one of the things I plan to do while I'm in Europe. I think I developed an interest in Italian history just to give me an excuse to go there as often as possible."

"And now you're researching Italian history, but in England," Jonathan observed. "I completely understand your attraction to Italy. My mother's parents had a holiday home in Tuscany. We'd holiday there almost every year. Our grandparents would take my brother and I there for the whole summer and our parents would join us in

August. We loved all of it–the food, the weather, the people. Now, with cheap flights, I go over as often as I can–well, until recently that is."

"Why did you stop going?"

"Too busy. I went back to full-time study for a year, and since then I've been preparing for the opening of my gallery."

By now they had reached Paddington Station where Lauren would catch her train. Jonathan looked up at the departure board and then at the station clock.

"We've got time. Come on."

He led her over to platform one. "Look there."

Lauren's face lit up. "Oh my God! It's Paddington Bear! From deepest, darkest Peru. I just loved Paddington when I was, well, not so terribly little, actually."

She looked solemn for a second then beamed again, "Thanks for walking with me, and for Paddington Bear. You've taken my mind off my worries for a few hours. And…," she hesitated. "And can I ask you to keep what I told you about the Leonardo diary to yourself? I shouldn't have mentioned anything, it just slipped out–I guess I was a bit stressed. We haven't announced anything yet, and it's up to the Earl to decide when and how we do."

As they shook hands, Jonathan maintained his grasp an extra beat as he reassured her, "Don't worry, I won't say a thing. See you at the opening."

He watched her as she made her way to her platform. He very much hoped this lovely American girl would turn up next week. But if she didn't, he'd call her.

1504

January 14th

Salaì is back. I learned today that he had turned up at the studio a few days before Christmas, when Dimmi was minded to allow him in, but Cecco prevailed and he was sent away once more.

"He has to learn, Master. He must behave and put an end to his endless mischief, he is not a child. And how can you discipline the younger students if they witness you always forgiving that wretch?"

But today Salaì went first to Cecco and apologised most profusely before begging Dimmi for one more chance. I saw Cecco look at Jacopo with a wry grimace. Did Jacopo coach Salaì? Whatever transpired, Salaì is back among us. For the rest of the day he worked quietly, causing no trouble, indeed never speaking. I wonder how long his contrition will last?

February 8th

At last to bed! We spent all evening tearing our studio apart. Late in the afternoon, Agostino asked me for the *pattern book, but it was not in its place in the locked cupboard. I do not recall mentioning the pattern book in these pages. It is a most important asset of our studio. In there, Maestro has created a veritable library of fabric patterns painted on pieces of vellum. The apprentices can find appropriate patterns for dresses, window and table coverings, vestments, banners—indeed any possible application that may arise. It is one of the signatures of our work that we reproduce in oils, the richest brocades, linens and silks, with uniquely complicated patterns based on geometry or nature as the occasion demands. And now the book was lost.*

Naturally, suspicion immediately fell on Salaì, but he swore by all the saints that he had not touched it in some weeks. Everyone stopped work and helped conduct a search of the studio. After we had looked in every possible location, Dimmi ordered us to turn out our sleeping quarters. All of our garments, our storage boxes, even the beds themselves were meticulously checked. Finally, the only place left was Dimmi's bedchamber. He insisted that the book was not there, but we persuaded him to allow Count and I to take a look.

Within two minutes, Count found the book where it lay— on the floor under Dimmi's bed.

"I must have been examining it before falling asleep," he stammered as we all stood looking at him with accusations in our eyes, it now being some hours after we should have taken our evening meal.

March 2nd

I do not understand the disdain shown by Maestro Michelangelo to my master. Dimmi is well liked by other artists, with whom he is widely known to be generous with his time and his money, even when we have too little of either to spare.

It is true he has no desire to sculpt in marble, finding it a crude and dirty craft. But as far as I know, he has confined this opinion to his notebooks and a few of us in the bottega.

And yet, from the first, Maestro Michelangelo has broadcast to all his dislike and disregard for my master. Today, by ill fortune, both men arrived at the grand salon in the Palazzo della Signoria at about the same time. Immediately, Maestro Michelangelo declaimed that my master's outline was unsatisfactory and unworthy of the room. He entreated those present to petition the Signoria to have the commission taken from my master, 'else we will be waiting until the Judgement Day for a work that gives pride to the city.'

This barb struck home because Dimmi does have a reputation for not completing much that he starts—and he himself knows this.[1]

---

[1] Ironically, Michelangelo failed to even start his fresco for the Palazzo della Signoria, although his design is known from a copy of his full-size cartoon.

In order to maintain the dignity of the Signoria, Dimmi ignored the baiting of the young fool and left the Palazzo.

As we hurried away, Dimmi spoke quietly to me, but with great venom.

"That ugly little bastard will come to regret his insults."

No one has been able to explain to me the source of this enmity. I mean to discover it.

March 10th

An interesting day.

This morning I took myself to the studio of Maestro Michelangelo. I made myself as inconspicuous as possible, and in time succeeded in approaching Stefano, who performs much the same tasks for Maestro Michelangelo as do I for Dimmi. We agreed to walk together during the midday break.

"Stefano, I have sought you out to learn the reason behind your master's enmity for mine. It seems to me that two such talented men should not be enemies, but rather friends."

"Is it not obvious? Your master produces almost nothing of worth and brings no lasting glory to our city or the holy church. He squanders his talent on masques and carnivals— mere distractions and fripperies! And yet, he preens himself daily in the piazza, expecting to be honoured by all he meets. Meanwhile, Maestro Michelangelo, who has not yet thirty years, labours tirelessly to create true works of genius in

marble and fresco. In Rome, he sculpted the Blessed Mother cradling the body of her son and it is now venerated by pilgrims from all over Christendom, and this when he was but twenty-four years old." [1]

We continued to exchange views for some time. It became clear to me that Maestro Michelangelo did indeed resent, not so much my master, as the perceived injustice that he himself was yet to receive sufficient recognition for his undoubted skills. And it is true that even now he spends many months, even years, in the quarries, hewing out the massive blocks of marble required for his art.

However, I also suspect that Maestro Michelangelo, who is disputatious, unkempt and malodorous, and whose broken nose is at one with his temper, is jealous of Dimmi's ease and elegance and the manner in which he is admired by men and woman alike.

Nevertheless, I would very much like to see his Pietà.

---

[1] *The Pietà in St. Peter's, Rome completed in 1499 when Michelangelo was indeed only 24.*

March 14th

This afternoon we held a small ceremony to unveil and hand over the portrait of Madonna Lisa del Giocondo. This morning, when young Maestro Sanzio visited us, he expressed great admiration for the painting.[1]

It is a delightful portrait of the young lady, who we have all come to admire and feel no little sympathy for, as none of us have regard for her over-bearing husband.

Mona Lisa sits modestly, three-quarters turned to the viewer and with a subtle smile playing on her lips. She sits in a pillared loggia and, if I have a criticism of the image, it is this: The background is too plain. Perhaps my master did not wish to deflect attention from the sitter. Or perhaps Agostino, for it was he who was assigned to paint the background, was just lazy or ran out of time.

In truth, the portrait flatters the lady, but that is as it should be. Her soul is lovelier than her face, and the painting presents this truth.

---

[1] Raffaello Sanzio, known in English as Raphael.

Image 6: The Isleworth Mona Lisa.

Paolo's chronicle clearly demonstrates that this is the Mona Lisa commissioned by, and delivered to, Francesco del Giocondo. Unlike the painting in the Louvre, this portrait is on canvas. Note the clearly defined pillars and rather empty background. (Private Collection)

Image 7: Sketch by Raphael after seeing Leonardo's portrait of Mona Lisa del Giocondo.

Note the pillars
(Louvre, Paris)

Messer del Giocondo expressed his satisfaction, as he should. Our fee was barely a quarter of what it should have been, the balance having been paid in political favour to win the Signoria's commission for the Battle of Anghiari. Indeed, so low was the price, my master instructed me not to take it to our bankers, but to distribute it in part-payment of our most urgent bills. He did give Count three florins in thanks for changing his mind about the portrait.

I find Signor del Giocondo a strange man. His manner is abrupt, and he feigns to find myself and the other assistants invisible. But he seems to truly appreciate Maestro's genius, even if he did drive a hard bargain with him. And he is ever solicitous of his young wife, ensuring she is comfortable and at ease at every moment.

March 15th

This morning Dimmi bade me deliver a canvas to Maestro Sanzio as a gift, to permit the young artist to commence the new commission he told us about yesterday. He has not the credit to buy his own materials. We have a good supply—I was able to purchase ten identical canvases last month and only three have yet been used.

September 11th

Maestro started today in a difficult mood. Last evening, almost home from a fruitless visit to the monastery at Pisa, we stopped at the tavern for some food. We joined a table of friends, artists *all. The discussion turned to the limitations of painting—those things that could not be captured by the craft. All agreed that a competent craftsman should be able to capture any emotion, although there was some debate about the use of symbols to represent such virtues as piety, purity and the rest. Someone, I do not recall who, suggested the impossibility of capturing the movement of inanimate objects—an arrow, or a stone, for example.*

"With a live creature, we can work with feathers, hair, fur, even clothes, to trick the viewer into seeing motion. But a stone in the air, or on the ground, is simply a stone."

Maestro da Sesto proposed perfectly still water. Maestro Sanzio nominated air. This suggestion was loudly disparaged as too obvious. Dimmi closed the debate with a self-imposed challenge.

"Cesare's suggestion of water suffers because water is never fully still in nature, and, even when constrained by man, it's presence can yet be deduced by the distortion it causes. Young Sanzio must allow that air may be perceived by its effects—whether the wind in the trees or the ripples on a pond. However, I will attempt to confound you, by painting glass, clear glass. Transparent, unmoving, glass. I will create an image where the glass is not visible, but yet perceived."

And now he feels driven to deliver on his boast.

"Why did you allow me to drink too much wine, Paolo?"

"You are too harsh, Master! Three or four times I attempted to lead us away home, but you would not listen. It is too unfair to now blame me for your predicament."

"Mmmm. In any event, how do you suggest I escape this trap? I have not the time for a painting with no client."

"Well, there is the new commission from the Cardinal, for a figure of Our Saviour, in benediction."

"What of it? I am asking about glass, not—"

I interrupted him. "I know, but what if you added something to the composition. Something made of glass. What if Our Lord is holding a glass of wine, as in the Last Supper? Or...an empty glass, perhaps clasped under his heart, a symbol of the sacrifice of blood to come? A bottle on a nearby table?"

Maestro stared at me, or rather through me—his mind was elsewhere.

"Of course! But not a glass, a transparent orb, standing for the universe—the stars, the sun and moon, the earth and all that is on it. Everything he created. To us, infinitely large, but to the Creator, a bauble held in the palm of his hand. Excellent, Paolo. Well done!"

* * *

This afternoon I visited my friend, Ugo. Ugo lives with his family in a comfortable apartment high in a building overlooking the Piazza di Santa Maria Nuova. While Ugo assisted his mother on some family matter, I stood alone on the balcony observing the world pass far below me.

Suddenly, I spied a familiar figure entering the piazza from the side opposite. It was Chiara. I watched as she crossed the busy expanse. Every few paces she would stop and greet a friend or a merchant selling their wares from a bench. Every person she met, smiled at her greeting and continued to grin as she took her leave. Even some soldiers leaning indolently against a wall, men who would be expected to call out to a pretty girl with some ribald comment, simply admired her passage and turned to each other with a shrug as she passed, struck speechless by the sight of her. A man, a foreigner by his strange dress, was standing alone by the fountain. He spied Chiara and, after a few seconds, straightened his back and went as if to step towards her. But before the motion was truly even begun, he looked at her once again and froze—and watched as she continued, heedlessly, on her way.

For myself, my heart was beating faster. My mouth had become dry. I was nervous. I was tempted to hurry down the stairs to greet her, but instead I too simply watched and admired until she vanished from my sight. I had been much affected by observing her, far below and unaware of my presence. I can laugh at my own self—truly, I am a lost cause! I will confide something here. Every time Maestro sends me on an errand in the city, I scan the crowds as I pass, excited that I might catch a glimpse of Chiara. Twice I have indeed spotted her in such a position that I was able to retrace my steps so as to appear to have accidentally crossed her path. Thus two days were transformed from the ordinary to the magical.

My behaviour is that of a child, or at least of a boy in the first flush of desire, but I cannot deny my feelings. I can be easy with her now, when we meet in the bottega or when I escort her home, but all the time we are together, my senses are flooded by her presence. And afterwards I am fixated, obsessed, with reliving every gesture, every look—all the while seeking, no begging, for a sign that her feelings for me are changing in the smallest degree. But while she shows me affection and, I truly believe, holds me in a special regard, still she sees me as a friend—a particular friend perhaps, but certainly not as a suitor.

As these thoughts spilled through my head, Ugo distracted me by appearing at my side.

"Look there, Paolo," he commanded, pointing.

Two floors below us, on the lowest balcony of the adjacent building, a woman appeared and lowered herself gracefully onto a chair. I could not see her face as a maid fussed around her.

"She does this every day when the sun is at its strongest and if there is no breeze."

I could not work out what I was seeing. Seeing my confusion, Ugo explained.

"She is wearing a hat which is only brim—it has no crown. The maid spreads her mistress's hair over the brim, and she

sits in the sun. Her pale skin is protected while her hair is bleached."

"But the brim must be enormous!" I exclaimed, "her hair is long, and yet it is held up by the hat?"

"Yes, she has very long hair and so she requires a huge brim to support all of it."

Ugo was laughing now at my expression. Soon enough, I joined him as I considered the simpleton I must appear.

"Some women will go to any lengths to appear fashionable, like our neighbour here. She spends two or three hours every sunny day, just sitting there."

September 15th

I fear the breach with Maestro Michelangelo will never be healed. My master served on a committee to decide the location for the sculptor's monumental 'David'. The many insults received have clearly accumulated in Dimmi's memory and, to his discredit, today he used his position to advocate a most unfavourable location for the enormous figure—where this excellent and beautiful sculpture would certainly not be seen to good advantage. Worse still, he was over-ruled.

'David' will stand proudly before the Palazzo della Signoria. To many, it seemed my master has acted with spite and weakness, a most terrible combination. Dimmi can be vindictive to those he perceives to have caused him offence.

Maestro Michelangelo is truly a genius. His magnificent statue is a work for the ages. When I consider the enormous effort and perseverance required to create such a figure, as well as the genius that directed his hammer, I wonder again if Dimmi is not in danger of leaving too scarce a record of his own unsurpassed talents. Indeed, I sometimes see hints that Dimmi may be troubled by these thoughts himself.

September 21st

This morning in the market, I negotiated with one of the candle-sellers and was pleased with the outcome—the price settled upon was considerably less than I had paid last time. As the transaction was completed faster than I expected, I decided to have my hair cut by my barber, Santino.

"How go things with you, Santino? And your family?"

"Well, thank you, signore. My second daughter is fifteen now—it is time I found her a husband. I don't suppose you are interested?"

I laughed. "I am too poor to take a wife, Santino, and anyway I prefer a quiet life. You are always complaining that your wife constantly tells you what to do and what not to do."

"Yes, but my young Giovanna is an angel and will make a fine wife for some lucky man."

"I am sure she will, just not this man."

Santino continued, "Tell me, are the rumours true? Did your master create a likeness of Mona Lisa del Giocondo reclining naked across his bed?"

As you can imagine, I was horrified to hear these words.

"Where did you hear such a wicked thing?"

"It is all over the market this morning. Some claim to have seen the image, but they don't agree as to her pose, so some are definitely lying, as is usual with these things."

"Well, you can tell them no such portrait exists. Mona Lisa would never permit such a thing, and shame on any who claim to have seen it."

I have a dreadful feeling about this. Francesco del Giocondo grows in influence every month. Our dealings with the Signoria are challenging enough without more powerful enemies ranged against us. I reported the exchange to Dimmi as soon as I returned. He gathered everyone together.

"Tell everyone what transpired, Paolo."

Once more, I repeated the exchange with Santino, word for word as I remembered them. Salaì hung his head in shame.

Dimmi leaned forward and, forcefully tapping the table to punctuate his words, he spoke intently, looking directly into the eyes of each of us in turn.

"It is essential we follow Paolo's lead. If you are asked, protest that any suggestion Mona del Giocondo would pose naked is an intolerable calumny—which has the great merit of being true. Do not be trapped in sophistry. 'Signora del

Giocondo would never do such a thing' must be your sole response to any question."

Everyone nodded in agreement.

October 14th

The harvest has been poor again. There was little rain in spring and summer was unusually long and hot. The prayers of the priests and the entire city had no effect. The bottega has been terribly hot, unbearably so as I have recorded. Even now there are days when no one can summon the energy to stir, although thankfully the nights are becoming cooler. But yesterday we learned there are children dying from hunger. This brings great shame upon the city. Our workshop has been more or less busy of late with commissions for various churches and guilds, so we have some money. This morning, Dimmi announced we would feed ten children or expectant women each day until there is some relief from the baleful situation. It means we will have only a small breakfast and one meal each day but, I am proud to record, none of our household complained at this sacrifice.

It has fallen to me to organise this project, a task I am happy to accept.

October 18th

Our programme to feed some of our citizens goes well. Gonfaloniere Soderini visited us this afternoon and commended our example. He has also agreed to provide a soldier to attend at the appointed hour as we have had some little trouble with youths and men appearing and trying to push themselves to the fore. It feels good to be doing something to alleviate the plight of some of the poor souls who come to us for succour. I wish we could do more.

October 21st

We had real trouble today. A noisy gang of men arrived, demanding to be fed. Our soldier guard proved no match for them, and they drove him off. I thought we would have to allow them to take the food until Dimmi emerged, a large staff in his hand. With a fleet thrust, he smashed the closest man in the face and sent him reeling, bright blood pouring from his mouth.

"Paolo," he commanded in a loud voice, "give these scum nothing. Throw the food in the fire before you permit them so much as a crust."

Now you must recall that my master is tall and much stronger than almost anyone in the city. He has sometimes accepted wagers to bend metal rods in his hands. Now, he looked defiantly around the group of surly individuals, all the *while under the watchful gaze of the mothers and children who should rightfully be enjoying our charity.*

Suddenly he pointed his staff at one man.

"Ah! Domenico Costa. I should have expected you. You will be the leader of this verminous band, I suppose? You boys! Behold this man. You are too young to remember the great wickedness that consumed our city a few years ago. Fra Girolamo[1] caused many deaths and even more unhappiness. Signor Costa was one who, with pretended piety, supported, indeed encouraged, that devil. He ordered the deaths and mutilation of several men and women, did you not, scoundrel? And now here you are, stealing food from the mouths of children and women heavy with child. This, boys, is the kind of man he is. Quick now, find a stone and aim it at his head."

He turned to the studio and called out, "Cecco, to me!"

With this, Dimmi laid about him with his staff. He was soon joined by Cecco, myself, and a gang of emboldened boys throwing stones as fast as they were able. Dimmi made directly for the man he had been taunting and caught him a severe blow across the head before the wretch made his escape.

At the conclusion of the melee, Dimmi was panting, but smiling.

---

[1] *Savonarola—he of the Bonfire of the Vanities.*

"Well done, you two. Costa made certain accusations and caused a painting of mine to be burned in the piazza. I have waited almost seven years to revenge myself on him."

I was secretly proud of the cut on my head, especially when Cecco assured me that it was not serious.

The Other Professor

The morning after her visit to the National Gallery, Lauren awoke refreshed, feeling much better than she would have believed possible just twenty-four hours ago. She had enjoyed her trip to London and meeting Jonathan. Now she was ready for her encounter with the Earl.

After showering and dressing, she went to William Chance's office, knocking politely before entering. She was taken aback to find him in conversation with a woman in her mid-fifties or thereabouts. Instantly she was on her guard.

The Earl rose to greet her.

"Good morning, Lauren. This is a friend of mine, Professor Jane Hunter, from the University of Oxford. Please relax and don't worry, we're not about to have a repeat performance."

Professor Hunter strode across the room and offered her hand. Her grasp was dry and strong.

"Good morning, Ms Patterson. William has told me of your discovery and of the unfortunate state of affairs now existing between yourself and your university. I hope to offer a solution. Won't you sit down?"

Lauren took the proffered seat. Jane Hunter took a chair close by and turned to face her.

The academic had a pleasant, intelligent face that became charmingly animated and expressive when she talked.

"I should explain that William approached me for several reasons. First and foremost, we have been great friends for many years. Second, I am the Gates Professor of Renaissance Studies and Senior Fellow of Magdalen College. And finally, I chair the Art History Committee of the Bodleian Library."

The professor gave Lauren a moment to digest her impressive credentials.

"What I wish to propose is the following: You continue to work here on the diaries until you have completed the first of your proposed stages–a summary and initial index. During this phase, I will assign you a technician who will make high definition images of each diary page. You will use these images to complete stage two, preparing for publication a straightforward transcription of the entire diary into period Florentine Italian, together with a translation into modern day English. In parallel, the original manuscripts will go into a programme to preserve and protect them in the Bodleian where, in due course, they will be made available for display and study.

"William has decided to transfer responsibility for all decisions regarding the manuscripts to the Library. A group of experts, from Oxford and further afield, will be assembled to produce a fully annotated edition of the Chronicles. Your summary and index will guide the range of required expertise. My presumption is that you will be offered a role in this group, as by then I'm sure you will have become the foremost authority on the diary's author. There, I've said my piece. What do you think?"

Lauren needed no time at all to consider her response.

"I think that sounds absolutely excellent, Professor. Thank you. Thank you very much. You too, William. I can't tell you what a relief this is. I'm sorry I involved you in the mess with Professor Hildebrand."

"It was a difficult situation, but of no one's making. And now Jane has devised an elegant solution. Perhaps it was a slightly painful path, but we got there in the end, and that's all that matters."

Jane Hunter was eager for information.

"Can you share your impressions of the diary so far, Lauren? I'm dying to read it of course, but you've already had that pleasure."

Lauren thought for a moment, organising her thoughts. She wanted to make a good first impression on the professor.

"I have to remind myself time and again that Paolo is a teenager. He seems so mature, so perceptive. Then again, the girls around him are getting married at fourteen and fifteen, or even younger. It's clear that, as soon as they hit puberty, the pressure is on to get married and have babies. And some of his male friends are off fighting at the same age–seeking glory and honour, and riches. They all seem so much more mature than I was at their age.

"As for the diary," she continued, "we're seeing Florence through the eyes of a clever and perceptive young man who is captivated by everything around him, and best of all, is disarmingly honest when recording his impressions. I've had a look at other abstracts online and, as far as I can see, Paolo's chronicle is much more intimate, more revealing, than any other I've come across from that period. He really bares his soul. Leonardo showed great insight when he told Paolo that keeping the diary would help him work out his own ideas, explore his feelings and emotions. He was absolutely right. I've never felt closer to anyone in my life. When Paolo wrote about his first time with a girl, I was sharing his deepest thoughts and emotions. It was almost an intrusion. I wish I had read it when I was sixteen," she finished with a smile—and then she gave a little laugh.

"I've referred to Leonardo da Vinci as if he was just another character in a story. And this is maybe the most remarkable thing about the diary. While Paolo admires Leonardo enormously, he really sees him, warts and all. This isn't a fawning historian writing about a giant of history—this is a young man reporting the foibles, as well as the genius, of his boss."

Professor Hunter shook her head. "Amazing. I can't wait to read it. One more thing, Lauren. We need to regularise your status, so you can secure a grant and continue to work under your current visa. I suggest you prepare a research proposal and funding request. I dare say they will be found acceptable."

It was with a lighter heart that Lauren returned to her comfortable and comforting study, to be transported once again to daily life in Leonardo's household—and to its dramas.

1505

February 12th

What a truly dreadful day this has been!

Late in the morning a constable arrived on a morbid errand: Salaì was required to identify a body pulled from the Arno.

"It appears to be a young Venetian you have recently become friendly with, according to the keeper of the inn on the other side of the river."

At these words Salaì was completely stricken and began to cry. Dimmi embraced him before turning to me.

"Come, Paolo, we will accompany Giacomo, he should not have to face such an ordeal alone."

It took a second for me to comprehend that Giacomo was Salaì. I had never heard anyone use any name for him but his nickname.

As we made our mournful way to the river and across the bridge, Salaì haltingly explained that, if his fears were confirmed, the young man was named Marcantonio, who had arrived in Florence some two months ago. He and Salaì had met while listening to a strolling player in a piazza and had quickly become firm friends. The two had been together last evening.

"We were with a few others, but as soon as the sun disappeared below the rooftops, Marcantonio announced he had to depart. He lives with Mona Ricardo and she insists her lodgers be in the house within thirty minutes of sunset. Oh! I cannot believe he may be dead!"

Once again, Dimmi comforted Salaì as we arrived at the far bank of the river. A small crowd had formed around the shape of a man, lying where the body had been dragged. A badly stained sheet covered the body. I shuddered to contemplate the horrors that doleful cloth had hidden over the years. The crowd parted for the Officer of the Watch and we followed him to the side of the corpse.

The constable knelt down and, looking up at Salaì, he not unkindly removed the cloth from the face.

"Is this your friend?"

Salaì could only nod as tears coursed down his face.

"And his name and family?"

"Marcantonio Balbi, of Venice. He is a musician, but has found little work in Florence since he arrived. He has a room with Mona Ricardo in Santa Croce. What happened?"

"It seems he fell into the river and drowned. No one saw anything. Perhaps he was drunk?"

"No! He had only two small glasses of wine, it is all he could afford—two glasses, twice a week. And he could swim, and very well. In January he won a wager by swimming *across the frigid river faster than the three best swimmers among us."*

"Well, unless he was pushed?" speculated the officer. "But if, as you say, he had no money, why would anyone push him into the river? Maestro, have you any idea as to what may have occurred?"

Everyone looked at Dimmi. He was well known for his interest in all manner of phenomena, although only we who worked with him had any true grasp of the range of his enquiries.

"Bring him to the Ospedale Santa Maria Nuova. I will examine him there. Paolo, Giacomo, return to the studio. There is nothing to be done here now. I will join you presently."

Our bottega was a silent, mournful place when we returned. For once Salaì was a figure of sympathy, and for a few hours we set aside the torments he had caused each of us at one time or another. Dimmi arrived less than forty minutes after our return and sent one of the maids to buy bread and cheese and we ate together at the long table, usually covered in drawings. No one was in the mood for working and the afternoon passed in quiet conversation as we sought to divert Salaì's thoughts from the terrible events of the day.

When Salaì was absent from the table for a few minutes, Dimmi spoke to the rest of us.

"*Cecco, you and Jacopo stay close to Salaì this evening. Take him out with you and make sure he comes home safe. Paolo, you will accompany me to the Ospedale.*"

In the late afternoon sun, I walked alongside Dimmi, anxious about our task.

"*There is nothing to fear from a dead body, Paolo. Indeed, the dead can teach us a great deal. You have seen the many drawings I have made from dissecting corpses—it is this knowledge that may tell us something of how poor Marcantonio died.*"

When we arrived at the Ospedale, we were greeted politely and guided to a room where Marcantonio lay on a plain table. He had been undressed and washed and was now covered by a clean sheet, which Dimmi gently removed.

I have seen dead bodies being taken in the cart to the cemetery, but I have never before stood close beside a corpse, cold and naked, shockingly exposed. It is impossible to look at such a grisly sight without pondering that one day, this will be me. I shivered and crossed myself three times.

I could see that Marcantonio had been a striking young man in life. Yet now in death, what dreadful changes had been so quickly wrought! His eyes, no doubt once lively and intelligent, were now horrible—pale, dead, terrifying in their awful emptiness. The skin that yesterday glowed with health now hung like an ill-fitting costume, mottled with disgusting patches of grey and puckered white areas, already foretelling the decay to come. Is this all we are, finally? What is that spark that animates cold, clammy flesh to life and love? The Church teaches that it is our immortal soul—invisible, unweighable, unfathomable. How I pray it is so! But where does it reside? And where is Marcantonio's soul now? Was he watching over us? Is he in sorrow at his early demise, or joyful at his arrival in Paradise? I refuse to even contemplate the alternative.

"Now pay attention, Paolo. We must proceed logically. Our task is to discover how this young man died. We will start with a careful examination."

"Maestro, why do you not suppose he actually did just fall into the river and drown?"

"He may well have accidentally drowned. But, consider. He was a strong swimmer. Salaì is convinced he was not drunk. How then does he come to fall into the Arno? The bridge has walls, low certainly, but walls nonetheless. How could he fall over them? If not from the bridge, then the riverbanks perhaps? But then, why would he make his way down one of the steep banks? He had left his friends because he was most urgent to return to his lodgings."

As Dimmi was speaking, he was thoroughly examining every part of the body. I merely observed.

I will pass over the detailed examination that ensued. Enough to say, perhaps twenty minutes had passed before I heard Dimmi sigh.

"Ah! Interesting. Come here, Paolo."

Dimmi had pushed away the hair over Marcantonio's right ear.

"Look inside."

Dimmi stepped away and guided me to look carefully at the ear, while he held the candle close.

"Take this fine brush and insert it gently—no, not the bristles, the other end. Slide it into the ear very, very gently, until you feel some resistance."

I found it extremely distasteful to violate even a dead body in this manner. But quickly even I realised something was seriously wrong. The slender brush had penetrated more than the length of my finger before it encountered any resistance.

I looked up to find my master staring at me intently.

"Very strange, is it not? He was in the water at most nine hours according to the officer, and possibly much less. No fish or other river creature burrowed this hole. I believe this wound was made by a fine stiletto or other instrument of almost exactly the size as the one you hold in your hand. But come, let us proceed to the final proof."

With that, Dimmi drew a freshly sharpened knife and cut an arc from the dead man's left shoulder all the way to his breastbone and on to his navel. Before I had truly absorbed the awfulness of this action, he started anew at the other shoulder and repeated his assault.

I could barely force myself to watch as Dimmi opened the cadaver's chest, revealing the awful confusion of our mortality. To my eyes, all was terrible, chaotic. Bone, muscle, blood and organs—everything obscene to my sensibility. And the smell! Even now Dimmi was not finished cutting, but now with a saw. Finally, I had to run from the room to retch time and again. I will never again be at ease when I see a butcher cut through a bone. That grating sound will forever bring back this night of horrors. Reluctantly I returned to the charnel house.

"Master, may I leave? Please?" I begged.

"Almost finished, Paolo. There, this is what I was seeking. As I am sure you know, these are his lungs. Now, I have the advantage over you. I have seen men's lungs before. Trust me when I tell you, these are the perfectly normal lungs of a healthy young man. If poor Marcantonio had drowned, his lungs would be disfigured by the river water that he inhaled as he died—even if he was unconscious. So, Paolo, we know how Salai's friend died, do we not?"

"Yes, Maestro. He was stabbed in the ear and then thrown into the river, dead."

"And what else may we assume?"

"I do not know. You found no other injuries, so…so there was more than one villain!"

"Correct. To be so accurate with the weapon in the ear, Marcantonio's head must have been held stationary. He bears no wound that would have rendered him unconscious— no severe blow to the head, no sign of throttling. Someone firmly grasped his head while another drove in the weapon. And Marcantonio was a vital young man, so we can assume the assailant holding him was exceptionally strong."

"So, the murder was deliberate, not an unforeseen consequence of a struggle?"

"Correct. More, I think the killers were experienced. A common thief would have simply struck Marcantonio on the head, or stabbed him in the back perhaps."

"Will the Watch be able to find the murderers, do you think, Maestro?"

"With no witnesses, probably not. Unless they can discover a motive, or someone is denounced. And something else. Why take the trouble to throw the body into the river? If from the bridge, the murderers took a great risk of discovery. If they brought him down the riverbank with much effort, why do so?"

"To wash away the blood and by so doing, hide the injury. If not for you, no one would have suspected anything but an accident."

"Correct, Paolo, you have deduced well. The murderers did not want anyone to learn of the deed, and that means they were not sending a message or warning to another person."

"Perhaps, Maestro, there is a clear connection between Marcantonio and his killers? They feared they would be discovered simply by the fact of the discovery of the murder."

"You may be correct again, Paolo! But that is an even greater puzzle to me. The young man was new to Florence, and scarce had time to make any grievous enemies. He had no wealth or power. A jealous husband, perhaps? Or perhaps he was blackmailing someone powerful? We must speak with Salaì in the morning. Come now, let us act for his poor parents, who must soon receive the most terrible news. Let us dress him for a Christian burial."

In the adjoining room, neatly stacked on a chair, sat the small pile of Marcantonio's clothes. I gathered them up and brought them into the room where he lay. With some effort we pulled on his hose, then turned to the terrible sight that was his upper body.

Dimmi had considered the problem. Any twisting applied to the corpse was likely to result in some of those dreadful parts spilling out. Just the contemplation is enough even now for me to taste once again the bile in my throat.

"We will tie this sheet tight around his chest before attempting to put him into his blouse and coat."

Together we wound Marcantonio tight as a swaddled baby. By the finish, I had become inured to sights and sensations that would have rendered me faint just a few short hours before.

Dimmi had the idea to cut Marcantonio's blouse in two down the back so we could slide each rigid arm into its own half.

"With his coat on, it will not be apparent his shirt is in two halves. But we need to get his coat on in one piece if we can."

As I lifted the blue coat, I stopped and looked closely at the vestment.

114

"*Maestro, I have seen this vestment before, as have you, I think. I am certain this is Salaì's coat. See here, this collar? I well remember Salaì boasting of his fur collared blue coat.*"

Dimmi snatched the coat from my hands.

"*You are quite right, Paolo. This coat was once mine. I gave it to Giacomo perhaps two years ago. We must consider this. Let us return, quickly now.*"

"*But Marcantonio! We cannot leave him like this.*" *I pointed at the sad sight of the dead man, coatless and with his shirt crudely covering his front.*

"*We will return and clothe him properly tomorrow. First I must talk with Salaì.*"

February 13th

"We *exchanged coats a few times, and jerkins also on one occasion. We are the same size and it was pleasing to wear something different on occasion.*"

This morning, Dimmi summoned Salaì and myself into his room, where we could talk privately. We explained to Salaì about finding his coat.

Dimmi looked at Salaì with a tender expression.

"*Giacomo, your friend did not die by accident. I am certain he was murdered, and his dead body thrown in the river.*"

Salaì stared at Dimmi, then at me, clearly confused.

"Murdered? You are certain? But…but why, who?"

I spoke for the first time.

"Maestro is absolutely correct, Salaì, he showed me the proof. Marcantonio was indeed killed deliberately. As to why and by what hand, that remains a mystery—"

Dimmi interrupted me, "Paolo is not being entirely honest. He has an idea as to why. But first, tell me, was Marcantonio seeing a woman? Perhaps a married lady?"

"No!"

Salaì was most vehement in his answer and then he blushed and lowered his head. In the lowest of whispers, he continued, "You will not speak of this, will you, Master? Or you, Paolo?"

Gently, Dimmi lifted Salaì's chin and looked directly into his eyes.

"Anything you tell us will be kept secret, will it not, Paolo?"

I nodded my agreement. "I swear it."

Salaì looked at us both again.

"Marcantonio preferred the company of men. You understand?"

"We understand. For myself I can say I care nothing one way or another. Paolo?"

I admit, I was confused. I have long been perplexed about this most vexed subject. Why would any man choose to lie with a male and reject the delights and tenderness of a woman's body? But so many plainly did; yet I could feel

116

nothing but revulsion at the very idea. However, at that moment, thinking of Marcantonio dead on that sad, lonely table, I realised in this circumstance at least, no, I did not care about his preferences.

"If he was killed for hatred of his nature, I would see his murderers hang."

Salai's smile was both tender and sad.

"Thank you, both of you. I am certain Marcantonio would have gone straight to his room when he left the inn. He was most anxious not to offend Mona Ricardo. In truth, she charges her lodgers very little and is endlessly patient if they cannot pay on time. She is rich, but she enjoys having her house full of life. She is more concerned about having well-mannered, cultured guests who obey her rules than having the rent paid on time. Marcantonio played music for her and depended on her generosity. He would have run all the way home to avoid giving her offence."

Dimmi nodded as if he had anticipated this answer, or something like it.

"There is another possibility we must consider, especially now you have told us about your friend's nature. Might he have been blackmailing someone, perhaps a powerful man with whom he had taken pleasure?"

"No, no, I cannot believe it. I am confident that no one else in the city knew of his inclinations. Although he had certain feelings, he never acted upon them, never. Merely thinking about it revolted him, he confessed to me. Perhaps a kiss? He told me this and I believed him then and believe

117

him now. You know, Maestro, you both know, I have lied on many occasions. I believe I would recognise a fellow wretch. I loved Marcantonio because he was the opposite to me in all things."

At this, Salaì wept a little, but Dimmi felt we had to continue. Salaì had to be warned.

"Paolo, tell Giacomo what it is that you fear."

I did not wish to say it, yet I knew I must.

"Salaì, sorry, Giacomo, I do not know if you are aware of the many rumours about in the city concerning the painting you made of Mona Lisa del Giocondo."

Salaì exploded. "That stupid, stupid portrait! I so regret…Master, I am deeply sorry, truly I am."

Dimmi calmed him. "I know you are. But hush, let Paolo finish."

I drew another breath. "Giacomo, it is possible, no likely, that the rumour of the painting has reached the ears of Francesco del Giocondo. I fear he may have ordered revenge upon you. Revenge that was, in error, visited on Marcantonio last night."

My words struck Salaì dumb. Then, as the implication became fully realised in his mind, he let out a heart-breaking cry.

"Then I killed him! I killed Marcantonio! I killed him as surely as if I had struck the fatal blow myself."

As swiftly as sorrow and guilt had overwhelmed him, I saw Salaì change before my eyes. Suddenly, I feared him. With dead eyes and no emotion whatsoever in his voice, he pronounced, "I shall kill del Giocondo and then surrender. My death will perhaps atone for my black soul. I will do it immediately."

I had utter faith that Salaì was intent on this path and I was equally certain he would succeed. As I began to contemplate this new situation, Dimmi took charge.

"You will not. You will do no such thing. Do you suppose for one moment your death will bring peace to the soul of Marcantonio? I do not imagine so. No, we must wait and study and plan. You will leave this matter to me. You know, Giacomo, that you have caused me much anguish over the years—you will not cause me yet more over this matter. I command you to swear you will not seek revenge against Francesco del Giocondo, I insist you trust me in this."

Dimmi continued to placate Salai. As he did, I searched for a more compelling argument.

For all of the trouble Salaì causes, I do not believe him evil. Rather he is like a wilful infant, concerned only for the moment and what seems convenient or necessary or pleasurable in that instant, with no thought for the morrow. But beneath all, he loves Dimmi and knows how much our master has tolerated his behaviour.

It was time for me to speak.

"Giacomo, if you do as you propose, and whether you succeed or fail, the story of the painting will become known to all, and very publicly. And, after the initial revulsion at your act, the city will turn on Dimmi. He is the one who first conceived of the naked image of Mona Lisa."

At this moment, there was a snort from Dimmi, and I realised I had used his nickname in front of him. It was too late to take back my words. I continued.

"You know I speak the truth. They may indeed hang you, Salaì—but Maestro will never win another commission in this city. We will be exiled."

After a ridiculous amount of time devoted to argument, Salaì swore an oath he would not seek revenge on Marcantonio's murderer.

Now I expressed my own concerns.

"So, is del Giocondo to escape justice, Maestro? And why should he not try once again to kill Giacomo?"

"There is no possibility of winning a case against del Giocondo. Even if he was not so well connected, so powerful in the city and the Signoria, the fact is, we have no evidence to connect him to the murder. Of course he was not present, and I am sure the men hired to do his bidding come from Siena or Pisa or some other city, anywhere but Florence. Or even more likely they will be banditi. In any case, they will be long gone. Unless someone close comes forward to denounce him, perhaps one in his household, del Giocondo will escape justice."

Dimmi looked at both of us to be certain we grasped the truth of what he was saying.

"Now, here is what I will do. I will seek private meetings with certain people: Dottor Machiavelli, Gonfaloniere Soderini, the Captain of the Watch and several other trusted men, including those of the Medici family with whom I am on good terms. To each I will set out our facts and suspicions. I will then meet with Francesco del Giocondo and tell him what I have done. I will make him understand that if anything should happen to Giacomo or anyone else in our bottega, the finger of suspicion and accusation will instantly fall on him. For that reason, I have secured the coat Marcantonio was wearing, safe from anyone. You must give me the coat of Marcantonio's that you must have, Giacomo. Your friend will be buried in his own vestments."

I have no doubt all will transpire as Dimmi foretold, but I cannot but feel unsettled that the murder of a complete innocent will go unpunished. Still, I must confess, Dimmi's final words chilled me.

"Giacomo, I swear that one day, though it may be many years from now, Marcantonio will be avenged on del Giocondo. That devil will pay for his sin here on earth, before he pays forever in hell."

May 6th

*I*t is now somewhere between night and morning. I write by the flickering light of candles but cannot even think of sleeping.

Had I written this report before sunset, it would have told a completely different story.

Since the death of his friend Marcantonio almost three months ago, Salaì has been but a shadow. He is absent for many days and when he does appear in our studio, he may as well be invisible. He speaks politely or not at all. He insults no one, he argues with no one. Nothing goes missing, nothing is inexplicably dirty. In short, the Salaì we knew had vanished, replaced by an imposter.

But this morning, the Salaì of old returned, except more— I mean more…more extreme. He was gay, he was loud, he was argumentative. He teased Jacopo to the point of madness. He insisted on providing our midday meal, and he gave Tessa an extra florin for her trouble shopping for our food. He commanded that we drink wine and sent out for more food even though we insisted we were completely sated. In truth, by the close of the afternoon, we devoutly prayed that the impostor Salaì would return—silent and mournful perhaps, but peaceful.

As the last rays of the sun were departing, Cecco looked around the room.

"Where is he?"

Such had been the day, no one thought to ask, 'Who?' We looked around and realised that for perhaps thirty minutes, we had been at peace.

Agostino spoke for all of us, when he pondered, "Is it too much to ask that he has collapsed, exhausted, and is now asleep?"

"Pray God that it is so," laughed Cecco.

I must note that today of all days, Maestro was absent from the studio. He was visiting the Cardinal in Bologna, seeking a commission. And so it fell to Count, except for me the youngest of our group, but in many ways the wisest, to act in Dimmi's role.

"Paolo, go check that he is well. Dimmi commanded we have a care with him."

And thus it was I found Salaì lying on his side, seemingly sleeping on our bed, except for a horrible foam emerging from his lips.

"To me! To me!" I screamed with all my strength.

My first thought was of Dimmi. We needed him, but he was not here.

Salaì was poisoned.

Then suddenly, it was as if Dimmi was standing beside me, calmly reminding me of all he had taught me. My cry had energised the others and they came bursting into the room.

"Cecco, make him sick," I ordered. "Put your fingers down his throat."

I continued, "Agostino, fetch the powdered charcoal from Dimmi's store, all of it. Count, we need milk also."

At the time I simply accepted that these older, more experienced men should immediately carry out my instructions. Thinking of it now, I am amazed they did not question me.

"Again, Cecco! He must vomit everything. Is he done? Yes. It seems so. Now, Jacopo, we need figs. Go to our neighbours and collect as many as possible. Ah, Agostino! Good, give me the charcoal. Go with Jacopo, get us figs and milk, we will need more."

All this while Salaì was breathing heavily. As Cecco laid him back down after expelling all we could force out of him, Salaì looked sickly pale, but he was vaguely aware of us.

Count appeared with milk in a goblet and, having anticipated my intent, he had also a spoon. I added fine powdered charcoal to the milk and stirred the unwholesome liquid.

"Can you hold him up while I make him drink this?"

Cecco raised Salaì to a more or less sitting position as I held the cup to his lips.

"Drink, Giacomo, drink this milk. It will be good for you. Yes, yes, it tastes strange, but it is good milk. Drink."

As I forced the horrible liquid into Salaì, first Agostino and then Jacopo returned with a basket of figs and another small jug of milk.

"Turn the figs to a paste," I ordered

Again, my seniors acted upon my instructions. But then Cecco asked, "What are you doing, Paolo? What are we doing?"

"I am doing what Dimmi trained me to do. He has seen men killed by poison—Salaì has taken poison. After the events of February, Dimmi trained me to recognise the symptoms and what to do in the eventuality that poison was introduced to our home. Perhaps our master could have determined which poison was used, I know not. But this is what he instructed me to do for all poisons taken by mouth—make him vomit up what has not been processed, bind what has been processed and force it out completely. This is the task of the charcoal and milk and now the figs. I will feed to Salaì the fig paste, to complete the last."

Although I still cannot imagine sleeping, with the dawn, Tessa has arrived to clean. I promised her two day's extra wages—she has a dreadful mess to attend to. I hope Dimmi will approve. I must lie down.

May 7th

Salaì is still alive, though terribly weak. Each of us attends a Mass to pray for his recovery. Two of his friends called, but Count explained, with gentleness, that he cannot yet receive visitors.

It is perplexing how quickly news spreads in this city.

May 8th

Dimmi has returned. He was instantly told all that had occurred, and he rushed to examine Salaì, who, it was clear, was much improved and able to take a small bowl of Tessa's good broth. Dimmi bade us leave him alone with Salaì, and he stayed in the room with him for an hour before emerging, looking grave. He called us to join him around the long table.

"He took the poison himself, by choice. As you will have guessed, he could not shake the shame of causing the murder of his friend. However, he is much moved by the efforts you all expended to save him from his folly. It has given him the first hint that perhaps he is not utterly beyond salvation."

He looked around us and smiled.

"You all did very well, I am proud of you."

Cecco spoke, "In truth, Maestro, it is Paolo you should praise. We merely carried out his instructions."

At this I blushed.

"*Paolo is a good student and has the instincts of a protector. He did well when faced with a crisis, as I knew he would.*"

With a nod to me, Dimmi concluded, "There is a small monastery of Franciscans in Fiesole. I will take Giacomo to them and ask that they care for him until he regains his physical and spiritual strength. They are simple men and calm, just what he needs."

Dimmi's return has lifted the burden of responsibility from me, a burden I am extremely happy to surrender. In a particularly dramatic fashion, I have come to appreciate the responsibility my master carries every day. Our entire household depends on him for our livelihood, our purpose, even our identity. We are 'assistant to Leonardo' or 'apprentice to Leonardo' or 'maid in Leonardo's household'. One day he will not be here. Who then will we be?

Jonathan

While Lauren was in her meeting with William Chance and Jane Hunter, Jonathan was in the back office of his soon-to-open gallery. He was supposed to be reviewing final arrangements for the launch party, not daydreaming with his feet up on his desk, chair precariously balanced on its back legs, as he leaned back and mused over his meeting with the intriguing American girl. She had made a bigger impact on him than she might have guessed.

The encounter had been fortuitously timed. Six months ago, in a part of south London still waiting for artisanal bakers and pop-up restaurants offering authentic Thai street food to replace its charity shops and unbranded fried chicken outlets, Jonathan had slowly lowered his phone to stare at the blank screen. With a shake of his head he turned to the young woman sitting on the battered sofa opposite, long bare legs tucked under her, a glass of chilled white wine in her hand.

"That was my father. My grandfather has died."

"Oh, Jon, I am sorry. Really. Come and sit beside me. What else did your father say? I mean, how did your grandpa die?"

"Old age, basically. He was 96, a good innings. The funeral's on Wednesday."

Sarah reached out and pulled him down beside her, keeping hold of his hand. Jonathan enjoyed the moment of sympathy and then asked, "Will you be able to come?"

"I'm sorry, no. I'm doing an in-house lunch for Barclays on Wednesday."

"Can't you get someone else to do it? This is important, Sarah."

"I realise it's important, but so is this lunch. It's for all the UK regional managers, all the top people in the company."

Jonathan knew he should probably leave it alone, but the fact was, he was fed up apologising for Sarah's absence at his family's events. No one said anything of course, but he knew they couldn't fail to notice—she rarely came to any of them. And this one was particularly upsetting. He would have liked her to be at the funeral, by his side. She knew how important his grandfather was to him. Had been to him. He pulled his hand away.

"Sarah, it's only a lunch. Surely Josephine could handle it—or you could contract it out for once."

Later that night, Sarah would feel a twinge of guilt when she replayed their conversation in her head. Jonathan had just had some awful news; perhaps this hadn't been the moment. But that would be later. Right now, she was defensive, and angry.

"It isn't just a lunch. It's Barclays. You know I've been after them for months. This is only the second job they've given me, and I want them as a regular client. I'm not like you, Jonathan—I can't afford to lose a prospective major client."

"What the hell do you mean, you're not like me? Look at this dump. Does this look like I'm rolling in money? Why do you always go on about how rich I am? Would I be living in this shithole if I had a choice?"

Jonathan swept his arm around to encompass their surroundings. The exhibition posters tacked on the walls among five or six decent original pieces couldn't hide the dreary wallpaper–made even more depressing by the stains from the regular inundations from the flat above, whose occupants struggled to come to grips with the decrepit washing machine in their equally wretched rented accommodation.

"But you *do* have a choice. You choose to rent out your lovely South Kensington flat and live here for maybe a quarter of what you're bringing in–all so you could finance your Masters. That's a choice. You've no idea how lucky, how privileged you and your family are, none at all. And it drives me nuts! It's not your privilege that pisses me off, so much as your complete blindness to it."

"This is all crap! Every single person in my family works damned hard."

Now Sarah was seriously agitated.

"Your parents made two and half million pounds profit when they downsized three years ago. And they *still* live in a lovely detached house in Henley, for Christ's sake! Where did you think the six hundred grand came from for your South Ken flat? And the same for Robert's, no doubt? Do you have any idea how utterly impossible it would be to *save* two and half million? Do you? That's nearly a hundred thousand pounds for every friggin' year they lived in that house. Profit. Clear. Tax free. For doing absolutely bugger all, except living in it. And where did they get the money to buy the house in the first place? A ginormous mortgage? Not likely! I'll bet no one in your family has had a mortgage for umpteen generations. No, I'll bet your grandfather gave them that house as a wedding gift. Or your mother's family did. That's the difference, Jon–property. Property handed down from one generation to the next, all the while making huge profits or bringing in rent."

Now it was Jonathan's turn to be angry, a rare occurrence.

"Where do you get off, talking about my family like this? And anyway, how do you know how much they made?"

"Duh! It's called the Internet–it's right there, for all the peasants to read."

Suddenly Sarah's tone changed completely. This wasn't what she wanted to say, what she truly felt.

"Jon, your family is lovely. And I don't hate what they did, what they do. Let's be honest, I'd like a piece of it myself. But that's not how it works. Your family, and families like yours, you understand how to hold on to it. That continuity, that certainty, gives you a natural confidence. You're so secure, you didn't need to go to Eton–Charterhouse was fine. And who needs to stress about getting into Oxford or Cambridge? Edinburgh, Durham, St Andrews–all perfectly acceptable choices for people who don't need to prove anything to anyone."

Sarah had unwrapped her legs and was now perched on the edge of the cracked leather sofa, a hand-me-down from Jonathan's parents.

"I bet the day you were born, your grandparents set up a trust fund for your school fees. So yes, I'm sure your father works hard enough at his law firm. But with no mortgage to pay, no school fees to worry about, how tough can it be? How much are you carrying in student loans? Personally, I'm still over thirty grand in the hole."

Jonathan's voice was harsh and cold.

"I have no student debt at all, Sarah, because, as you've obviously forgotten, the Army paid my fees, so I could have people try to shoot my arse while you were finding yourself on a beach in fucking Thailand!"

To her credit, Sarah was sheepish. "OK, OK, I was wrong about that. And you're a good person. I appreciate how kind and thoughtful you are. All I'm saying is, it would be good if you showed some awareness of just how incredibly fortunate you are. Then maybe you'd understand why I can't pass up the chance to win a possible mega client to come to your grandpa's funeral. I'm sorry, but I just can't."

* * *

On Wednesday night, after the funeral, Jonathan had gone to the pub in his grandfather's village with his older brother, Robert. It had been a bone of contention between the two brothers when, aged thirteen, Jonathan had put on a growth spurt and shot past his older brother, ending up an inch over six feet, a full two inches taller than Robert–and considerably broader. Where Robert was slim and effortlessly elegant, Jonathan was more at home on the rugby pitch than in a cocktail bar. A born leader, he inspired trust and confidence, and his easy charm and laid-back attitude meant he was regularly underestimated, as opposing rugby teams invariably discovered too late.

He gave his brother a potted version of the argument with Sarah.

"But why did she feel the need to look up the stuff about the house sale and your flat? Why does she care?" Robert asked.

"I'm not sure exactly. I suspect it was just a thing at the back of her mind that wouldn't go away. I'm pretty sure it started when I rented out the flat. That's when I mentioned I didn't have a mortgage."

"How did the course work out in the end, by the way?"

"It was great, I loved it. The Courtauld's a brilliant place."

Jonathan wasn't done with the Sarah argument.

"It's a bit galling, but I wonder if there isn't some truth in what she said. Did you feel rich when we were growing up?"

"No. Maybe I should have, but I didn't. Most of the people we were friendly with were pretty much the same, and some of them seemed bloody poor. Remember Crazy Charlie, two houses down the road?"

"God, yes! With his patched Barbour and his absolutely clapped out Land Rover. That thing must have done a million miles. Poor Edward, we really did give him some stick about his old man."

Now Robert looked thoughtful.

"Yes, but the weird thing is, Edward went to our school, which, looking back, is a bit of a mystery–where did the money for his fees come from?" he paused, then shook his head. "But that's the point. Among ourselves, we seemed normal, not rich–not like the people whose fathers drove Bentleys and bought 100-foot Sunseeker gin palaces."

"But the fact is, our parents did give both of us very nice flats. I had never thought about it before Sarah threw it in my face. I mean the idea that we're rich."

"What's going to happen with you and Sarah now?"

"I'm not sure. We were both pretty angry. She stayed at her own place after we fought. We'll see."

After the pub, the brothers returned to the house. After Robert went to bed, Jonathan crept silently around his grandparents' home. With the comforting tic-toc of half-a-dozen clocks keeping him company, he wandered from room to room, looking one final time at the collection of drawings and watercolours that his grandfather had assembled over his long life, all the while aware he would never see them all together again. Soon they would be distributed among members of the extended family. He now knew at least some of the drawings he had been familiar with since childhood were seriously valuable.

It took Jonathan a while to notice that the sketch of the girl with the basket was no longer in the collection. Somewhere among the artwork on the walls of this old house, there was a piece his grandfather had paid £50,000 for.

With a pang, Jonathan understood just how much he would miss the wise old man.

When Jonathan returned home from the funeral on Thursday afternoon, he spotted the note on the table as soon as he let himself into the flat. Actually, it would be a gross exaggeration to call it a note–the one-word message, 'Sorry', didn't qualify. In case there had been any misunderstanding, Sarah's key to his flat was lying alongside the sad piece of paper, making it perfectly clear what *'Sorry'* meant.

Something had been growing between them for months—he wasn't sure what it was. Money and class and resentment were all involved he was sure, but that wasn't the whole story. He realised he wasn't broken-hearted or even surprised. But he would miss her. He would miss her energy and drive; her enthusiasm for long walks, Arsenal and Chinese food; and her silent, comforting presence on the sofa as she re-read Jane Austen while he wrestled with a paper on the pre-Raphaelites. And his bed would be a lot colder at weekends, that much was certain.

Two weeks after the funeral, Jonathan was back at the Cotswold house, this time to hear his grandfather's will being read out.

"To my grandson Robert, I bequeath £250,000 plus my interest in Stow Stables in Newmarket. To my grandson Jonathan, I bequeath £250,000 and all of the works of art in my possession."

Jonathan's first emotion was delight at this entirely unexpected turn of events, immediately followed by a rueful sense that perhaps Sarah had been absolutely right. He was a lucky bugger!

1507

August 20th

I wrote nothing throughout our tedious journey from Milan back to Florence. As I have written, we had only lately arrived in Milan, yet here we were departing already. The weather throughout our travels was unchanging—a sullen heat that bore down on us all, man and animal alike. My master does not want to be back here and is annoyed we have been forced to leave Milan, a city most convenient to him, and to us. Only Count, Agostino and I have travelled with Dimmi, as we intend our stay in Florence to be short. We are here because of the greed of Dimmi's stepbrothers.

I wrote some years ago of the death of Ser Piero da Vinci, who left his first-born son not a single denaro upon his death. Instead, everything was shared among the legitimate sons. For all of these years, Ser Piero ignored the opportunity to legitimise Dimmi. Ignored or refused, I know not which. Even now, no one has dared to ask Maestro if they discussed the matter. In contrast, last year the kind and gentle Francesco da Vinci, my master's beloved uncle, died childless, leaving his entire estate to Dimmi. But now the stepbrothers have sued, and we have had to come all the way back to Florence to defend his inheritance. The brothers claim they should once again receive everything, as a result of an old agreement they say was made between their uncle and their father.

There is a melancholy spirit in our little group. Our delightful quarters in Milan are already no more than a fond memory as we are squeezed now into a cramped space, which is unbearably hot. We have brought a letter from the King of France, Lord of Milan, requesting that the case may be quickly resolved and my master freed to return to his royal service. We are hopeful this will be effective.

For myself, I am happy to be back in Florence, however briefly. The city has become my home, as it is to the one who still possesses my heart.

I have not seen her for eighteen months.

August 23rd

A day both happy and sad. Full of joy for everyone, but also of misery for me.

Chiara came to see us this morning. As before, I am overwhelmed simply by the sight of her. I have never succeeded in turning my emotions into those platonic sentiments so beloved by courtly poets. I play the part, but in my heart, my feelings and desires remain those of a thwarted lover, not a brother.

And I am no longer a boy. So, when Chiara skipped into our quarters, her greeting to me was friendly, affectionate *even, but with no warm embrace. Instead, she turned to Dimmi.*

"Padrino, I am so happy Providence has sent you here at this very moment. I am betrothed! My letter to bring you this news is even now on its way to Milan, but here you are!"

Dimmi swept his goddaughter into his arms and hugged her.

"Congratulations, tesoro. And when is the wedding?"

"We will be wed next month, the twenty-sixth. And I have a request, godfather. I have no dowry, but Alessio, my husband-to-be, has agreed to marry me nonetheless, and even though I am old. But it would give me the greatest pleasure if I could bring to our home, drawings made of us by the illustrious Maestro Leonardo da Vinci. This is my request for my wedding gift. This would be more than a blessing."

Dimmi smiled and clasped Chiara's hands in his.

"Cara, I have known you since you were but one day old and have loved you all of your life. You shall have paintings, proper oil paintings. It will be a marvellous delight to paint from my heart for once and not for the demands of an idiot client. You must bring your fiancé to see me. Not tomorrow, for then I must be in court, but the following day. I wish to see you both together."

This exchange seared a wound deep in my heart and the joy of seeing my beloved immediately turned to ashes. But I am proud to say I played my part.

"*Chiara, let me be next to offer my good wishes for your wedding. Sadly, your godfather requires me to be in Vinci at the time of your nuptials. We need a survey of the contested properties we have come to secure. But I look forward to meeting your betrothed in the coming days.*"

Chiara looked at me kindly. We both knew the tale of Vinci was a lie, but she conspired with me and did me the honour of accepting my congratulations.

And now I sit here in this tiny island of ever-shifting candlelight, surrounded by sullen silence and gloomy darkness, writing this report to I not know whom, and my heart is breaking still. The occasional echoing bark of a dog, the far away howl of a lonely wolf, serve only to magnify the silence and my sorrow. I had fondly hoped that the passage of years would, in the eyes of Chiara and the world, narrow the gap in age between the object of my love and myself. The distance between thirty-four and twenty-six would seem so much less than the gulf betwixt twenty-four and sixteen. Or so I have dared to believe.

But today, Chiara is twenty-eight, and I understand she feels the need to marry. Already she is far older than any virgin bride any of us know. I cannot fault her. While I have an honourable name, my family has no fortune. And Chiara deserves the comfort and security only substantial wealth can bring. She has sacrificed so much to the care of her mother and sister, it is beyond time when she must think to her own future.

But I will always love her and be devoted to her. In my most secret heart, I truly believe there will never be another for me. I have lived my days and nights comforted by the thought that one day we would be joined. How now should I compose my dreams?

I have just heard the first cock's crow. I should try to find some sleep.

August 28th

Today, I met Alessio Pacini.

He and Chiara arrived soon after we had finished our midday meal. We were still at table, listening as our master played his lira da braccio for us.[1] As Dimmi played most sweetly, he sang in his rich tenor voice. He was inventing a rhyme of Chiara and her love. Like many others over the years, the court in Milan had been amazed to witness Dimmi's talent as a musician, a skill they had never expected of the famous artist and engineer. He was quickly recognised as the foremost musician in the city.

When the couple appeared, Dimmi finished his song and Alessio immediately, and I think sincerely, applauded.

"Maestro Leonardo, your goddaughter has talked at

---

[1] A lyre, shaped and played somewhat like a violin.

length of your many talents, but never once did she mention your skills bestowed from Terpsichore!" [1]

Alessio makes a handsome figure, tall and well proportioned. He looks to be around forty, perhaps a little more, and I learned yesterday he is twice widowed, but with no children. He greeted each of us in turn as Chiara introduced us with a few gracious words. Even Salaì was on his best behaviour. I was, as you will imagine, conflicted in my emotions, but I focused on my regard for Chiara and behaved as I knew she would wish. I was warm in my congratulations.

Maestro had already decided he would paint the couple on canvas, a medium with which he is still experimenting. We still have several of the batch I bought some time ago, as they proved to be not popular with our clients. Although Maestro greatly likes the results of oils on canvas, most clients insist on traditional wooden panels for their paintings. But before Maestro would paint, he needed a preparatory sketch to fix his design.

Dimmi began to pose the couple in various ways. He had them standing, then sitting, then walking as if strolling through the piazza. Finally, he settled on an idea pleasing to him.

---

[1] A Greek muse of music and art. Her symbol is a lyre.

"Chiara, cara, sit on this stool, the high one. Alessio, if you would stand here beside her, your body turned almost to me, but your gaze fixed on your beloved. You are about to offer her your hand. But there must be a little space between you. This will be two paintings, not one."

"Chiara, I wish to try two approaches. First, turn your body towards me, but face a little to your right, with your head lowered. Now, begin to reach for Alessio's hand—just the first hint of the motion. He has only now declared his love and his wish to marry you. Your head was lowered modestly as he spoke. Perfect. Hold that for a few moments."

There was complete silence as Maestro drew swiftly, catching the moment, as we each examined our thoughts. Later he will spend many hours developing his idea. I will not commit my thoughts while she sat there, as I am ashamed of them. Jealously coursed through me in unceasing scorching waves.

Next, the maestro, for this is what he truly becomes at these times, crossed to the betrothed couple and with gestures and gentle touches, made more small adjustments here and there to their poses and their costumes until he was satisfied.

"Good. Now slowly raise your gaze to Alessio—stop! Look out to me, to the future, imagining your life together. Gaze directly at me, thinking about tomorrow and its joys, of the years you have toiled for your family. The many hurts received, now to be healed. Now you are truly the real Chiara!"

Image 8: La Scapigliata (The Dishevelled)
Always known to be by Leonardo da Vinci.
Before publication of Paolo's chronicle, the sitter was unknown.
However, the drawing's provenance is currently being re-
examined to confirm it is indeed the first, unused, preparatory
study of Chiara made by Leonardo and treasured by Paolo
throughout his life.
(Galleria Nazionale, Parma)

She raised her eyes and looked directly into the room. She
was at once desirable yet fierce, vulnerable yet adamant. I
thought of the day when she threatened Salaì with the deadly
stiletto, of the years of sacrifice as she tended to her mother

and sister. How could one person be so ravishing and at the same time, so formidable? My torment dissolved and I was completely enraptured. We were all enraptured.

Once again, we heard the whisper of Dimmi's charcoal as it flew over the creamy paper a second time.

Soon, Maestro shifted his attention to Alessio and repeated the sequence with fewer commands. Alessio was not an experienced model, and Dimmi knew it would not do to confuse him with too many instructions.

Finally, Maestro turned to Chiara once again.

"One more pose, cara, if you would, a simple one. Turn and look directly to the side, with no emotion. Just relax and stare into the far distance."

September 8th

We had some fun today, mostly at my expense. Over the years, some of the apprentices, especially Count, have encouraged me to copy this or that drawing–a face, a body, a chubby cherub. Occasionally the results are not completely terrible and one, a view of the city from the surrounding hills, was actually quite good, according to Count at any rate.

When Chiara and Alessio posed for Dimmi ten days ago, at the end he had Chiara take a pose looking directly to the side. I confess at the time I had been confused. Surely, he would not portray her in profile, a style he has single-handedly made old-fashioned–flat and uninteresting.

This afternoon, Chiara sat again for Dimmi, for her wedding portrait. But before Maestro started to draw, he erected another two easels beside his, and bid me come over.

"Today, Paolo, you will sketch Chiara. You take such pleasure in looking at her, it is time to turn your devotion to some purpose."

I blushed, and everyone, save only Chiara, laughed at my discomfort, and even she allowed a small smile to light up her face.

Dimmi continued, "I have made it easier for you. See here, I have made a profile of Chiara. You will copy this while I draw her as I posed her before. Profiles are relatively easy, so this will be a good exercise. When you are finished, I will re-use my canvas for Alessio's portrait."

Maestro placed his sketch of Chiara's profile on one easel and directed me to use the fresh canvas Count had prepared on the other stand.

I cheerfully worked alongside the maestro, aware there was a strange atmosphere in the studio, light-hearted and gay.

Agostino played and sang most sweetly for us as the day progressed, and everyone conversed in a light and happy manner, with many smiles and much laughter. After an hour or so, Dimmi decided to pause the work and Count was instructed to fetch some wine. We each had a glass in honour of the betrothal.

Even the cats and dogs were infected with joy, or so they appeared, for once playing without barking or fighting.

Have I written about the cats and dogs? Our master loves animals, all animals. When we have money, his favourite treat is to go to the bird market. He buys the singing birds, and, before the amazed stallholder, he opens the cages and frees them! As you can imagine, every stray dog in time finds its way to the bottega, there to be fed and allowed shelter from the winds and rain. At least the cats, of which there are always four or five, do useful work. There is never a mouse or rat in our studio or bedchambers.

The feeding of the dogs causes some agony to Dimmi. He is now a vegetarian.

Just a few weeks ago, he challenged Maestro Botticelli, "How can I love animals and then eat them? My body will not become a tomb for other creatures."

But he has learned that the dogs must have meat. It tortures him to decide. At present, the dogs are winning.

For myself, I like animals well enough, but I like them best grilled with olive oil and a little rosemary.

As I strained to copy his work, deliberately kept simple to make my task easier, I occasionally glanced at the genius working an arm's length from me on a much more complicated project. How does he do it? We both raise our hand to the canvas and we both make a stroke—and that is the end of the similarities. I leave a mark, yes, but it is not always possible to say I have improved on the blank space.

Meanwhile my master's canvas steadily evolves closer to perfection with each sure touch he applies. If asked, we would both say we were drawing, but in truth, there should be quite different words to describe our activities.

Every now and then, Dimmi reached across and made a line or two on my canvas, explaining why this or that correction would enhance my efforts. At one moment, he took his cloth and erased my clumsy effort to portray Chiara's graceful neck.

"Watch, Paolo. This takes practice, and confidence," he added as, with a single stroke, he captured her neck from chin to chest in a silken line perfectly encompassing the elegance and sensuality of that subtle form. Perhaps I should have been embarrassed at the inadequacy of my efforts, but all I could do was admire the sublime artistry demonstrated before my gaze. How could a single line achieve such perfection? I knew that, even having witnessed it, I will never have that fluidity, that sureness of touch. But then, I am in good company, for surely not many alive could match Dimmi's skill.

Finally, he stepped alongside me, then went over to a shelf and removed a piece of thin board, about a hand's width and a little more than one braccio long. It had been painted white and then lines drawn across it. He held the board against my drawing.

"Observe, Paolo. From the top of Chiara's head to the middle of her nose is the exact distance from her nose to the underside of her chin. From chin to her eyebrows is two thirds

of the total, from chin to below her nose is one third, as is nose to forehead. I derived these proportions from a study of Greek statues, and they conform exactly to those of my goddaughter whose proportions are ideal."

Having given mathematical confirmation to my long-held opinion that Chiara epitomised feminine perfection, Dimmi stepped back a pace to better examine my effort.

"Not bad, Paolo, not bad at all for your first attempt. Now watch once more."

He took the stick from my hand and within a few moments, as it seemed to me, he added a small posy of flowers held in Chiara's hands. There were no flowers in the room. He created each leaf and blossom from memory and his many studies of plants. They were perfect. You could almost smell them. He rendered her hands such that we knew she was cradling the flowers with just sufficient force to hold them steady. Then he took a single glance at Chiara and, in the blank space where I had been afraid to venture, he swiftly captured the charming confusion of her lustrous hair, today bound loosely atop her head. Now an unremarkable drawing had become something else—a flawed but charming depiction of a beautiful young woman.

Now Chiara teased me.

"Will your portrait be sold to a rich Milanese, Paolo? Will my likeness be admired by the French and the Lombards?"

I tried to come up with a witty response but failed. I stuck out my tongue at her.

September 26th – Lucca

My master is a considerate man. Today, I am in Lucca, where I have been sent to buy some pigments.

In Florence, at this precise hour, Chiara and Alessio are being wed. Maestro has promised to deliver my gift to the couple. It is a cup, carved from a wonderfully clear rock crystal, and with two silver handles.

I will cover most of the cost by assisting Maestro Barducci, a most excellent jeweller. He has been unable to collect a debt in Milan, and I believe I can resolve the matter.

She is married. I am undone.

Family Matters

Lauren kept her promise and took the train up to London for Jonathan's gala opening. The relief she had felt after her meeting with Professor Hunter had given way to excitement. The Paolo Chronicles were no longer a thrilling discovery, they were now the centrepiece of an entirely new chapter of her life. And what an opportunity! She had just translated a spectacular and privileged insight into the creativity and genius of one of the most remarkable figures in human history. And there was much more to come, she was confident.

Although she would never have given voice to her thoughts, Lauren knew that, as long as she didn't screw up, she was on the threshold of a major academic breakthrough. And she wasn't about to screw up. She had never before felt such an intense feeling of excitement, anticipation and sheer happiness.

The gallery was easy to find. Lauren was impressed that it was in a part of the city given over to expensive-looking galleries and the kind of antique shops and jewellers with no visible price labels and where prospective shoppers were carefully inspected via CCTV before being buzzed into the shop.

As she approached Access Art, she was surprised to see it was absolutely packed, with people overflowing onto the sidewalk, or pavement as she was learning to call it. In outfits ranging from understated elegance to idiosyncratically eccentric, guests stood in little clusters, chatting and drinking from tall wine flutes. She eased her way through the crowd and ventured inside where she accepted a glass of sparkling wine from a passing waiter. She squeezed her way over to look at the drawings, etchings and watercolours.

Now she was *really* impressed. There was hardly an item she wouldn't have loved to hang on her wall. Beside each artwork there was a small card indicating the artist or period and the title or subject matter of the work, together with a reference number. A smartly-dressed young woman handed her a laminated sheet of paper with the reference number of each item and its sales price.

She wouldn't be buying anything anytime soon.

After about five minutes, she heard Jonathan's voice right behind her.

"So, you made it? I'm glad."

"I did, and many congratulations. The art is absolutely amazing."

"Thanks. Come and meet some people."

In a whirlwind, Jonathan introduced Lauren to several of his friends. Names came too fast for her to retain. Fortunately, someone spotted her predicament. A slim brunette detached herself from the group.

"Jon, you're killing this girl. Go and schmooze some rich prospect and I'll take care of Lauren. Hi Lauren, I'm Geraldine, Gerry. I'm Jon's sister-in-law. And this is Robert, his brother. No more names for at least five minutes, promise."

Lauren laughed. "Thanks, my brain is about to explode. Hi, Robert, pleased to meet you."

"You must be the American girl, from the National Gallery."

"That's me. He was kind to me. I was under a bit of stress that day."

Geraldine took her arm, "You look pretty stress free now. Let's go look at some of the pictures."

For much of the evening, Lauren was an interested observer, watching the interactions between the various visitors as they came and went. One woman in particular caught her attention. She was in her late fifties, Lauren supposed–tall, slim, expensively dressed and in constant motion; greeting new arrivals, making introductions and ferrying individuals from one group to the next.

Lauren was admiring a watercolour of an English landscape when she became aware that someone was standing beside her. She turned to see it was the attentive hostess she had been observing.

"Hello, I don't believe we've met. I'm Jennifer, are you enjoying the art?"

"Very much so. I'm Lauren. This is a beautiful landscape, don't you think?"

"It's lovely. It looks like somewhere east–Norfolk perhaps, or Suffolk. No matter, it's gorgeous. Have you met the gallery owner, Jonathan? I can introduce you, if you'd like."

Lauren smiled. "That's OK, it was Jonathan who invited me."

As Lauren was saying this, her eyes drifted over to where Jonathan was standing among a small group of people. As she watched, his eyes scanned the room until he caught the attention of a man with a strong family resemblance. She saw Jonathan give a tiny inclination of his head, directing the man's gaze to the far corner of the room. Lauren too looked to where a red-faced character was gesticulating wildly. Even over the hubbub of several conversations, she could hear his strident voice.

"It's obvious that modern artists are all a bunch of bloody con men, selling utter crap to absolute idiots."

"Oh dear," Jennifer whispered into her ear. "Simon swears he never gets drunk but is regularly over-served."

Lauren chuckled. "He certainly seems to be enjoying his wine."

"It's OK, look. Roger is taking charge."

They watched as Roger smoothly engaged the drunk in conversation, draped a friendly arm around his shoulders and gently, but firmly, steered him out onto the pavement.

"Is that Jonathan's father?"

"Yes, they do look alike, don't they? And I'm his stepmother. Come on, let me introduce you to someone much more interesting than Simon."

At ten o'clock the last guests were finally ushered out the door as the catering crew were boxing up the last of the glasses and piling empty bottles into recycling bags.

Jennifer and Roger came over to the handful of people left: Jonathan, his brother and sister-in-law, his best friend, Mike, with his girlfriend Sue, and Lauren. As Roger shrugged into his coat, he smiled at his son.

"That went well, I thought."

"It did, didn't it. Thank God, it's over though, I'm exhausted." Jonathan replied.

"Well, we're off. Good night, all."

He stretched out his hand, "It was lovely meeting you, Lauren. I'm sorry we had so little time to chat. Next time, I hope."

Meanwhile, Jennifer was accepting good night kisses from Jonathan, Robert and Geraldine.

"Good night, Mike, Sue. Good night, Lauren, it was a pleasure to meet you."

They prepared to leave as the caterers ferried the final loads into their van. Jonathan looked around. All things considered; the place didn't look too bad. A quick run around with a vacuum in the morning and everything would be ready for his first real day in his new venture.

"Let's go for a curry, my treat," he announced.

Lauren was thoroughly disappointed at having to decline.

"Sorry, Jonathan, I can't. By the time we eat, I'll have missed my last train."

Geraldine stepped in. "Nonsense, you must come. You can stay with Robert and me. We've got a spare toothbrush and other essentials. You can catch the early train in the morning."

They had a fun evening, sharing endless platters of spicy Indian food washed down with cold beer. Jonathan was on a high from his successful opening. Eight items had sold and various people had promised to come back for a second look at one item or another.

Once again, at various moments Lauren found herself observing; watching the interplay between the others at the table. She could see the easy trust and familiarity between Jonathan and his friend Mike, and especially between the two brothers. She hadn't missed the fact that Jonathan must have told Robert about their meeting at the National Gallery. She was flattered and intrigued.

At the end of the evening, as they shook hands before Lauren went off with Geraldine and Robert, Jonathan was finally able to take her aside and ask how things had gone with the Earl.

"I'll explain properly next time I see you, but it's all good, really good. Fantastic, actually."

"Excellent! I'm happy for you."

"I watched your stepmother earlier. She was working hard for you, constantly mingling and making sure everyone was taken care of."

"Yes, they were great, they both really helped out."

Lauren realised that while Jonathan appreciated the help and support of his family, the reality was he took it for granted. She was sure that if pressed, his response would have been along the lines of: 'That's what families do, isn't it?'

* * *

Lauren's experience of family life hadn't left her with such a sanguine perspective.

She had grown up in a one-bedroom trailer park home with her mother, Julia, a waitress in the local diner. Shortly after her seventh birthday, she asked her mother why she didn't have a father.

"When I was seven months pregnant with you, I was friggin' huge and I told him we wasn't having no more sex until you was borned, and prob'ly for a while after that. He left next mornin'. Good riddance."

About a year after this memorable conversation, a drunk driver fell asleep at the wheel and his car drifted across the road to smash head-on into Julia's Toyota Corolla, totally wrecking the car and killing its driver instantly. When the Highway Patrol officer broke the news to Lauren, she had the presence of mind to give him the address of her mother's older sister, Helen, who lived in California. Lauren had had never met Helen, but for as long as she could remember, she had received birthday and Christmas cards every year, always with some money folded inside.

Helen arrived the following evening and stayed until the funeral, attended by barely twenty people: neighbours, co-workers and a few regulars from the diner, all of whom Lauren knew. Lauren was beginning to comprehend that she was seen as an oddball in the little town. Before she was old enough to have a key to the trailer, she would come to Julia's diner every day after school to sit in a corner booth and read. She didn't play much with the other kids her age, she just liked to read her books. The diners thought her polite, cute and way too smart and bookish for a young girl. It was a constant subject of gossip, how Julia had raised a daughter so unlike herself, except maybe in good looks.

Early the following morning, a taxi arrived to take Helen and Lauren to the airport. Lauren had a single bag, full of as many clothes as she could squeeze in, and a backpack containing her favourite books, Paddington

Bear and a small, pink, heart-shaped case crammed with tiny Polly Pocket figures.

Months later, a cheque arrived for $285. The covering letter explained that this was the proceeds from the auction of Julia's possessions.

Lauren had always been vaguely aware that she had relatives in Italy, even before she knew where Italy was, exactly. Once or twice a year, her mother would open an envelope covered with exotic stamps to find some money inside. The spring after Julia's death, a letter from Italy arrived for Helen. Instead of money, there were round-trip tickets to Italy for Helen and Lauren.

This would be the first of many magical trips to the small hill village in Umbria where Helen and Julia's grandfather, Fabio lived with his second wife, Lucia. Right from day she arrived on her first visit, it was clear that everyone in the village knew who Lauren was and had been expecting her. She explored every lane and garden, fed chickens and harvested vegetables alongside mothers and grandmothers, eating warm tomatoes freshly picked by her own hand. She got to take care of gorgeous brown-eyed babies while their mothers dusted and swept floors and showed her how to make pasta sauces. No one spoke a word of English as they chatted away to her nonstop. Within days she was replying haltingly with a few words. By the end of that first month, she had stopped apologising and could manage enough broken Italian to get through her carefree days.

When she arrived the following year, she picked up right where she had left off, and was able to demand updates on the progress of her babies.

After several more trips, it was decided that Lauren was old enough to travel by herself and every summer through her high school years, Lauren spent at least four carefree weeks with her Italian family.

* * *

The Paolo project was motoring now. Penny Hughes turned out to be a skilled archival photographer and a fun person. She and Lauren hit it off immediately. They quickly worked out a routine. As soon as Lauren was finished with a page, Penny made a copy and added it to Lauren's file. Now Penny could take each original to the Bodleian to be properly imaged and stored, while Lauren had a working copy to refer back to.

Indexing and summarising was going faster and faster as Lauren became more familiar with the sixteenth century handwriting and vocabulary.

A couple of Sundays after his launch party, Jonathan came to take Lauren to lunch in a country pub, and she was able to bring him up to date. As a special treat, she brought her laptop, and allowed him to read some of the highlights she had extracted for her summary.

He was impressed.

"Wow, this is fantastic stuff. The experts will be beside themselves. But it's also a great story, albeit a bit sad. You can just picture poor Paolo feeling sorry for himself in the middle of the night. Will he and Chiara get together, do you think?"

"Oh, I hope so!"

* * *

A few days later, Lauren's phone rang.

"Hi Lauren, it's Gerry. Jonathan's tied up all morning, but he asked me to give you a call. We're taking a picnic to Henley next weekend, would you like to join us?"

"What's at Henley?"

"Ah, you don't know. Well, Henley is a rowing regatta on the Thames, but really, it's just an excuse to dress up, drink Pimm's, eat strawberries and sit in the sun."

"I've absolutely no idea what a pim is, but it sounds like my kind of day. What kind of dressing up?"

"It's easy. Any smart summer dress will do. Think Great Gatsby on the Thames."

"That sounds very English. I'd love to come, thank you."

"Great. I'll send you a text with Jon and Robert's parents' address. We can meet there and leave our cars. It's only a short walk to the river and parking in town is impossible. Around 10:30 Saturday. Is that OK?"

Lauren had barely settled back to work after Gerry's call when one of the house staff came running in.

"There's a call for you, Lauren."

"For me? On the house phone? That's weird."

She followed him down the corridor to a sitting room where there was an extension. Lauren knew she had never given the Blythswood internal number to anyone. She knew this because she didn't know it herself.

She picked up the phone.

"Hello?"

With only a little imagination, the voice on the phone could have belonged to Jeremy Irons.

"Is this Lauren Patterson?"

"Yes, I'm Lauren, who is this?"

"Brian Andrews, *The Burlington Magazine*. We haven't met, Ms Patterson, although I believe I saw you at Jonathan's gallery opening. I'd like to ask you some questions about the diary you're working on, the diary of an assistant to Leonardo da Vinci. As you may know, ours is the most prestigious fine arts magazine in the world. If you would give us an interview, we would produce a wonderful article to help introduce the diary."

Lauren was taken completely by surprise and was absolutely not prepared for this development, but she handled the situation with considerable aplomb–and a lie, although only a white one, she told herself.

"I'm sorry, Mr Andrews, this is a terrible time for me to talk. I only took this call in case it was a family emergency. My aunt is seriously ill at the moment. If you give me your number, I'll call you back in an hour or so."

Lauren ended the call and sat down heavily.

"Shit, shit, shit!" she muttered out loud. "Goddammit, Jonathan, how could you!"

They weren't ready–*she* wasn't ready.

She ran through the house and found the Earl in his study.

"We have a problem. I've had a call from a writer on *The Burlington Magazine*, asking about the diaries. It's all my fault."

The Earl was commendably calm. "Don't worry, it had to happen sooner or later. Let's call Jane, let's see what she thinks we should do."

The professor took charge with her usual efficiency.

"How many pages do you still have at Blythswood, Lauren?"

"Lots—over a hundred I'd guess."

"Very well. Penny can collect them this afternoon and bring them to the Library. You'll have to finish your work there—we need to get the papers properly secured before word gets out. Tell you what, why don't you call the journalist back and invite him to come to the Library and meet with both of us? I don't suppose you'll want to join us, William?"

"Now you're trying to be amusing, Jane. Not likely, thank you."

"I thought so. But we can't give anyone an exclusive, it will cause too many problems down the road. *The Burlington Magazine* is a monthly, so we can offer him a week or so of controlled access before we send out a press release, putting the record straight and setting out our plans. That will also draw attention to the fact that the papers are at the Library and not with you, William. The week will allow Mr Andrews a head start on getting a longer piece prepared."

"Excellent," William Chance responded, "I do *not* want reporters camped on my door."

Jane Hunter spoke again. "Can both of you be available for a press conference on, say, the eighteenth? I'm sure we can hold them off until then."

Before Lauren could respond, William made his views known.

"No television. I have no desire to appear on TV."

"We can't exclude them, William. How about just the BBC? We'll give them onscreen interviews, but in return they release the footage for general use immediately after they've broadcast it."

William was clearly reluctant, but even he was finally persuaded that some accommodation would have to be made.

"Very well, but only the BBC. Fiona Bruce would be nice."

Jane Hunter laughed and then prompted Lauren, "What about you, Lauren?"

"I'm with William, the fewer media people I have to deal with, the better."

As soon as she got back to the haven of her study, Lauren called Jonathan.

The second he answered, she was off, her voice rising as she spoke. "I've been talking with a friend of yours, Brian Andrews. You remember Brian, the journalist, the art business journalist? The one at your party? The one who knows all about my diary, the diary you promised not to talk about. How could you, Jonathan, how could you let me down like this?"

As she finished her impassioned question, Lauren realised her voice was about to break, and she would not let him hear that. So, on her final word, and before he could respond, she ended the call. Seconds later, she saw his number appear on her screen as he attempted to call her back. She rejected the call.

1507 – Accused

October 11th

Disaster!

Chiara was here this morning, in floods of tears. She came running into the studio, utterly distraught, and immediately rushed into Dimmi's chamber. It happened I was there, reminding him of today's various appointments. Maestro looked up as his goddaughter came crashing in without knocking.

"Dimmi!" he commanded at once.

Through her sobs, she haltingly told us, "This morning, when the tamburi were opened, there was a letter accusing Alessio of taking pleasure with that wicked, infamous sodomite, Jacopo Saltarelli. Godfather, it is a lie, a most scurrilous lie. It is not true, it cannot be true. We…"

She stopped, embarrassed, and looked at me.

Dimmi addressed her gently.

"Chiara, you must realise by now Paolo has been utterly devoted to you from the day he first saw you. If we are to deal with this situation, we must use his talents. I promise you, he is cleverer than he looks."

Dimmi said this with a smile. I was not offended. I knew he was trying to give Chiara strength.

She looked at me once more, attempting to smile through her tears.

"I know. My protector."

Chiara pulled herself a little more erect.

"Since our marriage, we have had normal relations as between husband and wife. Alessio gives every indication of being pleased with me…by my charms. I refuse to believe he seeks men to lie with."

Dimmi took her hands in his.

"Leave us now, tesoro. Let us consider and make some enquiries. Come back in three days." [1]

October 14th

Three days have wrought terrible damage to my darling Chiara. Her eyes are dull and red-rimmed, sunken in deep shadows. Her hair no longer shines, instead hangs lank and lifeless around her tear-

---

[1] *Tamburi means drums. There were several slots dotted around Florence where anyone could post an accusation against another citizen into one of the tamburi. The slots were also called buchi della verità, 'holes of truth'. Documents deposited into the tamburi were read by the 'Ufficiali della Notte', the night watch. An accusation would lead to a public hearing, but guilt was not automatically assumed. The accuser's name was kept secret, but the accusation could not be anonymous.*

ravaged face. Worst of all, her entire spirit is diminished by misery.

Throughout this time, she explained, Alessio has been at home, never stepping outside his front door.

"He has changed, godfather, changed terribly, and so quickly. He sits all day and stares at het wall, drinking too much wine. At night…at night he is, he will not…or cannot be with me. Oh, godfather, and you too, Paolo; as you love me, please, please save us!"

"Come, come, cara. Have faith. Your protector here has had an idea. Perhaps this very afternoon, we will have a plan that may assuage your husband's situation."

What Dimmi referred to, was an idea I had, to request sight of the accusation in the tamburi. Maestro sent Bartolomeo and I to petition the Ufficiali. In view of my young age and his noble family, Count spoke.

"Signori, we are well aware that the authors of the accusations in the tamburi are, and must be, secret. We do not request sight of the name of the accuser, only of the specific details of his accusations. Tear off the name! Ensure the craven coward is protected! But allow us to study the falsities laid against our client and friend."

Bartolomeo's charm worked, as always. We returned to the bottega with the document, shorn of the signature of its author.

I urged our master, "Now, Maestro, now we are counting on you. From all of your studies and experiments, there must be something, anything, you can discover from this paper, this ink, this writing."

Maestro Leonardo stared at me with a strange look in his eye.

"The writing...the writing. Let us look again at the writing."

October 15th

A very busy day!

In the morning, Dimmi sent me to the markets and into the piazza. My task? To listen.

"Pay attention to everything, Paolo. Especially anything relating to Francesco del Giocondo."

"Del Giocondo? Are you sure, Maestro?"

"Certain. Listen, and pay attention to everything he says or is said about him."

And so, of course, I did.

I spent every hour walking the city, penetrating sections unfamiliar to me, places where the merchants gather to exchange contracts, gossip and news.

In general, these districts are more comely. Being far from the food markets, there is less smell. And fewer dogs and cats roam, searching always for scraps. Fewer dogs means less mess and again, fewer noisesome odours. It is well known that natives of the city may navigate by ear and nose alone. I *have learned that each gonfalone has its distinguishing sound or odour, whether it is the fish market, the leather workers, the goldsmiths or the bakers.*

The merchants' quarters were free of smells and its noise was low and constant—the sound of quiet conversations, heard but yet not heard, and with no competition from boisterous hawkers or noisy children. The sound of money, I have decided.

In following my master's strictures about attending to everything, I discovered something that may be important to my darling's case.

"There is only one item of interest concerning del Giocondo, Maestro. Suddenly, he is offering the finest English wool, landed at Pisa within the week and at an excellent price. Guaranteed. Everyone is interested, it seems. It is rumoured that a ship from Flanders is lost at sea, so a shortage is expected. A cargo of high-quality English wool will be worth a fortune."

"Well done, Paolo. It is as I expected! You have done well."

October 17th

Another busy day, even although it is the Sabbath. Last evening, I was too late returning to my room to write my journal. At the sixth hour, I crept from the bottega into the street. I confess I was nervous, but the need to salvage the reputation of Chiara's husband was stronger than my fear. I was on my guard for sight or sound of anyone. There is no reason for honest men to be abroad in the city in the dead of night.[1]

The night was clear, but not too cold. The new moon had been on Friday, so the tiny silver sliver in the sky gave almost no light at all. Thankfully, the Via Lattea was a bright band across the sky.[2] I have occasionally studied it with my master, but from the safety of a secluded garden or rooftop, not while alone in the dark city.

Gradually, my eyes became accustomed to the dark, and the starlight provided just enough illumination for me to avoid the largest impediments to my feet—and the ever-present mess of the dogs. It is strange to be about in the city at this unholy hour. The uncanny silence reminds me of how noisy the city normally is: hawkers selling their wares, musicians playing and seeking donations, children shouting and fighting like the dogs, and all against the never-ending background hubbub of friends and neighbours greeting, arguing, laughing.

I was going down to the Arno. I know that some youths go there at certain times to catch the fish moving between the river and the sea. Being too young to join the Fishermen's Guild, it is illegal for them to catch fish for the market, so

---

[1] *For Paolo, the day started at sunset. So in October, the sixth hour would be around 11 p.m. With no lights anywhere, the streets would be utterly black.*
[2] *Via Lattea = Milky Way*

they do it under the cloak of night, and refrain from taking so many that the Guild try too hard to stop them.

Maestro had heard a rumour concerning one of the young poachers, and this was my last opportunity to find him before the hearing.

This morning, tired, but elated, I reported to Dimmi.

"Maestro, there is something I discovered, perhaps not important. Your suspicions are well founded. You will not know Alessandro, he is a street urchin. He lives from day to day—an errand here, a stolen purse there, some illegal fishing, a foreign visitor delivered to one of the artists in the piazza. You know the kind I mean. Well, young Sandro has a new doublet and he boasts that next week, he will have a new jerkin to match, lined in silk in two colours, and with a velvet collar."

October 18th

*P*ay attention!
Never will you hear of a more excellent case. Never will you be witness to a more clever and complete *victory! Read!*

Let me set the scene. Maestro Leonardo stood before the assembled Signoria. The room was full, not a single seat was empty. Rank upon rank of benches held the principal men of Florence, all in their finest clothes. The room was ablaze with colour—flames of crimson, sunbursts of yellow, waves of blue and fields of dazzling green. I confess to taking some credit for this situation—I spent yesterday spreading word that the greatest mind in Christendom would, on the morrow, show proof of the corruption of the city and our Republic. Salaì will regret he was not witness to this spectacle; he is delivering a painting in Pisa.

As soon as Maestro stood to speak, an expectant silence spread throughout the great room.

"Messeri, we are here today, in this august chamber, to hear the case against my well-beloved friend, Messer Alessio Pacini. You are all aware that this chamber is not altogether without pain to me. Over there is the wall on which I have laboured to display the great victory of our republic. Today, I ask you to set aside any animus you may harbour against this unworthy and dilatory artist. Today, I appear as a petitioner and as an accuser—against one of your number."

As that shocking announcement sunk in, you could have heard a silk kerchief fall to the floor. Each man looked to his neighbour to share his bemusement. A public accusation was extraordinary.

Maestro stood erect, his purple doublet and golden hose a perfect ornament to this dramatic scene. He looked around the room, slowly, as if assessing every member. His was an impressive figure indeed. Then, with no warning, he spun to his left, shot out his arm and pointed to an individual while calling out in a strong voice,

"Francesco del Giocondo! Why did you lay this base accusation against my innocent friend, that gentiluomo, Ser Alessio Pacini?"

At the sound of the name del Giocondo, there was a great clamour. The president of the hearing, one Dottor Andrea Cellini, shouted over the noise.

"Maestro Leonardo, you have made an accusation without proof. I require you to withdraw your charge against Messer del Giocondo. No one knows the author of accusations in the tamburi. Withdraw your charge, sir, or face our punishment!"

"Dottor Cellini, please bear with me. Trust me, I know of which I speak."

And now Dimmi swept his hand to indicate the long table, behind which sat the good Dottore and the other members of the Otto.[1]

"Signori, pray indulge me. Let me quote from the accusation. 'I accuse Jacopo Saltarelli of being party to many wretched affairs and who consents to please those persons who request such wickedness of him, including one Alessio Pacini, merchant.'"

"Now, here is a loaded pen and a piece of parchment for each of you. If you would, please inscribe on your parchment,

---

[1] *The Otto di Guardia e Balia was a committee of eight men responsible for administering criminal justice in Florence.*

the words, 'to please those persons'. That is all. I understand that by themselves, these words are meaningless—but if you would, Messeri, indulge me. And on the back of the paper, please write your name."

It would be wrong to say there was awed silence at this point. No, there was a great murmuring, as the members of the Signoria speculated as to my master's intent. I caught sight of del Giocondo. He had a peculiar look on his face, more intrigued than fearful.

After a few minutes, it was clear that the Committee had completed its task.

"Signori, please gather close around the table."

As he said this, I noted a quick movement of my master's left hand.

"Regard, there are nine pieces of parchment before you. Yes, nine, not eight. By sleight of hand, I have added a paper, an exact but partial copy of a document I possess, which you may inspect for yourselves shortly. But for the moment, what do you observe? Let me make the task easier. I place on the table, the accusation we are today discussing. It is folded just so, to draw attention to a particular phrase, the one you yourselves have just written, but it is the actual accusation from the tamburi."

Now there was silence such as one rarely experiences in such a grand room filled by so many opinions. Time itself was suspended.

Finally, old Dottor Loredan was heard.

"Well, the accusation cannot be by this hand, or this, or this. It is clear that the authors of these manuscripts were taught in Venice, or at least by a Venetian tutor, by the shape of their 'p's."

"And look," this was Ser Malatesta. "Look here, this 'o' is unusual, a different hand completely."

And so it went on. Guided by my master, the Committee itself gradually eliminated every author, but one.

With a dramatic motion, Dimmi swept his hand across the sole remaining parchment and turned it over. Into the waiting silence, he held up the scrap of paper and dramatically called out the name written on the reverse, "del Giocondo!"

There was uproar and confusion, with supporters of the newly accused merchant calling over themselves in their anger. After a while, Dimmi succeeded in regaining control.

"And thus you see, Messeri, we derived the author, not from bribery or the calling in of favours, but by logic. Some years ago, del Giocondo commissioned a painting from me."

Everyone noted the disrespect in my master's words, as he referred to the merchant as one would a servant.

" 'I require a painting that will impress and please those persons who visit my home and see the work.' Those are the precise words in our contract, the words that allowed me to observe the shape, the form of his letters. When I saw the accusation document from the tamburi, I recognised immediately the identical choice of words and the distinctive way this writer forms his 'e' when it is the final letter in a

word. Here is the original of our contract, you may examine it yourselves to witness the accuracy of my copy. So, we know the accuser."

Maestro looked around the table, fixing each man with a quick look.

" 'And what of that?' you may be thinking. Consider. As many of you know, the merchant, del Giocondo, has boasted lately that he will have very soon, the finest English wool available to those who seek it–at a handsome price. Perhaps he will favour us with sight of the order he placed that is now bringing this bounty to him? No? I thought not. Is it a coincidence, I wonder, that the accused, Ser Alessio, my client, has just such a shipment of English wool, half paid for in advance by Ser Alessio and scheduled to arrive imminently? And will this contract be void if my friend is found guilty before then? Of course it will. And will we learn that del Giocondo has arranged to inherit the voided contract?"

Dimmi could have allowed the argument to rest at this point, but it seemed he was determined to exact the full measure of revenge on his enemy, as he now saw him. Ignoring the shouts and cries all around us, he nodded, and at this signal, the sergeant pulled from behind him, Sandro, the street urchin, struggling vainly to escape his grasp.

"And what of this creature? An accusation in the tamburi is not enough to convict a man, for which we may give thanks. No, a witness is required, one who will swear *to the facts. Attend to this ragamuffin's doublet. Do your sons wear any finer? Ask him about his new jerkin, expected next week. Is it lined with fur or with velvet? Or trimmed with silk? Will he swear on the Holy Book that Messer Alessio Pacini took him by the arse? Was he intending to bear false witness? Ask him."*

An even greater tumult broke out at this point, and when it was over, Alessio had been vindicated, and del Giocondo had been driven from the chamber, loudly, but vainly, protesting his innocence all the way. It had been an unseemly episode.

Alessio's reputation has been saved, and, as I write this report, it comes to my mind that, in some measure at least, Marcantonio has indeed been avenged.

Just as Dimmi promised.

Helen's Call

By late afternoon, Lauren was ready to call it a day. She had already given Penny the last of the unread pages and she was too distracted by the day's calamitous events to start on anything else.

She drove into Oxford and parked her car behind Merton College. She had only just begun exploring the ancient city. Meandering through its winding streets and pathways had been pleasantly soothing on her previous visits. However, on those earlier occasions, her mood hadn't been as black as today. She was feeling low and more than a bit sorry for herself. Jonathan had turned out to be as unreliable as her previous boyfriends. Yes, he was more charming, but, in the end, he'd turned out to be just as quick to take advantage of her.

As she walked along the side of Merton Field, she replayed her family's recent history in her head, reminding herself of just how disastrous many of the male figures had been, all the way back to Riccardo, her mother's Italian father. He and his American wife had abandoned their teenage daughters, preferring a life free of parental responsibilities. Riccardo's note reassured his daughters that they would be OK because, 'Your mom has stocked the fridge and paid the rent for three months. And there's $300 in the kitchen, which should take care of the bills until Julia gets a job. Then you'll have two paychecks coming in. You girls will be just fine.'

The girls never heard from either parent again.

Then there was her biological father, Ricky Patterson, who had given Lauren his name, his blue eyes and absolutely nothing else.

These thoughts were bouncing around in Lauren's head when her phone chirped. It was Helen calling from California.

"Hi, Helen."

"Hi honey, and congratulations!"

"What are you talking about?"

"Your diary, of course! Your Leonardo da Vinci diary. There was a report on *Good Morning America*. Of course, the journalist tried to suggest you were too inexperienced to be in charge of something so important–typical dickhead. I'm only surprised he didn't add you were too pretty as well. So come on, spill. Tell me about this diary. They didn't say too much about what's in it."

"Oh God! I don't believe this. Helen, do you remember where the report came from?"

"Sure, from Chicago. The reporter quoted a professor, I don't remember his name, I assume it was one of your old teachers."

"Was his name, the professor I mean, could his name have been Hildebrand?"

"No, I'm sure that wasn't it. A colour, Black, Brown… I'm not sure."

"Greensmith. Was it Greensmith?"

"Yeah! That's was it, Greensmith. Wasn't he your professor?"

"Helen, I gotta go. There's someone I need to call. I promise I'll call you later. Promise."

She opened her phone's browser and quickly went to ABC.com. There it was, a short item about the Chronicle. It was sketchy, but the gist was that the diary had been found, by luck, by an American student studying in England, and now serious US academics were worried that an unqualified individual was being allowed to keep this amazing resource to herself. There had been no announcement about the diary, and this was symptomatic of the secrecy surrounding the amazing discovery.

She called Jonathan. This time he spoke before Lauren had a chance to say a word.

"Lauren, thank God you called. I talked with Brian. He got the story two days ago from the States, from an American freelance journalist who was trying to track down more about a tip he had received. He asked Brian to do some legwork–they would share the story. Brian only worked out today that you were the woman he was looking for. He's happy to call you right now to tell you himself."

"Oh, Jonathan! I am so, so sorry. I should never have doubted you. I leapt to a conclusion and–"

He interrupted her. "It's okay. I mean, what a coincidence! That Brian should be the one he called. But the art world is a small one."

"Still, I shouldn't have been so quick to accuse you. Can you ever forgive me?"

"Lauren, it's fine, it really is. Forget about, please. Will we see you tomorrow, for Henley?"

"I... Yes, please, if you're still sure?"

"Of course, I'm sure. See you tomorrow. And Lauren?"

"What?"

"You're going to be famous! I'm going to tell everyone I knew you before you became a celebrity. They'll think I'm cool," he teased.

Lauren's mood lifted. "Very funny, wise guy. Hilarious. I'm going now, see you tomorrow."

She was still nervous about the prospect of dealing with the media, but that emotion paled next to the huge relief and delight she took from knowing that Jonathan hadn't betrayed her.

And she made an instant decision.

Despite Jonathan's teasing, she knew wasn't going to become a celebrity, not really. But, if she was going to be even a tiny bit famous, she would be famous as Lauren Tonelli, not Lauren bloody Patterson.

1508

January 8th

The painting of the Virgin and Saint Elizabeth progresses well. Since the terrible trial, Chiara has regained her former beauty, indeed she appears to me lovelier than ever, if that is possible.

No one sees the portraits of Chiara and Alessio.

Dimmi is supposed to be bending all of his energies to the commission of the Signoria, which continues to cause difficulties. Indeed, I begin to fear that this great work will never be completed.[1]

In any case, he does not want visitors to see he has started yet another major project, and one of his own choosing. The paintings of Chiara and her husband sit hidden in his bedchamber, where Dimmi works on them, alone.

---

[1] Indeed, The Battle of Anghiari never was finished. It is thought possible that some part of it may be hidden behind a false wall today. And so the great artistic duel between Leonardo and Michelangelo failed to produce a single fresco.

January 18th

My father came to the bottega today bringing me the sad news that my mother has died. I will write more about her on another occasion. For now, I record that she was a quiet, devout woman who took excellent care of me in my childhood and was devoted to my father throughout their life together. I will miss her.

February 1st

My master is a true gentleman. He knows I am saddened that once again, I have taken my farewell of Chiara. The legal problems with Dimmi's stepbrothers have been resolved and we return to Milan. As we turned for a final look at Florence, he put his arm around my shoulders.

"Paolo, we must talk. Your Chiara, our Chiara, is married and, now that we are leaving the city, I can tell you that I believe her to be carrying a baby. It is early, but she will know, or at least suspect, although I imagine she will not have told anyone. I will try to capture the suspicion she feels in my portrait, even if it was not there when she sat for me."

"Then how do you know, Maestro? Did she tell you?"

He laughed. "No, but while you gaze upon Chiara's lovely face and see only perfection, I see the smallest change in her complexion. The skin on her forehead is a shade darker. It is called the mask of pregnancy. In Chiara's case it will, I'm sure, vanish when she is delivered of her child. So, we can safely assume that relations with her husband have been restored. Chiara is building her life. It is time you did also."

"Perhaps in time my sentiments will change. For now, Maestro, I am sad, yes, but also happy in my love. But, as you have raised this matter, I have a request. When you began working on the wedding portraits, you made two studies of Chiara. May I have one, please?"

"Yes, Paolo, you may have the first." [1]

August 1st

My father is dead. My cousin Andrea wrote me the news. By now he will be long buried, so there is little point in a hurried return to Florence. However, there are some few matters to be settled which I must attend to before too long. It is an irony that I will again have business with Dimmi's oldest brother, since he has assumed the responsibilities of their father's business, and thus he became notary to my own father.

We live in a small world.

---

[1] The second study, the one actually adopted for the final portrait, is lost.

As with my mother's passing, once again I find I need time to condense my thoughts about the death and the life of my father. But I did calculate that, since the day I entered Dimmi's service, although we corresponded regularly, I saw my father only six times, and my mother twice. It is strange how time and distance may alter even the most precious relationships.

October 12th – Milan

Today, Maestro showed us the completed portraits of Chiara and Alessio, many months delayed by the welcome commissions we have had in this fine city. They are truly breathtaking—the greatest works he has ever produced. And it is not only I who say so. Everyone is agreed, even Dimmi himself.

"I painted these from my heart," he allowed, as he removed the sheet obscuring them.

Alessio is standing, facing somewhat to the side, his body turned a little towards the viewer. He holds in his hand a sheet of music. It is the music Dimmi composed for their wedding. Alessio is about to present it to Chiara. His right hand, clasping the music, is extended and his left also, palm up, reaching for Chiara's hand as she rises to embrace him at the moment of his proposal. His clothes are plain, except his stole is of fur—and such fur!

Even one who is not besotted with Chiara, as I freely confess I remain, will fall in love when he stands before the vision presented to him.

Chiara is seated. She has just received Alessio's proposal and is about to offer him her hand. A white lily lies cradled in her lap, and a unicorn sleeps at her feet. But it is Chiara's radiant face, and in particular, her eyes and mouth that will captivate all who stand before this portrait.

We understand that a second before, she had been contemplating the lily on her lap; like the unicorn, a symbol of innocence and purity. At the words of Alessio, she is raising her gaze towards him. But the painter has captured her in mid-turn, looking directly out, at us. Her startling blue eyes pierce us. She is already looking to her future as a married woman, and one day, perhaps soon, as a mother. There is a challenge in her eyes. Somehow, it is not comfortable to hold her gaze too long. A beguiling smile of anticipation is just beginning to form. Maestro has made her aware of the first stirrings of the new life growing inside her, even though this actually occurred only months later.

Like Alessio, Chiara's dress is plain and simple; pale wool of the finest, softest grade and beautifully rendered. My mind goes back to a day long ago—I am indeed tempted to stroke the folds of the dress to confirm what my senses tell me, that this is real fabric hiding, while also revealing, the shapely woman before me. The viewer is invited to study, not jewels and fine silks, but the couple's faces and through their eyes, their souls.

Behind each figure is a subtle landscape. In each canvas, a path winds through rocks until both paths merge behind Alessio, before a bridge crossing a swirling, turbulent river. The water in the river is in frantic motion and is surely wet. Across the chaotic rapids, a single road wends into the softly rolling Tuscan hills. The bride has joined her path to her husband's and now they take a single, smooth route to their shared, tranquil future.

And yet, artful though the backgrounds are, they serve to enhance and dramatise the two figures. By his mastery of light and shadow, Maestro has illuminated the subjects of the paintings, highlighting them as if lit from a window.

I confess a few tears escaped my eyes as I looked on Chiara's image. Not, I swear, in sadness, but in awe that my incomparable master has captured so faithfully the beauty of the face and the soul of the woman I worship.

Dimmi agreed to my request to deliver the portraits to Alessio and Chiara in Florence. I have need to settle the affairs of my late father and the visit will permit me to see Chiara happy and settled in her married life.

Image 9: Portrait of an Unknown Musician

Before the publication of the Paolo Chronicles, this was accepted as an unfinished autograph Leonardo. We now must concede that it is a partial, and not very good, copy of Alessio's full length wedding portrait. Admittedly the man portrayed seems younger. Perhaps Alessio's pose was adapted for another commission.

(Pinacoteca Ambrosiana, Milan)

Henley

On Saturday morning, Lauren arrived at Jonathan's parents' house, a picturesque cottage with roses climbing exuberantly over every wall.

Lauren couldn't suppress a 'Wow!' when Jonathan opened the front door. He was wearing a jacket of bold stripes–blue, maroon and pink.

"That's quite a jacket!"

Jonathan pretended to preen himself.

"This supremely elegant item of gentlemen's attire is an Old Carthusian blazer."

"You went to a school called Carthusian? That's an odd name for a school–wasn't that an order of monks?"

"I went to Charterhouse School. Former pupils, what you'd call alumni, of Charterhouse are called Old Carthusians."

"Why?"

"The original school was built…oh, never mind. Come on, there are people to meet."

They walked through the picturesque, albeit busy, town down to the grassy banks of the river. There Lauren was charmed by the sight of hundreds of people who had stepped out of an Edwardian painting. Girls wore a rainbow of pretty silk dresses in pastel colours, while the men outshone them in white, yellow, pink or blue slacks and ties and blazers as garishly striped as Jonathan's. Some young boys and old men even wore straw boaters. Dotted across every patch of manicured grass, parties were laying out picnic rugs and opening hampers, while strollers meandered from group to group, glasses in hand, greeting old friends and being introduced to new ones.

By noon, Jonathan and his group were settled on a shaded spot by the side of the Thames, sprawled across four overlapping tartan rugs, surrounded by hampers of food and drink. Lauren had brought prosecco and crusty bread and pâté as her contribution and soon she was relaxed and thoroughly enjoying herself.

Geraldine came and knelt beside her, handing her a tall frosted glass of what looked at first like beer, except it was garnished with cucumber, fruit and mint leaves.

"Here you are—Pimm's!" Geraldine announced with a flourish, before continuing, "And don't worry, you're not the only one who doesn't have a clue about what's going on—the rowing is completely incidental. There are dozens of races and no one except the friends and families of the rowers cares about any of them. Except when it's a team from your own college or school, naturally. Jon and Robert will get all excited around about half-past four, when the Charterhouse eight is due on the river. But it's traditional to clap when they announce a result over the loudspeakers, even if you can't make out a word and wouldn't care if you did."

After a while, Lauren found herself sitting alone with Jonathan.

"I really do have to apologise again. I was so wrong, and inexcusably rude."

"I told you, forget it, it's absolutely fine. How's the project going?" he asked, "I mean will the media attention complicate things?"

"Not really. It's just that neither the Earl nor I are keen about talking to the press, which we'll have to now, even TV apparently."

She saw a smirk developing on his face and poked his chest.

"Don't dare start your celebrity nonsense, I'm not looking forward to it one little bit. And speaking of TV, William said he liked the idea of being interviewed by someone called Fiona Bruce. What's all that about?"

Jonathan grinned as he replied, "Lots of guys his age wouldn't mind being interviewed by Fiona Bruce. She's…well, even my father says she's pretty cute."

"Men! Don't you *ever* grow up?"

"Probably not," he smiled. "Listen, are you really worried about the press conference?"

"It's pathetic, but yes, I am."

"Well, how about next weekend, Robert, Gerry and I rehearse you?"

"Rehearse me?"

"For the press conference. We'll be journalists and we'll ask you difficult questions. We can use my grandfather's old place, it's nearby."

* * *

On Wednesday, a few days after the Henley picnic, Jonathan was alone in the gallery, replying to one last email before he closed up. He heard the electronic beep announcing the arrival of a customer. He looked at his watch, 6:57 p.m. 'Damn', he thought, 'not again!' On Monday, a man had come in at almost exactly this time and Jonathan was unable to get him out the door until almost forty minutes after his 7 p.m. closing time. Worst of all, it had been clear within the first two minutes that there was absolutely zero prospect of a sale. He suspected the time waster had been filling the minutes before an eight o'clock dinner reservation.

Nevertheless, he put on his best welcoming smile and stepped around the corner. To a surprise.

"Sarah! I wasn't expecting you. I haven't seen you in…"

"Over six months. I know. Are you about to close up?"

"Yes, I am."

"Can I buy you a drink around the corner?"

"Well…yeah, sure. Just let me send this email. Take a look around if you want, I won't be a second."

Sarah walked slowly round the room. She called out to him, "This is wonderful, Jon. I heard you had opened, and I wanted to see your place. It's fantastic. Congratulations."

"Thanks. OK, that's gone. Let's go."

The wine bar was quiet, a lull between the last shoppers and the pre-dinner crowd. They sat at a corner table.

"You're looking well, Jon. Well, but tired."

"It's been pretty hectic, getting ready for the opening. You're looking great. How's the corporate catering business?"

"It's going pretty well, thanks, I've taken on two more people, just to handle… Yes, it's going great."

"Just to handle Barclays?" he smiled.

"Well, yes, but I'm here to apologise. The last time we talked, I was horrid, really horrible."

"It's OK, you–"

"No, Jon, it wasn't OK."

Sarah took a deep breath. "I had been lying to you for weeks. The truth is, my business was in all kinds of trouble. We'd had a case of food poisoning, if you can believe it, about a month before. I lost two big clients and the money was drying up."

"Why on earth didn't you tell me?"

"I told myself I didn't want to worry you. You were working all the hours God sent on your thesis. Anyway, what could you have done? But, and this is why I'm here, that wasn't really the reason. The truth is, I was ashamed. Your friends and your family, they're all so accomplished, so successful. Even when they're not making tons of money, they're musicians or artists or something else cool and impressive. I couldn't stand the idea of being a failure among them, in front of you. I wanted to be admired, the way I admired all of you."

"Oh, Sarah! I did admire you. I do admire you. You built your own business from scratch, with absolutely no help from anyone, I was always seriously impressed by that–I'm even more impressed now, by the way, now I'm trying it myself."

"Well, I always felt good when it was just the two of us. You made me feel appreciated. But when I was with your family, or your friends, I felt…I don't know–clumsy, not sophisticated, out of my depth. I felt that everyone was being terribly polite to me, all the while thinking 'she's quite nice, but not one of us–how peculiar of Jonathan to take up with her'."

"I wish you had told me all of this a long time ago–it would have explained a lot."

"I know. I've thought the same thing a million times. And when I heard about the gallery, I knew I had to come to explain, and ask. Ask for another chance."

Jonathan watched as the numbers on his bedside radio flickered to three o'clock. He was tormented by guilt. He shouldn't have done this. It wasn't fair on Sarah, and, even though he and Lauren were not romantically involved, nonetheless it felt like a betrayal. He no longer thought of Lauren as just another friend. This had been a huge mistake. Which is why he was immensely relieved to hear Sarah softly murmur, "It isn't the same, is it?"

He didn't reply immediately, but slowly turned over to face her. The glow of the radio was just enough to let him see her face.

"No, not really."

She was looking directly into his eyes, and he understood that while he remained very fond of her, he no longer felt as he had before.

He wanted to at least try to explain.

"That day, the day we argued, a lot of what you said was true. Afterwards, I began to understand just how much I did take for granted, I mean about my family, our wealth, my good luck. In lots of ways, the gallery is my attempt to build something by myself, by risking everything I have. I want to make this work, to prove to myself that I can. So, in a way, I have you to thank for where I am now. I suppose what I'm trying to say is yes, things have changed, but not because I resent anything you said that day."

When the first early light filtered through the curtains, he was still awake as Sarah slid out of bed. Ten minutes later she emerged from the bathroom, fully dressed.

There was a slight catch in her voice when she spoke.

"Goodbye, Jon, and good luck with the gallery."

Jonathan heard the front door close and lay awake, still feeling guilty.

* * *

On Sunday, Lauren, Jonathan, Robert and Geraldine were sitting around the kitchen table in the old house, its stark walls a reminder of the void created by the absence of Jonathan and Robert's grandfather.

"Already we've learned so much," Lauren told them as she tried to explain the situation. "Lots about the everyday life of Florence, of course, but mostly about Leonardo and his studio, all of which is incredibly important. Professor Hunter doesn't want to release much detail from the diaries right now, so I have to be careful about that. We want to direct attention to Paolo himself. She doesn't want information about Leonardo coming out piecemeal. We need to be especially careful about anything we say about the *Mona Lisa*. It's such an iconic painting, and when we do release the Chronicles, we'll probably come over as demeaning it. I mean, we won't really, but that's how the French are going to see it, I'm sure. And the British press are going to be all over that, so I guess that's our main concern right now."

Robert offered some advice.

"If the French are destined to become the enemy, who can be your allies? How about the Italians?"

Jonathan was sceptical. "The Italians? What are you thinking?"

"Well, this is Italian art and Italian people we're talking about. And their experts are bound to be involved right from the outset. Here's an idea. Make sure the UK correspondents for the Italian media are invited. Invite their questions and, even though they'll address you in English, answer in Italian and make clear your love for all things Italian, not least Leonardo."

They ordered in a Chinese meal and talked into the night. At eleven o'clock, Robert and Gerry went to bed, but Jonathan and Lauren decided to finish off the bottle of wine.

As Jonathan poured fresh glasses, Lauren asked, "I thought your grandfather was dead? I mean, is this your other grandfather's house?"

"Oh, no. My grandfather *is* dead, but my father has an Australian cousin. She's coming to teach at Oxford for a year, with her husband and kids, so the family decided to hold on to the house, so she can use it. Then I suppose it'll be sold, which is kind of sad."

"Your family seems close."

"We are. I've cousins on my mother's side who I see pretty often. My father's an only child, but he has lots of cousins and I see them and their kids, at least the ones who are in England. One was in the Regiment with me."

"The Regiment?"

"Ah! Of course, you don't know."

"Don't know what?" Lauren asked.

"Two years ago, almost, I left the Army."

He saw the surprise on her face. "That's right, the Army. I was a Captain in the Coldstream Guards. It was my entire life for a while. A lot of my friends who you've met are either in the Army or used to be."

"If it was so important to you, why did you leave?"

"Afghanistan was a mess, is a mess. I saw one of my men killed and another badly injured. He has prosthetic legs now. But it wasn't the casualties so much. Even while the operation was going on, we could see how pointless it all was. One day the Afghans will sort themselves out, or not, and we'll have little, probably nothing, to do with it. In all likelihood the Taliban will end up being part of the government and everyone will pretend it was all worthwhile."

He paused as memories came flooding back. "When you're out there, you ignore all that stuff. You're only focussed on the mission, on your team. But when you come home on leave, you read the papers, talk to people who were there before us. I finally faced the fact that my heart was no longer in it. And my enthusiasm was never coming back. So, I came out as soon as I could."

"And the gallery? It's a long way from the life of a soldier."

"It is, I suppose, but the idea had been in my head for a long time. My grandfather was a collector and got me interested in art when I was pretty young. My best birthday present ever was from him. I was fourteen. He took me to Cheltenham and outside the auction house he handed me £100."

* *. *

The young man began to thank his grandfather, thinking it was a bit odd that he had given him the money on the street. His grandfather interrupted him by turning him to face the building beside them.

"Look, this is the auction house. Let's go inside. It's viewing this morning, when we can look at all the lots. Then, after lunch, the auction will begin, and you can bid on anything you like up to £100. Let's go."

Catalogues in hand, the pair wandered around the cluttered rooms of the auction house. The majority of lots on display were beyond Jonathan's budget, most far beyond. But there were some drawings, old prints and a few Victorian watercolours with estimates between £40 and £200.

While they were in the fourth room, a man approached them.

"Good morning, Mr Granville. See anything that interests you?"

"'Morning, Frederick. Actually, I'm not looking for myself today. This is Jonathan, my grandson. It's his birthday, and this is his first auction. Jonathan, this is Mr Henderson, this is his auction house."

"Welcome, Jonathan. Your grandfather is an excellent teacher–pay attention to whatever he tells you."

"Yes, sir."

"What's your budget, Jonathan?"

"£100."

The auctioneer thought for a moment. "Let me show you something."

He led them into the smallest room in the auction centre, where he stopped before a tiny drawing. It was only about two inches square, but, surrounded with its plain white mount, it was closer to twelve inches on each side in its handsome gilt frame. The chalk and ink drawing was a highly detailed study for a cherubic child's head, but by now Jonathan knew it was likely to be an angel, or an infant from a religious painting–perhaps the baby Jesus himself.

"This is estimated at £60. First of all, the frame alone is probably worth that, although people don't think that way these days. We have no idea who the artist is. It's listed as possibly Italian, from the 16th or 17th century. We have to be cautious with our descriptions, but personally, I think it probably is from the 1500s, and see here, this odd little nose? It's quite distinctive, don't you think? It's entirely possible that one day you could find this face in a painting, maybe Venetian."

After another ten minutes carefully examining the tiny sketch, Jonathan had decided that, yes, this was the one. His lot was announced at ten past three.

The bidding turned out to be the most nerve-jangling experience Jonathan had ever been through. At one point his heart was hammering so hard he thought his grandfather must surely be able to hear it. Mr Henderson could probably hear it across the room. The opening bid was £45, and Jonathan was sure he was going to lose out as the bidding rapidly climbed to £80. In the end, his bid of £90 won the day against an online bidder.

"Gosh, that was exciting! Thanks, Grandfather, that was amazing!"

They were standing outside the auction house, Jonathan with his prize purchase tucked under his arm.

"I'm glad you enjoyed it. Now, what did you learn?"

Jonathan thought, but he couldn't come up with anything.

His grandfather looked at him very seriously. "Mr Henderson directed you to that piece, and he may have shaved the time available for another Internet bid. Now, I am a very good client, but when you're on your own, it will be for you to cultivate relationships with auctioneers, dealers, experts–all the people who can help or hinder you if they choose. While you're young, they'll be keen to help. I'll assist you, but in the long run, it will be down to you. And always remember, Jonathan–the art world is a small one. Reputations are easily won and lost. In all of England there are fewer than one hundred auctioneers, dealers, gallery owners who really matter. And they all talk to one another, if you lose the respect of one, you'll likely encounter difficulties with the others."

* *. *

Jonathan took a drink of his wine and smiled at Lauren.

"That auction really got me hooked. I started borrowing coffee-table art books from Grandfather and then from the school library. I was obsessed with finding the face of my cherub in a painting. Of course, I never did, although I've never completely stopped looking. In the process, I learned a fair bit about Italian art and four years later, I went up to Durham University to study art history.

"When I came out of the Army, I still wasn't sure what to do. I thought of trying for a job with an art dealer or auction house, but decided instead to do an accelerated Masters at the Courtauld Institute. And then my grandfather died and left me his art and enough money to open the gallery."

Jonathan gave Lauren a strange smile.

"I've been thinking about the conversation I had with Sarah, my ex, immediately before she dumped me. She basically said I was a spoiled little rich boy who had everything handed to him on a plate. I think the gallery was partly to demonstrate to myself I was capable of risking everything.

"Of course," he concluded, "I'm probably kidding myself. I suppose I'm aware I have a pretty big safety net in my family."

Lauren was having none of it.

"It's still a huge emotional risk. I mean, you'd be horribly disappointed if the gallery failed, wouldn't you? You'd feel that somehow *you* had failed, I'm sure. Risking your sense of self-worth is far more important than risking your money."

"I suppose. What about you? How did you end up doing a PhD in England? And on the Italian Renaissance?"

"In my final year at UC Santa Barbara, I came across a footnote reference to a woman called Margaret Pennant. I was intrigued by the idea of a successful international business run by a woman, at a time when the overwhelming majority of females had few property rights. Well, one thing led to the other. There was a long gap in between graduation and starting my doctorate. I tried corporate life for a few years, but discovered it wasn't for me. I started doing some research on my own, trying to find more information about Margaret. I had some idea there might be a magazine article in her story. Then I found out about her marriage into the Chance family and as I said, one thing led to another."

"Do you have brothers or sisters?"

"No. My Mom died when I was a kid and my aunt and uncle took me in. Helen and George had no kids, but I do have relatives in Italy. They're pretty distant cousins, but I got to know them really well and we're still in touch."

"We have something else in common then. My mother died when I was eight–cancer. Jennifer was her best friend. She, Jennifer I mean, wasn't married and she just kind of stepped in to help in the last six months of my mum's illness. It wasn't a huge surprise when they told us they were getting married."

"Jennifer seems really nice. Did you always get along?"

"We did, right from the start. I think because it was all about her and my mum at the beginning, about doing her best by her friend. That meant Robert and I had a close relationship with her even before she and my father became involved. And they were really smart about it. Things were never forced or hurried. By the time they talked to us, we were both relieved–we wanted Dad to be happy and life was just easier when Jennifer was sleeping under the same roof."

"What was your mom like? Do you remember her?"

"Oh yes, I remember lots of things. She was great, really great. She was funny, very sporty, and brilliant at organising everything. She was never stressed out, she had always thought of everything in advance."

He reached into his hip pocket and pulled out his wallet. Carefully, he slid out a folded piece of paper. Even more slowly, he unfolded the yellowed sheet and laid it on the table in front of Lauren. The creases were fragile, some torn part way through–the document had been folded and re-folded many, many times.

"The day before Mum's funeral, Dad gave Robert and me envelopes with letters from our mother. This was in there too."

Lauren looked at the paper. It was a copy of a hand written poem:

DO NOT WEEP

I want your memories of me–
And memories I crave.
Not tears, not fears, not sad regrets,
But love beyond the grave.

Remember me in years to come,
In all the sights you'll see.
As day by day unfolds the tale–
Not you, not I, but we.

So do not weep, but laugh and love.
Embrace each day anew.
Pursue your dreams, and have no doubt,
That I live on…in you.

"That's really, really lovely. It must have been a comforting thought for you both."

"It was. It is. This is a copy. You see, she wrote the poem out, once for me and once for Robert, but she wanted us to be able to carry it with us all the time. But she also knew how upset we'd be if we ever lost it. So, she made five photocopies of each and signed them all. That way, we could keep the original safe at home, and carry a copy with us. Robert still has all of his. I lost one years ago. But it's OK, because I've got the others. That's what I meant about always thinking of everything. There was also a roll of linen tape in the envelope–I really should repair this."

Lauren realised she was touched by the fact that Jonathan had shared what was obviously a hugely important memento. But then she wondered if she was over-thinking things. Maybe he showed the poem to lots of people. She wouldn't mention anything, at least not now. Instead, she turned the conversation back to the Chronicles.

"You know, there isn't a single mention of Leonardo's mother in the Chronicles, not one so far. His father and brothers pop up now and then in various references, but never his mother. And as for Paolo–he records he only saw his mother on two occasions between joining Leonardo when he was fourteen, and his mother's death."

Jonathan carefully re-folded his poem and replaced it in his wallet.

"Nothing absolutely certain is known about Leonardo's mother beyond her name. She was a poor country girl made pregnant by Ser Piero. In any case, we know Leonardo was brought up by his father's parents.

Being illegitimate then wasn't as scandalous as it would later become. So yes, he was another one who grew up without his mother. As for Paolo… You said you thought Paolo was from the countryside. It may have taken days to get there from Florence. They didn't have annual holidays I don't imagine."

After he showed Lauren to her room, Jonathan lay down on his bed and stared at the ceiling, thinking about their conversation and wondering how he truly felt about this intriguing American. Why had he shown her his mother's poem? Even Sarah hadn't seen that.

1508 – Return to Florence

October 27th

Everything is wrong in the home of Chiara and Alessio. Well, everything except the baby. The house is well appointed. But the spirit of the place is barren—a building, not a home.

Alessio hates the portraits. He complains that he wished the images to show them wealthy—bejewelled and successful, as befitting an important merchant and his wife.

Alessio has grown ever more bitter and angry since the sodomy accusation, even though a full year has passed.

"Yes, I was cleared, but still there is gossip. People prefer to believe the evil accusation and forget the hearing and its outcome."

I offered a counter. "But such people are of no worth, Alessio. Why worry about the empty sound of rattling barrels? People of distinction, people of worth, such people will ignore the prattle of fishwives."

His angry response dismissed me as one of no account.

"Paolo, you are young, you live now in distant Milan, you know nothing of which you speak. Stay and dine with Chiara if you wish. I will take my leave."

I was embarrassed. Not for myself, but for Chiara, who witnessed our exchange. Not a word of appreciation for the magnificent portraits, but rather, only complaint. No thanks to be conveyed to Dimmi, whose immeasurable gifts, princes would value beyond reckoning.

And to refuse to dine with a guest who has travelled eight days to bring this bounty to him is an inexcusable discourtesy.

"I am so sorry, Paolo," Chiara began. "Alessio has changed utterly. The accusation, the hearing, all of it has grown in his mind so that he dwells upon these matters every day. At first, after the hearing, he was relieved, joyous even and I thought the matter was firmly behind us. But then he began to be the butt of jokes and instead of laughing at them, or ignoring them, he fought back excessively."

Chiara looked away from me, to stare at the view outside the window, as she spoke again.

"He has taken yet another young mistress and flaunts her openly. And she is not the first, not close. I think he means to convince everyone in the city of his carnal interests. Because of all that transpired, I could perhaps forgive the mistresses—after all, he is hardly the first husband to misbehave. But we sleep alone, even when he is here, which is rarely. He tells me he wants the pleasures of the bed, but not with me. I do not know why, but he has come to hate me."

She cried, and I held her close. As I held her in my arms, I was overwhelmed by the warmth and promise of her body under my fingers. I fought the desire to lift up that lovely face and kiss away the evidence of her pain and sorrow. What those kisses may have led to… With a great effort, I forced myself to cease such thoughts, and do no other than provide an ear for her words and a shoulder for her tears.

After a while, her sobs subsided. She told me of her life since I had seen her last. She urged me to express her own fervent gratitude to Dimmi; she at least having an appreciation for the majestic portraits. For my part, I tried to amuse her with tales of the studio, and Salaì's latest mischiefs. She seemed to take some comfort from being able to release the words she has been holding inside for many months. After almost two hours of talking, I heard a baby's cry as, of course, did Chiara.

Instantly, she brightened, and I saw the first true smile since I arrived. It transformed her completely.

"Now you will meet my son, the light of my life."

After perhaps twenty minutes alone, I heard footsteps fast approaching and I turned, expecting to see Chiara enter the room. But it was Alessio. He looked around, angry.

"Where is my wife?" he demanded, most severely.

"What is wrong, Alessio? Why do you address me so harshly? Your wife has gone to attend to your son, who cried for her."

He gave no answer, but turned around and departed once again, brusquely passing his wife who was now arriving, baby in her arms.

"This is Leo. He was baptised Leonardo, for my padrino, but I call him Leo. What did Alessio want?"

"Chiara, I may be wrong, but I think he returned suddenly, expecting, or perhaps hoping, to find you and I…"

"Dio mio! You are probably right. He grasps something of your feelings for me and mine for you. He would love to catch me in the wrong. There are many people in the city with little regard for his treatment of me."

I stood up. "I must leave. I will not be the cause of yet more trouble for you."

She looked at me fiercely and commanded, "No! First, you will give Leo your blessing."

She smiled once more as she gazed at the babe, his eyes open and as blue as his mother's. He was swaddled in fine linens. Her voice became soft, intimate.

"His nurse has fed him, and he is clean. You may hold him, if you wish."

I sat back in my chair as she knelt before me and gently lowered the tiny body into my arms.

She did not straighten up and, with her face inches from mine, she looked directly into my eyes and urged, "Paolo, bury your face in his hair, in his neck. Breathe in his scent, there is nothing to compare with it, nothing."

I did as instructed, and she was right. Leo smelled of warmth and milk and love and innocence all at once. His skin and hair were so perfect, so soft, a caress to my face and to my heart. I swear he smiled at me.

And I suddenly understood what Chiara was doing. Through offering me this instant bond with her son, the fruit of her body, she was sharing a profound intimacy between us.

I looked over the tiny head of her son into those bottomless blue eyes and we both smiled. We understood each other, perfectly. Once again, our eyes were joined; my heart is truly, and now forever, bound.

October 29th

It is time for me to leave the city. I will return to Milan via the farm of my parents and arrange what remains of their affairs. However, I wanted to see Chiara one final time before my departure, so I sent a message that I would call on her this afternoon.

When I was shown into the salon, I beheld a strange sight. There was another young woman sitting with Chiara and she looked so like her, I thought my eyes were deceiving me. As I looked from one to the other, Chiara began to laugh.

"You are a picture of confusion, Paolo. Say something sensible or my sister will think you a fool. Pacifica, you remember my dearest friend, Paolo del Rosso, assistant to Maestro Leonardo, and much more intelligent than he appears at this moment."

"Pacifica. I saw you once or twice, many years ago, but you look very different now, very ..."

I stopped before I embarrassed myself even more. I was about to say that she was very beautiful—how could I say

209

otherwise when she was the mirror image of her sister. I calculated that Chiara must be the elder by ten or so years, but her uncanny skin and clear eyes had always made her seem much younger than her age, and so the two women could almost have been exact contemporaries.

Chiara was enjoying my discomfort, but she took pity on me.

"Come, sit down, Paolo and take a glass of wine with us. I must go to attend to Leo soon, but first you must entertain us with gossip from your life in Milan."

Under Chiara's gentle prompting I amused the two sisters with tales of the complicated and often scandalous life of the court in Milan. All the while I talked, I was aware of the extraordinary beauty of the two women before me.

"So, Pacifica, how is it I have not seen you these many years?"

"I have been living in Urbino with my aunt. When our mother died, I went to live with her sister. I long to return to my home. I shall do so next week."

Pacifica said this with some determination and was looking at her sister as she did so. I sensed tension between them.

Soon after these words, Pacifica rose to her feet.

"Allow me to attend to Leo and his nurse. Chiara, stay and take your leave of Paolo before he must depart. Paolo, I trust you come safely to your home in Milan."

With that, she slipped from the room, leaving me alone with Chiara.

"Did you enjoy meeting my sister again, Paolo? She is much changed since you saw her last, I think."

I looked at her and saw the strain in her eyes as she stared at me intently.

"What troubles you, Chiara? Tell me honestly, what is on your mind?"

There was silence as a debate raged behind Chiara's eyes.

"Oh, Paolo, how well you know me! I do not want my sister to return to Urbino. She has developed an infatuation with a nobleman, a Medici—Giuliano, youngest son of Lorenzo. He will take advantage of her, I am certain he will. Pacifica will not see that men such as the Medici marry not for love but for political alliances. Just before you arrived, she told me she would return to Urbino—she will bring about her own ruin. That is my fear. When you arrived, my heart lightened. I thought you might find her pleasing, and perhaps …"

When I left Chiara's house, I wandered the streets for some time, a confusion of emotions swirling around my head. I could readily understand Chiara's fears for her sister, and it took no genius to predict that I would be attracted to the facsimile of Chiara. And Pacifica has also a pleasant disposition. She lacks the special radiance of her sister perhaps, but she is graceful and amusing company.

211

But had Chiara not been trying to use me as her instrument? Yes, friends may play matchmaker, there is nothing dishonourable to that. But in this case, was the motivation our mutual happiness, or merely a hastily improvised response to a perceived imminent catastrophe? Could her motives be both at once? I was confused and even as I write this record, I remain unsettled.

Since my father died and I have come to my small inheritance, I have contemplated if I should find myself a wife, but there is plenty of time and, in truth, I am aware of a challenging reality.

In pursuit of my duties for my master, I often accompany him to the homes of wealthy and distinguished families. There I occasionally espy the daughters of these households. I am often struck by their elegance and beauty but, of course, I never engage them in conversation, unless they be young children. Their role seems to be that of demure ornaments to their fathers' homes, at least until they are married. The young wives are of much more interest. They share the physical charms of their younger sisters but are freer to discuss trivial matters with Dimmi, as an older, much respected citizen, if not with me. I watch them and they seem beautiful to me, beautiful and charming. And on many occasions, I sense the intelligence they cloak behind idle chatter. I believe that, if the occasion arose, I would enjoy exchanging real opinions and ideas with these women and I would enjoy…well, I would enjoy them in every sense.

On the counter to this, every day I pass words with girls close to my own age in the market or in a merchant's warehouse. These girls are rarely comely, often marked by a pox or a wound, and they are generally insolent and loud. Often, women I know to be much younger than thirty, seem to me ancient crones—already worn out by work and illness and the strain of trying to feed their many children in difficult times.

Of course, I am aware also of the existence of other, more virtuous girls, such as the daughters of Santino, my barber. These girls are kept apart, far from the risks and temptations of the street. They are, I am certain, occasionally attractive, sometimes able to read and write and often companionable. The problem is, the first time I would truly meet such a girl would be at our betrothal—and this is a step too far for me to contemplate. Especially with no mother or married sister to select someone compatible with my interests.

I am adrift between two worlds existing alongside one another but passing through each other with little or no meaningful contact. My position with Dimmi, my small inheritance, my education at the feet of a genius and, I may confide to this journal, my pride, all create an invisible barrier between my everyday society and myself. Yet the unbreakable rules of our heritage establish an equally unbridgeable chasm between me and the world to which I aspire.

And then there is the matter of Chiara. Am I doomed forever to compare unfavourably every other woman to the one

I have loved for so long? Would a marriage in such circumstances be fair?

Media

At two o'clock on Thursday afternoon, the university media affairs officer called the press conference to order. It had been agreed that the first question would go to the arts correspondent of *The Times*.

"Can you tell us, Ms Tonelli, exactly how you found the diaries, and how you felt at that moment?"

Lauren handled that one easily, and the follow-up questions: 'When did you realise how important the diary was? Why did you quit your PhD? How did the Earl react when you told him about the Paolo Chronicles?'

Then Lauren invited the London correspondent of *Corriere della Sera* to ask a question.

"Ms Tonelli, what opinion have you formed of Leonardo da Vinci from reading the diary?"

In colloquial Italian carrying a hint of an Umbrian accent, Lauren answered him.

"Leonardo da Vinci è stato uno degli uomini più grandi mai vissuti. Ma questo lo sapevamo. Quello che i diari rivelano è un essere umano ancora più grande; uno saggio, premuroso, generoso e leale - in effetti molto simile agli italiani di oggi."

The Italian beamed, while the English reporters looked on, mystified.

Lauren decided to put them out of their misery.

"Signor Verdi's question was very interesting. My answer was that Leonardo da Vinci was one of the greatest people who has ever lived. But we knew that. What the diaries reveal, is an even greater human being; one who is wise, considerate, generous, loyal–in fact, much like Italians today."

The press conference continued in a similar vein. Several questions were given to Italian reporters and each time Lauren replied in flawless Italian. There was also a journalist from *El País* and Lauren answered her question in Spanish. By the end, she had won over almost everyone, with the notable exception of the specialist art media, which continued to pepper her with aggressive and sceptical questions.

The final questioner was also hard to deal with, but for a different reason. She represented Reuters.

"Do the diaries provide any information regarding Leonardo's sexual orientation?"

Before Lauren could answer, Professor Hunter intervened. "We are not prepared to release any detailed information about the contents of the Chronicles at this time. As you will see from the press release, we have clear plans to publish all of the diary in due course."

* * *

Jonathan watched the press conference from the back of the room. When everyone had left, he found Lauren talking with Professor Hunter. After a few minutes, Lauren detached herself and came over to him.

"You were great!" Jonathan enthused, "there was nothing to worry about. Honestly, you came over completely confident and composed. And I didn't know you spoke Spanish."

"Robert's idea about using my Italian worked well, and the rehearsal covered quite a few of the questions. So, thank you. And I was raised in California, remember. My best friend in high school was a Latina. So yes, I speak Spanish. Some French too."

"Very impressive. Listen, is there somewhere we can talk for a second, and can you bring your laptop?"

They found an empty classroom and Jonathan explained.

"If I could read a few sections of the diary again, I have an idea I'd like to research."

"What idea is that?"

"Can I be all mysterious? I promise, I'll tell you as soon as I've checked it out."

1510 - Milan

February 8th

A Ser Lenzi visited our studio today for the express purpose of inviting Maestro to his home. It happened that I was the one to greet him and we conversed while we awaited Dimmi.

"So, Signor del Rosso, do you enjoy living here in our city of Milan? Is it more convenient to you than Florence?"

"Well, Messere, I am certain that Maestro Leonardo is more content here in Milan, so that, of course, has a considerable impact on my own feelings. Milan has been welcoming to us, I can have no complaint. But I am sure you will agree there is something about a man's home city always drawing him back. Republics are untidy, fractious and ill-mannered but, I confess, there are days when I yearn to be back in Florence."

We spent a pleasant period debating the merits of a republic until the barking of the dogs announced Dimmi's arrival. I made the appropriate introductions, then Messer Lenzi came directly to the purpose of his visit.

"Maestro Leonardo, I have been travelling in the north for these past two years, which explains why it is only now I come to extend an invitation to visit my home. I believe you know Maestro Bramante, sadly now departed from Milan for many years? He and I are in correspondence and he assures me you might enjoy hearing something of artistic developments in the Spanish territories in the north. In particular, I have returned with some works by an intriguing painter with a strange name, Hieronymus Bosch. You might find them interesting."

Messer Lenzi did not know that it took little to persuade Dimmi to accept an invitation—Maestro is a naturally convivial man, if intolerant of those he considers fools.

"I am sure it would be a pleasure to see works by an artist new to me. Thank you, Messere."

"And Signor del Rosso, you too must join us. I have much enjoyed exchanging views with you."

This is the first time in my life such an invitation has been extended to me by a man of the standing of Messer Lenzi. I am as delighted as I am surprised.

Dimmi was amused. "Why so surprised, Paolo? People here in Milan did not meet you as a smooth-cheeked youth. They encountered you as man, a man with talents and, I may say, a reputation for steadiness, wisdom and diligence. It is not so strange that Messer Lenzi would enjoy your company, as do I."

As I write these words, I experience anew the pleasure and, yes, pride I felt at this estimation of my character from one I admire so much. I confess I have long been aware that Maestro has developed a trust in my ability to perform my *tasks with efficiency and discretion. But I have not, and still cannot, think of our relationship as one with a degree of friendship. Perhaps I am wrong.*

February 12th

*T*his has been one of the most unusual and enjoyable evenings of my life. Where to begin?

The palazzo of the Lenzi family is most impressive. On our arrival at the twentieth hour, Maestro and I were met by Messer Lenzi himself and conducted on a brief tour of the main salon and gallery in order to see his collection of paintings and sculptures. There was much of interest, but Messer Lenzi was most urgent that we should see his new purchases, so we proceeded swiftly to a small room off the salon where he had hung his two new painted panels and where he had laid out on a handsome table, several sketches by the same artist.

My limited skills of description are wholly inadequate to describe the strange worlds portrayed in the works. Tables sprouted human legs and arms. Beakers had faces. Devils tortured sinners in ways at once gruesome and obscene, and these are but a tiny fraction of the mysterious creatures and shocking dramas portrayed.

After ten minutes of study, Messer Lenzi asked Dimmi, "Well, Maestro, what think you of this artist?"

Dimmi spoke slowly, clearly still considering his own reaction.

"He is proficient, inventive certainly. I cannot decide if his creations represent visions or nightmares."

"Visions certainly, I believe."

I spun around as a new voice interrupted Dimmi.

The speaker was a comely young girl who was now standing behind us, in the company of an older lady.

"Ah, gentlemen, may I present my opinionated daughter, Caterina, and my wife, Petruccia?"

As the introductions were being made, several things quickly became obvious to me. Caterina and her parents demonstrated an ease and deep affection with each other not always apparent in families, particularly concerning daughters. And although the mutual affection between the three was readily apparent, there was absolutely no deference shown by Caterina to either of her parents. Strangely, this did not reveal itself as disrespect or haughtiness, but rather as a confidence nurtured and encouraged by her mother and father.

As the evening progressed, I would come to realise that Messer and Mona Lenzi have highly unusual beliefs regarding the role of women, holding that females should have the same rights and freedoms as those accorded to their sons and brothers. For now, Dimmi brought the conversation back to the strange artist and Caterina's expressed opinion.

"Why imaginings and not nightmares, signora?"

"We wish to see them as dreams and nightmares because we cannot imagine deliberately conceiving and then portraying

221

these images. That is because our imaginations are limited by the teaching of our priests. The Holy Book gives us scant descriptions of angels or of devils, and yet every painting in every church has exactly the same depiction of these supernatural beings. Maestro Bosch has chosen freedom, freedom to imagine his own demons."

The conversation continued as Ser Lenzi gently guided us to the dining table, where other guests were already seated and engaged in active conversations.

Two of the guests were known to me, wealthy patrons of artists in Milan. Both men were accompanied by their wives, as was one of the strangers, a tutor to a noble family as I soon discovered. The final guest was Dottor Theodorus Apostolius, a professor of Greek, visiting from Rome.

Messer Lenzi rapped his knife on the table to draw everyone's attention and then generously introduced everyone at the table. I was the last person to be named, and at the conclusion of the introductions, Ser Lenzi continued,

"When I met Signor del Rosso last week, he communicated his opinion that, with all of its imperfections, a Republic is the preferred system of government. Dottor Apostolius, what is your view on this subject?"

Dottor Apostolius, it emerged, agreed with my own opinion, although with far more robust and learned arguments than I would have been able to summon. Dimmi, as expected, disagreed, as did Mona Lenzi and the tutor,

Signor Marchi. I found myself strangely pleased when Caterina joined my side of the debate.

In this manner the evening unfolded. When a topic was exhausted, or became overly heated, Messer Lenzi would call for attention and reveal an opinion previously expressed by a politician or friend or one of his guests—on the role of artists, the relative beauty of antique sculptures compared with the modern, the idea of a just war. Other than these initiating observations, Messer Lenzi said little except to draw a quiet guest into the conversation, generally myself or one of the wives. It was a display of considerable skill and wonderful generosity of spirit and I committed myself to learn from his example.

Although Ser Lenzi was reluctant to express his own views, the same could not be said of his daughter. Caterina participated fully in every debate. She was never harsh or loud, but always firm and confident. Her views were well-informed and elegantly expressed, with quotations from ancient and recent writers. Although she was most complimentary about Dimmi, frankly expressing her delight at finally meeting one she had heard so much about, she was unafraid to disagree with him. I could not but be impressed.

Towards the end of the evening, I caught the eye of Messer Lenzi and gave him a small nod of appreciation. In turn he raised his glass to me in a most friendly gesture. I was suddenly aware of the setting. Our host and two of his guests were extremely wealthy men, one indeed was a Visconti cousin. Meanwhile Dimmi, while of low birth, was one of the most eminent men in the Florentine Republic, and a close confidante of the King himself.[1] In contrast, the tutor and his wife, although honest people, were, by their vestments, clearly of limited means. And I of course, am a mere assistant.

I realised that Dottor Apostolius was the key to understanding the nature of the company. He was interested in everything we discussed, and his experience and great learning made him fascinating to all of us. Everyone, wives included, had an opinion to share, a story to contribute, and no one stood on their exalted position to demand greater respect or deference.

Messer Lenzi chooses his guests by the extent of their interests, not the extent of their fortunes.

And now I sit at my desk, attempting to arrange my thoughts for this journal.

The evening ended only because we had to obey the curfew. As we took our leave, Caterina shook my hand and spoke to me most easily.

"You must call on us again soon, Signor del Rosso, and I will show you the other works in my father's collection."

She said this as one might address a sibling. She was friendly but somehow managed not to seem improper, although on any other lips, her words would have seemed

---

[1] *King Francis I of France had deposed the ruling Sforza family and at this time controlled the Duchy of Milan.*

scandalously forward and inappropriate, given my sex and the chasm between our positions.

As we hurried homewards, Dimmi teased me. "The remarkable Caterina has her eye on you, Paolo!"

I protested, but I was, in truth, pleasantly discomfited.

But what will I do? Will I do anything to seek a friendship with Caterina? My confusion is in many parts. I have never had a conversation with a wealthy young woman before. My limited contacts have been among the daughters of the traders and merchants with whom I have dealings on behalf of Dimmi—and these could in no way be described as conversations, certainly not akin to the exchanges this evening.

The only female with whom I had enjoyed any true closeness is Chiara. And this, of course, is the other source of my confusion.

I am no longer the naive boy first enraptured by Chiara. And yet.

Despite the passage of the years, I still feel intense emotions whenever I think of her, which is daily. Her image is before me every morning and night. Two images in fact, the beautiful study made by Dimmi, and my own effort which, although laughably juvenile, brings back to me most vividly, the hours I spent that magical day, having been granted permission, so to say, to focus intently on the object of my love. And Chiara is most unhappy with her condition.

I must to bed.

February 18th

I visited Caterina today. I could say I finally resolved my confusion and decided to act. I could say so, but it would be a lie. The sad truth is, Dimmi bullied me.

"A charming, intelligent, spirited and rich young woman invited you to visit her. What in the name of all the saints are you waiting for? Go! Send the boy with a card that you will call this afternoon. Do it—or present yourself at the monastery and take vows."

March 10th

Today I was once again a guest in the Lenzi home. I have become remarkably comfortable with the family, remarkably quickly. On each occasion I am made most welcome and today I had the feeling of not being a guest so much as an intimate of the family.

March 19th

"Tell me more of Maestro Leonardo's scientific investigations."

Caterina and I were sitting in the shade in the courtyard of her house.

"His curiosity is boundless…"

I expounded for some length on Dimmi's various fields of particular interest and we talked of these for a while, until Caterina changed the subject.

"Has he never been married?"

By now I was familiar with Caterina's habit of asking direct questions, even those normally avoided out of a polite reticence.

"No, never. He seems rather uninterested. No, that is not true, he has several close female friends, but all are safely married."

"Safely?"

"Well, in the sense that there is no doubt as to the nature of their friendship."

"And what about you, Paolo? Why are you not yet wed? Uninterested?"

She said this with a friendly smile. I was being teased.

"I refuse to answer such an impertinent question from a sixteen-year-old girl who is also, I might point out, unbetrothed."

I suddenly thought I had stumbled. "Forgive me, Caterina, that was unwarranted. You may be betrothed, I should not have presumed."

She laughed, "Do not apologise, you are quite right, I am not yet promised to anyone. No one rich enough has come along to whom I am passionately attracted."

"So, he must be rich and attractive?" I teased in my turn.

But Caterina was completely serious in her response.

"Extremely rich, tolerably attractive and remarkably intelligent. If only you were rich, perhaps I would set my sights on you, Paolo."

This was such an astonishing thing to say that I could make no response. However, my hesitation was not remarked upon, as Caterina expanded on her answer.

"You will not know that my parents had a son. He was two years older than me, but he died when he was only twelve, of the plague. I resolved immediately that I would become their son and take responsibility for our family's continuation. My husband must join my name to his—our firstborn son will be Pietro Something-Lenzi. Pietro was my brother. We will marry our fortunes and we shall found a dynasty, so we must be fabulously rich. My son and his children will be as renowned as your Donati, Rucellai or Strozzi families in Florence."

Stunned, I sought a simple response.

"Why not powerful like the Sforzas or Medicis?"

"No, no, no. Politics is transitory, even if it does not seem so. And politics inevitably breeds violence and death. Only great wealth persists, if used wisely. And we will be wise, my husband and I. We will have houses and properties, discreet and well-tended. My family's name shall be immortal," Caterina finished fiercely.

I walked home in a daze. Such vision and determination, and from one so young. I am humbled. What is my vision for the future?

As to my emotions? I was flattered, just as I had been to receive her father's invitation, just as I am to be accepted into the family's circle. I will go back to the Lenzi palazzo, I will accept the invitation of Mona Lenzi to dine with the family next week.

More Pages

Lauren was rapidly running out of diary. In a few days she would have translated everything they had.

She told Jonathan in a phone call. He tried to be sympathetic.

"Maybe that's just it, he stopped. I mean, we've all done it, right? We start a diary and after a few weeks it tapers off, it's human nature."

"You know, it's strange. At a first glance you seem fairly intelligent. For Pete's sake, Jonathan! Paolo's been keeping this diary religiously for almost seventeen years. And no sign of ill health, or boredom, or…or anything. He didn't just stop! I hope nothing happened to him."

Jonathan backtracked. "Of course, you're right. I suppose the next step is to make sure there are no more pages in the house, maybe filed somewhere else."

"Ready to tell me what you're up to yet?"

"Nearly. I'll come up in a day or two and fill you in."

* * *

Lauren decided that a systematic approach was called for.

Penny had caught up with her imaging work and was recruited to join the search party. With Professor Hunter's help, four undergraduate students were dragooned into the team. Lauren announced that it was her intention to bring some serious organisation to the task.

"We'll be in three teams of two. Each team will take a floor in the main building. We need to examine every cupboard, every cabinet and drawer, every conceivable hiding place. We have the Earl's permission to look everywhere except the private quarters on the first floor of the east wing, which he is investigating right now. You've all seen what the diary pages look like. That's what we're after, more like that."

Lauren had assigned herself the top floor, a warren of tiny former staff bedrooms, utility rooms and storerooms. She and the only male student began to work systematically through the space.

It was Penny who made the crucial discovery on the second afternoon, on the first floor. As soon as she unlocked and entered the small dressing room, she was drawn to a chest of drawers in the far corner. She opened the top drawer to find it full of candles. The next drawer was also used to store candles, this time small tea lights. She noticed faded newspapers had been used to line the drawers. When she opened the third drawer, it was empty, and she could see the banner of a copy of the *Oxford Times* from 1896.

'My God,' she thought, *'this drawer was lined well over a century ago!'*

She considered the implications of this, the sense of continuity the family must have. She lifted up the paper to read what had been the news of the day 120-odd years previously. Instantly she saw that, under the old newspaper, the drawer had already been lined.

"Here, in here!" she called.

In the four drawers of the cabinet, they found nearly fifty diary pages. They had been laid in the drawers, fortunately overlapping, rather than cut to fit. The old newspapers had protected the sheets from damage except in one corner of the bottom where candlewax had somehow melted then flowed through the newsprint to form a thick square of congealed wax. The wax had stuck the newspaper and two diary pages to the bottom of the drawer.

The young man who had been teamed with Lauren offered a solution to the problem of extracting the sheets without causing any damage.

"I remember my mother cleaning up wax that had dripped onto the dining table. She used a hairdryer to soften it."

Lauren ran to her bedroom and returned with her dryer and an extension cord. Penny had removed the drawer and laid it upside down on the floor. After a few minutes of gentle warming of the drawer bottom, the wax softened enough to easily release the papers from its grasp. One more minute of heat applied to the newspaper and the two diary pages were safely detached and separated. All that remained was a greasy stain which would be left to the experts to tackle.

Penny's success spurred everyone on in the hunt for more pages. When all three teams announced an end to their search, without finding any more Chronicle papers, Lauren mixed the teams up and sent everyone back to searching once more, with everyone now on a different floor.

Remarkably, it was Penny who again made what turned out to be the final find in the rambling old house, this time in the library.

"I can't believe you guys missed it," she said, archly. "We only had to open about 300 books to find these pages. They were in this volume here. Take a look, it's fantastic. Someone before us read this diary, at least these pages."

The book was an English translation of 'A Treatise on Painting' by Leonardo himself. They converted the publication date, MDCCXXI, to 1721.

"So, someone in the family, maybe 200 or 300 years ago, was reading the diary and looked up a reference in this book. Then they slipped the pages in here, where, it seems, they've been hiding ever since."

"Well done, Penny, you're a star."

Lauren looked around the huge room. "I wonder what else might be hiding in here?"

1515/6 - Rome

July 14th

The heat in Rome is the work of the devil. There is dust everywhere—and the smells! I hate the south. The climate is unbearable, the people are savages, the food atrocious and Michelangelo's works are everywhere—most aggravating to my master. The city is a stinking cesspit of beggars and thieves, so much so that we must employ guards when we go about, to protect us from the constant threat of violence. With no one responsible for anything beyond the confines of the churches, abbeys, nunneries and monasteries, the streets are full of waste of all kinds and therefore also with dogs, rats and swine rooting about in the unholy mess. Why anyone would choose to live here is a complete mystery to me.

I do not believe Dimmi means ever to return to Florence. I am certain he has lost whatever love he may once have held for the city. In any event, with the return of the Medici, the political climate is not convenient.

That we are guests of the Duke signifies that Dimmi has no problems with the members of the Medici family themselves. However, many of their supporters are against him, not least Francesco del Giocondo, who, we hear, is restored to even greater power and influence. Fortunately, we *are housed in a villa owned by the Duke, on a small hill on the outskirts of this pestilential city.* [1]

Maestro has always been more comfortable with princes than republics. When we were alone after a meeting with the Duke, I asked Dimmi to elaborate on his preference.

"They are more lavish with their commissions, more flamboyant with their spectacles and there is only one mind to please," was his reply.

"But they are capricious, there is no constraint on their whims, no matter how cruel or unreasonable they may be."

"But they decide. A prince will answer 'yes' or 'no'. A council will debate, consider, postpone, reconsider, endlessly. All the while we wait. We wait, we spend our money and we wait some more."

"But so much of what princes desire is fleeting—pageants and spectacles to distract the populace and increase their own glory."

Indeed, the design of spectacular events occupies more and more of Maestro's time. He enjoys these commissions, although I fear they add nothing to his legacy, leaving as they do, no trace of the cleverness and originality that my master

---

[1] *Giuliano de'Medici, Duke of Nemours, had become the latest patron of Leonardo. The changed political situation in Milan had become threatening to Leonardo and so he left for Rome, where Giuliano provided him with a house.*

brings to these occasions. It was an error of mine to raise this point. Dimmi responded most sharply.

"You disappoint me, Paolo. These commissions that you despise and so readily dismiss, furnish much-needed silver to our household."

I sensed his disapproval, but the fact was, these distractions had long weighed on my mind.

"Yes, master, but they leave no trace. In the years and centuries to come, no one will look on these spectacles and be amazed. No one will look on them at all. They contribute nothing to your legacy. I hate them for this."

Dimmi paused and indicated that I should sit down. We had been standing at the table, looking at the plans for yet another procession.

He sat beside me and held my gaze.

"I thought you understood, Paolo. These works—the fêtes, parades, circuses, are as nothing. Diversions yes, a fleeting pleasure on occasion. And the portraits and altarpieces and murals—the same. They are nothing but a means of providing money. I have some facility and so I sell my skills. But what is important, what will be my legacy as you call it, are my studies. I would see every panel, every canvas go up in flames before I would lose even the slightest of my notebooks.

"Consider Rome, I mean the ancient Rome of Caesar and Cicero—better still, consider Athens. What is its legacy? A few hints of painted walls. Nothing of their portraits or landscapes, and yet they must surely have existed. What of their music? Nothing. And their buildings? Ruins.

Impressive, evocative, inspiring even—but ruins nonetheless. Yes, some little sculpture has survived undamaged, but carving in stone has never held much appeal for me, as well you know. And anyway, how many of the ancient sculptors can you name?

"No, Paolo, the true legacy of the ancients is in their writings. The dramas of Sophocles, the poetry of Virgil, the histories of Herodotus, the mathematics of Euclid, the wisdom of Plato—these are what we inherited to our great benefit. And these are the names we recall with honour."

He sat back in his chair as he finished more serenely. "When we accumulate enough wealth, we will settle somewhere quiet, you and I, and dedicate ourselves to a synthesis of my investigations. And if I do not complete the task, this will be your mission when I am gone, to complete the work. This is the true purpose of your training."

You may imagine my amazement at this exposition. I had no inkling of the truth of these matters. But as Dimmi spoke, much that had been a mystery became clear. Not simply his preference for the court of Milan, but his readiness to endure endless trouble by failing to complete his commissions, his enthusiasm for wandering around the countryside, his insistence on me accompanying him on these treks and to his dissections.

These are matters I must ponder at length. Is this to be my life? Am I content with this prospect? I thought of Caterina. Would she accept such a fate? But then, I was not blessed with a wealthy father. And in truth, as the years have

237

passed, so I have spent more and more time in the company of Dimmi, as the two of us wander the countryside, now with two or three guards for company—and they walking out of earshot. These sojourns have opened my mind to the astonishing breadth of his knowledge, most of it gained from his own studies, rather than from the writings of others. I have long since ceased to be surprised when he grabs my arm and pulls me to his table to show me yet another ingenuous device for fording rivers, a study of the properties of light in various seasons or his musings on the working of some inner pert of the body. Is there not honour in helping to organise this treasure trove of wisdom for future generations? I alter my opinion from one day to another.

In any event, Dimmi's aversion to Florence means that I am kept far from Chiara. Perhaps it is for the best. To see her every day may become too great a torment.

And now the Duke wants a painting, meaning still more time must pass before we escape to a more congenial location. It seems the Duke has a mistress. Well of course he has a mistress. To our certain knowledge he has at the moment at least three. This one, however, is even more indelicate than most. Under threats of dire torture, we have been sworn to secrecy.

The mistress in question, whom the Duke wishes to see immortalised by Dimmi, is none other than Sister Camilla Gherardini. When I write Sister, I mean Sister, not sister, although she is indeed, sister to Mona Lisa del Giocondo, née Gherardini. As Suor Beatrice, the sister resides as a nun in the convent of San Domenico near Florence. During the Duke's regular visits to the city, they manage to conduct their affair.

The Duke came to see my master this afternoon.

"Maestro, I understand you will be invited to accompany my brother, His Holiness, to Bologna and Florence. This will give you the perfect opportunity to meet Camilla and sketch her for your portrait, which I am certain will be a triumph!"

My master chose not to mention that he had already painted a member of the Gherardini family, no doubt because the subsequent history of his relationship with Camilla's brother-in-law had been so troubled. His Excellency the Duke is young and, if I may write freely, he is not over-burdened by knowledge. Nevertheless, even the Duke sensed Dimmi's reluctance, but he misunderstood the reason.

"Have no fear, Maestro. You will be under the protection of the Holy Father, and we will ensure the Medici family in Florence guarantee the good behaviour of their supporters."

"Excellency, some years ago, I painted a pair of wedding portraits for my goddaughter. For a number of reasons, I have painted little in oils since. It has been many years since I used my skills. So, although I accept your commission in thanks for the many kindnesses you have shown us, I must warn you, you may be disappointed."

Despite his little speech, as soon as the Duke had left us, Dimmi turned to me with a gleeful smile.

239

"This is an easy commission, Paolo, the kind I like—little effort to distract me from my projects. When we visit Florence, you will go to my uncle's old farmhouse where we stored everything and find a copy of the painting of Mona Lisa del Giocondo. I recall Bartolomeo produced quite a good version as a challenge. Let us hope the mice have not found it! In truth, I never liked Agostino's background to that painting. I will create a new backdrop, which will be much more interesting. I also regret my decision about those pillars. When the painting is framed, they clash with the frame itself. I should have anticipated that. Now I can correct the error. And let us hope the chased Sister is not too unlike in appearance to her chaste sister."

Dimmi does like his terrible jokes.

Thinking of the Duke and his mistresses takes my mind to Chiara's sister, Pacifica. As Chiara feared, her young sister did indeed become mistress to the Duke. Indeed, she bore him his only son, after which, from all we have heard, she had been dismissed from his court. I resolved to find her if she remains in Rome.

July 18th

Today I saw Maestro Michelangelo's Pietà. Twice. It is truly an extraordinary sculpture. No man may stand before it and not be moved by the tragedy experienced by Our Saviour's mother. The epic drama that *is the sacrifice of the Son of God is made human as the unbearable grief of a mother coming to terms with the cruel death of her son for the salvation of mankind.*

It is hard to believe Maestro Michelangelo was only twenty-four when he created this work of towering genius. I returned an hour after my initial visit, this time to understand how the artist had achieved his illusion. Illusion because, upon reflection, it would be impossible for a mother to tenderly embrace the body of her adult son. After a while I realised what Maestro Michelangelo had done to achieve his effect. Genius indeed.

September 2nd

Today I sat with Pacifica, having discovered her whereabouts from a handmaiden in the Duke's court, a pleasant widow with whom I have dallied a few times. Three days ago, the widow mentioned her friendship with the Duke's former mistress, and I had her tell me where I could find her.

Pacifica lives in a tiny house on the edge of the city. She is thinner than before and, although still beautiful, the outlines of her features are sharper, harsher. It took a moment for her to recognise me, after all, she has seen me but once since she was a child.

"Of course, the friend of my sainted sister, now I recall. Are you here on her behalf?"

"No, I have seen Chiara only rarely these past years. I am here on my own account to understand if you are well, if there is any service I may offer."

She looked at me strangely and waved to the only other seat in the mean room.

"Forgive me, Signor del Rosso, I receive visitors rarely. I have forgotten my manners. I recall you were in the service of Maestro Leonardo, are you still in this position?"

"Please, we are almost contemporaries and have been, let us say, connected, for many years. I would be happy if you called me Paolo. And yes, I am still in the household of Maestro Leonardo. We have been some time in Rome. Pacifica, may I speak freely? I have known you distantly for many years, and your sister is particularly dear to me."

"I fear you are about to impart bad news."

"No, no news at all. But I know of your child, I know you are no longer received at Court, and I know your child is not with you. For friendship's sake, I would like to understand your situation, if that is your wish. I have no power or influence, but Maestro Leonardo does enjoy access to the Court and the Duke, and he too would offer his help I know, if only for the sake of his goddaughter, whom he loves."

"I am touched by your concern, Paolo, truly I am. I have not enjoyed much concern these past years. If any man appears at my door, it is generally for a different purpose. Fortunately, I have neighbours who are quick to come to my aid.

"My situation, as you call it, is that I am here. My life is frozen in the absence of my son. He is taken from me and I am forbidden contact with him. But still, there are kindly women: nurses, maids and the like, who bring me news and alert me if my son is to travel abroad in the city with his father or uncle. I have seen him six times now. Briefly, of course, in a carriage or, once, on foot. I have not contacted him or spoken to him, but I have seen him."

"And you will not leave this accursed city to make a life elsewhere?"

"As long as my son is here, so I shall remain."

I thought for a while before speaking again.

"Once again I will be impolite. May I ask how you live?"

"As you can see, my needs are few. My sister sends me a little silver every quarter day and, if you can believe it, the wife of the Duke took pity and arranges a small allowance. It is not much, but taken together, it suffices."

"You fill me with sadness. You are young. You are, I will say it this time, you are beautiful. You could have many more children. Your son is kept from you, yes, but he is a Medici now. He will grow to wealth and power and when he is of an age, he will discover you himself and will not be denied access to his mother. Why not spend the years until that happy day seeking some joy for yourself?"

"I see now why my sister holds you in such high regard. Your words are, I know, spoken from kindness, and I thank you for them. But I fear you cannot fully understand the heart of a mother. My son is everything to me. If I leave this city,

I fear I shall never see him again. As for other children, I have no heart for it. I loved the Duke and, cruel though he has been to me, I love him yet. I wonder if perhaps you may not be one who can understand my feelings?"

We talked some more, but she would not be altered in her determination. We parted as friends and I implored her to send for me if the need should arise. I promised that Dimmi would petition the Duke to allow Pacifica some access to her son, even if only occasionally.[1]

January 5ᵗʰ 1516

uke Giuliano's commission was started today. I had accompanied Dimmi on his trip with the Pope, but while he sketched Sister Camilla, I went to play with Leo and Chiara. I never did see the lady.

However, as this chronicle did attest, I did find a copy of the Mona Lisa del Giocondo portrait, the copy by Count, judging by the fine beadwork represented on the lady's dress.

---

[1] *Duke Giuliano died young and his brother, Pope Leo X, raised his illegitimate son by Pacifica, Ippolito. Ippolito's cousin became Pope Clement VII and made the teenage Ippolito nominal ruler of Florence and, aged 18, a cardinal. He died, aged 24, possibly murdered on the orders of the following Pope or of his cousin and rival, Alessandro, who succeeded him as Lord of Florence.*

This morning, Maestro spoke, while looking pensively at Mona Lisa's image.

"Thankfully, Camilla is remarkably like her older sister. She is a little heavier now, which is excellent, it is easier for me to make the face fuller than to make it smaller. But truly, there is little to be done. I am tempted to put her into a nun's habit, but Duke Giuliano has been kind, so we'll leave her in Mona Lisa's vestments."

Dimmi sat down heavily.

"Oh, I am glad there is little to be done. My arm is worse, the travelling has aggravated it. I am finished with painting, certainly with large pieces." [1]

It is a strange thing, that he, who is the greatest painter of his age, has lost all interest in his art. His time now is taken up with his studies, for reasons I now comprehend, following our conversation some months ago. We tramp the fields and woods, spying the birds and animals. I cannot tell you how many hours, no days, we spend observing water. Yes, water. In streams, in pools, in falls. All the time, Dimmi is sketching and talking. 'Look, Paolo, see how it eddies and flows. Regard the way it accommodates that rock there, constantly testing it, finding ways to pass! And see, there is a fish under there—we cannot see it, but we detect the fish

---

[1] *It is generally believed that Leonardo had an accident, or possibly a minor stroke, around this time, although there is no explicit mention of this is the diaries.*

from the altered patterns on the surface of the water. Why do you suppose most fallen branches float, while a few sink? Dimmi!'

March 18th

Disaster!

Duke Giuliano is dead—without taking delivery of his painting and so, of course, without paying for it. No one else will want it. The nun has little money and the Duke's wife…well. Perhaps we can re-use it somehow.

Still, that little smile of hers is charming. A nun's secret indeed!

The good news is now there is nothing to stop us from going to France. Thanks be to God and St Zenobius. I still pray to the saint even though we no longer reside in his city. I do not imagine immortal saints are bound to earthly locations.

Image 10: The Louvre Mona Lisa.

According to the Paolo Chronicles, this is the portrait of Camilla Gherardini, sister of Mona Lisa and mentioned in de Beatis' journal, "one of a certain Florentine woman, done from life, at the instance of the late Magnificent Giuliano de Medici…"
(Louvre, Paris)

Promotion

Lauren was in the library at Blythswood House with the Earl and Professor Hunter.

"We've searched everywhere. I think we've found all the pages we're going to find."

The Professor nodded.

"You've done incredibly well, it's an immensely significant manuscript, the longest continuous diary from the period that's ever been found, not to mention the special role of the author. And the candid way he writes."

William Chance spoke up to agree with Lauren's assessment.

"We've thoroughly checked all of the outbuildings, there's nowhere left to look. How long will you need for your first pass through what's left, Lauren?"

"Not long, around a week or so. I should have my completed summary to you, Professor, within two weeks."

"Excellent! Which brings me nicely onto why I'm here this morning. I've received word that the funding for the research team has been approved. I've already spoken to all the prospective members and I plan to kick off with a two-day seminar at the end of next month, in the Library. That will introduce everyone, and we can set goals and responsibilities."

Professor Hunter smiled at Lauren and continued, "Well, I've talked with everyone except one person. Lauren, I'd like to formally offer you a position on the Paolo Chronicles Multidisciplinary Research Group and

I'd like you to give the opening presentation at the seminar. Here is the list of the other members."

Lauren took the sheet of paper from the Professor and ran her eyes down the list of names.

Professor Thomas Armstrong, M.A., DPhil, Professor of the History of Art, University of Oxford

Doctor Ursula Brownstone, B.A., PhD, Senior Researcher in Renaissance Studies, Harvard University'

And so it went on. All fifteen individuals were renowned scholars in art history, Renaissance studies, the history of science, or some other related field. Lauren recognised several of the names from books she had read or indeed been assigned as an undergraduate. She wasn't altogether confident at the prospect of addressing this group.

"Professor, are you sure I–"

Before she had finished her sentence, Jane Hunter interrupted.

With her expression even more animated than usual, she chopped the air for emphasis as she spoke, "I am absolutely certain you will prosper as a member of this group–as a *leading* member of this group. *You* found the papers, *you* fought to keep hold of them and *you've* been doing a sterling job summarising them so far, and in finding more of the manuscript. And I refuse to permit you to be intimidated by any of these people, do you understand? Mark my words, some of them will certainly try to intimidate you, just as they do with everyone they encounter, especially if they are young or female, and most especially, if they are both. Every time one of this lot says to you, *'if you refer to my last book on the subject'* or *'in my keynote address at the Princeton colloquium'*, trust me, they are out to impress and intimidate. Do *not* let them. This is *your* project and you have the complete confidence and support of William and myself, and we have the only two votes that count!"

Despite herself, Lauren laughed at this.

"OK, OK! Thank you, Professor, thank you very much. I won't let you down. What would you like me to address in my presentation?"

"I want you to set the tone and the context. The members of the group will naturally view the Chronicle through the prism of their own specialism. Before that happens, I want you to bring to life the person who wrote these diaries. Who was he? What was he like? How did he think? How should the team interpret the material through Paolo's eyes? When they read the diary, I want them to hear Paolo's voice, to see the entire forest before they get entangled among the trees."

"No pressure then?" Lauren replied with a smile.

"I didn't say it would be easy, only that you'll do a great job. And one more thing. I read the notes you sent me about the Rome entries. We must be careful about how we handle information from the diary from now on–this is explosive material. Anything that touches on the *Mona Lisa* will be extremely controversial."

Lauren went to the kitchen for lunch as usual. Although she tried to join in the conversations, she found her thoughts drifting away. Although Professor Hunter had previously hinted at her possible involvement, to actually be appointed to the research team was incredible, exciting, thrilling. To be recognised in this way was amazing–even if a bit intimidating. She had to share the moment with someone. As soon as she finished eating what little food she could stomach, she retreated to her study. It was too early to telephone Helen in Pasadena. She called Jonathan.

"That's fantastic! Congratulations, you must be thrilled. I know you found the diary, but Professor Hunter must have confidence that you've got a lot to contribute. We have to celebrate. Shall I come to Blythswood, or would you like to come up to London?"

"William and I are going to London the day after tomorrow, in the morning. William is meeting someone for lunch, but if you're free, maybe we could have lunch somewhere nice? And I want to hear what you've been keeping so secret!"

1521/22

March 27th

H ome at last!

So many delays in getting away from France. The King was deeply upset by Maestro's death. I sensed he wished to keep me close until he was certain he had extracted every smallest scrap of memory I have of my late and well-beloved master.

The incomparable Maestro Leonardo da Vinci, surely the greatest man who has ever lived. The breadth of his talents, the skill of his hands, whether drawing, painting or making music. And yet, an enigmatic man in many ways— kind, thoughtful, gracious. Quick to make friends and to enjoy their company. But with all that, lonely, I think. And a man who remembered every insult and who sought to repay it, even years later.

In our world, where connections are everything, he was denied so much. No distinguished family to support him, no neighbourhood bonds, no lofty position in a powerful guild. Even his city, Florence, held little claim on his affection. He fought always alone: for safety, for sponsors, for recognition. He once told me that it was absolutely necessary to avoid entanglements of friendship with others as this would necessarily steal time and energy from his projects. He was *happy to have acquaintances, but never true friendships. I believe Chiara and those of us in his studio were, in truth, his real family, and we looked to him for protection, not vice versa. Only in these past few years did he finally find his perfect patron in cultured King Francis. At last Maestro had freedom, security and scope for his visions.*

In our final interview, the King bade me sit beside his mistress, Comtesse de Foix, a charming and cultured lady who had been friendly with my master.

"Signor del Rosso, I have asked you many questions concerning Maestro Leonardo. But, in deference to your loss, I have avoided one issue. Before you leave us, and if you feel able, can you tell us of your final conversation with your late master?"

"It would be my honour, sire, for it includes something of the divine."

I paused to collect my thoughts. When you talk to a King, it behoves you to speak clearly.

"As you know, sire, the maestro knew he was dying. We talked of our memories—of the day I arrived in his service when but fourteen years of age. We smiled at the recollection of some of our former colleagues, of the oft-times insane desires of our clients. To be sure, matters of no real consequence, but the mortar of our shared life together. But then, he suddenly stopped speaking and I saw the emotion rise in his eyes."

" 'Paolo' he said, 'Our precious Chiara came to me in a dream. She could see that, although I try to make a brave

face of it, like all men, I had some fear of death—I will not deny it to you, old friend. She stood before me, beautiful as always, with that special smile she has. And then, Paolo, I sensed her looking deep into my soul where she saw my fear. Slowly, she raised her hand, and pointed far away. She was showing me the way ahead was merely another stage on our journey. When she saw I understood, she brought her fingers to her lips and sent a kiss to me, and as she did, I saw her lips form, 'Padrino'. When I awoke, my cheeks were wet, but my fears had left me, never to return.' "

There was a great sigh from the Comtesse, and I turned again to his Majesty, "Well, sire, you have seen the angelic face of Chiara painted, but sadly, you have never met her. She is married to another, but she is the love of my life. You will imagine the emotion he provoked in me. And then, Majesty, the final act."

I struggled to gain control over my own feelings, which were in danger of running too high.

"Maestro smiled at me. 'And do you still have my sketch and your own drawing of Chiara?' 'Of course,' I replied, 'they are with me every day.' 'Let me give you one more,' he said. 'Hand me a piece of chalk and some paper.' "

"And, sire, for fifteen or perhaps twenty minutes he worked on an image. He did not have the control he once did—but he could lose nine-tenths of his skill and yet remain twice as proficient as any other mortal. And then, Majesty, he gave me this."

I held out to his Majesty, a small drawing. Beside me, the Comtesse held a silk square to her face, staunching her tears.

Chiara stood, with her perfect smile, pointing the way for her beloved godfather.

Unlike Maestro's sketches for her portrait, it was not detailed. But to those who love her, it is unmistakably Chiara—gracious, strong, serene. She is sending comfort to one she loved so much, one who was in need of her in his final hours.

Tomorrow I will call on Chiara. It is two years since I have seen her.

Image 11: Woman in a Landscape (Pointing Lady).
Always known to be by Leonardo, this drawing is now believed
to be the final work of the maestro, the drawing of Chiara in his
dream, made for and presented to Paolo on Leonardo's
deathbed.
(Collection of HM The Queen, Windsor)

March 28th

D io mio, what a mess!
Alessio is a drunk. And being a drunk, his business is in rapid decline and he does nothing to arrest the fall. I fear that he, and more especially his household, which contains all that I hold most precious, will soon face ruin.

My Chiara is a mature woman now and has come into her glory. To her eternal beauty, life has added wisdom, patience and an unbreakable serenity. By her devotion and dedication, Leo is a fine boy, soon to be a fine young man.[1]

Chiara has passed beyond feelings with regard to Alessio and he is unable to cause her further hurt. He knows this and, strangely, he accepts it. They live more or less in the same house, but their lives are quite separate, except that Chiara tries to keep track of his business dealings, for the sake of her son.

We talked for much of the day. We reminisced about Dimmi and the bottega. She told me that her sister, Pacifica, had been murdered almost a year ago, by a man who forced his way into her house. Her neighbours in turn killed her murderer.

---

[1] At this date, Chiara is 42, Alessio 53 and their son Leo is a boy of 13. Paolo is 34 years of age.

"Some time before she died, she wrote, telling me of your visit to her. She was touched by your concern, as was I. All those years ago when I hoped that you and she might marry, I feel I was not so far from the truth of it. Her letter conveyed a great deal of regret about her life, and you. But Providence decided it was not to be. Her son at least is well and much favoured by the Medici, and by some agency she was permitted to see him twice before her death."

Leo is Chiara's priority in all things.

"You see, mio caro, if the business can but survive for only five or six more years, then Leo will be able to take over, and my son will have an opportunity to build his fortune and his life. But his father cannot, or will not, help himself, or his son."

"Does your husband still suspect our relationship?"

"No. He knows we love each other, but also that we are not lovers, at least as he would understand the word. He has no idea of the true depth of our affection and trust, none whatsoever."

"Good, then here is my plan. I will talk with Alessio. I will offer to take Leo as my apprentice, to teach him the ways of business, including the keeping of accounts. This will, in time, be useful for Leo and it will give me an excuse to involve myself in Alessio's affairs. I will explain that I will use the transactions of his company as material to teach the boy."

Chiara eyes were bright as she laid a gentle hand on my arm. "Forever my protector."

With her special talent for conveying emotion, she warmed my heart with the depth of her feelings.

"Always, and now Leo's also."

June 4th

O *ur plans continue to unfold. I make an offering every week to St Zenobius. I am sure it is helping.*

Leo lives now between two houses, his parents' and mine, and he seems happy with this arrangement. He is a clever boy and will soon enough outpace his master. Which is as it should be.

For his part, Alessio is enthusiastic about my suggestions concerning his affairs. He seems to have forgotten his suspicions regarding my intentions towards his wife. Or perhaps he no longer cares. Or more likely he heard and was impressed that the French Ambassador called on me again last week, bringing greetings from the King, and an illustrated book of folk tales his Majesty had promised me long ago.

As this is my private diary, I need have no false modesty. The truth is, I have already helped to alter the course of Alessio's business, steering it steadily away from the rocks that lay before us. Alessio is so pleased that he has decided I should be paid a share of the ventures I direct. My late master left me moderately well provided, but I accept the money—for the most part it will be there for Chiara or Leo if ever our ventures should fail.

The chief new problem I foresee, concerns the wedding portraits of Chiara and Alessio. They hang in a quiet corner of Chiara's bedchamber, where, she has told me, Alessio never enters these days. But he has heard rumour of the enormous prices the wretch Salaì received for my late master's works. And I am certain that many of the things Salaì sold are not by Maestro himself, but by one or other of the assistants.

Alessio has never grown to love the portraits, and he is much tempted to sell them. This must never be allowed. These are to be the inheritance of Leo and one day, his heirs.

August 2nd

I t is agreed, I go to England. One of our suppliers has died and his business dissolved. We need to secure our relationship with our only other source of fine English wool. Alessio refuses to travel, so I will go, and to my great pleasure, Leo will accompany me.

Chiara was most enthusiastic.

"It will be an adventure for you both, tesoro. And he loves you and would not wish to be separated from you."

"But he loves his mother more!" I exclaimed.

"Perhaps, but the love for a mother is different. At his age, it no longer manifests in a desire to be by my side every day. No, he should go with you and benefit from your wisdom. And it will be good for him to have met the Englishman. Do you suppose they are all uncivilised?"

"Perhaps a few, those who have travelled here, may have a veneer of gentility, but for the rest, I fear I despair. We will stay no longer than absolutely necessary and will wing our way back to the one we both love with all possible haste."

I have decided to bring this journal on our travels. Looking back, I see I have been writing this diary for twenty years. It has grown far too long. No grandson, no matter how loyal, will read so much, especially when so much is tedious. As we travel, I shall compress this chronicle into a much smaller volume, eliminating all that is petty.

I am also minded that I will likely never have a grandson. The passage of the years has done nothing to diminish my love and devotion for Chiara and now her son. It has become my settled state and I am content.

More and more, I consider Leo and his descendants my family. As I write anew, I will focus my chronicle on my late master and on Chiara. Those tales will be of interest, I am certain.

August 22nd

We leave for England tomorrow at first light. This afternoon Chiara brought Leo to my

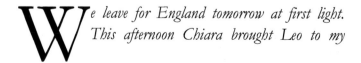

*quarters. He will sleep here tonight to ease our departure.
While Leo settled his horse in the stable, Chiara reached into
her purse.*

*"I shall miss you both, of course, but I am sure you will
enjoy your travels together. There is no one else to whom I
would entrust my son on such a long journey. I will pray daily
for your safe return. And I wanted you to have something
from me, a reminder of my trust and deep affection." She
took a breath. "Of my trust and my love."*

*With this, Chiara handed me a small silk purse. I
opened it to discover a beautiful heavy gold ring with a
dramatic stone engraved with great skill.*

*I am no longer a child given to overt displays of great
emotion, but I confess that as I studied her gift more closely
and considered her words, I was almost overwhelmed.
Thankfully, the return of Leo, full of excitement and
enthusiasm for our trip distracted us. I hope I conveyed my
feelings to Chiara by the intensity of my gaze as she took her
leave and departed for her home.*

December 4th - London

Mamma mia, this country is cold. And wet.
I have kept no journal since we left Florence, so
there is much to catch up on.

*We travelled first to Amboise, where we were received most
graciously by his Majesty, despite the strain of the war with*

the Emperor. Leo was much impressed by the King. For his part, I believe that King Francis was beguiled by Leo, and by the knowledge that his mother is the face in so many of the maestro's paintings.

"Come, come with me now, both of you."

The King led us to his private apartment. There we were able to gaze on the painting of the Virgin with her cousin and child. Of course, I had spent many hours watching Dimmi create this work of genius, but it was nonetheless a thrill to stand before it once again.

"Look here, Leo," I pointed out the angelic face he knows so well. "Not only is that the face of your mother, but perhaps only I can tell you that this entire composition was altered because of her beauty."

The King interrupted. "Truly? Please explain."

"My master's first design had the Virgin with her mother, St Anne, and our Saviour and St John the Baptist as babies. But, after regarding Chiara for a day for her wedding portrait, Maestro Leonardo decided that her beautiful face should be the model for the Virgin, and be made more prominent. And thus the composition changed completely. Now the Virgin's older cousin, Elizabeth, sits on her lap and the Saviour is represented by the lamb, the symbol of his future sacrifice for us as foretold in the words of John when he meets Our Lord years later, 'Behold, the Lamb of God.'"

We were given a letter of introduction from his Majesty for King Henry of England. His Majesty assured me that his cousin is a civilised and cultured monarch.

"He writes songs of surpassing quality and plays the lute most excellently. He enjoys dancing and indeed all of the arts, although music most of all. He is younger than you, Monsieur del Rosso."

Leo has been a charming companion and I have much enjoyed getting to know him even better than before. However, soon after we set out for England, he startled me as we rode along one fine cold morning.

"Signor Paolo, have you always been in love with my mother?"

He asked this most casually, as if enquiring if I was enjoying the view. I was taken aback, but I decided to be honest.

"From the moment my eyes first beheld her. And I have loved no other since, and nor will I."

"And what age were you then?"

"I was sixteen, your mother was twenty years and four. She was, well I will not say she was more beautiful than today, but she was truly the most dazzling creature I had ever seen. But, Leo, you must understand that we respect the reality that your mother is married to your father. We would never behave in a manner we would be ashamed to have witnessed by anyone. Do you understand what I mean?"

"I think so, yes. My father has never talked about these matters with me, but I have heard other boys, older boys, talking."

"Well, I am no great expert, I have been with only a handful of women in my life, but if there is anything you wish to know, you must ask. The man you are named for knew more about the bodies of men and woman than anyone who ever lived, and he shared his knowledge with me. Through him, I have learned to feel no shame concerning matters of procreation. One thing I will tell you unbidden. Half of what you have heard from older boys is greatly exaggerated, and the other half, completely fabricated."

"Thank you, I may ask another day. But for now, I am happy my mother has someone who admires and cares for her so much. It is good to know."

Tomorrow we will present ourselves at the court of King Henry.

December 5th – Hampton Court Palace

King Henry is indeed a most impressive sovereign. I was surprised at his familiarity with the reputation of my late master.

"Of course Maestro Leonardo's name is known to us. We have heard of his reputation for many years. Surely all of Christendom knows of his genius? My cousin, Francis, made *me jealous describing the works of the great man now residing in his palaces."*

King Henry too was delighted to discover that the face in King Francis's painting was the mother of the boy before him.

"You are fortunate to have grown up with such a noble mother. For myself, I was only seven years old when my blessed mother died."

He held up a clenched fist and raised each finger in turn as he continued. "She was daughter, sister, niece, wife and mother of Kings!"

Tomorrow, rest. Then to a place called Abingdon.

January 8th 1522 – Hampton Court Palace

*I*t is hard to say no to a King. Finally, we are to leave King Henry's court, tomorrow. I am confident we will actually depart this time, because the King himself has already left, so will not be here to offer us yet more of his hospitality. But I must not be ungracious. Yes, we intended leaving a month ago, but instead we have enjoyed being at court for Christmas and the Feast of the Kings.

And it has been such a wonderful experience for Leo. He has hunted, sung, dined and danced with a King and with his Lords and Ladies. If I am not mistaken, he has kissed the daughter of a Duke.

January 10th – North-West of London

Today we left London behind on our way to Walter Pennant's home. The weather is amazingly cold, even if dry. Days spent on horseback gives me time to think, and yesterday I resolved to settle something with Leo.

As we rode along a particularly sullen pathway through thick woods, I addressed him.

"It is impossible to predict what lies before each of us in our lives. Although I think it less and less likely, it is just possible I may yet marry and have children. But what then of the portraits of your mother? The two by Maestro Leonardo are, of course, precious, and while the poor effort of my own is of no worth, yet it is a memento of a particularly happy day and I would not wish to see it thrown away."

"Of course not, but why would anyone throw it away?"

"Consider. Most likely I will not marry and therefore will have no sons. But if I should marry, what would my wife make of portraits of another woman, one who has possessed my heart for so many years? Is it likely she would welcome this rival into her home? I think not. So, I am resolved. If I die a bachelor or if I decide to marry, in either case, upon the appointed day, you shall have my three portraits of your mother. Then I can be certain they will be honoured and preserved in your family, as they must. They will be kept with the wedding portraits of your mother and father, and I will *rest content. This is also true of my ring, a gift from your mother. This too shall pass to you."*

With that, I held out my hand, palm down, so Leo could see.

"I have noticed the black stone before, but I did not know it was a gift from my mother. It is handsome. Thank you. I do not know what to say."

"It is not necessary that you say anything. It is enough that we understand each other."

January 14th – Oxfordshire

alter Pennant is, I believe, a good man. He received us with great courtesy when we arrived at his home yesterday evening. His wife, Matilda, is kind, and he has a son, Hugh, only a year older than Leo. His daughter Margaret, the older child, is an impressive young woman, reminding me somewhat of Caterina Lenzi. Like Caterina, Margaret is confident and comfortable in discussion and both women have a strange ability to be honest, open and forthright without appearing forward or inappropriate. How can it be that the same words in different mouths can create such different impressions? I could see that Leo was much affected by

Margaret and he blushed when she asked him to teach her some words in Italian.[1]

The boys became friends immediately, helped by the fact that Leo has a wonderful ear for languages. He had picked up a good deal of French on our voyage through that country, and a month at the court of King Henry has already given him a fair amount of English. The boys get along in an amusing mixture of English, French and Latin. Walter, of course, speaks excellent Latin and so we converse in that tongue.

By various subtle and diplomatic hints, Walter has given me to understand that he was aware of the steady decline in Alessio's attention and he is delighted we troubled ourselves to travel all the way to England to re-assert our ambition to further grow the trade between us.

"The problem," he explained as we stood together looking over his fields, "is that more and more farmers are turning to keeping sheep and cattle for meat, where there is often better money. To satisfy even your present level of orders requires me to contract with no less than twenty farmers within four days travel from here. And still I must buy some wool on the open market, which is more variable. If, as you hope, your

---

[1] The term Paolo uses is 'lingua cortigiana' which was the common courtly language used throughout Renaissance Italy. It was most like the Tuscan dialect and so would be very easy for Paolo to speak and understand. There was no language called Italian or political entity called Italy.

demand more than doubles, I would have to consider giving up my own animals and becoming your full-time agent. I would need to have a great deal of confidence that your orders would not dry up."

We have agreed to talk more on this. But first, Walter wants me to accompany him on visits to every farmer who supplies him with wool for onward delivery to Florence.

February 2nd – Oxfordshire

I am pleased that my initial assessment of Walter was correct. He is a good man and honest. To my great surprise he was not afraid to disclose how much he pays for the wool he buys on our behalf, thus revealing the amount by which he increases the charge to me.

"If we are to develop our partnership, why would I keep it a secret? It is good for you to know my principles. Then if the market is difficult and I increase your price, you will trust that I have no option. From now on, I will send you a letter every two months, reporting on the state of the market here in England and in Flanders, for many of my neighbours deal there."

In this manner, trust grew between us and I agreed we would commit to long-term purchases while, for his part, Walter would ease out of farming himself.

"I would like you to come with me to York," he announced this evening. "It is a goodly way, but it is one of *the largest wool markets in England. There is much to see and many people to meet. If you wish, Leo can stay here with Hugh."*

April 19th – Oxfordshire

B*ack in Abingdon at last. The journey has been tiring. England is indeed uncivilised, but York is a handsome city, and its cathedral the equal of any I have seen. I am too tired to write any more this evening. Except to say that Leo is well and speaking English almost as though he was born here. He has developed a close and relaxed friendship with Hugh and, more surprising, with Margaret. He teases her when she makes an error in her Italian, but always with a smile and a word of encouragement. Seeing him today, made me yearn to sit with his mother. We have been away too long.*

And we have heard worrying rumours of war.

Connection

It gave Lauren enormous satisfaction to take the 1522 pages to William Chance's office. She summarised the contents.

"Here it is, William, this is your family's link to Paolo and his Chronicles. Paolo and Walter became close, as did Leo and Walter's two children. Margaret is the Pennant who married your Chance ancestor, the dates align perfectly. And someone, at some point, must have read the diary, or at least this last piece of it–it was found inside one of the oldest books in your library."

The Earl was delighted with the discovery.

"Something must have happened to Walter, and to Hugh for that matter. Otherwise the daughter would never have inherited. Thank you, Lauren, it's incredibly satisfying to have an understanding of how exactly the connection was forged. What happens now that the search for more of the diary pages is over? There's no point speculating why the significance of the diary wasn't recognised all those years ago by whoever read it. Who knows how people thought back whenever it was?"

"We're working our way through the entire library, in case there are any more fragments to be found. It's remarkable that the connection should finally turn up just as we have run out of diary. We can guess *how* the diary came to be here. Margaret must have brought it with her when she moved into Blythswood with your forbear. The puzzle is *why* it was with her in the first place, unless Paolo died before leaving England. That's the likeliest explanation. There's no suggestion he was planning to move here permanently, quite the contrary. But why did Leo not take it back with him? Unless he too died or remained for some other reason. We may never know."

* * *

The Earl had called an old school friend who was the curator of the Royal Collection, to tell him the story behind the drawing of the *Pointing Lady* in the Collection. Today he and Lauren were in London, having been invited to come and see the drawing for themselves in the Queen's Gallery where it was on display in a temporary exhibition.

It was an extremely intense experience for Lauren and the curator saw the emotion in her eyes.

"This is why historical research is so important," he told them. "This lovely drawing now has a whole new meaning and a much heightened impact. This will be transformed from being just one of many drawings in our Leonardo collection, to one of our star attractions. When the story behind this image becomes known, I predict there will be long queues of people coming to see her and being deeply affected as they contemplate the context in which the drawing was made and the wonderful, complex web of relationships underpinning the image. We'll probably have to move this drawing to somewhere more accessible than Windsor. This simple image directly connects three fascinating people and indirectly embraces others touched by it over the years, not least the King of France."

Afterwards, Lauren walked to Jonathan's gallery to collect him for lunch. When she arrived at the gallery, Jonathan was attending to a customer.

Lauren strolled around the room, once again admiring the watercolours and drawings for sale. She spotted Gerry coming off the phone and went over to greet her. She leaned into Gerry's ear and, in a low whisper, raised her concern.

"All the items marked *'Sold'* have been here since the opening. Are people not coming back to pay for them?"

Gerry laughed. "No, no. They're not actually sold. These are pieces Jonathan doesn't want to sell for one reason or another. Mostly, they came from his grandfather's collection, things he has an emotional connection to, and won't sell."

"So why are they here?"

"Well, we don't have as much stock as we'd like, so these fill gaps in the wall. Also, it gives a sense that things are selling – 'if you like something, better buy it quick before someone beats you to it!' "

Just then, Jonathan joined them.

"I hear Gerry's spilling our trade secrets. Come and see this drawing."

He ushered Lauren over to the tiny cherub's face.

"This is the face I've been hunting for twenty years–no luck yet, but I'll keep looking. Ready to go to lunch?"

As they walked towards the door, Jonathan waved to Geraldine. "See you tomorrow!"

He grinned at Lauren. "I'm taking the rest of the day off. Playing hooky, I think you call it."

They found a table in a quiet Italian restaurant, and, after they had looked over the menu, Lauren asked, "How is the gallery doing?"

"Pretty well, but I need to get us more stock, we can't sell what we don't have. But I've become distracted with something else. And it's all your fault."

He was smiling. "I needed to re-read some of the sections of the diary, the ones you showed me, and check some things, but now I think there is a chance we could find Paolo's portrait of Chiara."

"Really! What makes you imagine that?"

"I've been doing some research. Painting on canvas was a novelty in Leonardo's time, almost everything was produced on wooden panels. So, I'm pretty certain which painting Raphael was set to produce on the canvas he was given by Leonardo. I'm confident he used it for his painting of St Sebastian, which is in the Uffizi in Florence. And we know its exact dimensions. And, these dimensions match exactly those of a lovely portrait of a previously unknown young woman done by Leonardo called *La Scapigliata*, 'The Dishevelled One'. Paolo's description of Leonardo's first study of Chiara, the one he was given, exactly matches *La Scapigliata*."

Jonathan sat back, a satisfied look on his face.

"I still don't see how this leads to Paolo's painting–although I can see you're about to tell me," Lauren finished with a grin.

"Both these known works, plus Paolo's drawing and the wedding portraits themselves, were in all likelihood done on a batch of identical canvases, the ones Paolo boasted of buying. Most clients couldn't be persuaded to accept canvas, so I imagine they would be used in-house, as it were. If so, we know the precise size of Paolo's painting and we even know what Chiara looked like. She truly was beautiful, by the way."

Now Lauren was excited. "But doesn't that mean we could find the wedding portraits themselves?"

Jonathan shook his head.

"I'm afraid not. Even if they weren't known to be by Leonardo, a matched pair of Renaissance portraits would be extremely high-profile, and I've searched every database. They don't exist, at least not in any major private or public collection, and they haven't passed through a major auction house or gallery during the past hundred years or so. Of course, they could be hanging in some obscure monastery or in a minor stately home somewhere, perhaps obscured by five hundred years of soot and grime, but that doesn't help us locate them. There's a painting in Milan known as the *Portrait of a Musician* which matches the description of Alessio's portrait pretty well. But although it is attributed to Leonardo, it isn't finished, it's on a wood panel and it's the wrong size completely. It could be a studio copy or an adaptation. But Paolo's effort is another matter altogether. He describes it as being amateurish, except of course for Leonardo's additions. Such a drawing could be easily overlooked."

"Or lost or destroyed," Lauren added sadly.

"I know. Realistically, a mediocre sketch may well not have survived. Experts estimate maybe only ten or twenty per cent of all the art created during the Renaissance still exists. Just think of all the house fires, religious unrest, wars, civil wars, floods, revolutions. And can you imagine the art losses in major disasters like the Great Fire of

London, some of the big Italian earthquakes or the bombing of Dresden? But nevertheless, it's worth looking, don't you think?"

"Where would you start? It could be anywhere."

"I have an idea about that as well. If it *did* survive, I could maybe trace it, if we were lucky. Even back then, the Italians were sticklers for tax and estate records. When people died, everything was inventoried."

"How many generations are we talking about?"

Jonathan thought for a moment, "I suppose maybe seventeen, perhaps as many as twenty."

"It would take forever to track all those wills, even if you're *really* lucky."

"In theory we *could* try following the family. The reality is, after twenty generations in Catholic Italy, there could be many hundreds, many thousands of descendants, all over Italy, all over the world. But I want to try a shortcut."

Jonathan's eyes betrayed his growing excitement.

"We can reasonably assume that, as Paolo promised in one of the final entries, Leo ended up with Paolo's three portraits. Leonardo's deathbed drawing of Chiara is in the Royal Collection and his first, unused study for the wedding portrait, *La Scapigliata,* is in Parma. Both were first sold around the time when any sons of Leo's may have died, possibly to share out some of the wealth, or because they just wanted the money. But Paolo's portrait had no monetary value. Let's say it continued to hang on the wall of the family home. It meant a huge amount to Leo and then to his children, who probably heard the story of the portrait from Chiara herself. And this is a wealthy family we're talking about. So, as long as the house stays in the family, let's assume the painting hangs where it is. It has no resale value, but it's an image of an ancestor–why would you throw it away?"

"OK, I can see that. So how does that help?" asked Lauren.

"I just have to find out when the family left the house, if they ever did. Just think, the painting could still be hanging on the exact same wall! More likely of course, the family moved at some point. So, I find Leo's house and follow it through the property tax records. I don't have to look at every year. I can jump say, twenty or thirty years, until the family name of the owner of the house changes. If it changed because of marriage, I keep going. If it changed because the house was sold, I narrow down the date and try to find out where the family went next and repeat the same exercise. And yes, I realise the painting could easily have been taken by a member of the family who moved away. But, if the eldest son kept inheriting, he may have held on to the portrait as well as the family home. It's a long shot, but you never know. And there's nothing to lose."

Lauren had by this point caught up with Jonathan's thinking, and his enthusiasm.

"Are you going to Florence to look at the records? If you do, you could try to discover if Paolo and Leo returned safely from England. If they did, it's possible Paolo continued his diary in Italy, and it may be in a collection or archive somewhere."

"Yes, I'm planning to go in a few days. Why don't you come with me?"

As soon as Jonathan's words were spoken, the atmosphere altered. The unintentionally loaded question hung in the air until Lauren brought them back to earth.

"I'd love to, but I can't. I really need to focus on preparing for the seminar. I don't know whether I'm excited or terrified. I've been receiving welcoming emails from all these impossibly distinguished academics, nearly all men, of course. They're all terribly nice, but they nearly all point out how much they're looking forward to what they're sure will be a fascinating—one guy said 'instructive'—presentation. There's a WhatsApp group and it's all 'Tony this' and 'Peter that'—they all seem to know each other really well. I've got to make a good first impression. I need all the time I can get to research and prepare my presentation."

Jonathan realised that he was really disappointed. In the silence before Lauren replied, he had a vision of them exploring Florence together. It had felt good.

"OK. I'll keep you posted, and I promise I'll look for more Paolo papers before I get too bogged down in the hunt for the portrait."

"We should go and see Professor Hunter and tell her you're going to Florence. She's got great contacts everywhere."

They each took a sip from their wine glass. Lauren found she didn't want the conversation to end where it was.

"I meant it, Jonathan. I would love to go with you, really, I would, for lots of reasons. But—"

"I believe you, I do. And I'm glad you are, for lots of reasons too. But, you're absolutely right—this is a huge opportunity for you. You've worked hard for it and it will be a great start for your career. So of course you need to prepare."

"I expect regular reports while you're away."

"Don't worry. Now, I took the afternoon off because there's something I want to show you. It's a public secret."

With that enigmatic statement, Jonathan turned to the waitress who had come to take their order.

* * *

As they strolled along Piccadilly, Jonathan explained where they were going.

"Leonardo painted *The Last Supper* before Paolo joined Leonardo's household, but I thought you would like to see it."

"But it's on a wall in Milan, surely?"

"Well, yes and no. Who is the architect of St Paul's?"

"Christopher Wren. Even I know that. But–"

"Bear with me. Everyone credits St Paul's to Wren. But he wasn't a mason, or a carpenter, or any of the other trades that actually built St Paul's."

"Yes, but he designed it, it was his vision, his ideas."

"So, if someone built an exact copy of St Paul's, would that be by Wren?"

"Well…"

"How about if Wren had overseen the construction of another, identical St Paul's in, say, Winchester?"

"Yes, that would be by Wren."

"Well, another day we can talk about why one copy is by Wren and the other maybe not. But, what we're going to see is exactly like that imaginary Winchester St Paul's."

Jonathan led them into the Royal Academy and to the room where the recently returned copy of *The Last Supper* hung. As they approached the enormous canvas, he explained.

"Pretty much as soon as Leonardo finished painting *The Last Supper* in Milan, it started to fall apart. Over the years it faded and was vandalised. Then it was defaced when a door was driven through it. By the time that happened, it was unrecognisable. All in all, *The Last Supper* today is very disappointing. The colours have faded, lots of bits are missing, and it has been heavily restored, not always well, and sometimes disastrously. Almost nothing now visible was painted by Leonardo or his assistants.

"However, the good news is that that this copy, as well as another one now in Belgium, was made by one of Leonardo's apprentices *during Leonardo's lifetime*. We're not sure of the exact date of this copy, but it's fair to assume that the artist was copying the original, that he was supervised by Leonardo, and he had access to the maestro's preparatory studies. This is well accepted to be a near identical version of the work in Milan. It was actually used as a reference in the last restoration of the original. It's missing the top section, which is mostly ceiling, but, if this isn't a true Leonardo, I don't know what is. This is an incomparably better reflection of Leonardo's creative vision than the degraded, dilapidated image on a wall in Milan."

Lauren was astonished by these revelations. She had no idea this artwork existed, never mind in the centre of London. She stood before the painting and admired the vibrant colours, the dynamic poses of the Apostles, the overall dramatic composition. After a while she began to examine her own reaction. Did she care if Leonardo had applied the paints? Would she rather look at the much diminished original or this vibrant version? What would Christopher Wren have said?

"Why haven't I heard of this?" she asked.

"The art business, and it is a huge, global business, is built on myths. One myth is that some people are uniquely qualified to pronounce on what is Art. Another is that while certain copies or reproductions are valuable, the vast bulk are fit only for greeting cards. So, in my little area, we deal in etchings, engravings, mezzotints, woodcuts, aquatints. Although all are copies of one sort or another, these are all viewed as legitimate works, worthy of hanging in museums. Then there are photographic prints, linocuts, vintage travel posters and on and on. There is no fixed boundary between Art and rubbish. Another myth is that experts know what they are talking about. This despite the widely accepted fact that a significant number of works hanging in national collections are fakes, or originals restored and touched up to the nth degree.

"This *Last Supper* challenges the foundations of the art market. The market needs this to be worth a few tens or hundreds of thousands of dollars, not hundreds of millions. So, surprise, surprise, you've never heard of it."

"Wow! So, what's going to happen with the *Mona Lisa*? I mean when we publish."

"I just don't know. It may be unique. Its reputation is so enormous, it may withstand the exposure, even though now we know it was mostly painted by one of the apprentices. It's impossible to tell.

"And by the way, the whole Wren and St Paul's business can get even more challenging. Imagine someone discovered a complete set of contemporaneous, detailed drawings of how the Parthenon looked when it was built. Which would you rather visit? The largely destroyed ruin, or a completely faithful reconstruction of Phidias's original concept built from those drawings? On a full-size re-created version of the Acropolis? And should the drawings be used to reconstruct the actual Parthenon, blending original and new stone?"

They sat in silence on the leather sofa before the enormous painting. After a while, Lauren had to draw Jonathan's attention to something.

"The figure on Christ's right. Who is that supposed to be?"

"It's supposed to be St John. Unless, of course, you're Dan Brown." Jonathan finished with a smile.

"Just because Dan Brown says it is a woman doesn't mean it isn't."

"I'm teasing. I agree. When I saw this version for the first time, I was really struck by how much this figure looks like a woman."

"It *is* a woman! Her face, her hair, her complexion. All the guys are swarthy, as you'd expect from fishermen and farmers. But this face is delicate and pale."

Jonathan was nodding. "And look. This is the moment when Jesus announces he's going to be betrayed. Everyone is shocked, appalled. Everyone except her. She is sitting quietly, her hands in repose. She isn't the least surprised-"

Lauren interrupted him, "because she already knows!"

"That's what I think. I think Jesus told her before everyone else. Perhaps at breakfast!" he finished with a grin.

Lauren counted up the figures in the painting.

"But if that's Mary Magdalene, where is the twelfth apostle?"

"Missing. Leonardo was already breaking with convention in choosing the moment of Christ's announcement. Perhaps he didn't want to stir up any more trouble by adding a woman to the image, so he just sneaked her in. Who knows? I don't buy all the *Da Vinci Code* nonsense, but this image does seem pretty clear."

"I wish there was something in the diary to clear all this up."

"That would be very helpful!"

Lauren had reached a conclusion about another matter.

"I've made up my mind. About the Parthenon. It's a close call, but I rather see the Disney version first, then the real thing. That way I could visualise the original in all its glory, while still having the actual ancient stones in front of me. That would be cool."

PART
TWO

Florence

Jonathan was excited to be returning to Florence, particularly now, after his meeting with Jane Hunter. She was incredibly well-connected in the city and had promised to contact those of her contacts who would be most useful to him.

He had arranged things with Gerry and Sue–they would become junior partners and there were encouraging signs that the business would be able to pay them salaries in the near future.

* * *

When Jonathan arrived at Florence's archive on his first morning in the city, he was met by the Director himself, Dottor Danilo Foscari.

Dottor Foscari looked and dressed more like a matinee idol than an archivist. He was the archetypally handsome, smooth Latin, but when they sat down in his office, he was instantly highly focused and completely efficient.

"The Professoressa gave me some information concerning your enquiries here in Firenze. We read the reports about the discovery of the Paolo Chronicles. I must say, it is very exciting. All Italians look forward to reading them, hopefully very soon. In any event, we have been looking for any records relating to Paolo del Rosso, or the Pacini family. I can tell you that Paolo del Rosso appears in the tax records and in many business transactions. He was the manager, or director you might say, for the merchant, Alessio Pacini."

To Jonathan's surprise, Dottor Foscari took a pack of cigarettes from his pocket and, after offering one to his guest, proceeded to light up. It was strange to see someone smoking indoors. He saw the look on Jonathan's face.

"I should not, but what can you do?"

He gave a characteristic Italian shrug and continued with his report, between puffs.

"You may have read that in 1529 and 1530, we had some big troubles here in Firenze. The city was under siege and many merchants were ruined. There are no tax records for Alessio Pacini after the siege, but his business continued to prosper under the control of del Rosso. There are no tax records for del Rosso after 1534, but also no record of the deaths of either man, although we have found a will for Paolo del Rosso. Perhaps they all moved somewhere else?"

"What did the will say?" Jonathan asked.

"It is short. He leaves everything to Leonardo Pacini, son of Alessio, trusting he will take care of his mother. It is dated 1528, but there is no indication of when it was enacted. We know it was filed with the authorities at some later date, but we haven't yet discovered precisely when."

There was a longer pause now, while the director stubbed out his cigarette before picking up his phone to order coffees for both of them.

"Immediately after del Rosso disappears from the tax records in 1534, Leonardo Pacini appears as the new owner of his father's house and the dirigente of the family trading business. We can assume Alessio Pacini died, but we have yet to find a will for him. We have a large file of papers on the business, which was successful, and which continued to operate for many, many years. We only arrived at this point yesterday, so I cannot yet tell you the end of this story."

He closed the thin file he had been referring to.

"One thing more. When Leonardo Pacini arrived back in Firenze in 1534, he claimed four dependents for tax purposes: his wife, Teresa; a daughter, Paola; an infant son, Paolo; and his mother, Chiara."

This last piece of information moved Jonathan enormously. Somehow, hearing Chiara's name outside the pages of Paolo's Chronicle made her seem more real. And the fact that her son had christened *his* children after Paolo was unbearably moving. But where was Paolo?

"Now, signore, is there anything else I can assist you with during your visit?"

"Not for the moment, thank you, but if I could call on your help later, I would be grateful. Actually, Dottore, there is one other thing. Is there another archive in the city, perhaps more likely to hold personal papers?"

"Yes, the archive of the Cathedral, the Duomo. If one of your subjects or a descendant wanted to put family papers somewhere safe, they might have deposited them with the church. Especially baptismal records, marriage contracts, things like that. I suggest you try there. I will call them."

* * *

"Dottor Foscari requested that we should assist you, signore, but I fear you are in the wrong place."

The young priest was dressed conventionally, with no hint of clerical garb. Danilo Foscari had explained what they were looking for.

"We no longer have what you seek. In 1958 the chief archivist had a complete inventory of the holdings of the Opera prepared."

He saw Jonathan's blank expression.

"The Opera di Santa Maria del Fiore is the logistical arm of the Duomo, responsible for the fabric of the building and, for historical reasons, for the archive. Anyway, when the inventory was prepared, the documents we held for many individuals and families were transferred to the National Central Library of Florence. We checked already, and I can tell you that we did indeed have a file on Paolo del Rosso, it was one of those transferred. I have arranged for you to be assisted there."

* * *

The Library's senior archivist was waiting for him when he arrived an hour later.

"Signor Granville, it is a pleasure to meet you, I have read of the discovery in England. It is exciting to think we may have some similar material here. My assistant, Angela, is looking now for the file we received regarding Paolo del Rosso. It will not take long–we have a good catalogue, especially for the material transferred from the Opera. Meanwhile, will you take a coffee?"

They sat patiently, awaiting Angela. Jonathan gave the archivist, Dottoressa Ricci, an overview of the Chronicles.

"You are lucky to have the assistance of Professoressa Hunter, she is a very able person. We first met many years ago, when I took some classes in England, and she has been here many, many times, of course. When you see her, tell her Roberto still asks about her," she finished with a twinkle.

Fifteen minutes after his arrival, Angela appeared and introduced herself.

"I'm afraid I have bad news. We did indeed receive a file from the Duomo on Paolo del Rosso, but it was lost in the flood of 1966. We don't have a record of what was in the file, but whatever it was, it was completely destroyed."

"I'm sorry, signore," commiserated Dottoressa Ricci. "The flood of 1966 was truly terrible. I was only a child at the time, but I remember as if it was yesterday. The library had over one million items lost or damaged. Almost the half of Dottor Foscari's archive was damaged. And one hundred people died. Much was restored, is still being restored today, but much was lost forever."

Thoroughly dejected, Jonathan thanked the archivist for her trouble and Angela was asked to escort him out of the building. As Jonathan put his hand on the brass handle on the heavy front door, he suddenly turned to the young Italian woman.

"Angela, would you mind? Can you please look to see if you have a file on a Leonardo Pacini from about the same period as Paolo del Rosso? Please?"

"Of course. You can wait here. I will not be long."

She showed him into an empty meeting room on the ground floor, where he paced back and forth, too anxious to sit down.

Forty minutes later, Angela returned, pushing a library cart carrying a large, extremely dirty and badly scratched box.

"This file was also damaged by the flood, but it seems we were able to save it. I will leave you to examine it. Please use these gloves to handle the papers, they are very old and anyway, many are very dirty."

Jonathan put on the gloves before carefully removing the lid of the old box. He lifted out a sheaf of papers, examining them briefly then laying them aside. He was not nearly as proficient as Lauren in reading the ancient script, but he was confident that he would recognise any diary pages if they were here.

The papers in the box were in a mess, piled higgledy-piggledy in collapsed stacks. Jonathan had resigned himself to the laborious task of looking through them when he spotted the edges of a large heap of sheets tied together with a leather strap. He lifted out all of the loose papers on top of the bundle and placed them on the table. Once more he reached into the box, noticing a distinctly unpleasant smell emanating from the documents or maybe the sides of the box itself.

He was able to take hold of the bundle with two hands and raise it up to place it alongside the rejected sheets on the long conference table.

As he looked at the top sheet of the bundle, his heart sank. It was nothing like Paolo's handwriting He gently turned down the top sheet, but the next was equally unfamiliar. Some instinct made him turn down one more sheet before turning back to the box and there it was—a page of Paolo's lovely script, identical to the Chronicle pages he was so familiar with.

He was able to slide the leather strap off the pile of documents and confirm that, with the exception of the first two pages, the entire bound file comprised what was surely the balance of Paolo's diary.

There was no one else in the room to witness the huge smile that spread over Jonathan's face. Yes, he was interested in the discovering the rest of Paolo's story, but more than anything, he knew what this would mean to Lauren. He was so looking forward to bringing her this treasure!

* * *

"Dottoressa Ricci, I can read only some of these documents, but enough to know they are the continuation of the papers we have in England. Would it be possible to have this file sent to England, for study?"

Jonathan was sitting opposite the grey-haired archivist. Between them sat the bundle of old pages, once more secured by their strap. He was very aware of how much it would mean to Lauren to get her hands on the rest of Paolo's diary.

"Leave the file with me for a day or so. And let me also talk with Professoressa Hunter. If it is possible to loan the file, it would be to Jane Hunter and the Bodleian Library."

* * *

To calm himself, Jonathan took a stroll through the historic streets of Florence. As he wandered, he did indeed begin to relax and eventually fell into a reflective mood, conscious that Paolo, Chiara and indeed Leonardo, had walked the same streets five hundred years ago. Despite the passage of so many years, most of the old buildings had survived, certainly enough for them to find their way around the city centre if they re-appeared. Jonathan now realised that, prior to this visit, the people in the Chronicles had been characters in a story–rich, compelling characters, but not flesh and blood. Coming across them in the official records, walking in their city, brought them fully alive. And now his familiarity with their stories and the closeness he had developed towards them, coloured his appreciation of the city itself. Now he was walking in *their* city, in *their* home.

The faces around him, men and women going about their business, but especially the market people; the men repairing a broken water mains; an elegant, silver-haired lady patiently urging her tiny dog across the piazza; these were the exact same faces Paolo had observed as he sat for his haircut. These were the direct descendants of the characters who had admired Chiara as she crossed this very piazza under Paolo's adoring gaze–from perhaps that balcony up there.

But his strongest emotion, was regret that Lauren was not here, sharing the same powerful connection.

He had decided to wait for the archivist's decision before telling Lauren about his discovery of the diary pages. He wanted to be able to tell her what the next steps would be. He wandered back to the Palazzo Vecchio, to a little restaurant he had discovered, *Vini e Vecchi Sapori,* and ordered a small carafe of house wine while he looked over the dinner menu. With his obligation to Lauren and Professor Hunter discharged for the moment, the following morning he would be back at Director Foscari's office on the hunt for Paolo's portrait.

By now Jonathan had convinced himself that the drawing may indeed have survived. It was exactly the kind of object that family legends develop around. For as long as Leo lived, he would have told his children and grandchildren about his beautiful mother, goddaughter and model of the famous Leonardo da Vinci, the man he was named for. These are the family stories that persist down through the generations, especially when there is a physical object to symbolise the legend. Of course, ten generations later, the ancestor in the image could have evolved to become Leonardo's favourite mistress or his love child or whatever–but the family link to the legendary Leonardo da Vinci would be a source of pride, to be told and retold.

* * *

The following morning Jonathan returned to the state archive office to ask Director Foscari for advice on accessing the property tax records.

"Of course, of course. Better, one of our interns will accompany you. Just tell her what you are looking for. Now, please excuse me, I must deal with a budget crisis. Wait here, I will send in Joanna."

In a couple of minutes, there was a knock on the door and a poised young woman entered.

In perfect, slightly American-accented English, she introduced herself.

"Mr. Granville? I am Joanna Bonsignori-Lenzi, I will be pleased to help you in your research."

Jonathan stared at her, long enough for Joanna to become uncomfortable and contemplate leaving, when suddenly he collected himself.

"Forgive me. Can you tell me your name again?"

"Joanna Bonsignori-Lenzi. But please, call me Joanna."

"And I'm Jonathan. But your family name, Bonsignori-Lenzi, is rather striking."

"It is an old name. Not so ancient as some in this city, but quite old."

"And you're an intern here?"

"Yes, I'm a student. I'm studying medieval history at Harvard, but I spend my summers here in Florence, to learn everything about the archives. These are the richest archives outside of the Vatican."

"And you know the origin of your family name, I assume?"

"Oh yes, my family is very proud of the story, especially the women. My ancestor insisted her husband add her family name to his, and–"

He interrupted her.

"Caterina Lenzi. And was her first son named Pietro?"

Now it was Joanna's turn to be stunned.

"Yes! You must have studied a great deal of the history of Italy to know this much about just one family."

"Not really. I know just a very little about your ancestor in particular. You know of the recently discovered diary of Paolo del Rosso?"

He continued as the young woman nodded her head. "When I get back to England, I'll email you a copy of some pages from the diary. Paolo and his master, Leonardo da Vinci, met your ancestor, Caterina Lenzi. Paolo and Caterina became good friends and could easily have married, but Paolo didn't match up to all of Caterina's exacting requirements. So, Caterina moved to Florence?"

"No, no. I am not from Florence. My family is from Milan. Well, we have houses in London and in other places, but home will always be Milan."

Step one was to identify the house that was Alessio's, then Leo's. This took no time at all. The home of the Pacini family was a prominent building in a wealthy section of the Renaissance city. It turned out to be even easier than Jonathan had hoped to track the subsequent ownership of the house. Buildings have the convenient attribute that they don't marry, die, or move. Both of Leo's children had pre-deceased him. So, on his death, the family name of the owner became Brandini, the man who had married Leo's eldest granddaughter and thus became his heir. Sure enough, in the record of Leo's estate, there were several paintings including a portrait, *'of the mother of the deceased'*. From his research in London, Jonathan already knew that both of the other portraits of Chiara by Leonardo were in the hands of new owners by the date of Leo's death.

However, there was no reference to a portrait of Alessio. Was the portrait listed in Leo's will Paolo's drawing, or Chiara's wedding portrait? Could the wedding portraits somehow have left the family even before Leo's death?

Had they somehow been lost soon after they were created? It was so ridiculously frustrating.

An amazing number of Italian properties have remained in the same family for many, many generations. And so it proved in this case. An hour of work disclosed that the entire house stayed in the Brandini family until 1851, when a Giulio Brandini sold off part of the building. The family remained in a much reduced section of the property.

By 1885, there was a new owner.

They looked back, and there it was. Niccolò Brandini owned the smaller remnant of the house in 1879, but he had not paid the taxes on it for two years. In 1880, someone called Filippo Bartolo was paying the taxes. Bartolo was not related in any way to the Brandini family.

"Please, come with me." Joanna requested, leading him to another room in the labyrinth that was the old State Archive.

After a fairly quick search, she pulled out a sheet of paper.

It was a notice of the 1880 auction of the contents of the house, to be held by the city authorities, the proceeds to be confiscated in payment of unpaid taxes.

"Will there be a record of the auction?" he asked, hoping for a positive answer.

"Oh yes, in Italy there is a record of *everything*, you only have to know where to look. We need to go to another archive in another part of the city. Would you like to go there now?"

"Yes, please. Let's go."

Jonathan called Lauren while Joanna went to tell her supervisor where she was going.

"I'm making some progress. We've traced Leo's family home to 1880 when it was sold to pay back taxes. They also auctioned off the contents. We're on our way to another building to look for the records of the auction."

Joanna appeared, and Jonathan ended his call so she could explain where they were going.

"By the time of the auction, Florence was just another Italian city. The auction was handled by the city authorities, and they have their own records. Don't worry, I am familiar with those as well. The archive we have just left is the successor to the archives of the Republic and the Grand Duchy, although some contemporary records are still being added. It's confusing to outsiders, I know. Here we are, we should find the auction records here."

They were entering a brutalist modern building on the edge of the old city, with none of the charm of the old archive building. Still, the rooms and filing systems were more logically laid out.

Nonetheless, it took almost thirty minutes for Joanna to locate the record they sought.

"Here it is, look. It's rather sad, I'm afraid. The family had almost nothing."

Jonathan reviewed the pitifully short list. It was indeed depressing.

> *1 good table, wood*
> *2 chairs, wood*
> *6 plates*

4 cups

3 tall wine glasses

… and so it went on for sixteen lines. The meagre possessions of a once wealthy family. Jonathan was glad Chiara and Leo knew nothing of this drastic decline. The fourth item from the bottom was the one that interested him – *1 chalk portrait of a young woman, framed.*

"What does this mean?"

Jonathan was pointing to a stamp on the following sheet.

"Unsold. The table and the portrait were bought in two separate lots. Everything else was unsold and probably thrown away. In total, in today's terms, the auction raised less than twelve euros. Sad, isn't it?"

"Desperately. Can we photocopy these, or should I take a photograph?"

"We can copy them. Let me go and get the key for the copier room. I'll be right back."

As Joanna walked away, Jonathan turned the papers over. The rusted paper clip fixed to the auction list and proceeds sheet also held two slips of paper, which he immediately recognised as receipts for the sold lots.

Joanna returned in a few minutes and they photocopied the two larger pieces of paper and the two much smaller receipts.

"This would have taken days on my own. Thank you."

"It was my pleasure. Can you find your way back? I'd like to call in on my colleagues for a moment."

"Of course, and thanks again. I'll remember to send you copies of the diary entries mentioning Caterina."

Jonathan walked back across the city, past the Duomo, into Via dei Servi. At a Chinese restaurant he turned left, into Via del Castellaccio. Fifty metres on, he stopped and looked across the street. There it was–the home of Chiara and Alessio and subsequently Leo and his descendants. Although sharing an impressive arched entrance way, the old home was now two apparently separate buildings: a small apartment block, and next door a trattoria with its own entrance, and three floors of what looked like offices above.

It was a strangely moving sensation, looking at the home of these people he had become so familiar with, and for whom he felt so much affection.

He decided to call Lauren again, this time using video streaming.

He positioned his phone so Lauren was seeing the view as they talked. She too was affected by the sight of the family home.

"It's amazing to picture them walking in and out of that doorway, isn't it?"

"It is, and I may have traced the portrait to a buyer from Germany. I can't be certain, but there was a framed portrait among the contents of the house when they were auctioned."

"That's amazing, Jon, well done you!"

"Thanks, but let's not get our hopes up too much just yet. It could be a completely different painting, although, I must admit I have a strong feeling that it is Paolo's drawing. But it's very weird, the wedding portraits are mentioned nowhere, not even in Leo's will. Whatever happened to them, happened pretty quickly. Unfortunately, Alessio's will hasn't turned up yet. I think he may have sold them, just as Paolo feared. And somehow they vanished."

"What are you going to do next?"

"I'm going to eat in that trattoria, to see inside the house. In the morning I have to go back to the Central Library to see someone, then I'm coming home. Oh damn! My phone battery is about to die. I'll call you later tonight, from the hotel."

* * *

"It's not too late, is it? I mean, are you in bed?" Jonathan asked.

"I am actually, but it's not too late."

"Sorry. I met some interesting Americans in the trattoria and we got chatting and... well, I just got back."

"What was it like?"

"To be honest, disappointing. With all the restaurant paraphernalia and not very good cheap paintings on the recently panelled walls, I couldn't get any sense of the place as their home."

"That's too bad."

"Yes, but listen to this. Before my battery died, I was about to ask if you remember Caterina, the girl who impressed Paolo in Milan?"

"Of course, why?"

"You'll never guess. Her descendant is working in the archive, doing work experience from Harvard. She's the young woman who helped me find the tax records. And Caterina did exactly what she told Paolo she would do–she founded a dynasty. It's pretty clear the family is still seriously wealthy–they're called Bonsignori-Lenzi. Isn't that great?"

"That's amazing! What a small world. Paolo would be pleased."

"It is incredible to think of that young girl, deciding what she wanted from life and just going for it. And succeeding so incredibly well. I had no clue what I wanted to do when I was a teenager–even after I finished my degree. I suppose that's why I joined the Army. It was a way of putting off a decision, I think.

"It's not like we're a military family. It seemed exciting, I suppose. And it was. I did all kinds of things and I don't regret it. But it wasn't an especially considered decision. How about you? How did you choose your degree?"

"It turned out that going to California to live was really lucky. The University of California has a great reputation, and it's a public school. Tuition for in-state students is pretty reasonable, so it wasn't a hard choice picking my college. And I knew I wanted to study history, I had been a sucker for historical fiction for years and then biographies. Santa Barbara is great, and it wasn't too far from home. I could go back and see Helen and George any weekend I wanted."

"And did you? Or were you too busy partying?"

"I did actually. I wasn't much of a party girl–still not really. I made a few bad choices with boyfriends early on and that put me off for the rest of my undergrad years. What about you and the girl you mentioned, Sarah? What happened there?"

He told her about the break-up with Sarah and the attempted reconciliation, although he decided not to go into detail about exactly how the reconciliation had been attempted. He didn't want Lauren knowing he had slept with Sarah after they had met. He was always going to feel guilty about that.

"Anyway," he finished, "it's well and truly over now."

"I'm glad you called. It's been nice hearing your voice. I should get some sleep, I've got a busy day tomorrow."

"What are you up to?"

"I have to formally present my proposal for a PhD based on the Chronicles. Professor Hunter says I shouldn't worry about it, but I still have to get through it. And I'm working on my talk. The seminar is less than two weeks away, but I've more or less figured out what I'm going to do for my presentation."

"I'll be back tomorrow night. See you soon. Good night, Lauren."

"Good night, Jon. Safe travels."

Each of them had enjoyed the intimacy of their late night call. They would both have felt even better had they known that they each went to sleep thinking of the other.

Crisis

Soon after she settled at her desk the following morning, Lauren was interrupted by a knock on her door. She was mildly surprised when both the Earl and Professor Hunter let themselves into her study and sat down across from her.

Professor Hunter opened the conversation.

"We've got some unpleasant news to share, a problem of the University's making, and we're well aware of that. You will have the full support of the University in the days ahead."

This all sounded extremely ominous, but the Professor ploughed ahead before Lauren could react.

"A French publication, *Le Figaro Magazine*, has got a hold of images of some diary pages, the ones from 1503 covering the commissioning of the Giocondo *Mona Lisa*, the subsequent nude version, and Leonardo's change of heart. They seem also to have at least a rough idea of the content of the Rome pages dealing with the second *Mona Lisa*. They're going to run a story tomorrow, claiming the diaries are a sophisticated Anglo-Saxon forgery designed to destroy the reputation of the Louvre's *Mona Lisa* and damage the museum's status as the world's leading cultural institution."

"This is awful! How did it happen?"

"We don't know. The problem is that a lot of people have had at least some access to the papers. I mean dozens and dozens one way or another. I don't think we'll ever know."

"Well, we'll just have to defend the Chronicles, won't we? I mean, the timing sucks, but this kind of issue was bound to arise, we've always known that, haven't we? Out of curiosity, why do they say this is happening now?"

"Their conspiracy theory is that the billion-euro deal done between the Louvre and the Emirates was a big blow to the UK's prestige, and we want to make sure it doesn't happen again."

William Chance interrupted.

"There's another issue I'm afraid, Lauren. The article is going to suggest you are the key person in this fraud. The trailer ends with a promise that in the expanded story on their website, they'll set out scandalous allegations about the person who is the key player in the affair, and they printed their claim under a small photograph of you."

In the silence that followed, Lauren became aware that the Earl and the Professor were carefully observing her, trying to gauge her reaction.

"I don't know what you want me to say. What are you planning to do?"

Jane Hunter responded to Lauren's challenge.

"Fortunately, I had already done one useful thing, although I didn't realise at the time just how useful it would turn out to be. When I read the Rome diary entries, I sent copies of all of the content relating to the *Mona Lisa* to the Director of the Louvre, confidentially, as a professional courtesy. It is clear the diaries will have major repercussions for him, and it seemed to me unfair that he should be caught unawares when we publish. It was the Director himself who called me with the news about the magazine. He is appalled about the situation and assures me that he will be taking our side in the debate in France. So that will be really helpful."

The professor looked at the Earl and back to Lauren.

"And I wasn't expecting you to say anything. I was just, we were just, concerned about how you would react to all of this."

"Angry, anxious, a bit frightened. But until I see exactly what they'll say about the Chronicles, about me, I don't see how I can respond."

In truth, Lauren was terrified at the prospect of intense media publicity.

William Chance asked her if the magazine had been in touch with her.

"No, but then I've pretty much given up on social media–the volume of messages after the press conference was just overwhelming. I hardly look at it any more. My friends know to use text messaging to reach me.

Professor Hunter had more to say.

"As I said at the outset, this is the Library's and the University's problem, and my responsibility. We were too slow to enforce proper security over the diaries. I can only offer the excuse that I had no idea how explosive they would turn out to be. No matter, it was our fault, my fault. I suggest you refer any questions regarding the authenticity of the Chronicles to me. Part of me doesn't like to respond at all, but the fact is, the early pages have already been examined by experts on language, writing and paper of the period and everyone is content that the diary is exactly what it appears to be. So, we have lots of ammunition."

* * *

Lauren had no appetite and couldn't summon up the enthusiasm to go to the pub, where she knew some of the estate staff would be with friends and partners. She thought of calling Jonathan, but she thought he might be on his way back. She decided she'd rather talk when she knew just what the magazine was going to publish. And anyway, he'd be back tomorrow.

In the end, she spent the evening in her room, reading about previous forged manuscripts and art world scandals. She was rocked when she came upon a summary of the *Hitler Diaries* fiasco. Until then, Lauren had assumed that the sheer scale of the Paolo Chronicles was itself compelling evidence of them being genuine. Who would attempt forgery on such a huge scale? But here she was, reading about a deception involving almost sixty volumes of purported diaries which, for a while at least, had fooled experts. After this depressing reading, she forced herself to stop–and moved on to endless YouTube cat videos.

At one minute past two a.m., after she had checked several times, Lauren finally saw *Le Figaro Magazine* had made their latest edition available online.

Her French was good enough to understand that the article was as she had been told, with a bit more background that made no difference to the essential story–*The Paolo Chronicles* were fakes, and she was the principal architect of the fraud.

Lauren didn't fall into a fitful sleep until after five o'clock.

Result

"What's in here?"

It was now late afternoon on the same day, and Lauren was standing in her study, holding a smart, shallow cardboard file box, decorated in a gorgeous, marbled pattern. Jonathan had handed it to her–it was no deeper than a finger.

"Florence is famous for wonderful cardboard and *paper* products–or have you forgotten?"

Lauren looked at her friend and saw the smug expression on his face.

"Oh, my God! This isn't…?"

Jonathan laughed out loud.

"Take a look, why don't you?"

Despite fingers suddenly made clumsy, Lauren wrestled open the beautiful box; and there they were–more pages of Paolo's lovely script.

"They were in a file deposited by Leo, originally in the Duomo. Obviously, these are photocopies. Even so, you can see that the originals are slightly damaged, but not too badly. Dottoressa Ricci, from the Central Library, which now holds them, has agreed to loan the entire file to the Bodleian. It will be delivered as soon as they complete some formalities. You should have the final pages in a couple of weeks. These are just a taster."

To her horror, Lauren found that her eyes were welling up.

"I can't believe you got them. Thank you, Jon, thank you very much."

Her words sounded pathetically inadequate and her emotions overcame her once again. This time, to Jonathan's astonishment, Lauren dropped the box onto her desk, threw her arms around his neck and kissed him, fiercely.

"Wow!" he said when she pulled away.

"I'm not sure if you can truly appreciate everything this means to me. I'm absolutely certain Paolo's story isn't close to being over, I'm just certain of it. And after yesterday and last night…"

To her intense embarrassment, Lauren began to cry. Despite all her efforts, she couldn't stop, and she was immensely comforted when Jonathan wrapped his arms around her and held her tight as she sobbed against his chest. Best of all, he didn't ask what was wrong. He simply held her close until she regained control.

"I'm sorry, really, I am," she said, trying to repair the damage to her eyes with the tissue he handed her.

She told him about the magazine article and her fears about what was yet to come.

For his part, Jonathan didn't tell her it wasn't important. He didn't suggest she should ignore it. He didn't dismiss it because it would all be forgotten in a day or two.

Instead, he coached a tiny smile from her by pointing out, "Hey, now you've got more of the diary to get stuck into, and you can look forward to lots more soon. And then there's your presentation. Can I see it? How about a dress rehearsal? Wait a minute!" he finished abruptly.

Tenderly, Jonathan put a hand on each of Lauren's shoulders, and held her at arms' length.

"I just realised something. Don't you see? These pages," he indicated the box, "these pages *prove* the diary is genuine! Otherwise you have to believe that the Central Library in Florence is part of the conspiracy–*I* didn't find these pages, *they* did!"

His word tumbling over themselves, Jonathan explained how he had first gone to the Duomo, only to find they had a record of sending Paolo's papers to the Central Library, where they were sadly lost in 1966.

"I had the idea to ask about any papers relating to Leo. It's racing certainty that Leo's papers were transferred at the same time as Paolo's. I didn't bother checking, but I'll bet there's a similar paper trail for Leo's stuff. So now you'd have to believe the Duomo is implicated as well, and as far back as 1958, sixty years ago! We've got them, the lying bastards!"

Lauren felt as if a physical band had been loosened from around her chest. In the back of her mind was the thought that *Le Figaro* had promised more revelations about her, but now she knew whatever they wrote would be completely discredited by the very existence of the new pages.

"We need to tell William and Professor Hunter–they'll be so relieved too. God, I feel so much better! Let's go find William first, he's around here somewhere."

They tracked the Earl down in the kitchen and shared the good news with him. Lauren could only have the briefest of telephone conversations with Jane Hunter, who was in a meeting, so they agreed to meet the following morning at the Library.

By this time, it was after six o'clock and Jonathan stole yet another look at his watch.

"I need to be off, I'm afraid, family dinner tonight. I thought I was only popping in to give you the papers."

He finished with a smile. "Why don't you come along, it's only Henley?"

"I was going to have a look at these new pages and then have an early night. I didn't get much sleep last night. Oh! the hell with it. Yes, please, I'd love to come. Can I have five minutes to change and freshen up?"

"You can have ten, but that's all."

"You look lovely, really nice."

After a frantic fifteen minutes dressing, Lauren tracked Jonathan down in the library. She had repaired the damage to her eyes and was wearing a summery print dress and she was pleased with the effect it was having.

"Why thank you, sir. Now I can meet your folks. Who's going to be there?" Lauren asked as an afterthought, as they walked towards the front entrance of the house.

"Well, it's Jennifer's birthday, so Robert and Gerry will there too."

"It's your stepmother's birthday?" Lauren stopped in her tracks, incredulous. "When were you planning to mention this? What have you bought her?"

"Well, nothing. I mean, we don't buy our parents birthday gifts."

"Well, maybe you don't, but I will be. Come on, let's go–we need to stop somewhere so I can buy something. And send you mother a text at least to tell her you've invited me. You are hopeless, you know. What does she like? Flowers, chocolates, music, books?"

"Yes, all of those I imagine."

They carried the conversation on in the car. Lauren interrogated Jonathan long enough for him to reveal that one of his stepmother's passions was baking. While Jonathan drove, Lauren went online and found a French pâtissier in west London who offered advanced classes.

"As soon as we arrive, make some excuse and get the voucher printed, I've emailed it to you," she instructed Jonathan. "And stop at the next florist or supermarket."

The gifts were a success. Lauren handed over the voucher and the flowers, explaining that they were from both of them, and she smiled as Jennifer kissed Jonathan's cheek.

"Thank you so much Lauren, and you too, Jon. Although I don't imagine you had much to do with it," she observed with a knowing look. "They're a lovely surprise."

Dinner was informal, and fun. Jonathan prompted Lauren to tell the family a little about the Chronicles, which she enjoyed doing, especially after his father complimented her.

"It is fascinating to hear about them, especially as this one," Roger nodded at his son, "has refused to tell us anything at all!"

When Jennifer asked her about her original PhD research, she had to suppress a smile. Jennifer and Roger were treating their unexpected guest exactly as Signor Lenzi would have recommended. Just like Paolo had been, now she was being encouraged to shine by her hosts. What a wonderful family, she thought.

When Jonathan pulled up at Blythswood House's front door, he had to gently prod Lauren awake.

"Oh, we're here already! I'm sorry. I'm utterly exhausted. Thanks for a lovely evening. Your family is very special. And thanks again for finding the rest of the diary, for even more reasons than before. I don't know how to…" She stopped, her feelings too intense to articulate.

"Hey, it's fine, it wasn't so difficult, anyone could have found them."

"I'm not so sure. By the way, how did you persuade them to loan the rest of the diary?"

"Charm. Sex appeal. The usual."

She rolled her eyes. "Yeah. As if."

"I'd love to take all of the credit, but honestly, Professor Hunter had everything to do with it, she has a huge reputation in Florence. The file will be delivered to her. The Library is responsible for its safety, but I wanted you to see a taster. And by the way, you might want to ask Prof Hunter about a mysterious Roberto from Florence."

He leaned over and kissed her on the cheek.

"Good night. Pleasant dreams."

But, having collapsed into bed, Lauren dreamt she was back in the bank where she had worked for almost three years after graduation. She was running late for an important meeting to discuss her career, but she was becoming more and more comprehensively lost in the enormous building that was the bank's head office. Every doorway led to yet another long corridor or stairway, all taking her ever further from her destination. She passed lots of people, but she couldn't ask for directions because she wasn't wearing any shoes.

She was steadily becoming more and more agitated, when she stepped through yet another door and found herself in a large room where a lively party was in full swing.

She watched people dancing. She knew everyone—they all worked in the bank, including Jonathan, who was slow dancing with his girlfriend, a gorgeous Italian who worked in private banking, looking after the bank's richest clients. The young woman had a terrific figure and when she tossed her head to laugh at some clever comment of Jonathan's, Lauren noticed her full, sensual lips. Her hair was the colour of fine old wine. Lauren couldn't for the life of her remember the woman's name. In contrast to Lauren's tatty top, stained jeans, and filthy bare feet, the Italian was wearing killer heels and a stunning backless cocktail dress of the softest white silk. Suddenly, Lauren remembered she hated this woman and she was overwhelmed by a crashing wave of jealousy as Jonathan and the girl began to kiss passionately on the dance floor. He was running his hand over the woman's naked back when Lauren awoke with a start, the image of Jonathan and his Italian lover seared for a brief second before fading from her memory, leaving only a feeling of deep unease and a racing heartbeat.

She lay awake tossing and turning, before slipping back into a deep and dream-free sleep. Next morning, she had no recollection of her nightmare.

Response

At nine o'clock the following morning, Lauren and the Professor were huddled over Lauren's laptop, looking at Le Figaro's website.

"Oh dear, Lauren! They're saying you have some kind of malevolent hold over William. It seems you're a femme fatale who has spun a web of sexual dependence around him in order to perpetrate this fraud at the behest of some mysterious puppet masters–either the British cultural establishment or the mysterious owners of the Isleworth *Mona Lisa*, or both."

Jane Hunter looked up from the screen and into Lauren's eyes. They stared at each other for a long moment before first Lauren, then Jane, started to smile before both burst out laughing.

"What's William going to make of this?" asked Lauren through her giggles.

"Oh dear! He so hates publicity–this will only confirm every bad thing he believes about the media."

It was much easier to laugh now, in the knowledge they would release a powerful rebuttal of the story almost immediately. They turned their attention back to the story and their good cheer evaporated.

"Who is Jackson Greensmith?" Professor Hunter asked after a few minutes' more reading, "Is he the one who came here with your Professor from Chicago? He says here you have a history of mental instability. Basically, he's claiming you're a desperately ambitious, mentally unstable, sexually aggressive woman who has manipulated the whole business."

"That's him. Professor, I should maybe tell you that I did—"

"Stop! Stop right there. You are *not* obliged to discuss with anyone, any aspect of your history—personal, medical or anything else, just because of this nonsense."

In a softer voice, she continued, "Lauren, if ever you want to talk to me about anything, anything at all, privately, as your professor, my door is always open. But any such conversation will be entirely confidential, between the two of us, and under no circumstances, none whatsoever, will it become a matter for public discussion."

While Jane Hunter had been talking, Lauren was gathering her own thoughts about the new revelations. Where before she had been frightened at the prospect of becoming a public target of the media, now her fear turned to anger. The implication that she had secured her role with the Chronicles by seducing the Earl was entirely typical of an attitude that explained a woman's success in terms of her sexual appeal.

"Why don't we attack them, Professor? They've picked on me because I'm female. Let's go for them for that, as well as on the fact that the diaries are completely genuine."

Professor Hunter gave a broad smile.

"Excellent! I hoped you would see it like that! But, I suggest we do very little at all at the moment. The University will put out a release this morning confirming what we have already decided to do. The launch of the research team will be in a few days and will proceed as planned.

"And others will take up the fight on our behalf, and this will be much more effective. We have allies: the Director of the Louvre, the Italian media you won over so well, the British media and *Burlington Magazine*, which is very influential. Not to mention all of the members of the Research Group who are desperate to get to work. I recommend that we include in our release a short quote from you expressing sadness that chauvinistic and misogynistic attitudes still persist in sections of the media. And Jonathan is right, the discovery of the Florence diary pages will speak for itself and destroy their credibility. Then we ignore them."

The Earl had the last word when they called him.

"My knowledge of the American legal system is based entirely on Perry Mason and watching LA Law and Ally McBeal with Katherine. Based on this extensive and authoritative education, I suspect you may have grounds for a lucrative lawsuit against the University of Chicago for misuse of your medical records."

Later in the morning Jonathan called.

"How are you bearing up?"

"I'm fine, honestly I am. Today's stuff has just got me really angry."

Before she could continue, Jonathan interrupted, "They would never have written anything like this if you were a guy, you know."

Lauren experienced an unexpected wave of affection for her friend. "You're absolutely right–and that's what's making me so incredibly mad."

"Have you found out who leaked the diary material?"

"No, and Professor Hunter has decided not to try. There are way too many potential suspects and too many honest people would have the finger of suspicion pointed at them. Anyway, we'd probably never get to the bottom of it."

"Will you have to give another press conference?" he asked.

"No, I don't think so. She's called the Library in Florence to ask them to put out an announcement about the discovery of the Italian section of the Chronicles. That should put paid to the conspiracy theories. By the way, with everything that's being going on, I can't believe I haven't even asked what's next in the hunt for the portrait."

PART THREE

1935 – Munich

"Opa, tell me again about this one."

"Very well, mein liebes Kind. This one is by Canaletto. Do you know why he was called Canaletto?"

"No, but you're going to tell me, aren't you?"

Susanna loved having her grandfather tell her things—stories about him and her grandmother when they were young, and especially about the pictures he had lovingly collected over his long life. Isaak Abramowitch was 85 and he had been extremely rich for a very long time, despite having been born dirt poor in Latvia. He had not yet turned thirty when he began buying art, becoming an important collector who loaned many works to the city art museum.

"Giovanni Canal was a painter—like his father, Bernardo. So, to tell them apart, Giovanni became known as 'little Canal'—Canaletto. This is the Grand Canal in Venice, I bought this for Oma after our first visit to Venice. We went back many times, but that first visit was special. Look here, this is a gondola, a special kind of boat you only see in Venice. Oma and I took many trips in gondolas. Do you know why?"

The little girl was ready to show off. "Because the streets of Venice are full of water!"

"That's right, they are; and Canaletto painted them better than anyone else. We have another of his paintings, but it is on loan to the museum. We can go to see it one day."

Susanna's attention was already elsewhere. "Tell me about this one, *The Lady*."

"Well, this one is very special. This is the first artwork I bought. It was at an auction in Florence. It is only a sketch, a profile and it was very cheap, a few marks, but I was excited to win the bidding. Do you like it?"

"I'm not sure. The lady in the picture is pretty, but…"

"But the painting is maybe not so great, eh? But look here; look at the flowers she is holding. See how simple it is, only a few strokes, but how real the flowers are! And the lady's neck, how graceful! And look at this wonderful cascade of hair! So, this one I love because it was my first purchase and because she is very, very special."

"Who painted *The Lady*?"

"No-one knows. It is not signed, and it does not look like any other work I know. So, you are free to imagine for yourself. Who do you think she is?"

The girl looked at the image for several moments.

"A beautiful princess," she announced.

Her grandfather laughed and ruffled his granddaughter's mass of black curls.

"Not every lady in a painting is a princess, little one. But she could be a princess–that magnificent neck. A beautiful princess, like you."

"Show me another painting."

"No, not today. Look outside, it's a beautiful day. The flowers in the portrait have made me think. Let's go and take some roses to Oma, she would like that."

"OK," Susanna replied cheerfully.

Opa always told her a new story when they visited the grave of her grandmother, although Susanna found it difficult to picture her elderly grandparents as the dashing, romantic young couple in the tales he spun for her.

* * *

Less than two months later, Otto and Ruth Abramowitch and their eldest child, Ignaz, talked at length, really for the first time, about the deteriorating situation. Three weeks had passed since they had buried Isaak beside his wife. Now, they sat in the parlour, a formal room, appropriate for a serious conversation. The heavy furniture was not designed for comfort or to appeal to aesthetic sensibilities. It was selected to advertise that this was the home of a successful, but completely conventional family. No touches of modernism here, no experimentation with new ideas. The family that chose these furnishings would always opt for stability, security, continuity. Unfortunately, their taste in home furnishings wasn't helping the family in the current crisis.

"More of our friends have left, even more are preparing to go," Ruth observed. "The Kleins have gone to her sister in Paris, I think they will not return."

"Did they sell the house?" Otto asked.

"Not yet. They didn't want to draw attention to themselves until they were safely away. But they shipped their most valuable possessions and I assume their money.

Klara Frankl says her husband thinks there will soon be even more restrictions on Jews who want to leave. We will be denied taking anything of value she says. Her husband has heard rumours in the bank."

"Perhaps we should make some plans, just in case. But I can't leave at this time, the business would fall apart. These people will fall from power, I am certain of it. But I'll contact cousin Felix in Amsterdam. I will send him some money to hold for us, an insurance."

Ignaz looked around at the magnificent art on the walls. "You know there are rumours? People say Hitler is crazy about art. They may make it difficult to get back any of the loans from the museum or to move anything out of the country."

"Hitler will pass. We will deal with the art as well as we can."

* * *

"You don't like him because he isn't a Jew!"

Ruth sighed; her older daughter was slowly driving her mad.

"Esther Abramowitch, you are barely seventeen years old. If Max was Jewish, Buddhist or Hindu, it would still be improper for you to be sitting in the garden alone with an older boy without a chaperone. Do not test me further on this, young lady, or you will be confined to this house for a month! Now, go to your room and come down when you are ready to apologise."

At that moment, Ruth heard the crunch of the driveway pebbles under the wheels of her husband's car. Otto and Ruth lived in an imposing house in a district favoured by the wealthy citizens of Munich. Their neighbours were lawyers, bankers, business owners and senior civil servants and politicians. It was a world of manicured gardens, chauffeurs, housemaids and horses.

"It is done," Otto announced as soon as he arrived in the parlour where his wife awaited him. "Felix sent a telegram confirming receipt of the money and he tells me his friend, Pieter Geerts, head of Italian paintings at the Rijksmuseum, has agreed to formally request both the Canalettos, the Veronese and the Giorgione for their Venetian exhibition."

"Will they let the Canaletto out of the museum?" Ruth asked.

"They might. We'll just have to see."

The decision about the paintings went all the way up to the Reichsminister in Berlin. Berlin was at that moment in talks with the Rijksmuseum to borrow two Rembrandt self-portraits and so it was agreed that Otto's paintings would be sent to Amsterdam in 1938 for the following year's exhibition.

* * *

Several weeks later, Ignaz asked his father join in him in the parlour.

"I was going to wait a while before I discussed this with you, Father, but with the situation as it is, I need to act now. Since I graduated last year, every avenue has been closed to us—the professions, the big companies and as for our family business…well, I need to get out. And now, with the money from Opa…"

Ignaz took a breath and remembered how he had planned to raise the next subject delicately, but now circumstances had changed. "I want to leave Germany, and with Leah as my wife."

Ignaz waited for his father's explosion and was amazed when it failed to arrive.

"Congratulations, son. You are making the correct decision, and I'm sure Leah will make an excellent wife and mother."

And then to Ignaz's even greater astonishment, his reserved father rose from his seat and reached his arms out to his only son, who stood to be warmly embraced.

"I will do anything I can to help you. When do you wish to have the wedding? Have you talked with Leah's father?"

"No, I wanted to talk with you and Mama first. Leah and I would like to marry as soon as possible and get out of Germany. I know you have decided to stay for the business, but we would like to go to the United States, but anywhere outside Germany will do for now. I will talk to Leah's father tomorrow. And thank you, Father, thank you from both of us."

Six weeks later, Ignaz and Leah were married in the modest Eiseman home. Only their immediate families and four close friends were in attendance.

* * *

On a wet, miserable day shortly before the last day of the year, at around five in the afternoon, Otto and Ruth were disturbed by a storm of hammering on their front door.

Reaching the entranceway before any of the household staff, Otto threw the door open to find his daughter-in-law crying hysterically in the supportive arms of a portly man around his own age.

"Your son," the man began, clearly emotional, "your son came to the aid of these people in Petersplatz."

As he said this, the man swept his arm around to indicate an elderly couple sitting in the back seat of a dilapidated black saloon in the driveway.

By now, one of the staff had arrived. Otto took him by the elbow.

"Franz, go bring those people in the car into the house, smartly now."

He turned back to the stranger, "Come in, come in. Where is Ignaz?"

Before he could answer, Ruth arrived and took charge of Leah, leading her to a sofa where she collapsed, still incoherent.

The stranger stood in the hall watching Ruth while nervously twisting the brim of his hat.

"Your son, sir, is dead. They beat him to death in the street. I was passing in my car and witnessed the end of the assault on your son."

The man saw the question forming on Otto's lips.

"I assure you, sir. Until recently I practised as a doctor, I was a surgeon. Your son was undeniably dead. His brain…trust me, there was no possibility he could have survived the attack, none. He was a brave man, but…one thing, you should have her own doctor examine your daughter-in-law as soon as possible. When the attack was finally over, she kept crying, 'But our baby. I'm having our baby, Ignaz's baby!'"

1938 – Munich

Ruth couldn't help but feel a little anxious.

"Otto, tell us again about the paintings, what do we need to do?"

"Tomorrow the museum will send over the Canaletto that has been on loan. The next day the shipping company will collect all four works and take them to Amsterdam. We have to have our other three paintings ready for a final check before all four are sealed in the big shipping box in the hallway."

"What pictures are we sending, Papa?" Susanna asked.

"The other Canaletto, the Veronese study and the Giorgione."

In a small voice, Susanna now asked, "Will we be able to take the other pictures when we leave, Papa?"

A few weeks earlier, Otto would have sought to reassure his youngest child, but he recognised that now it was time for the truth.

"No, darling, I'm afraid not. We'll have to use them to bribe our way to Holland. I don't think we'll see them again."

Susanna fought to contain her tears. Now twelve years old, Susanna was wise beyond her years. She had had to grow up fast in the years since Hitler had come to power.

"Then we should send *The Lady* to the exhibition, it was Opa's favourite."

Ruth knew Susanna would feel the emotional loss of the paintings deeply, they had been at the core of her relationship with her grandfather.

"Even if we wanted to, we couldn't, darling. The only reason we can send these paintings is because permission was granted long before things became so bad, and only because the Rijksmuseum requested these particular paintings."

Otto too tried to prepare his daughter.

"I'm afraid we may have to sell even these when we get to Amsterdam. We won't be wealthy anymore I'm sorry to say, and *The Lady* isn't worth much."

"We should send *The Lady*, not to sell, but to keep."

They all heard the pain in the young girl's voice, but it was Leah, who had been silently cradling her son throughout these exchanges, who empathised more than any of the others with her young sister-in-law.

Ignaz's brutal murder had put an end to any thoughts of America. With Ruth, Esther and Susanna available to assist with the baby, it had seemed natural for Leah to move in with her in-laws, who in these desperate times also had access to more resources than her own parents. Now she saw how important it was to support Susanna.

"We could do it. The Veronese is a study of a woman's head and shoulders, not too unlike the subject of Susanna's *Lady*. Of course, the two works look nothing like each other, but I don't imagine the men from the shipping company will spot the difference. They'll see an old image of a young woman, just as they expect. And perhaps you could sell the Veronese here, quietly, and get some money."

Now Esther joined the conversation.

"But what about Amsterdam, Leah? They'll certainly see something is wrong."

Leah looked at her father-in-law. Otto was the only one who had any understanding of what might happen in Holland. Otto said nothing for several moments.

"Perhaps if I got a message through Felix," he mused. "The Director is sympathetic, or he would never have gone along with this at all."

"Do you mean he is Jewish?" asked Susanna.

"No, darling, he is a Christian, but a good man. I hope you'll learn there are good Christians out there, even if it doesn't always seem so."

"Let's do it!" Ruth exclaimed, "Let's do it for Opa and Oma and for baby Jacob, so when he grows up, he'll have a souvenir of his great-grandfather. *The Lady* is a part of our family, we must try to save her!"

Two days later, the shipping company porters did indeed give only the most cursory glance to the four artworks as they slid them the final few inches into the prepared slots in the shipping container. With barely a word to the tainted Jewish family, they did their work, signed a receipt and left. By now the family had no domestic help. Even if they could have afforded to keep staff, Christians were no longer allowed to work for Jewish employers.

The family business had been 'Aryanised', confiscated in other words, and the family were surviving on their depleted hidden savings. Otto's bank accounts had been sequestered and routinely raided for one 'tax' or another.

* * *

Later, when they were all safe in Holland, Otto would often observe that it was only due to the Nazi venality that the family managed to get out of Germany. Isaak's remarkable art collection had been targeted and one by one the paintings were taken into custody for 'protection'. Against this backdrop, Otto managed to sell, clandestinely, several of the less well-known paintings to other collectors for cash, including the Veronese held back from the shipment to Amsterdam, albeit at prices less than one-tenth of their true worth.

Finally, Otto was able to engineer permits for his family to leave for Amsterdam. At the last moment, threatened with withdrawal of their travel papers, he was forced to add his signature to the transfer of the family home as a 'gift' to a prominent Nazi lawyer.

1939 – Amsterdam

In May of 1939, Otto received a note asking him to call on Pieter Geerts, at the Rijksmuseum. Otto had, of course, visited the Venetian exhibition several times, smiling each time he saw the explanatory label beside *The Lady – 'Follower of Veronese. Venetian School, late 16th Century'*. Pieter couldn't attribute the work to Veronese, but neither could he ignore it completely if the plan was to work. Otto was aware that several other curators in the museum must have been turning a blind eye to the deception, he presumed at Pieter's request. The conspirators had become friends.

"Thank you for coming in, Otto. I have heard, fortunately unofficially, that the German authorities will soon present a demand that your paintings must be returned to Germany in three weeks, when the exhibition ends. They will claim that as you did not pay Flight Tax on three of them, and the fourth is the property of the Munich museum, the paintings are therefore confiscated."

"How will your government respond?"

"I wish I could say they will resist, but they have acceded to German demands in every case involving property of German Jews in the Netherlands. I'm sorry, my friend, but I believe they will hand over the paintings."

"How long before you receive an official instruction?"

"I don't know, it could be any day."

"What if I sold them before the end of the exhibition?"

"That's exactly what I was going to suggest. There is a dealer, Heinz Burgdorf, based in Switzerland. He is the

333

brother-in-law of Martin Bormann, Hitler's senior assistant, so he has some influence with the Nazis. He is a fascist himself, but there is no one else I can think of in a position to get this done in time. Believe me, if there was, Burgdorf would be the last person I would recommend. But I must warn you, to get this resolved in a few days will mean accepting a terrible price. People understand your general situation and know you have few options, if any."

Following a call from the museum, Burgdorf flew to Amsterdam the next day. After a quick visit to the exhibition, the dealer and Otto sat down in an empty office.

Burgdorf was a huge man, obese and well over six feet tall. Nonetheless, he was immaculately dressed and carried himself in the manner of a man who knows he holds every advantage.

"Three of your paintings are interesting, Doctor; the simple portrait is odd, but it has a certain charm. For all four, I can offer you three thousand English pounds, paid in England, so you will actually receive the money—I assume you will try to get to England sooner or later. If I gave you guilders, the German government would go to court to seize the funds."

"The paintings are worth far more than you suggest, Herr Burgdorf. Each of the Canalettos alone is worth much more."

"Let us not pretend we do not understand your situation, Jew. In a few days the paintings will be confiscated. There is no one other than myself able or willing to buy them. You will take the three thousand or you will take nothing. Decide."

Otto kept his temper and replied, "The portrait has little commercial worth, but it has sentimental value to my family. I doubt the authorities will have much interest in it, so I would rather not sell it."

Burgdorf made the process of selecting and lighting a cigarette a piece of theatre that consumed a long silence.

"As I understand matters, that item was sent here as a Veronese. Either it is, or it was smuggled out illegally."

As he said this, Burgdorf fixed Otto with a malevolent stare. Both men knew the drawing had nothing to do with Veronese, but Burgdorf was telling Otto that, in the 24 hours available to him, he had been able to find out the precise circumstances of the shipment from Munich. He was advertising the fact that he could instantly place a call to anyone in the Nazi apparatus and be listened to. He was demanding *The Lady* because he could.

The paintings were conservatively worth twenty or thirty times the amount he was being offered, but Otto was realistic, and receiving the money outside the grasp of the Nazis was a major factor in his decision to accept the offer. He set aside his distaste for the odious Swiss across the table.

"Your offer is accepted. I will telephone you at your hotel within the hour with details of an English bank account where you may deposit the funds."

"Good day, Doctor. I will not say it has been a pleasure, but I hope you Jews have learned your lesson. In future a lot more humility can be recommended for you people."

1960 – London

Susanna settled into her seat. The concert would begin in two or three minutes. She had been looking forward to this programme for weeks. She hadn't imagined she would ever get a chance to hear Hans Richter-Haaser perform live–she certainly wouldn't travel to Germany to hear him. Yet here he was, in London, playing a week of Beethoven sonatas. Heaven.

As the glorious sounds washed over her, Susanna was transported, lifted to that different plane where her mind wandered serenely, gently propelled by the divine music. She sat with her eyes closed throughout the performance. Much as she enjoyed his sublime playing, Susanna did not want to look on Richter-Haaser's classically handsome Teutonic face framed by his blond mane. He reminded her too much of similar faces in threatening uniforms.

Concerts had become Susanna's passion. She had been out on a few dates, always reluctantly and always arranged by a girl friend or, more recently, by Jacob, her nephew, who was only ten years her junior and who had only recently finished his law degree.

"Come on, Susanna, you can't use me as an excuse anymore, it's time you had a life for yourself. You can't pretend you're still looking after me, it will make me look bad in front of my clients," he concluded with a smile.

"Hmm! And what clients would that be, Mr. Big Shot lawyer?"

"I'll have clients, don't you worry. And don't change the subject. Why won't you return Harry's calls? You said you had a nice time with him, and he's a good man. Maybe not too handsome, but not so ugly either."

"I don't have to explain myself to you, young no-client lawyer. And it's nothing to do with how he looks, I'm just not ready, that's all."

Jacob forbore from pointing out that, at 36, Susanna was as ready as she would ever be. He loved his aunt very much and never for one moment forgot how much he owed her. She had kept him beside her night and day for years and had protected him ever since the dreadful day when they had left the rest of their family, never to see them again.

When they had arrived in London after their escape from Holland, scared, alone, already missing the family they had left behind, the Jewish resettlement agency wanted to place Jacob with a family of Dutch refugees. At sixteen, Susanna was expected to go to work and be more or less independent after a short period of adjustment.

But Susanna had refused to allow her nephew to be separated from her and by badgering anyone who would listen, she found an elderly couple who had had the foresight to leave Germany just ten months after Hitler came to power. Now they were in need of someone to help them manage their large home and be a companion to the wife, who was becoming more and more frail with each passing year. Susanna and Jacob moved into two tiny bedrooms on the top floor of the townhouse in Knightsbridge and within six months, Jacob was doing well in school and had a rather posh English accent.

Now the old couple were long dead, and Susanna had a small business looking after the affairs of elderly Jewish people; paying their bills, arranging workmen and carers and whatever other support they required. Every Monday she went into schools, mostly Jewish, but also to non-Jewish schools whenever she could persuade a head teacher to invite her. By telling them the story of the terrible fate of her own family, she sought to ensure that the new generations knew what had happened and how many seemingly normal people were involved.

As the years passed, Jacob did indeed become a successful lawyer and was able to provide a comfortable life for himself and for his aunt. He married, and Susanna doted on his children when they came along. She became in turn their nanny, baby-sitter, homework advisor and mediator in teenage arguments.

One summer's day, she was strolling along Dover Street when out of the corner of her eye, she spotted a portrait in a gallery window. For just a second, she thought it was her grandfather's favourite, *The Lady*. Her breathing stopped for the brief moment it took before she realised her mistake. On a second look, the drawing in the window bore only a faint resemblance to the image still strong in her memory. As she stood staring into the gallery window, her thoughts returned to her childhood and Opa's patience in re-telling the stories behind his collection, and most of all about *The Lady*. She was glad the old man hadn't lived to see his family destroyed.

With his growing wealth, Jacob had taken to commissioning copies of the paintings that had been in the family's possession before the war–many were so well known, it was easy to find high quality images that the skilled artists could copy from. Sadly, the artwork Susanna longed to recreate most of all, *The Lady,* was undocumented. The only image that remained was the one in Susanna's memory.

PART
FOUR

1524

April 10th

W ord came to me today that Salaì is dead. I had heard he had married, but now I learned that some weeks ago he was killed by a bolt from a crossbow, although I do not know the exact circumstances.

I am not entirely certain of my emotions relating to the death of Salaì. He was undoubtedly a scoundrel in many regards, and a thief and a liar. But he was beloved by Maestro and he could be tender in his care for Dimmi in the last years. However, I am certain he did somehow steal those of Maestro's paintings he took from France before returning to Milan. Dimmi would never admit that this was so, but he could not deny it either. To the very end he was disposed to forgive Salaì, no matter his transgressions. In any event, Salaì is now in the merciful arms of God, who alone can judge him.

May 3rd

A n exceeding disturbing day, the most unsettling of my life. I am not certain whether I can commit today's events to this chronicle. I will wait and *contemplate and decide when my mind is clearer. For now, I am too disturbed to make a decision.*

May 5th

I have decided that I must indeed record the matters which I discovered three days ago. If this chronicle of my life is to have any meaning, it must be as complete as decency allows. I cannot omit those events that show my errors and disappointments, no matter how grievous.

The day was normal enough until late in the afternoon when a young boy appeared at the warehouse and asked to speak with me in private.

"My master, Messer Francesco del Giocondo, humbly requests that Signor del Rosso call on him this day. He sends his sincere apologies but would have you know that he is very ill and cannot leave his bed. He hopes you will put aside any reservations you have, for charity's sake."

You will imagine my surprise at this request. I am accustomed to seeing del Giocondo about in the city, but we have not exchanged a word in many years. Although, as I thought about him, I realised I had not seen him these past months. Nonetheless, I determined to visit him and so I did accompany the young herald back to his master's house. I was led past Dimmi's portrait of Mona Lisa Giocondo to a gloomy bedchamber where I found Signor del Giocondo looking pale and drawn, lying abed, his head and shoulders propped against cushions. He had lost a great deal of weight *since last I saw him. He indicated a chair beside the bed and bade me sit.*

He spoke in a low voice, occasionally availing himself of a sip of thin wine.

"Thank you for coming, Signor del Rosso, I appreciate it. This is mostly water, but I can have the boy bring you a glass of wine if that is your wish."

I declined his offer and he waved the boy away. We were left alone in the darkened room, heavy curtains almost completely closed across all the windows. There was silence until, at length, the sick man spoke.

"Signor del Rosso, I am dying. I tell you this, not to obtain your sympathy, but to persuade you that what I am about to tell you is the truth. I have met my confessor, but he has withheld forgiveness until I speak with certain people to set well some evil I have done in my life."

Naturally this intelligence heightened my anticipation even more, and I leaned in to hear his words, which were quiet and soft. His breath smelled of sickness and corruption, but I could not pull away.

"You will recall the matter of the rumoured painting of my wife, in which she was said to be naked?"

I nodded my agreement.

"I discovered the truth of the matter, that Giacomo Caprotti produced such a painting at the time your master was creating the portrait hanging in my house today. I also

found out Caprotti sold his painting to my enemy and rival, Baldovinetti."

At this point he took a sip of the weak wine and gathered himself.

"I ordered the murder of Caprotti. I intended to confess this to him but yesterday I heard he has died. I am telling you as one who knew him and knows the circumstances around the events in question. I hope this will suffice for my confessor. I paid two men to do the deed, but, as you know, they killed someone else in error. Remarkably quickly, Maestro Leonardo discovered my guilt and made it clear that a further effort to kill Caprotti would certainly lead to charges against me. I put the matter aside. But others did not."

The effort of talking seemed to exhaust the sick man, and again he lay back against the cushions. I thought he may have fallen asleep until he roused himself and continued.

"More than two years later, we come to the matter of the accusation against Messer Alessio Pacini and the subsequent trial. I was found to have laid the accusation against Messer Pacini in order to take control over a valuable shipment from England. Signore, I swear as I face my own judgement, I did not make the accusation, or cause it to be made."

I was amazed by this announcement. "But the contract, the handwriting, the street urchin—everything pointed to your guilt, and you offered no rebuttal! Yet now you say that you were innocent?"

"Recall the situation at the time. A ship from Flanders was feared lost at sea—in truth it was indeed lost. The man who had insured that vessel had also insured two other ships still at sea, one being the ship from England with Messer Pacini's cargo. The insurer could not have withstood another loss, so for a handsome price I agreed to take over the policies on the cargoes of the other vessels. I was merely accepting the relatively small remaining risk against loss at sea, with the vessels almost safely in harbour. I gave no thought to the law which provides that if a man is found guilty of a crime punishable by death, any contracts are forfeit and the insurer may assume the goods. So, yes, I stood to gain from a finding against Messer Pacini. Although sodomites are rarely executed, the law provides that they may be."

I was not convinced.

"And the handwriting on the contract for the portrait? It was clearly judged by all to be identical with the accusation."

"It was, but it was not my contract. The portrait contract presented to the Otto was the copy drawn up for your master. There were two copies of the portrait contract, mine and his."

"This is ridiculous. There is no man in Florence whose handwriting was more distinctive than that of Maestro Leonardo. I know, because I was one of the few who could read it."

"I did not say it was his hand, merely that it was his copy. I think the hand may have been of Caprotti, who would later have been happy to conspire against me."

"Why then did you not simply produce your own copy in your own hand, and prove your case?"

"Because I did not have my copy. It had been lost from the office of my notary, who held safe all of my personal contracts and deeds."

"And the street urchin, I forget his name, with his new clothes and false witness?"

"You will recall, he was never asked to say anything, such was the tumult. In any event, if one could bribe him, so could another."

By now, my mind was reeling, but I had thought of one last objection.

"You say your notary lost your copy of the portrait contract. Why not have him come and swear to the facts?"

"My notary died the year after the contract was drawn up. You see, signore, my notary was Ser Piero da Vinci, father of my accuser. And by ill-fortune, the day after the affair I had to take ship to Spain on a mission vital to my business and was thus gone from the city for many months. On my return, I decided I had more to lose than to gain by re-opening the matter, especially as your Master and his household had by then removed to Milan."

I have now had two days to consider this testimony and I fear I believe it to be true in its essential parts. Dimmi was an extraordinarily clever man and quite capable of seizing the opportunity to bring down one he wished to visit his revenge upon.

Here is the manner in which I believe it unfolded.

Somehow, perhaps through gossip or a cultivated spy, Dimmi became aware of Giocondo's assumption of the insurance risk on Alessio's cargo. His curiosity about all matters may well have made him knowledgeable about the provisions of the law relating to such contracts.

Had he long ago removed del Giocondo's copy of the portrait contract from his father's papers or did he quickly visit his brother and somehow extract it, perhaps under the pretext of seeking some old family document? And he may well have had Salaì make his copy of the original portrait contract as a matter of normal habit, as I myself did for him on countless occasions. Perhaps I was busy on some other task.

Whatever the case, as soon as he became aware of the insurance situation, Dimmi set his plan in motion. Salaì willingly writes the accusation, and places it in the tamburi. Pretending to be acting for Giocondo, Salaì bribes and threatens Alessandro, yes, I have recalled the name of the street urchin, and everything falls from there. Salaì, as I now recall, was absent from the trial, no doubt so the boy could not see and identify him. The Otto found the handwriting on each document identical, because it was. But the author, or as I should say, the writer of both was Salaì, not del Giocondo.

And of course, Maestro had a puppet to hand to be used to 'discover' the incriminating facts—one Paolo del Rosso, devoted assistant, enthusiastic spy, dupe.

I loved him. How could he use me so? What now do I make of the kind words he gave me? Of the hours and days in France near the end, when I felt as close to him as to any human? Did he and Salaì speak of the way they used me? Did they laugh at how quickly I leapt upon his hints and suggestions?

And much more grievous, what of Chiara? How could he betray his goddaughter–destroying her husband, fresh from the altar? And behold the lifelong wreckage of her marriage as a consequence. Did he presume that Alessio would shrug off the rumours as Dimmi had long ignored the accusations about himself? Did he even concern himself with Alessio's feelings?

Shall I tell Chiara? I cannot, I will not destroy the love she holds for the memory of her godfather. There is no one I can confide in, save only this journal.

Dio mio, I am lost. I spend my nights preparing his papers for publication according to the agreement we made. It is tiresome work, made difficult by his terrible handwriting and by the chaos of the subjects–everything mixed, jumbled. Can I continue this work now?

May 8th

I *have resolved to put the Giocondo revelations behind me. If I torment myself further, I will only destroy my own peace of mind. I will put the matter behind me,* and I will tell no one of what I know, or suspect. I will certainly say no word to Chiara.

Maestro was a remarkable man, but he was mortal, fallible, imperfect. He had his weaknesses, as do we all. If he failed to consider the impact his actions would have on Alessio, I am certain he must have regretted the devastating effect he had on Chiara's marriage, even if the full extent of the catastrophe was perhaps not apparent in the months before we left for Milan.

But I will allow myself a respite from the endless task of preparing Dimmi's papers. They can wait.

July 28th

Signor del Giocondo did not die. After many weeks he was seen again in the markets, although much diminished from his previous healthy appearance. Today we met, by chance, both leaving church at the same moment. He looked at me with some concern, so I decided to approach him. I led him aside until we could speak privately.

"Signore, I am happy to see you recovering. I would not wish to be the cause of delaying your return to full health, so let me say that I view our last conversation as an extension of your confessional, and I will not breach your confidence. The matters we discussed, will, for my part, remain private between us.

He looked at me most intently before nodding his head.

"Thank you for your honourable words, Signor del Rosso. You are truly a gentleman."

1526

March 8th

What strange lives we live!

It seems that Chiara, Alessio and I are destined to live out our lives in a strange pavane, weaving our days together, existing in close quarters yet rarely touching, and then only with the briefest of contact.

In truth, and most bizarrely, it is I who forms the hinge of our lives. While Chiara and Alessio have the minimum possible interaction, I sit with Alessio one or two times each month, at my insistence and always with a secretary present to record my reports. I brief him on the complexities of what I regularly remind him is his business, although my own share has grown considerably. Some years ago, I persuaded Alessio that instead of draining cash from the business, he should pay me in shares of the company. In this way I have ensured there will be no dilution in Leo's interests, as he will, in time, inherit everything.

We are now the pre-eminent dealer in English wools in the city, even if the overall trade has declined dramatically, just as Walter forecast. Today, the larger part of our wool imports are merino fleeces from Spain. Leo and I have made several trips to that country, although we have never returned to dismal England.

This is the strange situation in which we three exist.

Almost every day I find time and occasion to visit Chiara and spend some hours in her company. Often, we have little to say, but take pleasure in observing together the busy city below her balcony. There is no hint of scandal attached to our relationship—it is widely recognised and no longer a topic of gossip except perhaps for the occasional visitor from another city. It is not that the passions of youth have left me entirely, but the flame burns less fiercely now.

I have used some of my modest wealth to establish a small household. Old Marco takes care of my two horses, and an ever-changing cast of young girls spend their day cleaning. Francesca, a pleasant and even-tempered widow, finds and manages the youngsters and takes care of my other needs, directing the household, preparing my food and, when it suits both of us, spending the occasional night in my bed. Although never discussed, I suspect Chiara has some intuition concerning these arrangements.

I realised today that in a month Leo will reach his eighteenth birthday. Since our extended visit to England, he has lived solely with me, finding it easier to maintain civil relations with his father if he sees as little as possible of his behaviour.

Chiara has decided that the time has come when she must involve herself in the matter of Leo's betrothal, even if it will be some years before he will be wed.

"I do not mean to arrange matters for him entirely, caro. Leo's match must be of his own choosing. But I shall ensure

he is introduced to young women who would make good partners and helpmeets in his life."

"Some of his friends have set up their own bachelor households," I offered.

Chiara nodded and laughed. "Yes, and I asked Leo if this was his intent. He looked at me as though I was a mad woman. Why would I leave the comfort and company of Paolo's household? I am the envy of my friends who see the benefits and freedom I have enjoyed for many years.' I replied to my son, 'But Paolo assures me that you take little advantage of this freedom. Is he protecting me from the truth?' 'Mother,' he responded with a weary sigh, 'it is the possibilities of my freedom that I enjoy. I have no need to carouse around the city, but I have Paolo's trust enough to make this decision for myself. And if any of my friends have taken too much wine, it is to our household they come for sanctuary.' "

Chiara stretched out her hand and laid it atop my own where it rested on the arm of my chair.

"And so you see, Paolo, your love and wisdom have succeeded. You have raised a fine son for us both, as I knew you would."

As this conversation unfolded, it gave me great pleasure. But in truth, I have unthinkingly viewed Leo as my son since that long-ago day when I breathed in his essence as a tiny babe.

May 14th

For all our history as a Republic, the city has ever fawned upon Dukes and Princes. There was therefore much notice and gossip at yet another arrival today of a messenger from King Francis. This past year the King has been held captive in Madrid, which has given him greater time to attend to his correspondence. I count myself fortunate to number among the regular recipients of letters from his Majesty. We exchange views on the latest engineering and artistic developments in the city, although it pains me to observe and report that Florence is not the nonpareil we once were. Maestro Michelangelo is the sole acknowledged genius remaining among us, kept busy on various commissions by the Medici to glorify San Lorenzo and themselves.

It is true that Dottor Machiavelli, who I now call friend, is still with us, but he is out of favour these many years and recently finished his magisterial, if somewhat tedious, history of Florence.

The King's messenger bore with him a gift, a beautifully illuminated volume of poetry, together with some gold, commission for two fine paintings I have recently secured for his Majesty's collection, and payment for a copy of the Dottore's discourse on reforming Florence, forwarded by me to Madrid.

I shall visit Dottor Machiavelli within the week to convey the King's compliments on his work—he will take great *pleasure from the knowledge that one so prominent has pondered his ideas.*

1527

June 5th

T his was a day sent to remind me how fortunate I am.

Some days ago I received a request to call on Messer Fratelli to discuss his orders for the coming season. The request arrived via Leo and so it seemed natural he would accompany me. Since the death of his wife, Messer Fratelli is known to avoid visiting the city, preferring to spend his days in his magnificent estate a few leagues to the west of the city, on the north shore of the Arno.

Early this morning I was pleasantly surprised when Leo announced that his mother would be joining us, as she was curious to see the famous Fratelli gardens of which she has often heard but has never seen.

Thus, it was a cheerful group of three who rode out of the city on a perfect spring day, a cool breeze setting off the warmth of the sun. We arrived at the magnificent Fratelli palazzo well before the sun reached its zenith. On our arrival, we were greeted by Lorenzo, the only son of Messer Fratelli and his late wife. I know Lorenzo well, he is a great friend of Leo and a frequent visitor to my home.

"*Signor del Rosso, I regret there has been a misunderstanding. My father is expecting you on this day next week. Today he is in Pisa.*"

Turning to Chiara, he continued. "Mona Pacini, Leo has told me that you are desirous of seeing our gardens. May I suggest you and Signor del Rosso take advantage of your ride here to take your leisure for some hours. You will find a light repast awaiting you in the Belvedere. And you, Leo, unreliable messenger, come join me for a swim, it is a perfect day."

Following this obviously rehearsed speech, Leo turned to Chiara and myself, and with a smile announced, "In three days it will be your birthday, Paolo. I could not think of a suitable gift until I received the request from Lorenzo's father. Please enjoy your afternoon."

With that, the two boys ran away laughing, leaving Chiara and I momentarily stunned and then delighted.

For the next four hours my darling and I walked through a dream-like wonderland of gardens, antique sculptures and carefully planned vistas over the river and the distant city. In the privacy afforded us, Chiara took my arm as we strolled; sometimes talking, most times content to savour the moments together. As promised, we found a covered table holding some cheese and ripe tomatoes, fresh bread, succulent fruit and a small flagon of fine wine, all presented under the shade of a Grecian Belvedere with stunning views over the river to the beautiful landscape beyond.

When, at last, we had to set off on our way back to everyday life, Leo received a kiss and a heartfelt hug from his mother and a smile and a nod from me.

It was a wonderful gift from a loving and thoughtful son.

1529

July 28th

L eo is in love. He has asked his mother to arrange a meeting with a young woman, Teresa, who he has been observing at Mass these past two months. In the way of these things, and without a word passing between them, the two young people have become aware of each other and Leo is somehow certain the attraction is mutual. Chiara gave me her report.

"I have noted the way she does not look at me," he explained to his mother.

Gently, Chiara asked precisely in what manner the object of his admiration had not looked at him in a particularly meaningful way.

Apparently, he sighed deeply.

"Mother," he explained as if addressing an idiot, "it should be obvious to anyone. Now please, I beseech you, talk with her mother."

September 4th

"*Truly, Paolo, Leo was quite right. Apparently, the young girl is indeed aware of him and is most desirous of meeting him formally with his mother and I present.*"

"*And how do you feel about this development?*" I asked.

We were sitting on Chiara's balcony, enjoying the warmth of the late afternoon sun.

"*I am not sure. The family is very respectable. The father is a prominent notary and both he and <u>his</u> father served on the Otto di Guardia several times. The mother assures me of the grace and virtue of her daughter, but then, she is unlikely to say else. And Leo is only 21. I had hoped he might be a few years older before this development came to pass.*"

I replied, "I talked with him a few days ago. He cannot readily explain the reason for his attraction, although he assures me the girl is exceedingly beautiful. Moreover, he describes to perfection that excitement, that thrill, he feels whenever he sees her, even if at some distance and among the throng at Mass. He certainly believes himself to be in love. I well remember the feeling."

"*My dear Paolo. It is arranged, I am to meet with Teresa and her mother tomorrow. I shall provide you a full report.*"

September 6ᵗʰ

C hiara was excited when we sat in our usual place once again.

"She is charming, beautiful and very clever. Oh Paolo! she would make a wonderful match for our Leo, truly she would. She reads widely, she admires the better art in our churches. She pays attention to her father's reports concerning commercial matters in the city. I cannot speak too highly of her. And, my love, both mother and father have a high regard for you. Do not look so sceptical! Teresa's mother was absolutely clear. She told me in these exact words. 'My husband has observed the progress of your house since Signor del Rosso became such an important figure in your affairs, and he is most complimentary. "Our daughter's fortune can be safely entrusted to one who has been trained and guided by such a man. I am satisfied with the match." Those were his words to me, and I assure you, signora, my husband is not a man to speak lightly of these matters.' So, caro, believe me when I tell you, you can be proud of your efforts over the years."

You may imagine my happiness at this intelligence and at Chiara's obvious enthusiasm for Leo's choice.

To think of Leo married! It seems only yesterday that I first buried my head in his hair and sealed my love and devotion to him and his mother. How the years have sped by!

PART

FIVE

Present Day - London

Since returning from Florence, Jonathan had been busy. He had returned to his gallery to find that his new partners had been getting along very nicely without him.

His sister-in-law Gerry gave him a report on what had been going on during his brief absence.

"Yes, Jon, sales are going well, but we need you to get out there and acquire some new inventory, one of the walls is looking positively threadbare."

"I will, I promise. The business with the Chronicles is close to wrapping up, and in the meantime I'm on the trail of something that could make us famous."

With help from the staff at the British Library, Jonathan had found a freelance researcher in Munich. The auction receipt he and Joanna had found in Florence had listed the buyer only as 'Isaak Abramowitch, Monaco'. Thankfully, Joanna had been there to stop him making an elementary mistake. She pointed out that, in 1880, 'Monaco' was much more likely to refer to Munich in Germany, than the present-day millionaires' enclave on the Mediterranean.

In only two days, the researcher sent him an email with her report attached.

'Your assignment was straightforward to complete. For obvious and tragic historical reasons, the genealogical records of prominent Munich Jewish families have been thoroughly researched and documented by various organisations.

The Isaak Abramowitch whose descendants are listed below, is certainly the man you identified in Florence. He was a noted art collector with a particular interest in Italian art.

The descendants of **Isaak Abramowitch** *(1850-1935) and his wife,* Fanny *(née Bergman) (1855-1932) are as follows:*

- *their only child,* **Otto Abramowitch** *(1883-1942)* *m* Ruth *(née Koller) (1892-1942)*

In Munich, Otto & Ruth gave birth to:

- *s* **Ignaz Abramowitch** *(1912-1938) m* Leah *(née Eisman) (1912-1942)*
- *d* **Esther Abramowitch** *(1918-1942)*
- *d* **Susanna Abramowitch** *(1924-) No trace of a marriage or death, none registered with any of the principal survivor organisations.*

In Munich, Leah gave birth to:

- *s* **Jacob Abramowitch** *(1936-2010) m* Klara *(née Bauer) (1941-2013)*

In London, Jacob and Klara gave birth to:

- *s* **Benjamin Abrams** *(formerly Abramowitch) (1963-) m Sophie (née Miller)*
- *s* **Albert Abramowitch** *(1965-) m Kirsten (née Berenson)*
- *d* **Cynthia Abrams** *(formerly Abramowitch) (1966-) m (1) Tony Petersen (div), m (2) John Johnson (div), m (3) Fred Murphy.*

In London, Benjamin and Sophie gave birth to:
- *s* **Jake Abrams** *(1993-) m Liz (née Bronson)*
- *d* **Rachel Abrams** *(1997-)*

Note: Albert Abramowitch and Cynthia Abrams both had children after they each emigrated to the United States. I have not attempted to trace these children pending your further instructions.

Just to confirm that, as far as I have been able to establish, Susanna Abramowitch is still alive, aged 94 years old and living in London.

The best of luck with your further enquiries.'

Jonathan had skimmed through the email, stopping only at the final note confirming that Susanna was still alive. He went back to check that Susanna would indeed have overlapped with, and known, Isaak. As he re-read the information, he suddenly noted the coincidence of dates of death of so many of the family.

More and more shaken, he realised that Susanna had lost both of her parents, her sister and sister-in-law, all in 1942, and this after the death of her brother in 1938.

Paolo's portrait was bound up with the Holocaust.

Jonathan called Lauren and brought her up to speed.

"I'm not sure what to do now, it seems wrong to poke about in this family's history. The fate of a drawing seems so impossibly unimportant."

"Maybe, but perhaps they would be desperate for information telling them more about their ancestors? Perhaps though, you shouldn't approach the granddaughter initially, you have no idea how it might affect her. How about the next generation, what age are they?"

Jonathan did a quick check.

"The next generation is dead, but the one after that are in their fifties. I'll start there and see where it goes."

An Internet search turned up an address and home phone number for Benjamin Abrams, listed as Ben. A little nervous, Jonathan called the number.

"Mr Abrams? We haven't met, but I wonder if I could come and see you about a matter regarding your ancestor, Isaak Abramowitch? It's a little complicated, but I promise, I won't take up too much of your time."

Ben Abrams agreed to meet Jonathan the following week, in the Costa Coffee near his home in St John's Wood. Jonathan called Lauren and invited her to join them.

Susanna

After brief introductions, Jonathan explained why he had requested the meeting.

"Did you read about the discovery of a diary belonging to an assistant to Leonardo da Vinci?"

"Yes, I did actually," Ben replied.

"Lauren here is the person who found it. I've been helping in a small way, especially in connection with an artwork mentioned in the diary. The author, Paolo del Rosso, tells of a day when Leonardo had Paolo copy a profile of his model, Chiara, a young woman with whom Paolo was besotted. Paolo del Rosso was more of a personal assistant than an artist, so as he drew, Leonardo would occasionally reach over and add a few strokes of his own to Paolo's efforts."

"This is no doubt interesting, Mr Granville, but–"

"Don't worry, I'm getting to the point, and it's Jonathan, please."

Jonathan took a sip of his rapidly cooling coffee and continued.

"Paolo kept his drawing of his beloved Chiara at his side all of his life. In time, his estate went to a man called Leo, Chiara's son and Paolo's protégé. I went to Florence and traced Leo's descendants down to 1880 when the family, now destitute, were evicted from their home and their few remaining possessions auctioned to pay unpaid taxes. Among the items there was an inexpensive portrait, which I'm pretty sure is Paolo's drawing of Chiara."

Jonathan paused and looked intently at Ben.

"Your great-great-grandfather, Isaak Abramowitch, bought the portrait."

Jonathan sat back to await Ben's reaction. He had to wait a while.

"What do you know about Isaak Abramowitch?" Ben finally asked.

"Nothing really, except some bare family facts and figures–his dates, those of his wife and son, and their children and descendants. That's how I found you."

"Isaak Abramowitch was one of the most important European collectors of Italian Old Masters in the years before the First World War. He owned paintings by Titian, Caravaggio, Raphael, Veronese and many, many more. And one way or another they were all stolen from his son, Otto, by the Nazis. I have spent much of my life trying, with a little success, to recover our family's birthright. Normally, one more painting by an unknown artist, even one from Leonardo's workshop, wouldn't necessarily be a priority. But if, as you say, Isaak bought your portrait in 1880, then it may be exceptionally important indeed to someone you should meet. Finish your coffees and come with me, please, both of you."

They left the coffee shop and made their way along St John's Wood High Street before turning into Allitsen Road where Ben led them up a few steps to the front door of a substantial detached house. When he took a key from his pocket and opened the door, Lauren and Jonathan naturally assumed this was Ben's home.

However, as Ben invited them to enter the hall, he called out.

"Tante! You have visitors, put down the sherry!"

Turning to Lauren, he explained, "I live two streets away. This is the home of my Aunt Susanna, actually my great-aunt."

An elegant old lady, her back ramrod straight, but using an ebony cane to assist her, now appeared from the doorway at the end of the hallway.

"Don't be impertinent, Benjamin, and I prefer champagne at lunch time, as you well know."

Susanna was smiling as she spoke.

"Now introduce me, or have you forgotten all of your manners?"

By now, Susanna had reached her great-nephew and they warmly embraced.

"Forgive me, Tante, this is Lauren and Jonathan and they have an interesting story to tell you. Jonathan, Lauren, this is my great-aunt, Susanna Abramowitch, granddaughter of Isaak. Come, let's go in here and talk."

Susanna led the way into a grand front room, flooded with afternoon light. She indicated an upholstered sofa beside a marble fireplace and took her chair opposite. Ben remained standing and turned to Jonathan.

"Please tell Tante Susanna your story, Jonathan, just as you told it to me. I'm going to fetch something from upstairs."

Jonathan repeated the story he had told Ben and watched as a slow smile developed on Susanna's face. Ben returned as Jonathan was finishing his tale.

"So, Tante, what do you think?"

"It must be *The Lady*. Opa would be so pleased! He loved that portrait so much. He sensed that it was special, at least parts of it."

Susanna turned to Lauren.

"It was his first purchase and he was very fond of it. He would be delighted his suspicion that a master had worked on it was correct–the flowers and *The Lady's* lovely neck. That's what we called the portrait, *The Lady*."

Lauren looked over to Jonathan, excited now.

"Can you say a little more, about the elements of the drawing?"

"*The Lady* was a nice drawing, but not first class. But Opa pointed out to me certain aspects that he believed were added by a very talented artist–the flowers in her hands and the line of her neck. Oh! And I remember now, her hair. Her hair was piled on her head and it looked so, so *natural*. Opa said only a real artist could have rendered her hair."

Jonathan had brought along a print outs of the 1507 diary entry where Paolo described the day in the studio when he drew Chiara. He handed the two pages to Lauren to read aloud to Susanna and Ben. As she read, Ben stepped over to his aunt and gently squeezed her shoulder.

Susanna looked up at him. "If only Opa was with us to hear those words. He would be proud, I think."

"And here she is," Ben announced, crossing to Lauren and Jonathan with an opened catalogue from the 1939 Rijksmuseum exhibition.

"Here," he pointed, directing their attention to a small black and white photograph.

They could barely make out the image of a young woman's seated profile. Apart from the flowers in her hands, little detail could be discerned.

Jonathan commented, "They had the attribution wrong. It wasn't from Venice at all."

"No, no, Jonathan," Susanna insisted, "that was Papa being clever."

Now Susanna told them of the scheme to get four of Isaak's works of art out of the grasping hands of the Germans by having the Rijksmuseum request them on loan–and her desire to switch *The Lady* for a Veronese study.

"The paintings were completely different, but we knew we could rely on the ignorance and laziness of the shipping company not to spot the deception. That is the Veronese over there."

Susanna pointed at a fine grisaille study of a woman's head, hanging above a chair in the corner of the room. Jonathan looked around at the paintings arrayed on the walls, many of which he recognised.

"These are all copies, not reproductions mind, but expertly hand painted copies of some of the pieces in Isaak's collection, all stolen from the family."

Jonathan looked around once more, awed at the riches represented before him. There were important national art collections with fewer Old Masters. It was hard to imagine one man collecting all of this priceless art.

Ben elaborated, "There are more, all over the house. Isaak was very wealthy, and art wasn't as expensive then as today, even adjusting for inflation. Although these are copies, we did recover the original of that Caravaggio, that Raphael and these two Titians. The Raphael was donated to the Tel Aviv art museum in memory of Isaak and the members of our family who were murdered."

Susanna broke the silence that followed.

"Benjamin, go and make some coffee, please." She looked at Lauren and Jonathan in turn. "Would you like to hear our story?"

Lauren replied for both of them, "Very much, please."

Susanna settled down to tell the story of her family. Recounting the story remained important to her, she still wanted as many people as possible to hear at first-hand about the evil perpetrated by the most civilised country in Europe.

"By the time Papa arranged to loan our pictures to Amsterdam, life had become difficult. And then my dear brother Ignaz was beaten to death in the street, all for coming to the aid of an elderly couple being terrorised by thugs. Papa's business had been stolen and anything of value was being steadily plundered. Finally, we decided to get out, to Amsterdam and safety. I begged Papa to send *The Lady* instead of the Veronese study and he and Mama agreed. The final paintings, including the Veronese, were later sold and the money used to bribe German officials to give us the exit passes we needed. Finally, we were safe."

"In Amsterdam, Papa was a consultant to international trading companies and for a while we thought everything would be bearable, although in 1939 Papa did have to sell the four Rijksmuseum paintings in a terrible rush before the Germans demanded them from the Dutch authorities.

But then, in 1940, Germany invaded the Netherlands and took control within days. At first, it wasn't too bad, but slowly things became frightening again and we tried to leave for Spain. A lot of Dutch Jews did get out, but not German Jews who had already escaped the Nazis."

At this point Ben came into the room with a coffee pot and four cups and poured for each of them as Susanna finished her story.

"Although many Dutch people helped the Germans round up Jews, the Dutch resistance offered to try to get children out. My nephew, Jacob, Ben's father, was only six when I took him with me to a house in the suburbs where a woman met us. We were moved from one home to another. Finally, we were hidden in a farmer's truck and spent four days being driven through Belgium and France and into Spain. A few weeks later, we escaped to England."

Lauren knew she was meant to ask the next question.

"What happened to the family in Amsterdam?"

"We only found out after the war. One day in 1942, Dutch policemen arrived and gave them ten minutes to pack one small suitcase each. They were taken to the transit camp at Westerbock and some months later they were put on a train to Theresienstadt where they were starved and abused. The Germans wanted Father to sign a piece of paper saying the Canaletto that had been in the Munich museum had been a gift and not a loan. He wouldn't sign, so they beat him to death, then raped my sister and sister-in-law before shooting both of them and my mother, as an example to others who were defying them."

Jonathan and Lauren were stunned into silence. In a single, matter-of-fact sentence, Susanna had exposed them to the unimaginable horrors of the Holocaust.

Jonathan pulled himself back into the comfortable, safe, London room.

"Why on earth did they care about his signature?"

"They were Nazis, they thought that way. Someone high up, maybe Göring himself, wanted it done. Apparently, his signature would have allowed them to get the Swiss to hand over the painting. It is impossible to understand the Nazi mentality. At the same time that their thugs were beating and killing Jews to steal everything we possessed, they employed armies of lawyers, passed dozens of laws–all to give everything they did a veneer of legality."

Susanna knew the question going through Jonathan's head, and knew he would never ask it.

"I cannot say for sure, but by the time he was killed, my father had been starved and been beaten many times. I suspect he knew the end was coming–Papa would not have been fooled by empty promises of favours or freedom. Perhaps at the very end we must cling to what is true, and he knew his signature would be a lie. Or perhaps he wanted to defy them after they had taken everything from him. Or maybe he misjudged his situation, believing that this was the one bargaining tool he could use to keep his family alive. We will never know."

Susanna took a sip of her coffee and glanced at Ben before turning again to the two young people on the sofa.

"I am the last person alive who knew them: Papa, Mama, Esther, Leah, Ignaz. And I won't be here for much longer. To you, they are only names, but to me... This is our challenge. Six million names—an impossibly long list of names, far too many to encompass. But it cannot be just a list of names. It is six million dreams and hopes. Six million individuals exactly like you and your friends and family. Young people like you, who never grew old, never had families, never went to the theatre, built businesses, wrote poems, fell in love."

"This is why Benjamin's work is so important, why he must continue. Every painting he recovers will forever have our family's story attached to it. And every story, every memento, every plaque or memorial or television programme or film becomes a part of our collective memory. I believe that objects help fix memories. *The Lady* is the key to my strongest memories of my grandfather. Our paintings will forever fix the memory of our family in the minds of everyone who ever looks on them. And the memory of Papa and Mama and Esther and Leah and Ignaz fixes also the memory of the entire six million. Their deaths can only be understood as five of the millions. And the world must never, ever be allowed to forget what happened to them, to all of them."

Susanna had spoken calmly throughout her narrative, displaying no emotion whatsoever. Her words had a powerful effect on Jonathan and Lauren. They could not imagine how many tears Susanna had shed before arriving at this state of control.

Suddenly Ben spoke, changing the subject and catching Jonathan off guard.

"Why have you gone to so much trouble to track down this drawing, Jonathan? How did you envisage this would end?"

"I'm not exactly sure, to be honest. If it turned out that the portrait was in a public collection, I would have been able to provide its true attribution. Lauren and I are pretty heavily invested in the characters in the diary and it would be nice if they could be recognised and remembered.

"And to be frank," Jonathan continued, "the publicity would have been good. I've recently opened a gallery, selling works of art. Becoming known as the person who found a piece so intimately connected to Leonardo da Vinci would have been good for business."

Jonathan looked at Susanna as he continued.

"Then, I received the information about Isaak's descendants and saw all those deaths in 1942."

He leaned forward in his chair. "I have a tiny drawing of a cherub's face. It's small, not important at all, but I love that drawing. It was the first piece of art I ever bought, on my birthday, with my grandfather. He took me to an auction and gave me £100 to spend and I bought my drawing. It launched my love of art and, well, I couldn't dream of parting with it. One day, I hope I'll have a child who will inherit it and have a connection to a man they never met, but who I loved very much. Last night I hoped you still had the portrait and I would be able to tell you its story. I thought maybe it would, I don't know, maybe that would be important to you."

Susanna nodded at him and smiled softly.

"It is, Jonathan, thank you."

Now Ben surprised Jonathan and Lauren.

"I know exactly where *The Lady* is. Let's go upstairs and I'll explain."

Susanna stood up and took Ben's arm and Lauren and Jonathan followed them out into the hall and up a wide staircase. The walls in the hall and up the stairs displayed yet more copies of amazing works of art. Although Jonathan had read about the great collections amassed by wealthy collectors of a previous era, he had never before grasped just how extensive and astonishing the art hanging in their homes must have been. Now he was getting an idea.

He followed the others into a large upstairs room he thought must once have been two bedrooms. Now it held a large partners' desk in the centre of the floor and over a dozen four-drawer filing cabinets against one wall. Another two walls held nothing but metal shelves straining with old auction catalogues, museum guides and large format art books.

"This is where I keep my research. My own house is too crowded," he smiled at his aunt.

"I have information on where around forty of Isaak's works are today and where another twenty or so were at some point or other between 1945 and today. In addition to the paintings I told you about, I'm pretty confident we'll recover or settle at least another five or six in the next year or so, not counting the four from the Rijksmuseum."

Ben pointed a one particular filing cabinet.

"These top two drawers hold material about the four items sent to the exhibition in Amsterdam."

He had brought the old catalogue upstairs with them and he now placed it on the desk and opened it to another page marked with a yellow sticker.

"This is the Giorgione that Otto sent. This is one we're settling on right now, it's so tainted."

He continued, "Under threat of having the four paintings confiscated by the Germans, Otto was pressured to sell them to a Swiss dealer called Heinz Burgdorf at a price far, far below their market value at the time. Burgdorf was a horrible man, the brother-in-law of a prominent Nazi, Martin Bormann. A few years ago, I discovered that Burgdorf gave the Giorgione to Bormann, as payment for Bormann suppressing any difficulties surrounding the two Canalettos. The two German groups responsible for confiscating Jewish artworks were both planning to get their hands on the Amsterdam paintings, but Burgdorf beat them to it. After the war, the Giorgione painting wound up in a public collection in Cleveland, Ohio and we're finalising legal paperwork whereby the museum will buy the painting from us at an agreed price, which won't be huge, it isn't a great painting and was almost certainly finished by another artist after Giorgione's early death."

He turned a few pages of the catalogue.

"These Canalettos were the other items loaned and then sold by Otto. The two Canalettos and *The Lady* were taken to Switzerland, where Burgdorf planned to sell them. But things went badly for Burgdorf. He tried to cheat Hermann Göring over the purchase of a painting, thinking his brother-in-law would protect him if Göring ever found out. Göring did find out and Burgdorf learned too late the limits of Bormann's loyalty. With his life in danger from Göring's agents in Switzerland, Burgdorf had to put his paintings in storage and flee to South America, where he spent the rest of the war."

Ben opened the top drawer of the filing cabinet and extracted a photograph.

"This is Burgdorf in 1946. It is the last known photograph of him. By then he was back in Berne, but he had become a recluse. He never reopened his gallery and it seems he sold only a few paintings piecemeal until he died in 1957. He had married another émigré in Argentina when he was well into his fifties and they had a son, Franz, who inherited the estate, including the paintings."

Now Ben indicated the next drawer down.

"This holds the various reports and legal exchanges between us and Franz Burgdorf's lawyers going back almost twenty years. Basically, Burgdorf's position has always been that his father bought all the paintings legally for a fair price and he therefore has good title to them. He has always refused to provide an inventory of what he has, but myself and other people working to reclaim family property have put together a list of 46 works we can prove Burgdorf senior acquired from various Jewish sellers at a time when Jews were being systematically persecuted. Some courts are now taking the position that there should be a presumption of duress in all such transactions and are voiding the sales."

"It must be difficult to document many of these transactions after so many years," Lauren observed.

"It is. In some cases, it's impossible. But not all cases are equal. In the years during and after the war, there were thousands of artworks coming onto the markets, by no means all from Jewish owners. All kinds of people were trying to turn their assets into cash to buy food in order to survive. People in countries occupied by the Germans, latterly Germans themselves and then, of course, eastern Europeans who found themselves under Soviet control after 1945. And many buyers were truly innocent, simply acquiring art. But not in all cases. Art of the quality of Isaak's collection had a high profile. If major public institutions didn't investigate the provenance of their post-war purchases, it was because they didn't want to deal with the truth. And they should have. Major collections, like Isaak's, were well documented and well-known among professionals. And people like Franz Burgdorf know very well how their pictures were obtained, they simply choose to deny everything and challenge people like me to prove otherwise."

At this point, Susanna interrupted.

"What my nephew is too modest to tell you, Lauren, is that thanks to him and a few others like him, Franz Burgdorf is in a difficult situation. Benjamin and his friends have succeeded in getting laws changed, in getting all the major auction houses and dealers to refuse to handle any of the 46 works that they have identified. And now, I'm delighted to say, Burgdorf is very ill and needs expensive medical treatment and he has, we believe, almost no money. Fortunately, he can't sell *any* of his paintings because for the past six months, the storage facility where they are housed has been sealed by a Swiss court until the various disputes, including ours, are resolved."

For a second Lauren found it strange to hear this charming and refined old lady delighting in the fact someone had a serious medical problem, but then she thought of what Susanna had been through and what she had lost.

Jonathan turned to Ben. "And how long before your case with Burgdorf is resolved?"

"Not long now, we're getting close to a settlement, even if it is a horrible compromise. At last month's meeting in Berne, the other side made an offer. We could take our pick of the three paintings, with the other two going to auction at Sotheby's and the proceeds split 50:50."

As Ben said this, he was looking at his aunt, who in turn was gently smiling back.

"Benjamin knows how much I love *The Lady*. He is holding out for taking back one of the Canalettos while the other side would have to agree to have *The Lady* independently appraised and we would buy her back at a fifty per cent discount. The second Canaletto would be sold and the proceeds shared."

Benjamin crossed the room to stand beside his aunt and rested his hand lightly on her shoulder.

"It comes to much the same thing as their offer, except we'll be certain to get *The Lady* back, and this is one picture that will never be sold again, it will stay in the family. Our next negotiating meeting is the week after next at Sotheby's, here in London, and I'll make it clear this is our final offer. I don't think Burgdorf will argue, Sotheby's are ready to advance him money against his share of the Canaletto sale."

Jonathan and Lauren left with a photocopy of the page of the Amsterdam catalogue and a promise that Ben would be in touch whenever the dispute was resolved, to update them on the fate of Paolo's portrait.

They walked to a nearby café and found a quiet corner table. Jonathan brought out the photocopy.

"It isn't a terribly good image, probably because the curator would have been embarrassed, given that he was participating in a kind of fraud by going along with an attribution he knew to be wrong. But here it is, Paolo's portrait of Chiara. It's amazing to think we may actually see it for ourselves soon."

"But no thrilling discovery for you–that must be a bit disappointing?"

"Yes and no. Of course, it would have been great if the painting had been hanging in Susanna's house and we had been able to read them the relevant entries from the diary and show them Leonardo's touches. But just knowing it survived is wonderful, and I believe Ben will get his hands on it. He's incredibly tenacious, you saw the lengths he goes to, to track down his family's possessions. Are you OK, Lauren? You seem a bit distracted."

"I'm sorry. I am a bit distracted I suppose. Susanna's story was so shocking. She tells it in such a matter-of-fact way, but to contemplate what happened… And I received an email while we were in the house. The rest of the diary pages you found in Florence are arriving next week. We're going to get to the end of the story."

The Seminar

Lauren took a sip of water and looked at the room full of expectant faces before her. Thanks in large part to a rehearsal with Professor Hunter, she was much calmer than she had anticipated. Now that the day had finally arrived, she was thrilled to be at last properly sharing her excitement about the Chronicles. She caught Jane Hunter's eye and began her presentation.

"When I was a young girl, I often visited my Italian relatives in their hilltop village in Umbria. Often I would stand in the square and wish history was a movie I could rewind and observe the life of the village 100, 200, 500 years ago. I wanted to see those long-dead people going about their business in the same streets and buildings that I was exploring every day.

"The Paolo Chronicles make that girl's fanciful wish a reality. Only instead of a static camera set up in the square of a nondescript village, our camera has followed Leonardo da Vinci for the last twenty years of his life. And while I have no doubt that the scenes relating to Leonardo will be the highlights of the movie, I defy anyone not to be captivated by Paolo's own drama, which continued long after his master's death.

"I don't mean to make you all feel guilty, but if I hadn't been spending so much time preparing to meet this distinguished group, by now I would have finished my first reading of the Chronicles."

There was a ripple of laughter at her complaint, one all the academics could relate to.

Lauren continued, "As it is, I can't wait to start reading them again from the beginning. I predict that like me, you will spend your first reading being constantly distracted by one remarkable insight after another. I'm looking forward to re-reading everything and simply absorbing the panorama that Paolo lays out before us.

"For now, I'd like to share with you, my impressions of our movie's writer, director and narrator, that wise and estimable man, Paolo del Rosso."

Lauren spoke for a further twenty-two minutes, and at the end of her presentation, the applause was warm and sustained. As the other panel members introduced themselves, she discovered that, far from being intimidated, she was looking forward to hearing these experts interpret and explain some of the incidents and stories in Paolo's diary.

William Chance, Penny and Jonathan had watched from the back row of the seats. The Earl was first to congratulate Lauren when the meeting broke up for lunch.

"I was very proud of you up there," he said, shaking her hand. "You certainly proved your point to those Chicago professors!" he finished with an uncharacteristic wicked grin.

"You were sensational!" Jonathan exclaimed; his eyes bright with excitement. "I can't wait to read the whole diary from beginning to end. You helped me step back and gain some perspective. Now I can properly grasp the huge importance of what you've been doing, Lauren. I'm a bit in awe of you now."

At this, Penny, who standing behind Jonathan's shoulder, looked at Lauren and gave her a very knowing wink.

Paris

A couple of days later, Jonathan turned up at Blythswood, once again unannounced.

"I didn't expect to see you for a while," Lauren observed, "I thought you'd be catching up in the gallery."

"I have been," Jonathan replied, "but I can't concentrate."

"Wondering what's going to turn up when Ben's legal team is finished?"

"No. Well yes, of course, but that's not what's bothering me."

"So?"

"I have to go to France, to an estate sale on the outskirts of Paris, on Sunday. There will be some great etchings that would be perfect for the gallery."

He paused, stared momentarily at Lauren before continuing in a rush.

"I wondered if you'd like to come with me? It'll only be three days," he added quickly, "a long weekend."

Both of them knew that this was not a casual suggestion, friend-to-friend.

Jonathan was anxious Lauren might say no, he knew how busy she was. Before she could, he spoke again.

"We could talk. I would like for us to talk, about things."

"About what things?"

"About you and me. I feel there are things to discuss and I thought if we were away from everything…"

There was a long pause before Lauren answered him.

"Yes, I agree. But," she added, "promise me nothing will be said or happen that will stop us being friends. Can you promise me that?"

He had a huge grin on his face as he replied, "Promise. Scout's honour."

* * *

They took an early Eurostar on Friday morning and were in Paris by mid-morning. On the train, Lauren surprised Jonathan.

"I told Professor Hunter where we were going, and she has arranged something for us. I know we're here to get away from everything and talk, but this is special, I thought you wouldn't mind. We're going to visit the *Mona Lisa.*"

Thanks to Professor Hunter's professional courtesy to the Louvre's Director, they would be part of a select group that would be permitted to visit the *Mona Lisa* at six o'clock, after the museum closed. Such was the constant demand from VIPs and celebrities, the museum found it easier to schedule an extra hour for a private viewing of their principal attraction every Friday, rather than try to accommodate ad hoc requests.

Jonathan and Lauren arrived at the immense palace at two o'clock, intending to spend the afternoon looking at a few of the other treasures of the world's largest collection of art.

Jonathan was broadly familiar with the collection and he led them straight to the *Virgin and Child with St Anne*.

"There she is," he whispered. "I think Leonardo made the right decision, don't you?"

Chiara was sublime as Mary. She was in her trademark pose, looking down at her cousin, miraculously delivered of a son, John the Baptist. At this time Mary knows she too is carrying her own miracle child.

"When you were flirting with me in front of the cartoon in London, you teased that I should go to Paris to see this. I would never have imagined we would be here together, especially in these circumstances. I have to pinch myself sometimes, it seems too surreal."

"I was *not* flirting, but I know what you mean. It's incredible to have learned so much about the painting and about the model and her godfather."

Lauren stared at the painting.

"I don't understand how people ever thought that this was Mary sitting on her mother's lap. The rear figure is obviously much the younger of the two women. No doubt this will be another controversy when the Chronicles are published."

She slipped her hand into his.

"And you *were* flirting, Jonathan Granville. Don't deny it."

Jonathan suggested they go to see the collection's Raphaels.

Standing in front of the powerful *Portrait of Baldassare Castiglione* he explained, "This is one of the only other two works on canvas by Raphael. And now we know a little more about him as well."

"Isn't it amazing that he and Leonardo and Michelangelo all lived in the same place at the same time and knew each other?"

"It is—and all three were left-handed. Not a lot of people know that," he finished in his best Michael Caine voice.

"What was that?"

"That was my Michael Caine impersonation."

Lauren was completely bemused. Jonathan gave a rueful smile.

"Maybe you have to be English."

"I guess," she replied, obviously not convinced.

At five-thirty Jonathan was thinking they should begin making their way to the room where the *Mona Lisa* was displayed. Before he could walk across the gallery they had been visiting, Lauren called to him.

"Jon, come here a moment."

He came over to where Lauren stood before a baroque painting of the Virgin and Child surrounded by perhaps thirty chubby angels. It was exactly the kind of overblown religious imagery Jonathan detested.

"Look here, at this one. Look at his nose."

Jonathan looked, and there it was—the distinctive cherub's nose he had been looking for ever since the long-ago auction.

He laughed out loud. "My God, Lauren, you're right! Twenty years I've looked for this, and you find it in an afternoon."

He glanced at the accompanying description. "Rubens, not Venetian at all, not even Italian."

"What made you think it was Italian anyway?"

"Well, I could say it was the style of the painting, which does look Italian by the way. But the fact is, we see what we expect to see–and I was told when I bought it that it was probably Venetian. So, I looked to confirm that. Mind you, Rubens did spend years in Italy and loved Italian art, so it wasn't so far away after all. I can't wait to tell Mr Henderson."

"Can I be all American and tacky and ask what this does to the value of your drawing?"

Jonathan smiled at Lauren.

"Well, it's my very first drawing and it connects me to my grandfather, so, unless the wolf is actually *inside* the door, I won't be selling. But, since you ask, if I *was* to part with it, I'd now be asking maybe £15,000 or £20,000. Rubens is an important artist. Of course, I'll have to do more work now–on the image, the paper and the provenance of the thing. But all going well, that would be the ballpark figure. I owe you a really good dinner, at the very least."

With that he leaned in and kissed her cheek.

"Don't think for one minute a peck on the cheek and a nice dinner is going to cut it, buster! You'll have to do a lot better than that."

Jonathan laughed, and took her arm.

"Come on, let's go upstairs."

This was Lauren's first visit to the *Mona Lisa*. Jonathan had seen it a few times before, but for maybe thirty seconds at a time, surrounded by hordes of people intent on trying to frame themselves in a selfie with the iconic image. For most visitors, the painting was an object to be ticked off their bucket lists rather than a work of art to be appreciated.

This time was different. The room was library quiet and there were only four other guests.

They stood before her, thinking of the story they now knew from Paolo's diaries, imagining Paolo rummaging through the old barn and finding this copy of the earlier painting. They could picture Maestro Leonardo carefully appraising his assistant's efforts before applying himself to creating a transformed image with a proper background, no pillars and a more sympathetic face, with that enigmatic smile hiding the scandalous truth.

Standing there, they were both overcome by the change in perspective brought about by Paolo's Chronicle. The art world would be turned upside down when the diaries were published.

That evening they enjoyed an excellent meal in a tiny restaurant near their hotel. Comfortable in the knowledge they had two more days together without distractions, they felt no urgency to jump straight into the conversation they both knew they would have. Instead they had a relaxed, companionable evening enjoying good food, accompanied by delicious wine.

When it came time for dessert, Jonathan ordered a half bottle of Chateau d'Yquem, an extremely expensive

Sauternes. Lauren was shocked by the price listed on the menu.

"I tasted this once–it's amazing. And it's part of your reward, remember," Jonathan pointed out with a grin.

"Well, in that case, you're allowed."

On Saturday morning they awoke to grey skies and steady rain. When they met for breakfast, Jonathan suggested that since the weather was foul, Paris's covered arcades would provide a pleasant experience; exploring the nineteenth century's version of indoor shopping malls.

The weather stubbornly refused to improve, so they used the afternoon to visit the Monets in the Marmotton Museum.

They sat quietly in the large subterranean oval room, surrounded by the incandescent images. Remarkably, they had the space all to themselves. As Lauren studied Monet's masterpiece she was startled to see the water ripple and move as she looked at the canvases. Somehow the artist had contrived to create the illusion of motion in a still painting.

The serenity of Monet's images worked its way into Lauren's heart, sending her thoughts drifting back over the months she had spent in England, and still further back, to Chiara and her world. How would she and Chiara cope if they magically swapped roles for a week?

Lauren imagined that Chiara would cope better than she would. She couldn't see herself dealing too well with the lack of privacy and security. Not to mention hot, clean water and a million other everyday creature comforts. And living in an even more male dominated society than her own. On the other hand, would Chiara find modern life devoid of spiritual and cultural depth? Would the incessant, meaningless, 24-hour noise and clatter outside this oasis of calm overwhelm her?

In the calmness that washed over her, Lauren suddenly knew what she wanted to say to Jonathan. Taking her eyes from the panorama before her, she turned and took his hands in hers.

She spoke in a quiet, but strong voice. "I know why you asked me to come to Paris. And the answer is yes. Yes, I do have feelings for you beyond the wonderful friend you've become, strong feelings, actually. But I was serious when I said I don't want to lose you as a friend if, if things go wrong. So, if you still want to talk, could give me a little more time? Then I'd be more confident things *won't* go wrong. I've never had a proper, serious relationship. I've had a few boyfriends, each disastrous in his own special way and you're different, I know you are. And I don't want to make a mess of us. But we're so near to the final chapter of the story of the Chronicles *and* the portrait. I can't properly deal with something else so important at this moment—and what happens to you and me *is* important and deserves *all* of my attention. I really, really don't want to screw up."

She let go of his hands.

"Would that be OK?"

Jonathan reached up a finger to gently tuck back a wayward strand of Lauren's hair before leaning in to kiss her softly on the lips.

"That would be absolutely fine."

1530

August 3rd

All is lost! The army is defeated, the Signoria incapable of action. The butcher, Maramaldo, approaches the gates of the city and everyone fears his brutality. At last we have been able to persuade Alessio the time has come to flee while we may. He is fearful of losing his position, his business. He is a fool. He has been a loud-mouthed supporter of the Republic and will not long survive the return of the Medici. But Alessio is weak–fat, soft and weak. The virile man who wed Chiara vanished years ago.

Meanwhile, I have few concerns for my own safety. When the immediate violence subsides, I will return to the city and manage our business as usual. Gradually, I will transfer control to Leo.

But Alessio caused trouble to the bitter end. After many delays, Leo secured horses and carts. We loaded everything essential and Leo assisted his mother, an island of calm as usual.

In no time, everything was prepared for departure. Except, of course, Alessio, who was taking an eternity to decide between this cloak and that jerkin, until finally Leo took an armful of vestments from him and threw them aside.

"Father, we are leaving. Now. We are leaving with you or without you."

I had charge of the paintings: the wedding portraits, my own profile of Chiara and my most precious possessions, the two sketches of Chiara by my former master and given to me, plus four or five other good paintings the family owned.

I will follow tomorrow, after ensuring our staff are all safe. We will rendezvous in an inn some little distance from the city gate. The plan is for me to travel with the family for a few days, until the worst of the violence subsides, before returning to manage the company until it is safe for Alessio to return.

With Chiara and Leo in the carts, Alessio finally pulled on his cloak to follow his son. First however, to my surprise he turned and grasped my arm.

He leaned in close to me and I could smell the sour wine on his breath and the unpleasant odours from his body.

"Paolo," he croaked, "the wedding portraits are to go to my brother in Rome. The Pope himself has promised an extraordinary price. See to it before you leave."

I nodded my head, while my heart began to race. There was absolutely no way I would follow this instruction. But what to do?

I waved them away—husband, wife, son and their domestic servants.

August 4th

It is done! I worked throughout the night. First, I extracted the wedding portraits from their frames, then removed the canvas of Alessio from its wooden bearer.

I then did the same with my own puerile effort and blessed my younger self for striking a bargain to buy ten canvases and frames of identical size.

With a final look at Maestro's transcendent image of Chiara, I carefully laid a sheet of heavy silk on top of her portrait and mounted Alessio's image on top of this, nailing it all around the shared stretcher. Another sheet of silk and my own pitiful effort was laid atop everything and nailed to the now thrice-loaded stretcher.

With some effort, the combined painting was squeezed back into the frame that had held my clumsy effort, the plainest of the three.

I worry about Alessio. I worry about the brigands prowling the city. This is Florence, even thieves recognise quality. The portraits have to be hidden and saved.

When I arrived at the warehouse the following morning, having carefully locked up the Pacini home, our staff were assembled, obviously scared. I addressed them in the storeroom, now empty of wool and fabrics.

'Friends, for everyone's safety, we will close down for a few days, perhaps a week. Go home, stay indoors with your wives and children and remain quiet, this trouble that started *last night could become dangerous. But when the Medici return, they will want the city calm and prosperous once more, the better to pay our taxes. All will be well. In light of last night's disturbances, I have decided I will sleep here, to ensure there is no mischief done to our warehouse. Here are twenty florins for each of you, to aid you in the coming days. God speed and I will send for you all again soon. Matteo, can you wait, please?"*

Matteo was usually in charge of loading the carts. He is the strongest man I know. And he lives alone.

"Matteo, I am supposed to meet Ser Pacini and his family outside the gates. Now that I feel I must stay here, will you take to them the donkey and cart with their paintings and reassure them that I am well? And make sure you give this letter into the hand of the signora herself, no one else. Afterwards, if you are agreeable, I would be grateful if you would return to assist me. Though we have run our stocks to zero, the mob may try to burn the building, even if it is empty."

I have decided to keep Maestro's final sketch of Chiara— I cannot bear to part with it, even now, and it is small and would be easy to hide.

The letter explained my change of plan, and I also included a letter to the King, introducing Chiara. I was completely certain his Majesty would protect someone so special to one he loved. I asked her to keep safe my portrait and the study of her by Maestro Leonardo until we are together again. I wrote nothing about the wedding portraits, in case Alessio asks to see the letter.

August 9th

I t is over. The Medici are back in charge and, as I expected, the violence stopped as quickly as it began. Many of the merchants are ruined—any who held large stocks were targeted by the mobs. There is a little damage to the Pacini house, nothing too serious, but I shall move into it for the moment, until I can be sure it will not be targeted or even taken, if it is empty.

August 12th

M atteo brought me some surprising intelligence this afternoon.
It seems word had gone throughout the various Medici factions that our warehouse and homes were not to be damaged during the recent upheavals. The command had come from one of the most prominent supporters of the Medici family, Francesco del Giocondo.

Fate is indeed strange. After the passage of so many years, it seems that Signor del Giocondo and I are, if not friends, perhaps loose allies. Today's intelligence reflects the reality of life in our city—the existence of networks of obligations and favours that can rule our lives. My late master either failed to appreciate this reality or, more likely, found it impossible to establish himself at the centre of a network of support and alliances. His stubbornness in failing to execute so many of the commissions offered to him caused many would-be friends to despair and his habit of seeking revenge on any who he believed had injured or slighted him, made minor rivals into bitter enemies.

Would the lives of Alessio and Chiara have been different if Maestro had not concocted his deception and revenge against Giocondo? Or was Alessio possessed of a fatal weakness that would have emerged under some other prompt? It is impossible to say with certainty. Our lives are governed by so many minor and major events, both planned and unplanned. It is pointless to speculate what if this or that action or accident had been avoided.

November 4th

A s I am a Christian, I try not to be happy about the news we had today. Alfonso, the brother of Alessio, has died in a fire that consumed his house.
He had been a widower for some years and lived alone in Rome.

My plan, poor as it was, was to claim that the wedding portraits must have been lost on their way to Rome. I had been listening to every report and recently had finally identified a citizen of our city, a trader in silver, murdered on his way to Rome. This unfortunate individual would, *retrospectively, have been reported to be my courier. Now, this plan is not needed.*

A fire! The perfect supposed ending for the portraits. Alessio will have no cause for suspicion now. Perhaps the Almighty is on my side. I shall give thanks to St Zenobius for interceding on my behalf.

Although perhaps a saint would not have petitioned for a fire and a death? But again, perhaps Alfonso was a wicked man?

November 27th

Another excellent missive, this time from France.

Chiara and her family are safe in Chambord, and secure in the court of the King. And even more wonderful intelligence–the King has granted a generous pension to Chiara personally, not to her husband. Did the wise King discern the weakness in Alessio, or did Leo speak with his Majesty? Or perhaps it was his memory of the final dream of my late master?

I do not believe it will be safe for Alessio to return for many months, perhaps years. The political situation remains tense, and he has powerful enemies.

November 28th

S ad news from England, Walter is dead. He was not old, the plague took him and his wife. I shall say novenas for them for thirty days. His daughter, Margaret, is running the business. She has never married and has been working alongside her father for many years. She assures me all will continue as before. In her letter, she sounds confident and competent, which is reassuring. She also passed on fond wishes and prayers from her brother, Hugh, now confessor—secretary to a senior prelate called Thomas Cranmer, but himself also very sickly.

1532

February 19th

Leo arrived today, unexpectedly, and with astonishing news. Alessio is dead. He died last month, of a weak heart.

"He hated the court, hated France. My mother is worshipped by everyone. However, it was soon clear that that affection did not extend to my father. In any event, he is gone and, to be honest, Paolo, he is not missed. What will you do now?"

"I will go to your mother. I will ask her to marry me."

To my great happiness, Leo embraced me.

"At last! Nothing could make me happier, nor I know, my dear mother. You have both waited so long, no one deserves to find joy and happiness more."

"I need to wait here for a month. We have a huge shipment coming from Margaret, I must attend to it before I hand everything to you. Unless you are planning to stay?"

"Forgive me, Paolo, I cannot. I was delayed in Milan for weeks. My second child will soon arrive. I must return now and look to my family. We will await your arrival and, I trust, your wedding, and then we will move back to Florence and continue our business. Will you live in France?"

"I will be guided by the wishes of your mother, but I must say, a few years with Chiara in the court sounds tempting. But she will want to settle near you and her grandchildren, as do I. We will be back in Florence ere long, I am certain. With Alessio gone, his political enemies will turn their attentions elsewhere. Chiara will return to a warm welcome. Her time at court will give her great status, she will have no trouble whatsoever. For now, I will give you a letter for your mother, and I will leave my papers and belongings in your home. Matteo will live there until your safe return."

These thoughts brought back a painful memory.

"Every now and then, my memory goes back to my earlier diaries. Why was I such a fool? Why did I drag so much paper across Christendom? I know the answer, but the fact is I did nothing towards my project to make my diaries into something someone might actually read. Over twenty years of memories gone, left behind when we fled for our lives. And do you know, Leo? Even though England was suddenly involved in the war, I do not think we were ever in serious danger."

Leo, as always, tried to cheer me up.

"You had me in your care, a heavy responsibility. I thought Walter might have found them, perhaps with one of the neighbours who hid us that week."

"I too had hoped—but I must stop re-living these memories. I promise you, when I reach France, I will write down the most important stories, those concerning Maestro Leonardo and your precious mother. It will be better anyway, *a shorter form that you, and one day your children, might actually want to read!"*

February 21st – Letter from Florence

*M*y dearest, darling Chiara,

I send this with Leo, who will be with you some weeks before my arrival.

I will not play the hypocrite and pretend sorrow for Alessio's death.

My darling, I yearn to hold you in my arms and at last kiss those lips that have beguiled me for so many years. My love for you is as ardent as the day I first beheld you and was smitten. Just as ardent, but now much deeper. The years have shown me just what a remarkable woman you are, and how lucky I am to be in your affections.

As I write this letter, my little sketch is propped before me. I look at it every day and it is the last thing I see as I take myself to bed each night.

I refuse to dwell on the years that have gone, instead I shall think only of the happy years before us.

By the time this reaches you, I trust we will have another grandchild. I say we, because for many years I have thought of Leo as my son and will equally take his children as my family. I am such a lucky man, to have such a son.

Leo is impatient to be away and so I must keep this message short. I will be at your side soon, and I will bring you news of a most wonderful surprise.

I send my love ahead as my ambassador.

Look for me within the month.

Yours forever,

Paolo

April 15th – Letter from Lyon

istinguished Signora,
My name is Sebastian Gryphius, a printer and seller of books in Lyon. It falls to me, dear lady, to bring you the very worst of news. Your friend, and I believe your love, Signor Paolo del Rosso, is dead.

One week ago, that most interesting, learned and cultured man arrived in my city, en route to you in Chambord, as he explained. Unhappily, he had recently endured a fall from his horse, and needed to rest for some days, before continuing on his quest to you, concerning which he was most insistent.

I need not tell you how enjoyable was his company, how memorable his stories. Indeed, with his permission, I had invited a small group of our most distinguished citizens to my home to take lunch, to afford them the opportunity of meeting Signor del Rosso themselves. It was because he did not appear at the appointed hour that I went to find him, fearing his injuries may have impaired his movements.

Indeed, his wounds must have been far graver than he, or I, suspected. Upon entering his chamber, I found him dead.

He was, Madame, lying abed, peaceful, as if asleep.

Set before him was a small leather travel frame holding the image which I believe to be a likeness of yourself. I enclose his sketch, together with his ring, in the hope they may afford you some consolation in your time of grief. I await your instructions for the disposition of the rest of Signor del Rosso's effects.

It is with deep sadness I bring you this news. Even on such a short acquaintance, I was made aware of the great depth of feeling Signor del Rosso had with regard to your good self. I am deeply sorry to be the bearer of these grievous tidings which I fear will bring you immense grief.

It was my great honour to have known him. It is my burden that it was such a short acquaintance.

I remain your servant,

Sebastian Gryphius

An Ending

In a quiet, humidity-controlled room in the Bodleian Library, Lauren reached into the file box and removed one of the final sheets of Paolo's Chronicle. Unlike the Blythswood papers, the Florence pages had been stored in order, so Lauren had been able to read the Chronicle in proper sequence. She could readily see there were only a few sheets left and she was torn between two conflicting emotions–eagerness to read the end of the story, which she still desperately hoped would find Paolo and Chiara together, somehow–and sadness that there would be no more fresh pages to read.

As Professor Hunter had anticipated, Lauren felt she understood Paolo better than anyone she had ever known. His gentle strength and utter devotion to those he loved was inspiring. Contemplating this remarkable, thwarted, romance also provoked her to think about her own feelings for Jonathan. Since Paris, he was rarely far from her thoughts.

When she came to the entry describing Paolo's night spent hiding the wedding portraits, her immediate thoughts were again of Jonathan, *'That's why he couldn't find trace of them in Florence. They weren't sold, they were hidden.'* She would tell him this evening, or maybe at the weekend when she was looking forward to seeing him.

But all romantic notions were blown far away as Lauren read the letter from Sebastian Gryphius. Now she thought her heart would break. Penny, who was sitting across the table looked up when she heard Lauren cry.

"Oh no! No, surely not!"

"What is it, Lauren, what's wrong?"

Lauren's eyes were brimming. "He died. Paolo died, without ever being with his Chiara. After all those years of loving her so very much. It's just too sad. Listen."

Slowly, she read the letter aloud, translating as she went along, something that had become second nature to her by this point. Even on a second reading, Lauren couldn't stop the tears spilling down her cheeks.

Her voice was desolate as she looked up from the letter. "It's like some terrible Greek tragedy. I feel so sad for them. All those years, and to be so close at last. It's *such* a disappointing ending. I so wanted them to be together at last. And he died before he could tell anyone what…Oh my God! We can't be too late, we just can't!"

Lauren's hands shook as she fumbled in her bag for her phone.

"Jon, where are you?"

"On a bus in London, why? Is everything OK? You sound…"

"Everything is terrible, but also maybe OK. You need to get hold of Ben Abrams–immediately."

"Miss Abramowitch, it's Jonathan Granville. Is Ben with you? He isn't answering his mobile and no one is answering his home number. It's incredibly important that I speak with him."

"I'm sorry, Jonathan, Benjamin is in town, at his meeting at Sotheby's."

He jumped off his southbound bus and feverishly, Jonathan keyed in Ben's number again, letting out an exasperated moan when his call went directly to voicemail. Ben was either talking on the phone, out of coverage or, God forbid, had turned off his mobile. He spotted a black taxi.

"New Bond Street, please."

Jonathan looked repeatedly at his watch and vainly retried Ben's number every few minutes as they crawled through London traffic. Several times he thought of getting out and taking the Tube, but then a bus lane would open up and they would make good progress for a few minutes. When, finally, the taxi ran into a solid jam of cars in Berkeley Square, Jonathan crammed two £20 notes through the cab's partition.

"Keep the change," he yelled over his shoulder as he threw open the door, narrowly missing a cyclist.

When he arrived at the entrance to the auction house, Jonathan took a moment to compose himself before approaching a glamorous young woman sitting behind a highly polished reception desk. He was just about to ask for her assistance when he caught sight of Ben coming out of the lift and heading towards the entrance.

"Ben!"

Ben looked up and came over to Jonathan. They stepped away from the desk.

"What brings you here?"

"I've come to find you. Is your meeting over?"

"Yes, just finished. What's going on Jonathan?"

"Damn, damn, damn! I don't believe it. I can't believe I'm too late."

Jonathan's anguish was written all over his face. After all this, all their work, the lying son of a Nazi was going to be the beneficiary of the greatest art discovery of all time. It was so unbelievably unfair. He looked so distressed that Ben was concerned for him.

"Come over here, sit down for a moment. What on earth is upsetting you so much."

"It's the portrait, *The Lady*. It's hiding something, something amazing and now…"

Ben was astonished to realise that Jonathan was having to focus to retain his composure.

"Well, that's OK, we can fix that. What is it hiding?"

"But it's too late, when *The Lady* is examined, everything will be discovered."

"For God's sake, Jonathan, tell me what the hell you're talking about. It isn't too late for anything. Now come on, what is *The Lady* hiding?"

Jonathan had rehearsed how he would tell Ben the story of the wedding portraits and Paolo's subterfuge, but the crushing disappointment he was experiencing meant the story came out in disjointed bits and pieces. He stumbled to the end of his explanation.

"So Paolo died without telling anyone what he had done with the wedding portraits. No one knew, not Chiara, not Leo, not Isaak. But this is all a waste of time. I wanted, *we* wanted you and your family to end up with the wedding portraits, but now you won't get them at all. This will all become a huge legal nightmare. If only you hadn't turned off your phone during your meeting with

Burgdorf's lawyers—I've been trying to call you for over an hour."

"But I haven't met with Burgdorf's lawyers yet."

Ben looked at his watch. "That meeting doesn't start for another fifteen minutes. I've been meeting with the lawyers from Cleveland, finishing up the Giorgione agreement. Sotheby's loaned us a conference room since I had to be here anyway. I was just stepping out for some fresh air before going back in."

Jonathan couldn't quite believe it. Relief overwhelmed him and he reached out a hand to grasp Ben's elbow.

"Thank God! You can still claim *The Lady*!"

"Listen, Jonathan, each of the Canalettos could be worth somewhere around £15 million. You're asking me to gamble a fortune on a hunch."

Unveiled

Five days later, Jonathan, Lauren, William Chance, Ben, his wife Sophie and Tante Susanna were nervously awaiting the arrival of *The Lady*.

In the end, Ban had been late for his meeting with Burgdorf's lawyers as he and Jonathan went over and over the arguments for passing up a Canaletto worth millions, for *The Lady* and the *possibility* of what she might be concealing. In the end, it was the thought of how he would feel if Jonathan was right, but he allowed two Leonardo painting to go to a man he had come to despise that convinced Ben to take the chance. He went into the meeting and surprised his lawyer by demanding immediate enactment of the proposal that Burgdorf's lawyers had made at the previous session. They of course agreed, and Ben formally selected *The Lady* for immediate delivery from Switzerland, hinting that Susanna was adamant her family heirloom be returned to her immediately, fearful that she wouldn't be reunited with the drawing before her death.

As a result of Ben's seemingly irrational and emotional selection, *The Lady* was about to be delivered to this room, the restoration workshop of the Courtauld Institute. They were all standing around a large stainless steel table, each lost in their own thoughts.

Ben was still unsure whether he had done the right thing. He had not been able to reach his brother or sister before making is decision, and he felt the weight of responsibility in gambling such huge stakes on the research of two young people he barely knew.

Now, awaiting the moment of truth, Jonathan too was nervous. However, his thoughts were disrupted when he felt Lauren take his hand and lean in to whisper into his ear.

"This weekend, no matter what happens, let's do something, go somewhere together–somewhere neither of us have been before, and make it our own."

"What did you have in mind?" he whispered back.

"Have you ever been to York?"

"Nope. Why York?"

Lauren squeezed his hand, "Because Paolo liked it, and I trust his judgement. Just like I trust yours. Don't worry, it's going to be fine."

He looked at her, overwhelmed by gratitude and love. He nodded and returned her squeeze.

The murmured conversations in the room ceased as they heard the door handle turn, but it was only Professor Hunter and Penny. Lauren had insisted they should both be present when the painting was examined.

"Sorry we're late, our train was held up. No sign of the portrait yet?"

At this, one of the other two people in the room spoke up. Ben had decided that from here on, *The Lady* should be comprehensively documented. He wanted an irrefutable chain of evidence should the provenance of the piece and whatever it may reveal ever be challenged. Accordingly, there was a professional videographer and sound engineer ready to capture whatever transpired.

"One of our team is in reception. They'll call me when the package arrives, so we'll be ready to start recording the instant that door handle begins to turn."

The sound engineer had no sooner uttered these words than his phone began to trill. He answered it.

"They're on their way. Just remember, we'll be capturing video and audio from now on."

Sure enough, a minute or two later, the door was opened by the Director of the Institute, leading in three of her colleagues, followed by two men carrying a wooden case.

"If you would lay it on the table, please?" Joan Ferguson, the Director, requested. "Mr Abrams, they need you to sign a receipt for the drawing, so let's quickly expose it so you can see it is the item you expected."

With the shipping case safely on the table, one of the deliverymen produced a battery-powered screwdriver and removed the eight screws holding down the lid of the case. As they lifted the lid, everyone could see the inner cardboard box that was now extracted from the outer case and laid beside it. Finally, the cardboard lid was eased off to reveal a framed sepia coloured canvas with the image of a seated young woman in profile, a small bunch of flowers in her hands. There was a gasp from Susanna and Ben turned to his great-aunt, a question in his eyes.

"Yes, that is her, that is *The Lady*. To see her again after so many years! Thank you, Benjamin. And you too, Jonathan. I can hardly believe it! Opa's favourite!"

Ben signed the receipt for the painting and the deliverymen picked up the two parts of the wooden case and followed one of the Courtauld staff out of the room.

The tension rose another notch.

Director Ferguson and one of her colleagues carefully removed the portrait from the cardboard box and placed it on the table.

After several minutes studying the image, the Director turned to directly face the camera.

"This is a portrait of a young woman's seated profile, executed in chalk, on a canvas that was once white, but is now seriously discoloured. It is no more than moderately well executed, but with obvious evidence of a superior hand here, here and here in particular."

As she spoke, the Director indicated the unbroken curve of the woman's neck, executed in a single, confident line, with a previous, hesitant attempt erased but parts still barely visible. She also drew attention to the natural confusion of the woman's hair and the simple, but naturalistic, posy of flowers held lightly in her delicately rendered hands.

Joan Ferguson now gently assisted Susanna to join her in front of the camera.

The elderly lady radiated dignity and an inner strength belying her years.

"My name is Susanna Abramowitch, daughter of Otto Abramowitch, the owner of this artwork when it was loaned to Amsterdam's Rijksmuseum in 1938. My grandfather told me the story of this portrait many, many times when I was a child and we examined it together on several occasions. This the drawing purchased at an auction in Florence by my grandfather, Isaak Abramowitch. We called her *The Lady*."

As they had rehearsed, Jonathan then spoke, explaining briefly how the diary had been found in Blythswood House, how he had found the concluding sections in Florence and how he had traced the history of the portrait to the tax auction there in 1880 and to a buyer, Isaak Abramowitch, of Munich. Ben then outlined the deception that took the drawing to Amsterdam; the forced sale of the four paintings in 1940; the subsequent murders of his family in 1942 and his own attempts to recover his family's property over the past 20 odd years. He concluded with details of the settlement he had reached with Franz Burgdorf, leading to delivery of this portrait.

Finally, Lauren spoke.

"According to Paolo del Rosso's Chronicle, this simple portrait hides two other works—oil paintings created as a wedding gift by Leonardo da Vinci, Paolo's master and loving godfather to Chiara Brandano, the young woman in the drawing and the bride-to-be in the portraits. Paolo loved and protected Chiara and her son for his entire life and when, at a time of civil unrest, the wedding portraits were in danger, he used his own drawing to hide them. Tragically, Paolo died before he was able to tell anyone what he had done. And now, we hope to unveil the two paintings hidden for almost 500 years."

When Lauren finished speaking, a hush descended over the room. The two Institute technicians carefully turned the Paolo drawing over, laying it face down on the table. Two powerful lamps were wheeled close, to illuminate the back of the frame and canvas. In the continuing silence the technicians and Director Ferguson studied the frame for several minutes until the older of the technicians pointed.

"Here, here and I think, here. If we remove these, it will lift out."

The Director nodded and the two men gently but firmly used their tools to remove three strips of wood securing the canvas stretcher within the frame. It took only a few minutes to free the old stretcher and lift it out, laying it face down again. Now the two restoration specialists worked together efficiently to remove the rusted pins holding Paolo's creation to its wooden stretcher.

"OK," announced Joan Ferguson, "on three. One, two, three."

The two technicians carefully flipped the painting once more so that Paolo's portrait of Chiara faced them again. After a moment, the two men gently lifted the canvas holding Paolo's effort from its stretcher and set it down carefully on the far side of the table.

Now they were all looking at what appeared to be a blank canvas.

Before anyone else could speak, Lauren reassured the room.

"That isn't a canvas, it's the sheet of silk Paolo used to protect the surface of Alessio's portrait."

Slowly and deliberately, Joan Ferguson lifted the silk sheet from the stretcher, revealing the canvas beneath.

And there it was.

Looking as fresh as the day Leonardo had unveiled it in his studio, the portrait of Alessio glowed with colour.

"The Milan musician!" Jonathan exclaimed and Professor Hunter and Director Ferguson nodded vigorously.

"But so much better," added Jane Hunter. "Incomparably better!"

After ten minutes admiring and filming the portrait of Alessio and discussing its merits, Lauren could bear it no longer.

"Can we please get on with it? Please?"

The earlier process was repeated until once again Joan Ferguson raised another sheet of protective silk.

Without having given it any conscious thought, Jonathan wrapped an arm tight around Lauren's shoulders. He could feel a few tears running down his own cheek.

There was a long silence as everyone in the room absorbed the impact of the stunning portrait of Chiara. She was the sublime embodiment of vibrant femininity. Demure but confident; intelligent, beautiful and strong. Her eyes held the viewer's gaze in a disconcerting challenge: *'You think you know me? You do not. I am much more than I appear.'*

They could see in her expression that Leonardo had anticipated her being pregnant with Leo–the son who would be named for her godfather and mentored and loved by Paolo throughout his life.

But then the realisation of the tragedy about to unfold crashed over them. Thanks to the intrigues of Leonardo, the promised joy and music and love lasted but an instant, to be replaced by a lifetime of yearning for another, a yearning fully reciprocated, but never satisfied.

"She is so beautiful and so vibrant," Penny murmured. "Poor, poor Paolo. To love such a woman his entire life and never be truly with her."

"But what a love story," Lauren protested. "They knew great happiness as well as sadness and here she is, protected by Paolo one final time and now destined to be immortal."

Ben nodded and added, "And what a painting! She could almost speak to us."

Lauren gently corrected him. "She has already spoken to us, Ben, through Paolo's Chronicles. I feel I have always known her, and now to actually *see* her—it's wonderful."

Jonathan couldn't take his eyes off the sensuous curve of Chiara's painted mouth. It was exquisite. "What will you do with the paintings, Ben?"

"I don't know. This a lot to process. I need to talk with the family. I listened to your story, Jonathan, but until this moment, I didn't truly grasp the reality of what this would mean. Two paintings by Leonardo da Vinci—and such paintings!"

Director Ferguson addressed Ben.

"I have had the privilege of studying most of the world's great works of art, some here at the Institute. I have never seen such a magnificent work on canvas. These will be set alongside the Sistine Chapel as the absolute pinnacle of Renaissance painting."

She continued, "With your permission, Mr Abrams, the next thing I must do is call the head of security. We've never had responsibility for anything remotely as valuable as even one of these paintings, never mind two of them. And we need our conservation team to get these portraits looked after immediately, especially the two loose canvases."

Lauren's thoughts were in a turmoil. This was the climax of her amazing adventure with Jonathan, but, she hoped, not the end of their story. She knew she loved him and, on an impulse, reached up to kiss his cheek. His delighted reaction told her everything she needed to know. However, there was one final chapter to be shared with everyone.

She disengaged from Jonathan and sought the cameraman's attention once more.

"Before you do that, Director, can I read something? This is a copy of the document found with Paolo's papers in Florence. I'd like you all to hear what it says."

November 23rd 1590

My name is Leonardo Pacini–Rosso, commonly known as Leo, formerly a merchant of this city. I have lived 82 years. I pray not many more, if God is merciful.

This letter is to be kept with the papers I today deposit into the care of the priests of the cathedral, papers relating to the noblest man it was ever my honour to know, Messer Paolo del Rosso. A man whose name I took upon his death, he having no natural sons.

I discovered three days ago, that Brandini, husband of my granddaughter, and thus my heir (my own darling son and daughter being dead these eighteen years) has sold the likeness of my dear departed mother, executed by Maestro Leonardo. While it made a handsome amount, this portrait was beyond price to Paolo and to me, yet it has been sent away with no more thought than selling an old mare that can no longer be ridden. In the dispute that followed, Brandini boasted he had also disposed of the small sketch of my mother, done by Maestro Leonardo on his deathbed and also given to Paolo. In an echo of Paolo's own death, this small drawing was the last item held in the hands of my mother as she died, connecting as it did her godfather, her true love and herself. Given in payment of a gambling debt, for shame.

I have betrayed Paolo's trust. He passed these treasures to me because he believed I would protect them and preserve them in our family. And now they are both gone, and also, I suspect, Paolo's ring, which I cannot find.

It is clear therefore, that Paolo's diary cannot be entrusted to the barbarian who must inherit it.

I have added to Paolo's own papers, two letters received by my mother, one sent by Paolo himself shortly before he died, and the other, the dreadful missive that told us of his passing.

Brandini believes me to be senile and incapable of action. So, upon my death, he will be aggrieved to discover that I have willed the half of my estate to the priests of the cathedral, Santa Maria del Fiore, to say a Mass every day for 100 years for the souls of my beloved children and those of Paolo and my darling mother, in the hope and belief they will finally be united in Paradise.

I wish I had the skills of a poet to memorialise the love of Paolo and Chiara. They would live forever in legend alongside Petrarca and Laura, Dante and Beatrice. Paolo loved my mother his entire life and was forever focused on her safety and happiness. He salvaged our family's business and set it on the prosperous path it followed until recently. He opened the doors of the court of the King of France to us, thus ensuring the warm welcome and high regard my mother enjoyed on our return to Florence.

For her sake also, he loved me as a son and became the true father I earnestly desired. He taught me those things a boy must learn if he is to become a man of honour. He made me his heir, which brought me a surprising fortune. Whatever success and reputation I have earned, has all been my inheritance from my guide and my friend.

And yet, Paolo's tragic fate was to encounter death, alone in a strange city, at the very moment when he was about to finally find happiness in the arms of his beloved.

Paolo never attained great fame, although he was admired and held in high regard by Kings. This diary that Paolo kept, that part not lost many years ago in England, here delivered to the church fathers to be kept safe, will, I have no doubt, be of interest to future generations who wish to understand how we lived. It is too painful for me to read it—the very thought brings back too strongly the memory of that spirit I miss so much.

Paolo's modest reputation ensures that my grasping heir is not tempted to sell Paolo's own portrait of my dear mother, which I can see before me now, having had it moved into my bedchamber. It is a better likeness than Paolo believed, because his skill was greater than he thought and because he painted it in the springtime of his love for its subject. It has no monetary value. But it has a true value far greater than anyone else now alive can appreciate.

This gentle portrait was created at the command of the man Paolo admired above all others. It is a portrait by a true lover of the object of his devotion.

My earnest hope is that one day the story of Paolo and Chiara will become known, and this portrait recognised at last for its true meaning and worth.

Leonardo Pacini–Rosso

Firenze

Year of Our Lord, Fifteen Hundred and Ninety

Postscript

The store had no shop window. It was on the second floor of a 1930's building on Manhattan's 57ᵗʰ Street. The only clue to its existence was a small brass plate in the entrance lobby and the multiple security systems protecting the front door. Its monied clientele knew where to come to find a unique piece of antique jewellery or objects d'art from every period of human history.

The client was well-known to the owner, one of his best customers. He was a collector who, like most obsessives, could never have too many of, in his case, antique rings. The plain gold watch peeking out from his cuff was a Patek Philippe. The understated timepiece, his plain wedding band, and, on occasion, his Harvard class ring, were the only adornments he ever wore. His expensive collection was not for wearing, but for display in his Park Avenue apartment, in the custom case he had commissioned from a craftsman in Rome.

The man never needed an excuse to visit the store, but tomorrow was his birthday, so on this occasion his wife was with him, and she would make the selection. This was to be her birthday gift to him.

She stretched out an exquisitely manicured finger.

"That signet ring, the one with the black stone."

The salesman unrolled a black velvet cloth onto the glass countertop before reaching into the display case. He positioned the heavy ring on the cloth then switched on a powerful lamp.

"The stone is obsidian, which is created in the cauldron of a volcanic eruption. It is extremely hard, but rather brittle. Remarkably few old stones survive intact."

He adjusted the lamp slightly and rotated the ring slightly to better display the intricate carving on the black stone which, even under this intense illumination, swallowed the light that fell upon it.

"It is extremely rare to see obsidian engraved in such intricate detail, it's a difficult material to work. This ring was made by an extremely talented Italian craftsman, around the beginning of the sixteenth century. As you can see, the motif is a heraldic dragon."

The woman peered at the stone. "What is the significance of the dragon?"

"The dragon represents courage, but on this ring the true meaning is to be found in the creature's other distinguishing attribute. The dragon fiercely protects its treasure–if necessary, to the death. This ring holds a secret, a message that would be seen only by the its owner."

The salesman lifted the ring and lowered it, stone down, onto the woman's upturned palm, to display the underside of the bezel. The disk of obsidian was mounted on a gold base, which was now revealed.

"Can you see? There is another engraving, here on the inside of the bezel. At first glance, it looks rather like a tree. Actually, it is two conjoined letters: 'C' and 'P', set within an endless braid. And can you make out the motto engraved around the shank? The letters are tiny and worn almost smooth–but they say: *Il tesoro più grande non è visibile*."

The greatest treasure is not visible.

Notes & Acknowledgements

This book is published by me, its author. I hope you enjoy it and if you do, I hope you will help bring it to a wider audience.

If you are inclined to help, you can do any or all of several things:

1. Recommend the book to your friends. (If your friends include Richard & Judy, Oprah or the chief buyer for Waterstones, so much the better.)

2. Leave a review on Amazon.

3. Leave a review on Goodreads.

4. Give a copy to all your friends at Christmas.

Thank you.

Brian McPhee

This is my third novel and by far the most challenging to complete.

I owe a considerable debt to patient readers of my early drafts, including my always reliable cousin, George Dunn, neighbour Michael Delahaye and especially, The Cool Cats Book Club of south east London: Helen, Tom, Seb, Isobel, Cate and my daughter and regular editor, Marianne Moulder-McPhee. This time around I have also benefited from the insights and suggestions of my new son-in-law, Adam Moulder.

As always, my principal sounding board and (to steal Stephen King's expression) my constant reader, has been my long-suffering wife, Sheila.

Amy Durant and Lesley McDowell of Jericho Writers (formerly the Writers' Workshop) read the first version and provided measured encouragement and very useful professional input. My thanks to them.

My Milanese friend, Paola Spagnolello, helped with Italian language and idiom issues.

Ed King, a fellow expat, generously shared his experience and knowledge gleaned from a distinguished career in the art world. My apologies to Ed and his fellow experts—I have taken great liberties with the handling of historic documents and fragile artworks. I fear this book will never be a training guide for conservators!

The cover was designed by my brother, Stephen McPhee (check out lumartos.com for some amazing images).

However, most important of all was the contribution from a wonderful editor, Kaytie Lee. Kaytie's advice and guidance was revelatory. Her understanding and insightfulness were an enormous help. I cannot thank her enough.

* * *

This is a work of fiction, and I have taken considerable liberty with history, cheerfully filling in many blanks while trying to avoid complete distortions of the facts that we do know.

Sadly, Chiara and Alessio are entirely fictional, as is Paolo, and thus his Chronicles.

Paolo was inspired in part by Francesco Melzi, son of a nobleman, assistant and apprentice to Leonardo and a very competent painter in his own right. He was talented and loyal, and he served the memory of Leonardo honourably as his literary executor.

Salaì was Leonardo's apprentice, and he seems to have been a complete rogue. If Leonardo had a male lover, Salaì is the prime candidate. Salaì inherited or 'liberated' a number of Leonardo's paintings.

Mona Lisa del Giocondo (née Gherardini) had a sister named Camilla who became a nun and was involved in a scandal involving youths climbing up a ladder to kiss and fondle the young nuns–a rather more minor transgression than becoming the mistress of a Medici! Francesco del Giocondo was comfortably off and well-connected–but it is something of a mystery why Leonardo agreed to paint his wife when other, much more obvious petitioners were being turned down.

Pacifica Brandano was the mistress of Leonardo's patron in Rome, Giuliano de'Medici, and bore him his only son, Ippolito, who did indeed have a stellar, if short-lived career. A small minority of experts think she may be the subject of the second *Mona Lisa* that hangs in the Louvre.

According to Martin Kemp (*see below*), the best candidate for Leonardo's mother was the fifteen-year-old Caterina di Meo Lippi, an orphan. The baby was brought up by his paternal grandparents and Caterina essentially vanishes from the Leonardo story, although she did get married and had other children. Leonardo records a visit from a Caterina just over 40 years later, and, one year later still, he paid for the funeral of a Caterina. Whether either or both of these women was his mother, is unknown.

The wording of the accusation in the *tamburi*, alleging a charge of sodomy against Alessio, is taken essentially verbatim from the *tamburi* accusation laid against a youthful Leonardo. The charges were dismissed.

Leonardo was a committed and passionate vegetarian, believing that eating meat was immoral. He was very handsome, and he knew it.

The beautiful sketched portrait known as *La Scapigliata*, which I co-opted as the preparatory study for Chiara's wedding portrait, which was then treasured by Paolo, was painted on wood, not canvas.

Machiavelli was a friend of Leonardo and helped him win the commission for the Signoria mural. And Michelangelo Buonarroti really did have a serious antipathy to Leonardo for some unknown reason. Leonardo did recommend an unfavourable location for Michelangelo's *David*. Raphael made the study of the early *Mona Lisa*, but he did not paint St Sebastian on canvas. (Although he did paint a rather insipid version on a panel.)

It is a true mystery why Leonardo's father failed to legitimise him–a fairly straightforward procedure at the time. And Leonardo did have to return to Florence to defend the inheritance bequeathed to him by his uncle–a compromise solution was arrived at.

Piero Soderini was the Gonfaloniere of Florence; Leonardo's father, Ser Piero da Vinci, was the notary to, and neighbor of, the Giocondo family; and Sebastian Gryphius was the most important printer and bookseller in Lyon in his time.

Even with advances in modern forensic science, definitively distinguishing between pre- and post-mortem immersion in water can be extremely difficult, and virtually impossible with the technologies and knowledge available even to Leonardo.

The official archives of Florence are carefully maintained in a very modern building. I assume that at one time, they were indeed stored in a rather chaotic old structure.

I recommend that anyone visiting London should visit the Royal Academy and its wonderful *Last Supper*, which is much superior to the original in Milan. And those who are dismissive of the idea of restoring the Parthenon (with, for example, copies of the [completed] Elgin marbles) are presumably of the view that Notre Dame should be left without a roof, never mind a spire, following the terrible fire.

There is an enormous volume of books on Leonardo and his times. I would particularly recommend Walter Isaacson's biography, *Leonardo da Vinci* (Simon & Schuster 2017); *Daily Life in Renaissance Italy* by Cohn & Cohen (Greenwood Press 2001); *Leonardo's Lost Princess* by Peter Silverman (John Wiley & Son 2012) (which, if nothing else, will make you think twice about so-called authoritative art attributions); and *A Florentine Diary from*

1450 to 1516 by Luca Landucci (available as a free online read or download). Two excellent books on the *Mona Lisa*: *Mona Lisa* by Martin Kemp & Giuseppe Pallanti (OUP 2017), and *The Mona Lisa Myth* by Isbouts & Heath Brown (Brown & Pantheon 2013).

The chapters relating to the Abramowitch/Abrams family and their travails were in part informed by *The Orpheus Clock* by Simon Goodman (Scribner 2015) and *The Munich Art Hoard* by Catherine Hickley (Thames & Hudson 2015). The fictional family name was chosen to honour the late Maja Abramowitch, Holocaust survivor and author of *To Forgive...But Not Forget: Maja's Story* (The Library of Holocaust Testimonies, Valentine Mitchell 2002).

There is more in my blog *(bmcpwriter.blog)* about the *Mona Lisa* and the various controversies surrounding some of Leonardo's masterpieces. For the record, I don't believe Leonardo dragged a painting around Italy and France for twenty years, but nor do I think he painted over an old portrait that had been stored in a barn!

ABOUT THE AUTHOR

Brian McPhee lived in Glasgow, Scotland until he was 21, when he moved to London. In his early 40s, he moved with his wife and daughter to a neighbourhood near Annapolis, Maryland, USA, the model for the fictitious community of Kingsbay in his first novel, *Bunco*.

The family hold UK and US passports.

He and his wife currently live in Monpazier in southwest France.

EMPRESS

Empress is the epic story of a legendary ship and two generations of a family whose fate is intimately bound up with her.

The saga travels from a shipyard on the River Clyde, to the tropical seas where the rich and famous cruise in dazzling opulence, to the perilous waters of the Atlantic Ocean in World War II. The dramatic conclusion is set against the glamorous backdrop of the Cannes Film Festival in the 1960s.

EXTRACT

This novel was inspired by a true story

From the Wikipedia entry for the Empress of Britain
(Extracted June 2017)

'In 1995, salvagers found Empress of Britain...The bullion room was still intact. Inside was a skeleton but no gold ...'

1962

UNDER THE ATLANTIC OCEAN

After three failed attempts to open the massive door, the team had spent twelve tedious hours cutting an inspection hole into the wreck's bullion room.

Now the lead diver warily slid his head through the new opening, mentally cursing his bulky full-face mask. A few seconds later, Steve eased in an arm and switched on his powerful flashlight.

He was looking down on what had become the floor of the strongroom when the great ship had finally settled on the seabed.

There was nothing to see.

He drifted a little further into the hole, mindful of the sharp edges waiting to cut him or his dry suit.

Now he could see the entire floor. Apart from a small pile of debris in the far corner, it was completely bare, empty.

No gold, nothing.

As he began to gingerly back out, Steve felt something brush the back of his head.

"Oh God! Oh God! Oh sweet Jesus!"

With one panicked heave, the diver shot back from the opening, arms thrashing wildly, a maelstrom of silver bubbles bursting from his exhaust vent, heading exuberantly for the surface. His abandoned flashlight swung at the end of its thin tether, casting weird shadows that danced and swayed around the comforting circle of artificial light.

"Steve, Steve, calm down. Think about your breathing. Come on, man. Breathe."

Andy came alongside his boss and saw he was regaining control; his breathing returning to normal.

"Look, look at the bloody thing."

Steve's trembling finger pointed to the dark opening.

Andy turned to look, and his own stream of bubbles ceased for a very long moment.

Dreadfully slowly, the head of a corpse was falling past the freshly cut hole. It was not quite a skeleton; here and there ragged strips of pale flesh clung tenaciously to the bones. As they watched, appalled but spellbound, the head drifted out of view, followed by the rest of the body, clad in a black diving suit, much like their own. Just before the ghastly apparition disappeared, they glimpsed a rubber swim fin trailing from a skeletal foot.

1928

CLYDEBANK, SCOTLAND

The women leaned heavily on their windowsills, strong arms red and chapped; hand-rolled cigarettes held lazily between nicotine-stained fingers. They had paused their assorted conversations; words thrown from one window to the next, or all the way across the street or, by twisting unnaturally, to a neighbour on a higher floor.

For some reason, the man had ordered his taxicab to stop thirty yards back along the road. He unfolded himself from the cab and looked up at the serried windows. The women stared unflinchingly back.

The stranger was aware of the watchers following his progress along the uneven pavement. They carefully calibrated his meticulously crafted appearance; the shine on his shoes, the subtle sheen of his hat, the flash of white above the grey gloved hand carrying a soft leather briefcase emblazoned with a golden crown. This one was accustomed to privilege and power.

The stationary taxicab radiated sharp clicks from its cooling engine. It would wait for the passenger's return journey to Glasgow Central Station and the early evening London train. The man's visit north would be as brief as he could possibly make it.

The visitor reached the corner and froze. After a beat, he slowly raised his gaze to properly take in the leviathan before him. The enormous, unworldly hull soared high over the grey tenements, dominating the mean streets around, even the sky itself. It was truly an awesome sight, vastly more imposing than he had pictured in his wood-panelled Whitehall office. The cliff face of steel was taller than Nelson's Column, as long as three football pitches.

The pyramids of Egypt, the cathedrals of Europe, New York's skyscrapers–all were planted firmly in the earth. The colossus before him was expected to glide across the oceans under man's direction. It struck him as preposterous that something so massively solid would even float.

As he slowly walked towards the behemoth, the man briefly caught, and then lost, a panorama of the entire vessel. He retraced his steps to appreciate it properly. But he looked in vain: there was simply no way his imagination could grasp the entirety of the hull–its immense scale defeated him.

The cranes looming over the abandoned hull were themselves enormous, the largest ever constructed. There were eight of them marching down each side of the ship, towering over it, spanning its width; each ready to hoist materials inboard to be lowered into the depths of the great vessel.

But for now they stood motionless, silent sentinels awaiting the command to spring to life.

As he moved closer, the civil servant could pick out details in the scene before him. Most prominent and revealing were the mournful streaks of rust staining the massive sheets of metal cladding the ship.

It was ten o'clock on a Wednesday morning, but the shipyard was eerily silent. No men clambered over the hull, driving in red-hot rivets; no incandescent sparks cascaded from welding torches. The great iron gates barring the rail tracks were padlocked. The powerful yard locomotives, which should have been operating continuously, ferrying materials to the work crews, stood sullen in their sidings. Scraps of metal, shards of broken bottles, shattered wooden cases; were all reflected in fetid black puddles. Great wooden beams lay scattered carelessly everywhere. Scrawny grasses and rank weeds exploded from ominous black crevices; finishing touches to the scene of desolation.

In the echoing distance the man could hear the faint cries of children; there was a school somewhere nearby, he guessed. But the fathers of the schoolchildren were sitting silent at home, or were milling around the Labour Exchange; a soulless place where hope came to die. Even highly skilled men, who had long ago swallowed their pride, were lucky to pick up a couple of days' labouring work now and then.

Hull 384 spoke to everything wrong with the times and the country. Conceived as a monument to national pride and wealth, Hull 384 had instead become the manifest symbol of the decay of a community and the dizzying decline of a once-proud nation–and a silent howl of rebuke to politicians and business leaders.

The man from the Finance Ministry lifted his eyes once more to the magnificent bow, looming high over his head. As if on cue, a shaft of sunlight sought out a patch of bare metal and the reflection illuminated the detritus and decay around him.

To the curious watchers, the man was tiny, insignificant; but the papers in his elegant briefcase would transform Hull 384, the yard and the lives of the families in the rows of tenements.

For Hull 384 was to be resurrected. Steelworkers, joiners, painters, engineers, plumbers, electricians – thousands of men of every trade and none would be employed once again to realise the dreams of her designer. She would be launched and fitted out here, on Scotland's River Clyde.

Then the fastest, most elegant, most luxurious liner afloat would bear the rich, the famous and the powerful across the oceans and around the world.

Printed in Great Britain
by Amazon

35690919R00262